Goldblatt's Descent

Goldblatt's Descent

MICHAEL HONIG

ATLANTIC BOOKS
London

First published in Great Britain in 2013 by Atlantic Books,
an imprint of Atlantic Books Ltd.

This paperback edition published in Great Britain in 2014
by Atlantic Books.

10 9 8 7 6 5 4 3 2 1

A CIP catalogue record for this book is available from the British Library.

Paperback ISBN: 978 0 85789 703 9
E-book ISBN: 978 0 85789 702 2

Printed in Italy by Grafica Veneta SpA

Atlantic Books
An Imprint of Atlantic Books Ltd
Ormond House
26–27 Boswell Street
London
WC1N 3JZ

www.atlantic-books.co.uk

Goldblatt's Descent

1

THE PHONE STILL HADN'T rung. Typical, thought Ludo.

It was a small white phone and it sat smugly, toad-like, on a desk strewn with laboratory forms, patients' notes, test results, and large cream-coloured X-ray folders. Ludo stared at it resentfully.

According to the timetable she had been sent, a round was supposed to be starting in the doctors' office on the ward on the seventh floor, but no one else was here. It was Ludo's first day on Professor Small's unit. She had already bleeped the specialist registrar three times. Bleeps were supposed to be answered. That was the theory, anyway.

Ludo was still staring at the phone when Goldblatt came in. She glanced up at him.

'And you are...' he asked.

'The new senior house officer,' said Ludo.

'How convenient. I'm the registrar.'

'Then maybe you can tell me what's supposed to be happening.'

He shook his head. He couldn't tell her what was supposed to be happening because it was his first day on the unit as well. He sat on the edge of a desk. 'Malcolm Goldblatt.'

'Ludo.'

Goldblatt frowned. Ludo? Wasn't there a game called Ludo? He was sure there was. He wished he could remember how Ludo was played or what it was or anything at all about it. There were so many facts he had known at various times in his life and that he had forgotten. Yet it was never possible to be certain, before you forgot them, which ones you would later need and which you could safely consign to oblivion, and often you mistook one for the other. That was the irony of it. But it was only one of life's ironies, he knew, and not the greatest.

He glanced at Ludo again. She was going red with some kind of embarrassment that he couldn't fathom. Maybe she was named after the game. Maybe she was conceived after a game. Maybe she was conceived *during* a game...

'Ludka,' Ludo blurted out. 'All right? It's short for Ludka.'

'Ludka?'

'Ludka Madic.' She pronounced it with a hard c at the end, and had gone redder, as if she had just revealed her most harrowing secret. But she hadn't. That came next. 'It's Serbian.'

'Then you should say Madich, shouldn't you?'

'Everyone gets it wrong,' replied Ludo sourly, 'so I just say Madic.'

'You shouldn't deny your heritage.'

'Why not?' demanded Ludo with what seemed very much like heartfelt bitterness. 'Everyone hates the Serbs.'

That was a sweeping statement, thought Goldblatt. On the other hand, a statement wasn't wrong just because it swept. This was only a few years after the war in Bosnia had been brought to an end following half a decade of determined condemnation by the nations of western Europe and an equally strong determination by the troops of those nations to get out of the way whenever civilians were being massacred. There was probably more truth than lie in Ludo's remark.

'I don't hate the Serbs,' said Goldblatt. 'For the record.'

Ludo turned away and looked back at the phone. Goldblatt watched her. She had porcelain blue eyes and the lids hung low over her irises, giving her a kind of doped appearance. She had thick white skin, with a couple of spots of acne on her cheeks. Her long dark hair hung loose down her back. She was wearing a white doctor's coat, and she sat with her arms folded across her chest. A purple woollen skirt stretched over her thighs.

'Have you bleeped anyone?'

Ludo rolled her eyes, not bothering to reply.

'I'm going to take that as a yes.'

Ludo had finished her previous job in Leicester the day before, and had woken up at four o'clock to be in London in time to start her new job on Professor Small's unit. The hospital had said they would give her a room for up to a month while she found a place of her own, but when the taxi dropped her at the accommodation block she couldn't get in. She had had to stand in the cold until someone happened to come out and she could sneak inside. Then she found a note with a number to call for out-of-hours' assistance pinned to a board behind a little desk, and it took half an hour for someone to turn up once she had rung it. The only assistance he could give was to tell her that her room wasn't ready and he didn't know where she could leave her bags, so she had to leave them behind the desk, where he grudgingly allowed her to deposit them, and hope no one would steal them. Then she had come up to the ward, and the specialist registrar wouldn't answer her bleep and there was no sign of anyone, not even a house officer, and all she needed now – *all* she needed now – was for some registrar to turn up and tell her not to deny her heritage as if she was a Serbian nationalist or Radovan Karadžić's daughter or cousin or had even met him or something.

Actually, she had met Radovan Karadžić, but that was when she was eleven and her parents had forced her to rehearse for a folk dance with some other girls at the Serbian cultural centre in London, and they all performed in front of him and a bunch of other lecherous-looking guys who had come on a visit from what was then Yugoslavia. Her parents were big on Serbian culture. One of the men had squeezed her bum as they lined up in front of them after the dance, although she couldn't remember if that was Radovan Karadžić or one of the others. At that stage Radovan Karadžić was just another one of those lecherous guys, no one special, some kind of a poet or something, and it wasn't until years later when everyone was saying he was a war criminal that her mother reminded Ludo that she had danced in front of him. It was true, her father said, she should be proud of it. She wasn't proud of it. It made her sick. But she was eleven at the time and it wasn't her idea, anyway. And who could have known what the tall man with all that silver hair was going to turn into and that she would have to live the rest of her life with the terrible secret that she had danced for a war criminal and had possibly even had her bum squeezed by him?

'It's so unfair,' muttered Ludo.

'What?' asked Goldblatt.

Ludo didn't reply. Goldblatt guessed there were many answers to that question, and he was fairly certain he didn't want to hear any of them. He pondered his options. On the one hand, he could launch into a discussion of the atrocities and assorted illegalities of the Balkan war with his new senior house officer, who appeared to be an aggrieved Serb nationalist with a chip the size of Bosnia balanced precariously on her shoulder. Or on the other hand...

'Did you say you bleeped the SR?'

Ludo nodded.

'What's the number?'

Ludo pulled a piece of paper out of the pocket of her white coat. '403.'

'How do you bleep here?' asked Goldblatt.

'Dial eleven, then the bleep you want, then your extension,' she replied, reading mechanically from the paper.

Goldblatt picked up the phone. Ludo watched him as he dialled the numbers and then put it down again.

'There's meant to be a round,' said Ludo.

'When?'

'Now. That's what it says on the timetable. Don't you have a timetable?'

Goldblatt didn't have a timetable. They might have sent him one.

Ludo examined the piece of paper. 'Wednesday, nine o'clock, round.'

'Here?'

'That's what it says. Starting in the doctors' office on the ward.'

'Well, that's definitely here,' observed Goldblatt.

Ludo glanced at him impatiently, then stared at the phone again. 'It really pisses me off when people won't answer their bleeps.'

Goldblatt looked around the doctors' office, hoping that if he didn't respond the whining tone that had crept into Ludo's voice would recede. A pair of desks stood on either side of the room with a shelf bracketed to the wall above each one, accompanied by an unmatched assortment of office chairs and a metal trolley on wheels with hanging files containing the medical notes of the patients on the ward. An X-ray box and a whiteboard were fixed on the wall opposite the door. To all intents and purposes a standard issue doctors' office, not excepting the horrendous mess of notes and papers scattered across every available surface as if left behind by the retreat of some kind of medical tsunami.

'It *really* pisses me off when people won't answer their bleeps,' Ludo repeated, apparently mistaking his silence for encouragement. The whining tone had got worse, and it was downhill from there. Ludo went back to the sound of her alarm clock waking her at four that morning – even though strictly speaking she was supposed to be whining about people not answering their bleeps – moved methodically on past the businessman who supposedly ogled her in the train all the way down from Leicester, the taxi driver with the hacking cough who had probably infected her with something on the drive to the hospital, the wait in the cold outside the accommodation block which would almost certainly have exacerbated whatever she had caught in the taxi, and the strong likelihood that, even as she whined, her bags were being stolen. She whined at a regular, measured pace with the air of a professional, and obviously had the stamina to go on for hours.

Goldblatt had a dismal premonition that this wasn't going to be the last time he heard that tone in Ludo's voice.

'Tell me about the first patient,' he said, desperate for it to stop. He threw a glance at the notes trolley. 'Simmons,' he said, reading the name on the first folder. 'Tell me about Simmons.'

Ludo stopped in mid-whine and stared at him in disbelief. 'How should I know about Simmons?'

'I'm your registrar. You're my senior house officer.' Goldblatt looked at his watch. 'It's ten past nine. How long have you been here? You haven't done a thing.'

'I've been talking to you!'

'Exactly. I expect you to know your patients before you sit around talking to me, Dr Madic. I expect you to know them inside out. You'll know their haematology, their biochemistry, their serology, and their hepatology. You'll know what tests have been done, what tests have been ordered, and when the results are going to be back. Is that clear, Dr Madic?'

Ludo's mouth had fallen open. Goldblatt wondered how much more of this rubbish she was going to fall for. He thought he might as well find out.

'I don't expect Professor Small to hang around while we familiarize ourselves with her patients. Do you? The Professor deserves a little more respect, Dr Madic, and you'd better start showing it.' He shook his head in admonition. 'Simmons,' he announced, as if he had come in earlier to check the notes and actually knew something about the patient, 'a seventy-two-year-old woman with a past history of Wernicke's encephalopathy and cerebellar dysfunction secondary to—' Goldblatt stopped, scrutinizing Ludo's paralysed face. 'Give me the causes of cerebellar dysfunction.'

Ludo looked around helplessly.

'Come on.'

'Multiple sclerosis?' she whispered.

'In a thirty-five-year-old, maybe. In a seventy-two-year-old? I think we can start with something a *little* more common, don't you?'

'Stroke?'

'Yep!' said Goldblatt, sticking out his thumb. 'What else?'

'Ah...'

'Come on,' said Goldblatt. 'Stroke.'

'Didn't I say that?'

'Alcohol,' said Goldblatt, snapping out his index finger. 'Tumour, hypothyroidism, heavy metal poisoning.'

All of Goldblatt's fingers were extended. Ludo was watching him, eyes narrowed in hostility.

'And?' said Goldblatt. He closed his fingers and extended his thumb again. 'And?'

Ludo sneered. 'And what?'

'Lithium toxicity. How many times did you fail your first part?'

'Five.'

Goldblatt stared at her. He was impressed. Or perhaps that wasn't quite the right word for it. The first part of the exam for membership of the Royal College of Physicians, which was taken two to three years after qualifying in medicine and starting work as a doctor, was the gateway to the multi-year-long obstacle course known as specialist training. The second part exam came a couple of years later. If you failed the first part six times, you were barred from trying again – your career as a specialist was over before it had begun. It was a tough exam, and it was no shame to fail once or even a couple of times. But failing five times and turning up for a make-or-break last attempt... Goldblatt had never met someone who had actually done that, although he had heard that such people existed. The way you hear of people who take twelve hours to finish a marathon but keep going to the end and then you wonder, honestly, why they bothered.

'That's quite something,' he said eventually.

'Thank you,' said Ludo tonelessly.

'That really is... special.'

Ludo rolled her eyes.

'Simmons,' said Goldblatt. 'Seventy-two-year-old woman with a history of cerebellar dysfunction secondary to lithium toxicity, who was admitted four days ago for a suspected myocardial infarction complicated by inframammary candidiasis.'

Ludo looked at Goldblatt suspiciously. 'What do you mean, complicated by inframammary candidiasis?'

'Thrush under her boobs, that's what I mean. Don't you talk medical?'

'I know what you mean. You just said she's had a heart attack. Who cares if she's got thrush under her boobs?'

Goldblatt gazed at her sternly. 'She cares. So I care. And that means you care, Dr Madic! Have you ever had thrush under your boobs?'

Ludo grimaced.

'All right, suit yourself. Don't tell me. Find out about Simmons. Make sure you can present her to the Prof at the round.'

'When?'

'Now. When do you think?'

Ludo got up and yanked Simmons's file ungraciously off the trolley. She sat down and opened the file on her lap. Goldblatt watched with interest to see what would happen next.

'Simmons,' she read in a disgusted voice. 'A twenty-eight-year-old male admitted with mild jaundice and pain in the right knee.' She looked up at him.

Goldblatt shrugged. 'Must be a different Simmons.'

Ludo grinned. 'You just made that up, didn't you?'

So she smiles, thought Goldblatt. Apparently at evidence of deviousness and misrepresentation. In other words, lying. That was interesting. And worrying.

Ludo closed the file and put it on the desk. 'So, what are you doing here, anyway?'

Goldblatt bounced the question back at her.

'Half time SHO for the dermatologists, half time for Professor Small,' she replied smugly. 'Should be the easiest job I've ever had.'

'That's your reason?'

Ludo grinned again.

Goldblatt watched her. Why didn't that surprise him?

'What about you?' said Ludo. 'I heard the registrar job's just a locum position.'

Goldblatt nodded.

Ludo smiled insinuatingly at him. 'Couldn't get a real job?'

Goldblatt smiled back. Ludo Madic, he thought, had a strange way of winning his favour. Not that she was necessarily obliged to try, but since he was the registrar, and she was only the senior house officer, she might have wanted to consider that for the next few months her life on the ward – for better or worse – would be in his hands.

Goldblatt was just about to point this out when the door opened. Immediately a procession was on its way into the office. First came a pudgy, blonde woman who bustled in with a white coat flapping around her. Next came a slim, short man in a dark blue suit, with a reddish moustache. And last came a small person who could only have been a house officer. Everything about her said House Officer. Papers spilled out of the pockets of her white coat. Her short red hair stuck up in tufts. Her glasses had slipped halfway down her nose, and she followed the others in with a look of bewilderment and trepidation that she didn't even try to conceal.

'Sorry we're late!' announced the pudgy bustler. 'I'm Emma Burton the specialist registrar. You must be Dr Goldblatt. And you must be Dr Madic. This is Dr Morris,' she said, indicating the man in the suit

Dr Morris shook their hands.

Emma-Burton-the-specialist-registrar, without stopping to explain what she had been doing for the last hour while her specialist-registrar-bleep had been bleeping its bleeping bleeper off in her pocket, lunged straight for the notes trolley.

'Since everyone's new today, Dr Morris,' she announced at the top of her voice, 'I'll present the patients.'

But Goldblatt wanted to know what was wrong with Simmons. There had to be more to the story than mild jaundice and a twinge of knee pain. No one had come into hospital for such trivial problems since the late medieval period – or at least since the latest round of bed cuts in the National Health Service. And it was unlikely to be inframammary candidiasis, Goldblatt knew, because he had made that up himself. Besides, Simmons was a male, if you could believe Ludo, so he didn't have any *mammas* for the candida to grow *infra*.

'What's wrong with Simmons?' he asked.

'Nothing's wrong with Simmons,' retorted Emma briskly, spotting his file on the desk and seizing it in both hands. 'He's got hepatitis.'

'What sort of hepatitis?'

'What difference does it make?'

'Are we giving him alpha interferon?'

'Good question,' said Dr Morris. 'Would you give him alpha interferon, Dr Goldblatt?'

'That depends, Dr Morris.'

'Have you read the paper from the Mayo Clinic?'

'The one in the *Lancet*?' asked Goldblatt.

'No, the *New England Journal*.'

'In October?'

'November.'

'Ah, this was October,' said Goldblatt.

'October?' said Dr Morris.

'In the *Lancet*.'

'Not the *Annals of Internal Medicine*?'

'It could have been *Hepatology*.'

'*Hepatology*?' said Dr Morris, trying to recall.

Goldblatt watched Dr Morris keenly. There was nothing like a good brisk game of Bluff the Journal to set the pulse of a doctor racing in the morning, and it was obvious that Dr Morris was an enthusiastic practitioner of the art. Goldblatt foresaw many happy hours of invention and suspense.

'You must give me the reference,' said Dr Morris and turned to Ludo. 'Tell me the causes of hepatitis.'

Ludo sagged.

'Here!' yelled Emma. She pulled a piece of paper out of Simmons's folder. 'No need for interferon. His hepatitis serology is negative!'

'Negative?' said Goldblatt.

'Negative?' said Dr Morris.

Emma gave the paper to Dr Morris, who glanced at it and handed it on to Goldblatt. Goldblatt scanned it and handed it back to Emma.

'Close the door!' Emma said to the house officer.

'Where's Professor Small?' asked Goldblatt.

'She's not here today.'

'Where is she?'

'Cardiff,' said Dr Morris. 'Or Bristol.'

'Oxford,' said Emma, in the tone of someone who knew.

'When will she be back?'

'Tomorrow.'

'Will she do another round tomorrow?'

Dr Morris laughed.

'No,' said Emma. 'We'll do the round today without her. We always do the round without her when she's not here.'

'Do we?' asked Goldblatt.

'Yes,' said Emma.

Dr Morris laughed again. 'We might actually look at the patients.'

Emma smiled. It was the smile of someone who didn't think that anything was particularly funny, but thought she'd better smile anyway.

'Shall I start?' she asked.

'No,' said Dr Morris. 'We need Sister Choy. We can manage without the Prof, but there's no way we can manage without Sister Choy.'

'But I know all the patients, Dr Morris!' protested Emma.

'I know you do,' said Dr Morris. He looked at the house officer. The HO looked back at him uncomprehendingly. Dr Morris glanced meaningfully towards the door.

'Oh!' said the HO, and went out to find the ward sister.

2

THE WARD WAS ONE of three on the seventh floor. It had a U-shaped configuration, with three four-bed rooms opening off the outer side of each arm of the U, and a six-bed area housing high-dependency patients running along the base. Opposite the six-bed space was the nurses' station. The inner block of the U housed four single-patient rooms, a treatment room, and the various other cubicles and chambers that are a necessary part of any ward: patient bathrooms, supply rooms, sluice room, staff WC, and nurses' tearoom, as well as the doctors' office and the specialist registrar's office. Of the thirty-four beds on the ward, sixteen were allocated to Professor Small's unit.

Dr Morris couldn't wait to get out there.

'Come on, let's see them,' he said, interrupting Emma as she began a rundown of the patients once Sister Choy had arrived in the office.

Emma looked at him doubtfully. 'Now?'

Dr Morris was already standing up. 'Aren't the patients ready?'

'They're ready,' said Sister Choy pointedly.

The patients were ready. Emma wasn't. The Prof's round always started off in the overcrowded doctors' office with two hours of discussion about the patients before anyone ventured out to press the flesh. Today, with an HO, an SHO and a registrar who had all started that morning, it was Emma's one chance to be the absolute, complete, solitary, and indisputable source of information during this discussion, demonstrating once and for all her complete and utter indispensability to the Prof. But where was the Prof on this important day? Oxford! She had gone off to give a talk in Oxford, leaving Dr Morris in charge. Dr Morris, Emma suspected, was unlikely to appreciate her complete and utter indispensability. Not as the Prof did, anyway. It was selfish of the Prof. She had probably done it on purpose. And now Dr Morris wanted to rush straight out on to the ward. He didn't want to listen to all the information she had learned about the patients for the occasion. She had stayed late the night before and turned up at seven that morning to check it all again, just in case the Prof had to cancel her talk at the last minute and turned up unexpectedly.

But there was nothing Emma could do. Dr Morris was a consultant. He may have been a very new and young consultant, but right now, he was all they had. And Emma didn't argue with consultants.

'All right,' she said reluctantly.

'Good,' said Dr Morris. He glanced at the HO with a smile. 'Come on,' he said, as if inviting her to a rare and delectable entertainment.

Most consultants spend as much time seeing to their position and prestige on a round as seeing to the patients. In some cases, that's all they do. Not Dr Morris. He headed out with the rest of the team trailing behind him, and proceeded to lead a round that was the deftest, most efficient, most useful round that Goldblatt had ever seen a consultant lead. Almost perfect. He did ham it up a bit with one old lady who accused him of being too young to be a consultant. It was amusing while it lasted, but since Dr Morris did look too young to be a consultant – and since there's nothing old ladies enjoy more than metaphorically squeezing the cheeks of their doctors and telling them they're too young to be their doctors – Goldblatt sensed that the joke would wear thin if Dr Morris planned to provoke these comedies every week. But even with the amateur dramatics, they got through their sixteen patients in under an hour, which was some kind of a record, Goldblatt suspected, judging by the look of dismay on Emma's face and the look of delight on Sister Choy's.

'That's it, then?' said Dr Morris brightly, as they headed back into the doctors' office. 'Anything else?'

Emma glumly shook her head.

'Good,' he said, rubbing his hands enthusiastically. 'There's a fascinating patient I've got to see on the fifth floor. Anyone interested in coming with me?'

Everyone looked away, desperately scanning the floor or the walls for something urgent to do. A consultant's invitation to 'come and see' an allegedly fascinating patient was usually code for 'come and write down a list of investigations that you are going to have to perform, follow up, record, and inform me of, while I wander off to make some money in the private patients' wing.'

But Dr Morris, as they would soon learn, genuinely just wanted to know if anyone was interested in sharing the experience of seeing an interesting case. No? All right. He'd go by himself. And then he was off, heading briskly for the stairs.

The HO started pulling pieces of paper out of her pockets, looking for the lists she had made of things she had to do. She had started on the unit only that morning, like Goldblatt and Ludo, but had arrived early enough for Emma to grab her and drag her off to see the Prof's private patients before the round. Now she had a whole raft of investigations to organize.

Emma sat down and began pulling patients' files out of the trolley to add to the notes the HO had scribbled down during the round.

'I'll do some of those,' offered Goldblatt.

'That's OK,' replied Emma. 'I know how the Prof likes her notes to be written.'

'So you won't want me to do any,' said Ludo.

'We should talk, Emma,' said Goldblatt.

'What about?'

'How we're going to do things. How we're going to divide responsibilities.'

Emma stopped writing and thought about this. She stared at the open folder in front of her.

'We should talk about how we're going to do things,' Goldblatt repeated, wondering if she was having some kind of neurological event.

'I heard you,' Emma said.

'And?'

'What do you want to talk about? Can't we talk about it now?'

'If you like,' said Goldblatt, sitting down.

'I've got to go,' said Emma suddenly.

'I thought you wanted to talk about it now.'

'No,' said Emma. 'Now's not good. Now's... bad.'

'All right. Let's do it this afternoon if you're too busy now. Two o'clock?'

'Two's all right, I suppose.' Emma glanced at Goldblatt shiftily. 'What did you say we're going to talk about?'

13

'How we're going to do things.'

'The Prof's not here today.'

'I know,' said Goldblatt. 'Is that a problem?'

'Not for me,' said Emma. 'Is it a problem for you?'

'No. I'll see you here at two.'

'Fine,' said Emma. She got up and hurried out.

Goldblatt watched her go. Then he looked at the others. 'Coffee?'

The HO, still sifting through her papers, shook her head.

Ludo sighed. 'I thought you'd never ask.'

'You still haven't told me,' said Ludo, after she had claimed to have not a penny in her pocket and Goldblatt had bought them each a coffee.

'What?'

'Why you've taken this job. Your post's only a locum job, you know.'

Goldblatt did know. He wondered how Ludo did. She'd only been on the unit for two hours.

'A girl's got to do her homework,' Ludo remarked, as if she could guess what Goldblatt was thinking.

Goldblatt glanced around the cafeteria. Most of the tables were taken up by groups of nurses on their morning breaks.

'Well, Malcolm?'

He turned back to Ludo. She was watching him expectantly. The way a wolf watches a lamb straying to the edge of a sheepfold.

He didn't want to go into it. Not now, anyway, and certainly not with Ludo, of whose existence he had been thankfully unaware until he walked into the doctors' office that morning. It was a long, frustrating road of locumdom that had led him to this job on Professor Small's unit, and he was beginning to wonder if he would ever get off it.

'I'll tell you something else,' said Ludo with a strangely lascivious twinkle in her eye.

'What?'

'Emma's a locum as well. The SR left two weeks ago. And you know what Emma was doing before that?' She paused for effect. 'Your job!'

Goldblatt shrugged. Plenty of people got their first specialist registrar jobs as locums. He'd done SR locums himself.

Ludo leaned closer. 'Emma had only been the reg for four months. And you know what? It was her *first* registrar job.'

'Her first registrar job?'

Ludo nodded.

'And they made her the SR?'

Ludo nodded again.

'Are you sure about this?'

Ludo raised an eyebrow.

'Ludo, you're not making this up, are you?'

Ludo smirked. 'I'm telling you, she was the reg until two weeks ago. And four months ago, she was an SHO like me.'

Goldblatt frowned. 'Why did the SR leave?'

'I don't know,' said Ludo, and through her tone alone, without uttering a single further sound, she managed to add one more word. *Yet.*

'Must have been in a hurry,' mused Goldblatt.

Ludo watched him with greedy expectation. 'You're going to *love* taking orders from Emma, Malcolm. When did you say you're meeting her?'

'Two o'clock.'

Ludo smiled. She sipped her coffee, watching Goldblatt over the rim of her cup.

At two o'clock the doctors' office was deserted. Goldblatt sat down to wait.

For the next ten minutes, nothing happened to disturb the serenity of the office except for one brief interruption when Sister Choy put her head in looking for the HO. Sister Choy grunted in disapproval when she saw that only Goldblatt was there and went out muttering venomously about house officers who were never around when they were needed. Eventually Goldblatt bleeped Emma. Four seconds after he put the phone down a bleep went off inside a white coat that was hanging behind the office door. He went around the corner to the specialist registrar's office and knocked. He tried the handle – locked. He came back to the doctors' office. After a while he rang the Prof's secretary, who didn't know where Emma was and sounded as if she operated a policy of ignorance on matters of that type.

Shortly after two-thirty, Goldblatt heard voices in the corridor outside. The HO came in, looking hungry and harassed. She took hold of the notes trolley and began to wheel it out of the office.

'Where are you going?' asked Goldblatt.

'I'm doing a round,' replied the HO, stopping in the doorway.

'But we did a round this morning.'

'I know,' said the HO.

'Then why do you want to do another round?'

'I don't.'

'Then why are you doing one?'

'Because the SR wants to do one. She says she just wants to be sure everything is all right. She says Dr Morris was very quick today. She says the Prof is always much more methodical. She says the Prof's coming back tomorrow and she'll want her to tell her about all the patients.'

'Don't you have any other work to do?' asked Goldblatt.

'Yes,' said the HO.

'A lot?'

'Yes,' said the HO.

'How many new patients do you have to clerk?'

'Three.'

Clerking a new patient on to the ward – taking a history, performing a full examination, writing up the notes, organizing investigations, and commencing treatment – could take an hour for each patient, longer for an HO on her very first day as a doctor.

'Have you had lunch?'

'No,' said the HO, who hadn't stopped since the end of the round with Dr Morris that morning.

'That's no good.'

'Isn't it?'

'No,' said Goldblatt. 'Put the trolley back. I want you to eat lunch. I want you to eat lunch every day.'

'I don't think Dr Burton does.'

'Listen to me. I'm going to tell you something important. Nothing comes between you and your lunch except a cardiac arrest. Anything else can wait.'

The HO stared at him, scrunching up her little nose to keep her glasses from slipping off.

'What?' asked Goldblatt.

'You said you were going to tell me something important.'

'That was it.'

'What? That thing about lunch?'

'Yes. It's important. Trust me.'

The HO looked at him sceptically.

Goldblatt sighed. It *was* important. The HO, barely an embryo of a doctor, had no idea.

'Dr Burton's waiting,' said the HO.

'Put the trolley back and go and have lunch.'

'Is that an order?'

Goldblatt nodded.

The HO put the trolley back.

'Where are you meeting Emma?' asked Goldblatt.

'Bed one.'

'Simmons's bed?'

The HO nodded.

'OK. Go. Have lunch. Then come back. Sister Choy was looking for you with an axe. Beg forgiveness. Lick her shoes.'

'I haven't licked Dr Burton's shoes yet.'

'Lick Sister Choy's shoes,' Goldblatt advised her. 'They're much more important for you. I'll look after Emma.'

'Will you lick her shoes?'

'No,' said Goldblatt.

'Good,' said the HO.

Goldblatt found Emma standing beside Simmons's bed, closely inspecting the barely yellow whites of his barely hepatitic eyes.

'The house officer has three patients to clerk,' said Goldblatt. 'I've told her to have lunch and then go ahead and do them.'

Emma turned with a start. Her face went red. 'I was just going to go through the patients quickly with her.'

'We were going to meet at two.'

'Were we? Oh, I meant to call you. I was so busy, my bleep hasn't stopped.'

'This bleep?' said Goldblatt, holding out the bleep he had taken out of the white coat in the doctors' office.

Emma stared at it.

'403?' said Goldblatt, reading the number on the bleep.

Emma flushed even more violently. She snatched the bleep out of Goldblatt's hand.

He turned and walked back to the office.

Malcolm Goldblatt had signed up to a five-month locum job on Professor Small's unit. He had been doing locum jobs, filling in at various hospitals for unexpected absences – the longest had lasted six months and the shortest had been a weekend on-call over the New Year – for the previous eighteen months. That was a problem. To complete specialist training and be able to hold a consultant position you had to show a minimum three years in recognized hospital posts – and locum jobs didn't count towards that. Even if they were in the same hospitals, on the same units, supervised by the same consultants, doing the same work as the jobs that did count for training, the Royal College of Physicians recognized only what they called substantive jobs, posts that were obtained after going through a formal interview process, not the shortcut appointment procedure that was used to fill locum positions. Or to put it another way, the nature of the interview meant more to the Royal College than the nature of the work. Time was passing, but, as far as the College was concerned, Goldblatt was standing still. And the more time that passed, the stiller he stood. The longer you spent doing locums, the harder it was to persuade someone to give you a substantive job. Eighteen months was pushing it. By the time this job on Professor Small's unit finished, it would be almost two years. He *had* to get a substantive post at the end of it.

So to put it bluntly, all Goldblatt really cared about in this job was getting a reference from the Prof that would help him get that post. On the way through, it would be good if he could minimize the duplication of work between himself and Emma, and ensure that the SHO and the HO got one coherent message from them. And making sure the patients got the right treatment would be nice, of course. But he didn't care who ran the show, or what tasks were allocated to him, or what tasks Emma wanted to do herself. He was going to ignore the fact that Emma was apparently an SR who had hardly even been a registrar, and had only four months' experience of running a ward at that level compared with his four years. He was determined to be tolerant, understanding, flexible, reasonable, measured, and calm. Sweetness and light. It was only five months, he told himself. He could manage that.

He had watched as Emma wrote in the notes that morning. Traditionally, SRs aren't the ones who do that at the end of a consultant's round. But if Emma wanted to do it, that was fine by him. Traditionally, SRs spend their times in clinics and come to the ward only for their consultant's ward round and their own weekly round with the team, but if she wanted to run the ward herself, that was fine by him as well. Whatever made her happy. Goldblatt had supervised enough HOs and run enough wards to last him a lifetime, and, if it gave Emma a buzz, she was welcome to it.

'I don't want to do it,' said Emma, after she had followed him into the doctors' office. 'That's the registrar's job. I'm the specialist registrar.'

'Of course you are,' said Goldblatt.

He picked up a loose piece of paper from one of the desks. If this was like every other doctors' office he had ever been in, a good number of the sheets that littered the desks would be stray laboratory results that had come back to the ward days too late to be of use to anyone and had never been filed. Goldblatt looked at the date on the page. Three months ago. He then scrunched the paper into a ball, aimed at the wastepaper basket beside Emma's foot, and threw it. The ball hit the rim and fell on the floor. Goldblatt got up and retrieved it, went back, and missed again.

He held out his hand for Emma to toss it to him.

She picked it up, unscrunched it, and smoothed it out.

Goldblatt took another piece of paper and scrunched it up.

'OK,' he said. 'We'll do it by the book. I'll do the ward. I'll arrange the admissions. You do your clinics and a ward round once a week, just like an SR.'

'I am the SR.'

'Right. That's how we'll do it, then. No problem.'

But there seemed to be a problem. 'The admissions are very difficult,' said Emma.

'OK. Do you want to do them?'

'I didn't say I want to do them.'

'OK. Then I'll do them,' said Goldblatt, in a tone that he imagined someone would use if they were tolerant, understanding, flexible, reasonable, measured, and calm.

'I'm just warning you that they're difficult.'

'How difficult can admissions be?' Goldblatt tossed the paper ball at the bin. In! He picked up another piece and scrunched. 'Admissions are admissions.'

'Stop doing that!'

Goldblatt looked at Emma in surprise. 'What?'

'That! You're destroying patients' notes.'

'Am I? You mean this is important?' Goldblatt unscrunched the result sheet that he had just scrunched. 'McCarthy,' he read. He looked up enquiringly at Emma. 'Do you know a McCarthy?'

'She was on the ward a while ago,' muttered Emma.

Goldblatt looked at the wrinkled paper again. 'About two months ago.' Goldblatt scanned the numbers on the page. 'Emma, her urea level's fucked! It's *double* the upper limit of normal. Here, look. Should we do something about it? It could be dangerous.'

'Very funny,' said Emma.

'It was only two months ago. She might still be alive.'

Goldblatt gave Emma another moment to save McCarthy's life. Then he rescrunched McCarthy's results and tossed them at the bin. He missed. The scrunched ball lay beside Emma's foot. Emma was staring stonily ahead. Goldblatt wondered if she was going to cry.

'Was McCarthy a relative of yours?'

'No, she wasn't a relative of mine! Look, the admissions are very difficult. It's very time-consuming. You don't know the Prof. She's very demanding, and if you can't get one of our electives in she'll expect you to manipulate the beds and try to—'

'I don't manipulate beds,' said Goldblatt, as if it was some big principle he had. Actually it did sound like a big principle. Goldblatt thought it sounded like quite a good one. He tried it out in his mind a number of times. I *don't* manipulate beds. I don't *manipulate* beds. I don't manipulate beds. I don't – I simply do *not* – manipulate beds.

Yes, it was good. But he'd betray it for sex. It wasn't that good.

Emma snorted. 'You don't know the Prof.'

'You're right,' said Goldblatt. 'She didn't even bother to come to my first round.'

Emma looked at him with narrowed eyes.

Come on, Emma, he thought. We're on the same side, right? It was funny. Admit it. It was at least a little bit funny.

Emma didn't seem to think so. She stared at him bitterly, arms crossed. 'The admissions are very stressful,' she burst out suddenly. 'I can't tell you how close I've been to resigning. I could just walk out of here right now, I'm telling you, and it would be a relief.'

Goldblatt watched her speculatively. No, he decided. Walk out? Right now? A relief? He wasn't going to fall for that. It wouldn't have fooled an amateur, much less a hardened professional like himself.

'I don't manipulate beds,' Goldblatt said again, almost believing it himself now.

'Then what are you going to do?'

Goldblatt sighed, climbing down off the high horse he had fabricated since Emma seemed to show no sign of wanting to join him up there. 'Look, Emma, you know how it's supposed to work. If we haven't got a bed and a patient's sick enough to come in, they can come in through Emergency. If not, they wait their turn. Isn't that how you do it?'

'Yes, of course, very simple,' said Emma mockingly, not exactly answering the question.

Goldblatt shrugged. 'That's how I always do it.'

'And what about the patients? They'll ring you up.'

Goldblatt shrugged.

'In tears. Some of them have been cancelled two, three, four times.'

Goldblatt shrugged once more.

Emma stared at him resentfully. 'Well, maybe you can do it,' she said at last, 'but I can't.'

Goldblatt shrugged again. There was far too much shrugging going on, he knew, and it was beginning to worry him.

'I can't do that to patients,' said Emma, 'I just can't do it.'

'Why not?'

'Because I can't.'

'That's not an explanation,' observed Goldblatt. 'It's just a repetition of what you've already said. Why can't you?'

Emma didn't answer.

Goldblatt continued to watch her.

'They're the Prof's patients!' burst out Emma at last. 'The Prof knows which ones to bring in.'

'But they don't get in, do they?'

'Yes, they do.'

'No, they don't. You said they get cancelled two, three, four times.'

Emma glanced at Goldblatt furtively. 'Not always.'

'But often?'

Emma didn't answer.

'Don't they?'

Emma sat there for a moment longer, staring at the white coat hanging behind the door. Goldblatt waited.

'Right!' she said crisply, slapping her thigh.

Goldblatt looked around the room to see what was right.

'Right!' said Emma again, and stood up. Obviously her slap on the thigh had set off a powerful wave of energy, and she wasn't going to pass up the chance of surfing it out of the office.

Goldblatt picked up another results sheet and began to scrunch it. 'So you want to do the admissions?'

'No,' said Emma, 'I'm the SR. The reg does the admissions.'

'OK, I'll do the admissions,' said Goldblatt.

'Fine,' said Emma.

'Fine,' said Goldblatt.

'Fine,' said Emma, and walked out.

Goldblatt thought about the conversation, scrunching up another old results sheet. He had been cooperative, hadn't he? He had been reasonable, measured and calm. Emma didn't want to do the admissions, so he was doing them. That was fine by him. Fine by her as well, apparently.

He couldn't quite put his finger on it, but something about the exchange didn't really seem quite as fine as all that.

*

'So, how was it?' asked Lesley, when he got home that night.

Lesley was his girlfriend, or his partner, or whatever the correct terminology was for someone you had lived with for two years. She was a barrister, and Goldblatt never had any idea when she was going to be home. Sometimes mid-afternoon, sometimes not until after midnight. Today when he walked in she was in the kitchen, chopping up things for a pasta sauce.

She was a tall woman with blonde hair, which she had tied back in a ponytail before she started cooking. She had changed out of her work clothes into one of Goldblatt's old shirts and a pair of grey track pants.

'Well?' she said, concentrating on the chopping board.

'It was...' Goldblatt searched for the word.

'What?'

'Fine.'

Lesley stopped chopping and turned around.

'It was fine,' he said. 'Really.'

'Really?'

'Watch out with the knife, Les. You're scaring me.'

Lesley looked at him for a moment longer. Then she went back to chopping. 'It's not going to be like the last job, is it?'

Goldblatt laughed.

'I'm serious, Malcolm. It's nothing to laugh about.'

It wasn't. They both knew how important this job was. After so long as a locum, he was deep, deep inside the last chance saloon, and the drinks weren't getting any easier to come by.

He sat down at the table and watched Lesley chopping. Even in an apron and sloppy old clothes, she was sexy. Of course, she'd be sexier without the sloppy old clothes. Or any clothes. Or the apron. Or maybe without the clothes but with the apron...

'There's a bottle of red on the table,' she said, without turning around.

Goldblatt got up and went to a drawer for the corkscrew.

Lesley stopped chopping again, half an onion in one hand, and caught his eye. 'So it really was all right, then?' she asked. 'Was it? Really?'

Goldblatt shrugged. He picked up the bottle and twisted the corkscrew into the cork, thinking about Emma. 'It's just like any other unit. Every place has its idiosyncrasies.'

'What does that mean?'

'Nothing. Oh, don't cry, Les.'

'It's the onions, you idiot!' said Lesley, wiping at an eye.

Goldblatt laughed. He put his arms around her and drew her close. She resisted for a moment, then settled back into him. Then she shrugged him away and went on chopping.

Goldblatt got out a pair of wine glasses. 'Anyway,' he said, pouring the wine, 'I haven't met the Prof yet.'

3

The next morning, Goldblatt settled down in the doctors' office with a coffee and the newspaper, giving the first patients in the clinic downstairs a chance to gather before he went and opened shop. In burst a thin, anxious-looking woman with a silk scarf draped over her shoulders.

Goldblatt stared. What kind of a hospital was this? Couldn't he even enjoy a cup of coffee in the doctors' office without being disturbed by every Tom, Dick and Harrietta who wanted respite from the ward?

'Dr Goldblatt, I presume?' said the woman, exuding an exaggerated, unctuous femininity that almost made Goldblatt spit out the coffee in his mouth.

'Could be,' said Goldblatt suspiciously.

The woman laughed, as if that was the most amusing thing she had heard for years.

'I'm Professor Small,' said the woman. 'Dr Goldblatt, thank you so much for coming.'

No. She said: 'Dr Goldblatt, thank you *so* much for coming,' as if she, Professor Small, was a famous society hostess, and the rubber-skidded vinyl floor of the cramped doctors' office was the marble-slabbed lobby of her mansion, and as if he, Malcolm Goldblatt, was a movie star or concert pianist or at least a major entertainer who had done her the *greatest* favour just by deigning to appear.

Goldblatt frowned.

The Professor was holding out her hand. Goldblatt stood up and shook it.

'Well, I'm very glad to be here,' he said, which is what he supposed a major entertainer would say to a famous society hostess in the circumstances.

'Are you? Are you really?' enquired the Prof anxiously.

Goldblatt shrugged. He would be, if only she'd let him finish his coffee in peace.

'I must rush,' said the Prof, managing to inject a tone of real regret into her voice. 'I just wanted to pop by and say hello. I'm sure we'll work very well together.'

Goldblatt nodded. He had no idea why the Prof was so sure. There were a number of people with whom, regretfully, he had not worked well in the past, and first impressions, he had discovered, were a poor indicator of the harmoniousness of future relations. Still, he appreciated her optimism.

'And we must have a talk about how we can help to make sure your next job is a substantive one,' she said on her way out the door, leaving little time – in fact, none – to discuss when this talk might actually take place.

And then she was gone.

Goldblatt sat down again. He picked up the paper and started to read. But it was no use, the tranquillity of the office had been shredded. He got up and headed for his clinic on the first floor.

The phone call came when he was with his last patient of the morning.

Goldblatt interrupted his conversation with the old lady sitting on the other side of the desk and answered the phone. For a moment he couldn't place the voice. It had a wheedling, whining quality, and he was tempted to hang up in disgust. But whoever was on the other end of the line knew his name.

'Dr Goldblatt,' said the voice for the second time.

'Yes,' said Goldblatt, and he smiled apologetically at the old lady in front of him, who was in the middle of telling him how she had broken her hip falling out of her wheelchair. The old lady nodded. In the NHS, she knew, the chances of a doctor hearing out the entire story of your hip fracture without a single interruption were pretty slim.

'Dr Goldblatt,' said the voice on the phone again. 'This is Professor Small. I wonder if you could do me a favour.'

Goldblatt doubted it. He rarely did favours for people who asked for them so brazenly.

'I have a patient with me in clinic who needs to come in. Are there any beds?'

Goldblatt rolled his eyes theatrically at the old lady. She responded with a conspiratorial smile, thinking there was some troublemaker on the phone. She didn't know how right she was. There were beds, of course, but none that was empty, if that was what the Prof meant. Goldblatt had been forced to cancel three admissions that morning before clinic, following a brief but torrid conversation with Sister Choy. From what Emma Burton had told him the previous day, that was probably the norm.

There was no point beating about the bush. 'No, Professor Small. We have no beds.'

'Dr Goldblatt, I have a patient with me in clinic who needs to come in.'

'We've already had to cancel today's admissions, Professor.'

'Malcolm, my patient really must come in,' oozed the Prof.

Malcolm?

'All right, send her to Emergency,' said Goldblatt. 'I'll see her after clinic and sort things out.'

'But she might wait hours for a bed in Emergency,' said the Prof.

It was true. It was truer than true. There wasn't any *might* about it. She *would* wait hours for a bed in Emergency.

'And she might end up anywhere in the hospital.'

True again. There wasn't a bed for her on the Prof's ward, that was for sure.

'Malcolm, I wonder if you would do me a favour,' the Prof continued to ooze. 'Do you think you could manipulate our beds and get this lady in on our ward? I'd be so grateful.'

Goldblatt didn't answer straight away. The Prof's gratitude was a powerful incentive. But what about his principle, his big, important principle that he had invented only yesterday and which he had enjoyed repeating to himself so much. Was he going to throw it away at the first temptation? Was he so capricious? So fickle?

He gazed at the patient on the other side of the desk. What would she think of him if she knew he was even considering that? But she had other things to worry about. Her dentures had slipped out of place, and she was busy working her lips surreptitiously in and out and over each other in a desperate attempt to reposition her teeth without using her fingers.

'Dr Goldblatt?'

He sighed. 'Professor Small, I'll see your patient in Emergency as soon as I'm finished here. I promise. I won't be long. I'm with my last patient.'

Professor Small had gone very quiet. There was only a tiny, mouse-like breathing on the other end of the line.

'Don't worry. If she's sick enough to come in, I'll get a bed for her somewhere.' Goldblatt waited for the Prof to say something.

'Oh.'

'What's her name?'

'Broderip,' whispered the Prof.

'Is that B R O D E R I P?'

'Yes.'

'I'll call Emergency and tell them to expect her, shall I?'

The Prof didn't answer. Goldblatt heard the muffled sound of a conversation on the other end of the phone. First the Prof's voice, then another.

'Dr Goldblatt, don't call Emergency,' said the Prof eventually. 'Mrs Broderip will think about it. I'll get back to you.'

The Prof hung up. Goldblatt put the phone down. He stared at it for a moment. He had a hunch that the Prof's patient – who wanted to think about whether she should take up the offer of being admitted – might not be *quite* as sick as the Prof had represented.

By the end of the day, he hadn't heard anything more about her. Goldblatt thought he had handled the situation pretty well. He had found the Prof's wheedling, whining tone oddly nauseating, but he had managed to hold down his breakfast and provide a textbook response, he thought. In fact, he was quietly confident that he had probably earned quite a lot of credit with the Prof for his calmness and rationality.

Or not. The next morning, when he arrived to do his round with Ludo and the HO, Goldblatt found a new patient propped up comfortably in bed twelve, enjoying a cup of tea and the fine panorama of north London that was visible from the seventh-story windows of the ward.

Goldblatt stared at the name-label on the chart in disbelief.

'Where did she come from?' he demanded hoarsely of the HO.

'Hornsey,' the Broderip informed him helpfully from her sickbed. 'The registrar didn't want me to come in. Ooh, if I catch that boy I'll give him a piece of my mind. Professor Small says to me: "Don't worry, Mrs Broderip, *I'll* get you in." Course I've been under her for years, I have. Started with her when she was just a doctor. Doctor Small she was, and now she's a professor. Hasn't she done well for herself? Still, she deserves it. She deserves everything she's got, that's what I say. Lovely person. Isn't she lovely?'

Goldblatt kept his opinion to himself.

'I won't stay long, love,' said the Broderip. 'Be no bother. It's just the Fatler's,' she informed him confidentially.

'She means she's got Fuertler's Syndrome, Malcolm,' whispered the HO.

Goldblatt glanced pointedly at the HO. He was just about capable of working that out, even after only two days on the ward, since hardly any of the Prof's patients had anything else.

'That's the one, love. Had it for years, the Fatler's. Still, can't complain. Suppose I should be grateful. Never had it as bad as some of them others. Awful, what it does to some of 'em. Gets 'em on the face, you know. Not me, touch wood. Bit on the arms, bit on the legs. Not too bad, considering. Got a little patch on me tummy, as well. I come up yesterday for the check-up and Professor Small says am I feeling tired? Well, who isn't? So she says I better come in for a bit. Have that Surlane profusion.'

'She means the Sorain infusion,' whispered the HO.

'That's it. You see, she knows. She's a clever one, this one. The Prof says: "Do you good, Mrs Broderip." Do me good. I knew her when she was just a doctor, you know. Isn't she lovely, bless her? She's lovely, isn't she?'

'Yes, she's lovely,' said Ludo, as Goldblatt grabbed the HO's collar and dragged her away.

Fuertler's Syndrome – or Fatler's, if you were Mrs Broderip – had been gifted to the world by Jacob Fuertler, a Viennese dermatologist who published a landmark paper in 1908 describing the illness in three Viennese women. The cardinal manifestations of this rare disease are skin lesions that range from a brawny thickening at one extreme of the spectrum to thinning and ulceration at the other, with the colour of the affected areas ranging from a deep brown discolouration to an almost entire loss of pigment.

No one really understood what caused the lesions in Fuertler's Syndrome. Acres of Fuertlered skin had been cut out, sliced up, and peered at under the microscope, but no one knew why they occurred in the first place. People with Fuertler's Syndrome have unusual antibodies in their blood, but are these antibodies cause or effect? Do they provoke the disease, or are they produced as a response to fragments of damaged cells released into the tissues? No one had been able to settle the question.

In addition to skin changes, Fuertler's patients sometimes develop various other problems. Chronic tiredness, dryness of the eyes and mouth, and low-grade inflammation of the joints are common. Nerve problems occasionally occur, with tingling in the hands and feet, and some patients develop mild muscle weakness. Less commonly, irregularities of the heartbeat, thyroid dysfunction, low-level anaemia, and mild deficiency of the blood's clotting components are seen. These problems are almost always manageable with treatment, never quite going away, never quite causing any trouble. The combination of skin lesions with internal problems means that the disease is sometimes treated by dermatologists and sometimes by physicians in other areas of internal medicine. In keeping with medical tradition, each group typically derides the other's ability to manage the illness – although in the case of Fuertler's Syndrome, with faint enthusiasm. Outside the tiny world of committed Fuertlerologists, no one is much interested in treating the disease. They are greatly outnumbered by those who couldn't care less about it and would gladly hand it on to anyone prepared to assume responsibility. Fuertler's Syndrome is an ungrateful illness. It grumbles along with its tapestry of depressing and disfiguring skin lesions, and its accompanying panoply of irritating but minor ailments, rarely doing anything to cause alarm, rarely repaying the treating physician with discernible signs of improvement.

On the other hand, there is one really serious complication that does occur in Fuertler's Syndrome. Pulmonary fibrosis, a thickening of the lung tissues blotting out the delicate membranes across which oxygen passes to the bloodstream, develops in a small percentage of cases. In the majority of these patients the process of fibrosis eventually comes to a halt, leaving them with nothing more serious than breathlessness on exertion, but in rare instances the fibrosis is aggressive, progressive, and resistant to treatment. Even the most powerful forms of chemotherapy are unlikely to arrest it. For these patients, after every conventional therapy has been exhausted, the only option is a lung transplant, but it's generally believed that the fibrosis will recur in the transplanted lung and therefore, given the scarcity of lungs for transplant, Fuertler's patients are hardly ever offered the operation.

Nothing that Goldblatt had seen suggested that Mrs Broderip was one of those rare cases, and much that he had seen – her hale and hearty demeanour, her robust complexion, her impressive weight – suggested the opposite. The HO gave a clear, succinct and passionate account of Mrs Broderip's arrival, her ruffled red hair standing on indignant end and eyes blazing with resentment. Ten minutes after Goldblatt had left the previous evening, Emma Burton had rung her up and told her that she had cleared a bed for a patient called Broderip, and the HO had better stay around to clerk her in because she was being admitted as an emergency from clinic, and the Prof had a special interest in her. No, it wasn't good enough for the on-call person to clerk her in. The HO had to do it herself. And four hours later this 'emergency' from clinic, who had taken the Underground back to Hornsey to get a nightie and prepare dinner for her husband – who couldn't be left alone just like that, love, without so much as a hot meal to give him strength – turned up, and the HO had been waiting all that time just to clerk her in.

'So don't blame me!' said the HO, fingering her stethoscope as if she was going to swing it at the first person who made a wrong move. 'I was here until ten o'clock!'

Goldblatt nodded. He had no intention of blaming the HO.

It had been too easy, he realized. How could he imagine that his reasonable, measured, and calm response could have any effect on a prof? Especially a prof like the Prof.

'Let's go,' he said to the HO.

They went back out on to the ward, where Ludo was still with the Broderip.

'She is lovely,' Ludo was saying.

'She is, isn't she?' said the Broderip.

'Come on,' Goldblatt said to Ludo.

'Don't you think she's lovely, Malcolm?' said Ludo.

'Come on, Ludo,' he repeated through gritted teeth.

'See you soon,' called out the Broderip cheerfully, and went back to sipping her tea.

They did the rest of the round. The HO pushed the notes trolley back into the doctors' office.

Goldblatt sat down. He glanced at the notes trolley and saw the Broderip's name on one of the files. He shook his head.

'What's wrong, Malcolm?' asked Ludo knowingly.

Goldblatt didn't reply. He looked around the doctors' office. Tatty brown Manila folders lay amidst the papers and X-ray folders that littered the desks. He gazed at one of them. Suddenly he felt like throwing it out. Goldblatt's first instinct was to throw most things out unless they had a clear and useful purpose that he could identify within ten seconds, especially in hospitals, where every document exists in duplicate except for those that are really necessary, which often don't exist at all. He practised wholesale disposal whenever he could, particularly with medications. This was a legacy of six months that he had spent as a registrar on a Geriatrics unit, where every patient came in clutching a bag bursting with drugs, a good portion of which had side effects that were far worse than anything they were supposedly meant to treat. Most of the others had been prescribed to counteract the first lot. From his very first day on the unit, Goldblatt had joyfully slashed long lines across the medication charts, often cancelling half a dozen drugs at a time.

'Let's get rid of these, shall we?' Goldblatt said, picking up one of the brown folders.

The HO's face was buried in the drug formulary, where she was trying to work out whether a drug called Cetirizine, which one of their patients was taking, could give you a rash. Goldblatt thought he should let the HO discover for herself that Cetirizine was normally prescribed as treatment for a rash. With luck, that would teach her to find out the easy way next time, by asking the patient why she was on it.

Ludo glanced at the folders doubtfully. 'What are they?' she said.

'No idea,' replied Goldblatt, gathering the rest of the brown folders up from the desks.

'Shouldn't we look before we throw them out?' asked Ludo.

'Why?'

'To find out what's in them.'

'Do you want to know?' asked Goldblatt.

Ludo shrugged.

'I had a professor of Ophthalmology when I was a medical student,' recounted Goldblatt, sitting back and switching seamlessly into old-timer mode. 'He had a saying I've never forgotten. "If you don't look, you won't see it". Has a nice ring, don't you think? "If you don't look, you won't see it."'

Ludo watched him suspiciously. 'Isn't that obvious?'

'Yes. So obvious you might never realize it for yourself unless someone told you. Ask yourself how many times have you not quite managed to see the full retina with your ophthalmoscope – or listened to every part of the lung fields with your stethoscope, for that matter, or got every limb positioned so you can test every reflex properly – and you've said to yourself, it's OK, I've seen enough?'

Ludo rolled her eyes. Probably every time she examined someone, thought Goldblatt.

He glanced at the HO, who had looked up from the formulary and was watching him. 'Never cut corners in examination,' he said. 'Never just assume it's OK. The one time you make that assumption, I can guarantee you, will be the one time you're wrong.' He repeated the mantra solemnly. 'If you don't look, you won't see it. They only gave this professor four lectures to cover all of Ophthalmology, and he didn't really expect us to remember any of it, but he wanted us to remember that. That, and one other thing he kept telling us to remember.'

'And?' demanded Ludo derisively, pretending she didn't care what the old ophthalmologist had said.

'He was right. We didn't remember any Ophthalmology.'

Ludo and the HO jeered.

'Now, this is Goldblatt's variant of the rule,' said Goldblatt, holding a finger up in the air.

Ludo and the HO waited.

'If you don't want to see it – don't look.'

Ludo frowned. The HO glanced questioningly at her.

'If you don't want to treat the renal failure in a terminally ill patient who's got two days to live and *really* doesn't need your treatment, don't do the test. If you don't want to reinforce someone's obsession with their blood pressure, don't put on the cuff. If you don't want to see it – don't look. Both of the principles are right. The trick is to know when each one applies. Look – or don't.' Goldblatt held out the folders to Ludo. 'Here you are.'

Ludo stared at the folders, as if transfixed by some barely resistible force emanating from their brown covers. They were just folders. But Goldblatt had done something to them. Suddenly the act of taking them had become an enormous, wrenching test of moral courage.

Ludo wasn't big on moral courage. And failing tests was one of her specialities.

She squirmed away, shaking her head. Some primal survival instinct told her that to take the folders was dangerous, to receive them was to create an unseverable bond between herself and those folders – whatever they were – which might exert malign and unforeseeable consequences over her far into the future.

Goldblatt held them over the rubbish bin.

'Don't!' cried Ludo.

'What?'

'Don't throw them out, Malcolm.'

Goldblatt smiled. Perhaps the bond had already been created. 'All right.' He tossed the folders on the floor under one of the desks.

'What was the other thing?' asked the HO.

'What other thing?'

'The other thing the Ophthalmology professor told you.'

'Beware the unilateral red eye.' Goldblatt turned to Ludo. 'And the causes of the unilateral red eye are...?'

'Please, Malcolm,' whined Ludo.

He put out his thumb, ready for the first answer.

'Look at the time! I've got a Dermatology clinic,' said Ludo, and walked out.

Goldblatt glanced at the HO. 'Incidentally, the Cetirizine Mrs Lamb is on. The one you were looking up. In the formulary. It's the cure, not the disease.'

The HO frowned.

'It's the treatment for her rash.'

'Oh. Right.' The HO paused. 'I would have worked that out.'

She soon left on what would become her daily visit to the Radiology bazaar to barter over the X-rays that hadn't been performed the previous day. Goldblatt pulled the admissions book out of a drawer in one of the desks. Thanks to the Broderip's miraculous appearance, he now had one less bed than he had previously assumed. He looked at the names of the patients who were scheduled to come in that day and chose the one with only two previous cancellations. Everyone else had three. He paused for a moment, took a deep breath, and dialled.

A woman answered the phone.

'Hello,' said Goldblatt. 'Is this Mrs Anderson? It's Dr Goldblatt here from Professor's Small's—'

Goldblatt stopped. Mrs Anderson was already crying.

As he listened to Mrs Anderson weep, Goldblatt could just glimpse the Broderip through the open door of the office. Propped up in what could have been Mrs Anderson's bed, she had finished her tea and fallen asleep, mouth gaping, snoring contentedly.

It took ten minutes to console Mrs Anderson. He promised to reschedule her quickly and swore the delay wouldn't worsen her condition. Even so, she was still sniffling when he put down the phone. He stared at the undeservedly snoring Broderip, and thought of the weeping Anderson. There were too many Andersons and too many Broderips, he thought. There were too many Andersons and too many Broderips, and they were inextricably linked by a cruel and immutable mathematical relationship...

He had discovered a new law of medicine, if not of nature! Because what was the Broderip–Anderson Principle, as Goldblatt immediately named it, if not such a law?

But what was the message buried in the Broderip–Anderson Principle? There was no joy to be had from it, no reason for him to smile. It was a monumentally depressing discovery. And yet, the very simplicity of the Principle's flawless, depressing perfection – its essential truth, so elusive yet so obvious when laid bare – gave Goldblatt a grudging satisfaction, much like the guilty pleasure that he imagined his medical predecessor and fellow humanitarian, Dr Guillotin, must have felt when he heard the first dull thud of a head falling from the block of his newly invented machine.

Broderip–Anderson. Goldblatt toyed with the name. He could see it in his mind's eye. He was dissatisfied. It lacked something. Not exactly a name to die for. Not even a name, as Khrushchev might have said, for a shrimp to whistle for. What was in a name? Everything. Shake-speare, who famously denied it in print, was either a complete madman or more probably was trying to keep a commercially sensitive discovery to himself. Goldblatt frowned. The name needed something. Exoticism, mystery, allure. Anderssen, he thought suddenly. Yes. Anderssen. There was something Scandinavian and tall about it. Blond, bearded, with the kind of craggy, bleak, Kierkegaardian intellect that could cook up such a principle. Or lithe, slim, blonde, and ready for sex. Whatever. Anderssen it was.

The Broderip–Anderssen Principle. Perfect!

No, it wasn't perfect. It was far from perfect. Not the principle, but the events that had led to its discovery.

It wasn't just the Prof, flying in the face of his utterly rational and calmly delivered response to her request to admit the Broderip. Profs fly in the face of rationality all the time. It was Emma Burton. Hadn't they had a conversation? Hadn't they agreed who was going to do what? Hadn't they concluded the admissions were going to be handled by him? And hadn't it all been – not to put too fine a point on it – fine?

Or had he just imagined the whole thing?

4

WHILE GOLDBLATT WAS SITTING in the doctors' office on the seventh floor, pondering his awful discovery of the Broderip–Anderssen Principle, Professor Small was sitting in her own office on the first floor. She too was pondering. Not the Broderip–Anderssen Principle – of which she hadn't yet heard – but its discoverer. As she pondered, she swivelled her chair around and stared at something stuck on the wall.

If anyone had been able to see the Prof when she was alone in her room, they would have often seen her in this posture. At first glance, the thing on the wall looked like a huge ruler made out of cardboard. It was about eight feet high, and numbered in hundreds up to 1800, which was written in bold figures at the top, with closely spaced lines dividing each hundred into units of ten. A thick column of red rose from the bottom to about half its height.

The Prof herself had conceived, designed, and created this scale many years earlier, after an epidemiologist called Dr Murdoch in Glasgow had estimated for her that there were approximately 1800 patients with Fuertler's Syndrome in Britain. It was the Prof herself who had progressively filled in the lower part of the scale with scarlet paint as the number of Fuertler's patients on her clinic list grew. Month after month, year after year, she had raised the level of the red column, adding a new band of paint whenever she had accumulated another ten patients. If you looked closely, you could see the lines where each band of paint had been added to the one below it, like the rings on a tree telling the history of its growth. The red column had reached 960. It had been at 960 for over five months, and the Prof still had to acquire another three patients before she could get her tin of scarlet paint out of the drawer in her desk and take it to 970. And above 970 there was still such a long way to go. There was so much white, an empty, yawning wasteland begging to be filled in. And the Prof wanted to fill it in. She yearned to fill it in. She could never rest, she knew, until the very last bit of white had been obliterated, and the column of red rose all the way to the top.

The Fuertler's Scale was a great motivator for the Prof. But it could also be a great depressor. Like the proverbial glass of water, sometimes it looked half full, and sometimes half empty, reflecting the Prof's own mood. It was also an incredibly silly object to have on the wall of her office, like some kind of display marking the progress of a church charity appeal, and the Prof felt embarrassed when people came into her room and saw it. She suspected that they talked about it later. Sometimes she wondered if she had outgrown it. But can you ever entirely outgrow the icons and amulets you have clung to in earlier, more desperate times? You can disown them to others, but can you disown them to yourself?

Andrea Small had tried once to take it down, but simply hadn't been able to. She had never tried again. After all, she had created it. Sometimes she talked to it. 'Scale,' she would say when everything was getting too much for her, 'what am I going to do?' The Scale never answered, of course. The Prof didn't expect it to. She wasn't mad, after all.

In short, the Prof's relationship with the Scale was probably the most profound emotional involvement in her life. It was certainly the most complex.

When the Scale seemed half full, it was like a comrade in arms, an old, trusted girlfriend who had been with her from the very start and was the only one who could really understand everything she had been through. And when it was half empty, it was like an old, estranged girlfriend who had turned on her and not only knew every secret of what she had been through, but mocked her for it with all the cutting cruelty that only an estranged girlfriend can wield.

When the world looked at her, Andrea imagined to herself, it didn't see her doubts, only the perfect façade she projected to the outside. It saw only the cool, efficient, learned, and thoughtful scientist, the sensitive doctor, the visionary professor, and the elegant dresser. As Imelda Marcos had been to shoes, so Andrea Small was to silk scarves, preferably from Liberty. She always wore one draped over her shoulders, or, if she was wearing a white coat, bunched around her neck. The silk scarf, she felt, was a central element in the image she portrayed to the world, alluding to her exquisitely feminine taste and sensitivity, while underlining her seriousness and position for all the world to see

But the doubts were there. Bottled up inside her, they boiled and bubbled, frequently threatening to explode, even as she maintained the perfect façade for the sake of her patients, and even as the column of red on the Scale climbed steadily up the wall of her office like some Dorian Gray thermometer of her inner uncertainty. Would the column rise any further? Nothing lasts for ever. As it had risen, so, one day, would it fall?

The perfect façade was just that, a façade that she pushed along in front of her like a heavy shield on castors. And the constant effort of pushing it meant that she could never forget what really lay behind it.

It had been like that ever since the day twenty-nine years earlier when Andrea Small arrived in Liverpool to start her medical training and found herself surrounded by big, loud, brash boys who had never voluntarily admitted ignorance in their lives, many of whom later ended up as alcoholics, adulterers, and professors. But it made no difference how they ended up. She had been thrown on to the back foot from the very beginning, and had never recovered.

No matter how much medicine Andrea knew, it was never enough when faced with someone louder and noisier than herself, even when she knew that person was an inveterate bluffer and liar and never spent any time learning anything properly. She was always waiting for the moment when there would be harmonious discussion and a peaceful interchange of ideas undisturbed by the blistering heat of rivalry. But that utopian time never arrived. When she was a medical student, she thought all the bluff and bluster would end when she graduated and became a member of the profession. And when she was a house officer, she thought it would end when she was a senior house officer and had full registration. And when she was a senior house officer, she persuaded herself that surely it would end when she had passed her specialist exams and was a registrar. And so on. And finally she realized that it would never end and that the cruel, caustic world she inhabited was the one in which she would always live, a world of incomprehensible bravado in which she was the only one, it seemed, who was aware of her own deficiencies, and, like some kind of self-nominated modern-day Christ, had taken on the burden of self-doubt for everyone else.

This was wrong, of course, as all the alcoholism and adultery later proved. But these weren't ways of coping with self-doubt, they were ways of seeking oblivion from it. Whereas Andrea, who rarely drank and hardly ever committed adultery, wasn't able to find oblivion from her self-doubt, and therefore experienced it down to the very core of her being.

She picked her way gingerly amongst the loud, brash, future adulterers and alcoholics in Liverpool, bouncing like an easily bruised pinball between their blustering buffers, and on through specialist training in a succession of hospitals. Somehow she survived, although as to the cost, the final account was still in the making. She learned to avoid, evade, ignore, and repress, and these skills, combined with her natural abilities to insinuate and ingratiate, got her through. Thirteen years after that first day in Liverpool, she was appointed as a consultant in London on a unit run by a physician called Dr Edward Wilkinson.

But that wasn't the end of her torment. It wasn't the beginning of the end. It wasn't even the end of the beginning.

Dr Wilkinson was a prickly, old-style general physician who prided himself, erroneously, on his ability to treat everything. His unit wasn't exactly a powerhouse in the hospital, more of a backwater where little had changed for decades or even centuries. But Edward Wilkinson was a pillar of the local medical community and, like any pillar, no one dared to knock him down. It was likely that he had selected Andrea Small, after the previous young consultant on the unit had fled to New Zealand, because he wanted someone he could dominate, someone who wasn't going to criticize the antique practices he still employed – exactly the opposite type of person, oddly enough, to Dr Morris, whom Andrea would choose when her own turn came to select a junior consultant seventeen years later. And Dr Wilkinson, who was an excellent judge of character as well as an accomplished bully, had chosen well. He quickly exposed Andrea's insecurities as a new consultant and picked at them incessantly, ensuring that they would never heal. He regularly humiliated her in front of the registrar and house officer on ward rounds with complicated questions that he looked up deliberately on Tuesday afternoons, and asked her to examine patients with subtle physical signs that she invariably failed to detect. Ducking and weaving to avoid the flak that Dr Wilkinson spat at her, she never really had a chance to develop the manner and cool confidence of a consultant. She lost faith in her ability to diagnose any but the most flagrant and advanced cases of the most common diseases. When Andrea looked back on that time now, it was barely believable that she had survived, let alone that she went on to rise to a professorship.

It was Fuertler's Syndrome that came to her rescue. Fuertler's Syndrome – a disease so vanishingly rare that only 1800 people in all of Britain were estimated to have it – that finally allowed her to create a façade that would stand up to the unrelenting corrosiveness of the world that surrounded her.

If one didn't know the details, one might easily be forgiven for thinking that Andrea Small's ascent to a professorship had taken place according to some cunning and prescient plan that she had made up as a medical student, and that her decision to specialise in Fuertler's Syndrome was the most cunning and prescient thing about it. As time had gone by, she had begun began to speak as if she actually had made the plan, saying things like: 'When I first decided to start treating Fuertler's patients...' But the truth was that she had never 'first decided' anything. Instead, she had inherited a Fuertler's patient from Dr Wilkinson, as many other junior consultants had inherited a Fuertler's patient or two from a senior consultant on their unit who had got sick of seeing them turn up year after year with their mystifying skin lesions that never went away. The difference was that Andrea Small then inherited a second Fuertler's patient from a senior consultant on another unit, who referred the patient to her on the flimsy pretext that, having recently taken on one Fuertler's patient, she obviously had an interest in the disease. This too happened to other junior consultants, but having a patient pressed on you from another unit wasn't the same as having to take one from your own boss. Even junior consultants had the right – and some in the profession might say the responsibility – to send the patient straight back to the unit they had come from. But Andrea was too unassertive to rebel against this flagrant act of exploitation and resentfully acquiesced. Doctors, like most mammals, can smell weakness. Acquiescence in accepting an unwanted patient is like posting an advertisement for more. Two additional Fuertler's patients followed, then another, by which time Andrea Small had accumulated the entire Fuertler's caseload of the hospital, and had become, to the amusement of the consultant body, the hospital's Fuertler's 'expert'. Andrea thought this was merely one more joke that life was playing on her.

But at some point she began to realize that this apparent joke might not be a joke at all. In fact, it might turn out to be the best thing that had ever happened to her. People still laughed about her being the hospital's Fuertler's expert, but to her own surprise, after a couple of years, she saw that this was precisely what she had become. A couple of newly diagnosed Fuertler's patients turned up on her doorstep. She began to get referrals from other consultants around London, only too happy to offload their Fuertler's patients to the new expert down the road. To everyone's amazement, she took them.

In those days, before she became a great Fuertlerologist, Andrea Small still had enough grasp of reality to recognize that Fuertler's Syndrome isn't a very important disease in the great medical scheme of things. But at least it was a disease. More importantly, it was her disease. She began to understand how precious is a disease which one can call one's own. Andrea's expertise in Fuertler's Syndrome gave her an independent position from which to face Dr Wilkinson's assaults. The frequency with which Dr Wilkinson attacked her over it, mocking and deriding this foolish, unimportant illness, showed how valuable it was. Andrea realized that the very deficiencies of her disease, its rarity and unpopularity, could be its strengths. They concealed a small yet apparently perfectly usable door to security and success.

The more Dr Wilkinson laughed and mocked her for it, the more secure she felt. Dr Wilkinson could laugh all he liked. Fuertler's Syndrome was hers! Hers! It was beyond his poisoned grasp. One day he would be gone, but Fuertler's Syndrome would remain.

Eventually Dr Wilkinson did go. He marched crabbily off into retirement, and Andrea Small, with her thirty Fuertler's patients, inherited the unit. And thus she might have remained, head of a small, unexceptional unit with an unusually large caseload of Fuertler's mixed in with the usual panoply of diabetics, heart failures, bronchitics, arthritics, and the others who make up the clientele of a general medical unit, if not for the arrival on the scene of Margaret Hayes.

Andrea Small would never forget the day she met the person who was to play such a large part in her life.

A big, solid woman with over-rouged cheeks and dyed brown hair in a beehive hairdo knocked on her door. The big woman came into her office, which wasn't much bigger than a cupboard in those days, took one look, and said: 'We'll have to do something about this.'

'About what?'

'About this office, Dr Small,' said Margaret Hayes. 'It isn't big enough to swing a cat in.'

Andrea was half inclined to throw this big, bustling, beehived busy-body out of the office to which she seemed to have taken such a dislike.

Fortunately, Margaret Hayes didn't give her the chance. 'I have come to you with a proposition,' she said.

'What proposition?' asked Andrea, wondering if it had anything to do with cats.

'My patients have spoken very highly of you, Dr Small,' said Margaret Hayes, who readily adopted a proprietorial tone.

'Which patients?' asked Andrea, feeling confused.

'Mine,' said Margaret Hayes. 'A number of them attend your clinic. The Foundation feels that it is time to make a commitment to one hospital as a centre of excellence.'

'Which Foundation?' asked Andrea.

'The Fuertler's Foundation, Dr Small. I am its secretary, and I have come to make a proposition. The Foundation feels that the time has come for a centre of excellence for Fuertler's patients. Fuertler's patients are being denied the excellence that other patients have. Is this right? Do you have the ability to head that centre of excellence, Dr Small? Think about it.'

Andrea thought about it. 'Yes,' she said.

Thus, in one exquisite moment of mutual bluff, a partnership was born. Margaret Hayes had been in charge of the Fuertler's Foundation for all of two months, having taken control from some drooping lily who had been running it so effectively that Andrea Small, the only doctor in London who would confess to having an interest in Fuertler's Syndrome, had never even heard of it. Its membership numbered all of eleven. This was something Margaret Hayes didn't tell Andrea on that fateful day. Andrea, on the other hand, knew as much about running a centre of excellence as she knew about performing cardiac surgery, which is something she didn't tell Margaret Hayes. Margaret Hayes had perceived very clearly that she required a medical alliance to cement the place of the Foundation in the hearts of the nation's Fuertler's sufferers, preferably with someone pliant, needy, and undemanding, and within a minute of meeting Andrea Small she guessed that she had found the right person. Andrea, who knew nothing about alliances and had never even thought about what kind she might want to have, merely sensed that something exceptional was on offer – even if the offer was being made by a big, brash blusterer who had turned up in her office like a beehived version of the boys she had known in Liverpool – and she could either take the chance or spend the rest of her life regretting it. They were both right.

In short, it was Margaret Hayes who was responsible for the fact that Andrea Small's cunning and prescient plan to become a professor – the one she had never actually made – moved ahead as if on schedule.

Margaret Hayes set about developing the Foundation with skull-crunching energy. How could she rest while her people – people with Fuertler's Syndrome – were in need? Not one of them, not a single one, was getting care that was good enough. How could they? There *was* no care that was good enough. The Foundation was their only hope for improvement, their one chance, and the responsibility of it weighed so heavily on Margaret Hayes's shoulders that she sometimes almost groaned with pleasure.

The Fuertler's Foundation grew, and, as its satellite, so did Andrea Small's unit. As Margaret broadcast the news to her growing membership, Andrea's fame as a Fuertlerologist spread over England's green and pleasant land. And over Scotland and Wales too. Patients began to mention her name to their consultants, wondering whether they could be referred to her. Their own consultants couldn't have been happier to oblige. The red column on the Scale in her office began its dizzying rise, slowly at first, then accelerating. Patients streamed towards Andrea's clinic from all over the country. And every patient who streamed through the door brought an extra payment to the hospital from their local funding authority. For the first time, Andrea Small noticed, the hospital administrators listened to what she was saying. For the first time, they began to agree with the things she wanted to do.

She set about the total Fuertlerization of her unit. Throwing her growing financial weight around to the full, she progressively divested her unit of its general medical functions. First, she turned her own clinic list into a Fuertler's-only zone, leaving other patients to be seen by the SR and registrar. Then she squeezed funding out of the managers for a couple of specialist assistants to help in her Fuertler's clinic as the number of referrals continued to rise. She stealthily transferred old non-Fuertler's patients, many dating back to the days of Dr Wilkinson, to other units, employing any pretext she could concoct. Then she achieved her greatest coup. Over howls of protest from her fellow consultants, she succeeded in withdrawing her unit from responsibility for emergency medical patients. The labour of her junior doctors was still allocated into the rosters for the overnight on-call slogs, but the patients her doctors admitted went to other units, and Andrea herself had no responsibility for their ongoing care. With this step, the process was complete. Other than the clinics of the registrar and SR, and the occasional admissions that came from them, the unit had been Fuertlerized. Andrea herself was insulated virtually completely from contact with any other disease, which had been her dream ever since Dr Wilkinson had pulverized her faith in her ability as a general consultant. The sixteen beds of her unit on the seventh floor were as a shrine to Jacob Fuertler, occupied almost exclusively by the patients he had loosed on the world.

But what were they doing there?

Other than the tiny percentage of patients with severe pulmonary fibrosis, Fuertler's patients had hardly ever needed admission before Andrea Small's unit had turned into a centre of excellence. Not that her patients with pulmonary fibrosis weren't important to the Prof. They were. The fact that Fuertler's patients could get such a grave condition, and could even die of it – even if it was only a fraction of a percentage point who did – somehow made Fuertler's Syndrome a more important disease than it would have been if all there was to it were blotches on the skin and an occasional blip in the heartbeat. But Andrea rarely had severely ill patients like that on her ward. To be honest, she wasn't altogether comfortable with the thought that they were lying around in her beds and might actually die in one of them. To be even more honest – which was something she was prepared to be only in the locked privacy of her office, for obvious reasons – they scared her witless, and reminded her of those horrible days with Dr Wilkinson when she had people dying of heart attacks and lung cancers and emphysema and all kinds of awful things all over the place and had no idea what to do about them. She therefore had her patients with pulmonary fibrosis transferred immediately to a respiratory specialist called Dr de Witte at the East Surrey Hospital, despite the fact that the East Surrey Hospital was eight miles away and there was a perfectly fine clutch of respiratory physicians right there in the hospital with a unit only two floors below her own ward. A unit on which Dr de Witte himself had once worked, and which he had left a few years earlier after failing to get the appointment as unit head. The reason that Andrea continued to send her patients to him, even after he had left, was a mystery to all but those who knew the most intimate details of the Prof's private life – or would have been, had they not spread such scurrilous rumours about her and Tom de Witte, a number of which were definitely untrue.

But what about the other patients, the ones not blessed with pulmonary fibrosis? Were they never to be admitted? Margaret Hayes insisted that they should be. Andrea agreed. She devised a six-monthly work-up of fifty-four tests looking for every conceivable problem that was known to develop in Fuertler's Syndrome and for quite a few that weren't. There were ECGs and echocardiograms and thyroid scans and pulmonary function tests and X-rays and so many blood tests that any patient who came in was guaranteed to take home at least a borderline case of anaemia as a souvenir of their stay.

There was no particular reason that Andrea had chosen six months as the interval for the work-up. There were no scientific papers that demonstrated that work-ups at six-month intervals, or twelve-month intervals, or any other intervals, increased the rate at which Fuertler's problems were detected or, more importantly, improved the way in which these problems could be treated, and Andrea herself didn't initiate any studies to verify this. Six months just sounded about right.

The hospital management didn't object to the work-ups, whatever the scientific evidence or lack of it. Why would they? Every patient admitted to the ward brought a payment that was far larger than the payment when the patient merely came to clinic.

Naturally, the work-ups were an opportunity for important scientific investigation. The progress and test results of every one of Andrea Small's patients were carefully recorded on data sheets contained in special folders. As often as possible, Andrea got one of her SRs to write up the findings into scientific papers that were usually rejected by the more reputable journals because of poor statistical method.

With financial support from the Fuertler's Foundation, Andrea also set up a little one-room lab and got funding for a Russian post-doctoral fellow called Bolkovsky to produce papers that were published with her name on them. And yet not even this was enough for Margaret Hayes. As time went by, it became intolerable to her that as the head of the Fuertler's Foundation's centre of excellence, Andrea Small was still not a professor. It was just one more example of the discrimination that the entire medical profession practised against her disease.

Andrea didn't disagree. Even after all she had done, she felt that her colleagues still didn't take Fuertler's Syndrome seriously enough. But Andrea wasn't sure that trying to secure a professorship was the right answer. She knew that Professor Dennis, the Dean of the Medical School, and Professor Gold, the Director of the Department of Medicine, didn't consider her research or her contribution to the medical school to be of sufficiently high standard to justify a professorship, and she didn't think it would improve the seriousness with which her colleagues took Fuertler's Syndrome if it became known that she had been rejected for one. Not to mention the seriousness with which they took *her*, which wasn't all that it could be, either.

Margaret Hayes knew better. Without even consulting her, Margaret spoke to the hospital's Director of Finance. The Director of Finance recognized an irresistible argument when he heard one, especially one that was coupled with a threat to take away the very thing that made it irresistible. The Small unit had become one of the hospital's most lucrative earners. Shepherded by Margaret Hayes, the Fuertler's faithful flocked to it from the four corners of the country. But as Margaret didn't fail to point out to the Director of Finance, there *were* other Fuertler's practitioners in the country – one or two, anyway – including a certain Dr Jenkins in Leicester who was champing at the bit – literally *champing* – to receive the Fuertler Foundation's recommendation.

The Director of Finance spoke to the Chief Executive. The Chief Executive, who had recently had to sit through an Andrea Small tirade on the allocation of physiotherapy sessions, didn't think much of her. He thought more of the Dean of his Medical School, whose opinion he trusted on academic matters, and he thought more of his Director of the Department of Medicine, whose opinion he trusted on clinical matters. But he also thought a lot of his Director of Finance, whose opinion he trusted on financial matters. The campaign for Andrea Small's professorship, which might easily have been misconstrued as a professional question, actually turned out to be a financial question. Or a question of financial blackmail, to put it another way. Or financial common sense, to use a less pejorative term.

So Andrea Small became a professor, exactly on schedule with the cunning and prescient career plan that she had never made. But did it change anything? Did it drain the acid pool of self-doubt that boiled and bubbled behind the façade? Or did it make it boil and bubble even faster?

By now Andrea had become a leading light in the tiny international world of Fuertlerologists. She spoke at conferences, she wrote review articles. Yet despite all of this, despite everything she had done, despite the fact that her unit was indisputably the only centre of excellence for Fuertler's Syndrome in the entire country and also happened to be one of the highest earning units in the hospital, despite her newly acquired professorial status, Andrea Small had a strong suspicion that her consultant colleagues still didn't take her seriously. They didn't sufficiently respect her, nor the disease to which she had dedicated her life.

Much of her energy over the past couple of years had been spent in a drive to make sure that they did. She had manoeuvred to achieve the appointment of a second consultant, Dr Morris, and only now had successfully completed a campaign for a senior house officer post to be funded on her unit. And yet still her suspicion was not allayed. Like a meerkat constantly scanning the horizon, Andrea was alert to every nuance and sign of disrespect, and often detected them. Even the new locum registrar she had just employed, Dr Goldblatt, after just one or two brief conversations, gave her that same horrible feeling of not being respected that she had felt so often before.

It was at times like this, when she felt insecure, that she would turn around and gaze at the Scale, hoping it was going to be one of those days when it appeared half full rather than half empty, hoping that it was going to be one of those days when it was like a trusted comrade rather than a treacherous friend.

She gazed at the Scale now, thinking about Malcolm Goldblatt. He was only a locum registrar, and the circumstances being what they were – the SR having walked out with hardly so much as a week's notice – she had needed someone in a hurry. He had faxed his CV in response to the urgent advertisement that the hospital had placed, and it was all done over the phone. Not a proper interview, nothing even approaching the exhaustive selection process before a full panel that would have been required for a substantive job. Considering the CVs of the other candidates who had applied, she thought she had been lucky to get him.

So what was it about him? A certain insolence. She had found him drinking coffee in the doctors' office. Nothing wrong with drinking coffee in the doctors' office, of course. Everyone did it. But the *way* he had been drinking it...

And the conversation on the phone about the poor patient who needed to come in from clinic. What was *that* about? She could hardly imagine a more unreasonable response. What was wrong with the boy? Perhaps he had misunderstood her. Yes, a misunderstanding.

No, it wasn't a misunderstanding. He had actually told her to send the patient to Emergency. To Emergency! On the surface, certainly, perfectly sensible, and probably exactly what he was supposed to do according to the hospital handbook, if such a thing existed – but completely absurd! She had had to call Emma, who had told her he had some problem with manipulating beds, of all things. For heaven's sake, what was he there to do if not manipulate beds?

Why couldn't they all be like Emma? Compliant, if not shamelessly sycophantic, and terrified of rebuke. Why couldn't they all be like her? But they weren't. Very few, anyway.

Dr Goldblatt clearly wasn't.

The Prof got up. She went to a filing cabinet and pulled out his CV.

Yes, it was impressive. Undergraduate degree at Cambridge. First class honours. HO and SHO jobs at good London hospitals. First part exam for the Royal College of Physicians, then the second part... Then he'd gone off to study law. Law! Honestly, whatever was he thinking? First class honours again, then a stint at some kind of non-governmental organization. Then back to medicine. The Prof shook her head. Medicine, law, medicine... What was wrong with the boy? He must be intelligent. Intelligent, certainly. But peculiar.

The Prof swivelled around and gazed at the Scale, thinking about the conversation she had had with Goldblatt on the phone. Perhaps she should have a talk to him. Perhaps she ought to say something to him about it.

She looked back at Goldblatt's CV. She thought about the way he had been drinking his coffee, the sound of his voice on the phone when she had called him in clinic.

The finely honed skills of avoidance and evasion that had served Andrea Small so well since the early years of her career were always primed to kick in. So deeply ingrained were they that she was no longer even aware when she was practising them.

No, she thought. No need for a talk. It was definitely a misunderstanding.

5

SIMMONS, THE TWENTY-EIGHT-YEAR-OLD MALE with mild jaundice and knee pain who had briefly turned into a seventy-two-year-old woman with cerebellar dysfunction and inframammary candidiasis, was a scabby, drug-addicted hepatitic who, Goldblatt soon decided, needed to be an inpatient about as much as Goldblatt did himself.

It's a sad fact of the profession that most doctors dislike drug addicts, and dislike even more having to deal with them. Experience soon teaches that a drug addict generally values only two things about a doctor – his prescription form and his signature – and more particularly the combination of the two, which is the key to a garden of a thousand delights for which they will cheat, lie, threaten, and deceive. Goldblatt treated them when they were genuinely ill, as he would treat anyone, and as soon as they were well enough he kicked them out.

It wasn't that he had no sympathy for them. How could you not feel sorry for these chemically corroded shipwrecks of humanity – when you didn't actually have one of them in front of you alternately begging and physically threatening you for a Temazepam capsule? It was the fruit of practice, one of the many lessons medicine had taught him. After feeling for lymph nodes deep in someone's armpit, for example, the smell of sweat will linger on your fingers for twenty-four hours, no matter how often you scrub your hands. That was one of the lessons medicine had taught him, and it saved a lot of fruitless and repetitive handwashing. Never write off a stroke patient in the first two days. That was another important lesson. Avoid drug addicts and kick them off your ward. That was just one more lesson, like all the others.

Medicine had started educating him in this particular lesson quite early in his career. Three weeks after he had started as a house officer, to be precise. Psychologically, Mother Medicine chose a perfect moment to begin her instruction, the first Sunday night that Malcolm Goldblatt ever spent on call.

When Goldblatt looked back on himself as he was then, Goldblatt the HO, that Goldblatt of his first Sunday night on call nine years before, he saw an almost unbearable vulnerability. It was almost too excruciating to contemplate. He wanted to cup his hands around his mouth and shout across time to that earlier, innocent self, shout all the things that he had been forced to learn since then, save himself some of the pain that awaited him. But it was impossible, of course. And it wouldn't have made any difference even if it were possible, that was the tragic thing about it. The Goldblatt of that night nine years before, the current Goldblatt knew, wouldn't have listened. The Goldblatt of that night hadn't thought of himself as inexperienced and vulnerable. He had thought of himself as rough, tough, and ready – a lot rougher, tougher, and readier than the current Goldblatt thought of himself.

But in reality, of course, he wasn't.

Just after two o'clock in the morning of that first ever Sunday night of his career on call, after he had already been on call on the Saturday night as well and had had a total of about an hour's sleep, the first ever drug addict of Goldblatt's experience as a doctor walked into Emergency.

The fact that this man actually walked in was pretty astonishing since he was sick enough to be dead, and logically speaking the fact that he actually walked out again three hours later after the nurse on duty took away his Distalgesic tablets should have been even more astonishing – because if some miracle had taken place to cure him in the intervening time, Goldblatt, for one, had missed it – but by that stage Goldblatt couldn't care enough about him to be astonished or even moderately interested. He had spent half the night with this prematurely aged, wizened, tattooed, and self-abused homunculus of twenty-five who had emerged from whichever cardboard box he had been inhabiting with earrings through his nipples and track marks down his arms, a fever of forty-one degrees, and a heart that shuddered and heaved and shook 120 times a minute as it tried to pump blood into the vessels of his lacerated circulation. Most of it was going the wrong way. There are four valves in your average human heart and at least two of the four in this particular human were half eaten away by infection. Or endocarditis, as the medical terminology goes. Goldblatt's registrar told him to do an 'endocarditis work-up', told him what anti-biotics to give, and went to bed. The 'endocarditis work-up' should have taken forty-five minutes. It took three hours. The drug addict, whose name was Bates or Bent or something else that was short and began with a B, kept begging for morphine. Every time Goldblatt asked a question, all he got was a whining supplication for the drug.

'Morphine, doc,' BatesorBent kept saying, feigning dizziness, nausea, and even death, which Goldblatt feared was imminent. 'I'm withdrawing. I'm going cold turkey.'

'Where's the pain?' Goldblatt kept demanding.

But the cold and cringing turkey in front of him didn't have any pain, and didn't have the presence of mind to pretend that he did. All he would say was that he was withdrawing. Goldblatt couldn't give him morphine for withdrawal, and BatesorBent should have known it. It's one of the basic facts of any self-respecting drug addict's existence that a doctor can prescribe opiates only for pain. BatesorBent really must have been sick to have forgotten it. But that didn't help Goldblatt, who was new to the job and still remembered things they had told him at medical school, like the fact that he could be struck off for inappropriately prescribing opiates to addicts. Apart from that, if it meant he could get the work-up done and get some sleep, Goldblatt wanted to give BatesorBent the stuff probably even more than BatesorBent wanted to get it. Over and over Goldblatt asked him if he was in pain, but the dumb bastard simply refused to say the magic word.

Eventually Goldblatt grabbed a fistful of BatesorBent's paltry flesh and squeezed it hard on the pretext of examining his thigh.

'Where's the pain?' he demanded desperately.

'I don't have any pain, you fucker!' cried BatesorBent, wincing. 'I'm fucking withdrawing! Don't you know anything?'

'Then I can't give you morphine,' Goldblatt said.

'Fuck you, you fucking fucker!' yelled BatesorBent, whose range of obscenities was proving to lack both inventiveness and variety.

Goldblatt shoved a needle through a minefield of track marks into a vein to draw blood.

'Is that morphine, doc?' he asked.

'No,' said Goldblatt.

'Fuck you, you fucking fucked-up fucker,' shouted BatesorBent, and jerked his arm away, spraying blood teeming with viruses and bacteria over Goldblatt's face and in a long, speckled arc across the screens around the bed. Goldblatt wiped his face with his sleeve and picked up another needle with grim determination.

He did the work-up. It was five o'clock in the morning by the time he finished it, and he was ready to fall into bed with BatesorBent and his FleasorLice if there was even a moderate chance of getting some sleep – but he did it. Somehow he had even managed to get BatesorBent to let him site a drip in one of the few veins that hadn't been destroyed by years of drug injection, and had given him his first doses of antibiotics, and there was some chance that this treatment would start to save the tattered remnants of his heart valves and possibly his life. And that was when Goldblatt made his mistake: not only did he allow himself to feel that he had achieved something, but he allowed himself to expect appreciation.

He really was vulnerable and inexperienced. Mother Medicine had one of her lessons in store for him and was about to pour it all over his head like a big tub of lard.

He had left BatesorBent after the triumphant conclusion to his three-hour endocarditis work-up, and was on his way to wash the dried blood off his face. A nurse passed him, going in the other direction, and smiled mechanically before disappearing behind the screens around the bed. An August dawn was beginning to brighten the windows. Goldblatt came out of the bathroom and sat down at the nurses' station to write his notes. Suddenly he heard a familiar voice.

'Fuck you!'

Goldblatt froze.

'Fuck you!' he heard again from behind the screens. 'Let go of that!'

The nurse said something.

'Fuck you, you cunt!'

Goldblatt wondered whether he should go behind the screens to rescue the nurse. The voice kept swearing. It was coming to him as if from somewhere in the distance, from behind clouds. Goldblatt felt an immense tiredness sweep over him and begin to drown him. The effect of two consecutive nights of almost total sleep deprivation suddenly hit him. The nurse was being murdered by the drug addict behind the screens, but he couldn't be bothered getting up. It wasn't physical. He was awake. But something inside him had laid its head down and given up.

He could still remember it now, all these years later, exactly as it felt. Everything was disembodied. Voices came from far away, sound and image dissociated, perceptions floated in and bounced off him and floated away again. The things that happened next seemed as if they were taking place somewhere else, far away, beyond his reach.

From his position behind the high ledge of the nurses' station, Goldblatt saw the screens around the bed jerk open. BatesorBent appeared in the gap like some kind of feverish stick-creature, dressed once more in his filthy black jeans and T-shirt, his blond hair standing on end all the way down to its black roots, and the drip that Goldblatt had inserted still protruding from his arm. He tottered towards Goldblatt and stopped in front of him, mistaking him for someone who cared about what happened to him.

'That fucking cunt took my Distalgesic tablets away.'

Goldblatt stared at him.

'Did you hear me? What right's she fucking got? Cunt! They're mine. I'm not staying in this fucking place without my fucking tablets!'

'You're in no fit state to leave the hospital,' the nurse's selfless voice called after him, as she emerged from behind the screens where BatesorBent had probably knocked her over and stomped on her face to get away. 'We can't be held responsible for the consequences. That's our medical advice, isn't it, Dr Goldblatt? I'm warning you, you'll have to sign a self-discharge form!'

BatesorBent obviously didn't appreciate the full seriousness of having to sign a self-discharge form. Someone should have told him before they let him on to the ward.

'Fuck you! Fuck the whole fucking lot of you fucking fuckers!' he shouted, and walked out.

'Dr Goldblatt!' demanded the nurse.

Goldblatt watched BatesorBent bounce against the swinging doors of the ward a couple of times before he made it out. Three sleepless hours of his work disappeared.

Goodbye, Three Hours of Work. It was nice to have met you at two in the morning.

The nurse glared furiously at Goldblatt. He was still watching the ward doors that BatesorBent had left swinging, mesmerized by the pointless inertia of their diminishing movements. There was nothing left inside him but exhaustion, emptiness, and resentment. The weekend on call, the two nights of sleeplessness he had already endured, had cleaned him out of anything higher and more human, reducing him to the level of bare, snivelling, animal survival.

Goldblatt thought, Three Hours of Work, I hope you fucking die.

And at that moment, he meant it.

A folder appeared under his nose.

'Make a note!' ordered the nurse.

Goldblatt made a note, watching his hand move the pen, and wondering what difference the words were going to make.

The nurse tore the folder away and examined it.

'I'm going to record this in the nursing notes,' she said. 'You can be sure of that, Dr Goldblatt. That man's ill. Seriously ill. I'm going to record exactly what you did to stop him leaving.'

'That won't take very long,' Goldblatt observed listlessly.

The nurse shook her head in disgust. 'That man may very well die.'

'True.' Goldblatt turned to the nurse, suddenly awakened, intrigued by her attitude. 'Why do you care? He called you a cunt.'

'Dr Goldblatt!' she screamed. 'I've never been so insulted in my entire life. I've worked as a nurse at this hospital for seventeen years and—'

Goldblatt had worked there for barely seventeen days and already it felt as if it had been too long. 'It was him who called you a cunt,' he pointed out with useless logic. 'Not me.'

'Dr Goldblatt!' she shrieked again, her voice rising an octave. She began dialling for the security man.

Goldblatt got up and walked away. He could hear the nurse shouting at him. Something in his brain refused to register the words. He didn't want to hear anything more from her or from BatesorBent or from any of them.

He did hear more, of course, when the nurse's formal complaint made its way to the medical director. That took about a week. By then Goldblatt couldn't see the point in the whole matter because unless he had sought urgent medical help elsewhere, BatesorBent was almost certainly dead. Without treatment, the infection in his heart would have blown one of his valves completely within a couple of days of walking out of the hospital. He was probably lying lifeless under a pile of refuse somewhere with a needle stuck up his arm. Possibly the same needle Goldblatt had put there.

When he said that, the medical director asked if that made him happy.

'No,' said Goldblatt. 'I pity the poor rubbish collector who's going to find him. He'll probably need therapy for years.'

The medical director growled. He was an old-school type and didn't set much store by therapy.

For a while after that, Goldblatt often thought about BatesorBent, wondering if he should feel guilty at his own indifference when he had watched that tottering stick-figure staggering out of the hospital. Or disturbed by it. Or ashamed of it. He told himself that surely BatesorBent would have gone somewhere else for treatment. He wouldn't have just buried himself under a pile of rubbish and died. But that comfort – or delusion – didn't change what he had thought at the time. Goldblatt didn't see himself as the kind of person who didn't care if another person died. But that was what he had become, at least for that moment. It worried him. He grappled with the realization. Eventually he came to the conclusion that if you reduce a human being to such a state of exhaustion, stress, and terror at having to cope with tasks far beyond his competence in conditions of such physical brutalization – as he had been reduced on that long distant Sunday night – then you can't expect him to feel anything. Anything but indifference, which is precisely the point he had reached.

But it took a long time, and many more nights on call, for Goldblatt to arrive at that conclusion. And in the meantime it didn't occur to him to wonder that no one spoke to him – no one apart from the medical director who wanted to know if he was happy that BatesorBent was probably dead in a cardboard box – to ask him how it felt to have been reduced to that state of catastrophic indifference, worse, how it felt to have watched that man walking out and to find himself actually wishing that he'd die.

His thoughts, his guilt, the conclusion he eventually reached – he went through all of it alone.

BatesorBent wasn't the last of the drug addicts that Goldblatt had treated over the years, not by a long shot. Like any hospital physician, he had seen an unending parade of them. They checked into hospital when it suited them, and they discharged themselves just as soon as they thought they had wheedled and whined, cajoled and cheated as many different drugs out of the staff as they could. They practised an incredible pharmacological promiscuity, taking anything they could get their hands on, narcotics, stimulants, opiates, depressants, antidepressants, hypnotics, analgesics, anaesthetics, anxiolytics, antispasmodics, anything that had a chemical in it and was rumoured to have an effect on mood, perception, or coordination. They took them in any formulation they could get hold of, tablets, solutions, suspensions, injectables, powders, pills, suppositories, anything that could be swallowed or snorted, injected or inserted.

In a way, you had to admire them. The lengths to which they went in order to obtain a few chemicals were nothing short of fantastic. And the precautions they took to conceal their caches were almost unimaginable. Many were the rectums in which a few pilfered, foil-wrapped tablets of codeine had been stashed to be retrieved when needed. It was almost funny. But not funny enough to outweigh the satisfaction of kicking one of them off your ward.

Goldblatt didn't know what Simmons had stashed up his rectum. He had no intention of finding out.

Simmons had dyed blond hair with an inch of black root, shifty brown eyes, a square face, and one quarter of what appeared to be an unfinished dragon tattoo etched across his thin white chest. He had a mild case of hepatitis, presumably induced by one of his pharmaceutical adventures. Emma Burton had seen him in clinic with a referral for knee pain – Simmons, no doubt, was hoping to score a six-month prescription of codeine that would last him about a week – had noticed a slight tinge of yellow in his eyes, and had rushed him in, writing up a four-hourly order for a huge dose of codeine in the process, which was a great inducement for Simmons to stay and enjoy the hospitality. So perplexed was Gold-blatt by Emma's action that he had spent a good twenty minutes on his first day on the unit looking through Simmons's notes to try to work out why he wasn't simply the mild, kick-me-out-of-hospital hepatitis that he appeared to be. He *was* the mild kick-me-out-of-hospital hepatitis that he appeared to be. The fact that he had been sitting in bed one on the Prof's ward for almost a week said a lot more about Emma Burton than it did about Simmons.

In the meantime, Simmons was sturdily recovering from his illness through a concentrated lack of medical intervention. Exactly how long Emma was planning to continue this policy wasn't clear – perhaps until the last faint tinge of yellow had disappeared completely and, like William Prescott at Bunker Hill, she could see the whites of his eyes. Or at least until the Prof saw them on her next round.

Simmons strongly supported this policy, and had already taken steps to reinforce it, overdosing on a bottle of antidepressants that he had snatched from the nurses' drug trolley two nights after he had been admitted to the ward. This initiative had earned him a day on the intensive therapy unit in case his heart seized up. It didn't, of course. As an experienced practitioner, Simmons knew exactly how far he could go before he over-dosed on an overdose. Back on the ward, he was probably already planning his next manoeuvre. In case there had been any doubt, this proved that Simmons obviously had an uncontrollable predilection for swallowing large amounts of chemicals with unpredictable effects, and for his own protection, if nothing else, Goldblatt reasoned that the kindest thing any doctor could do was to remove him from this drug-rich environment.

Simmons disagreed. When his three new doctors turned up with the notes trolley on their second day on the unit he immediately identified Goldblatt as a seasoned opponent. Like most people, he didn't know what to make of Ludo. With the instinct of a true street-fighter he identified the weakest link in the chain.

'It was a suicide attempt, that thing with them tablets,' he said to the HO, scratching at his quarter-tattoo and lying shamelessly.

The HO looked at him sympathetically, remembering all the things she had been taught in medical school about showing sensitivity, empathy, and understanding to suicide attempters. The first thing was to gain their trust, she remembered, and to gain their trust you had to listen patiently and be perceived as non-judgemental. The HO put Simmons's notes down on the bed and listened patiently with her most non-judgemental expression on her face – a conspicuous frown and a fixed stare. She looked as if she was trying to contain a fart. Her gullibility shone from her eyes and Simmons latched on to it with an unerring grasp.

'You're the house officer, aren't you?' he asked, just to be sure.

The HO nodded.

'I couldn't go on,' Simmons continued, giving the HO a beseeching look and shamelessly batting his stye-bulbed eyelids. 'This hepatitis and all.'

The HO nodded again.

'I didn't tell them,' said Simmons. 'I told them it was a mistake. But it wasn't,' he confided. 'I feel I can talk to you. It was a suicide attempt. I should have told them before, I know, but I couldn't.'

'I understand,' said the HO.

'Do you?' said Simmons, with a maudlin display of halting gratitude, so pathetic and contrived that even an HO should have picked up on it. 'I didn't tell them before. I felt... ashamed.'

'It's all right,' replied the HO soothingly, 'you've told us now.'

The HO picked up Simmons's notes and took her pen out of her pocket.

'Stop,' said Goldblatt. It was always advisable, he had learned, to find out how much work an HO was going to need. This particular pantomime had gone on long enough. 'What are you doing?'

'I'm just going to make a note of what Mr Simmons said,' replied the HO.

'Don't make a note,' said Goldblatt.

'Make a note,' said Simmons.

'Don't,' said Goldblatt.

'Do,' said Simmons

The HO looked around in confusion. She glanced at Ludo. Ludo gravely shook her head. If Simmons's assault on the bottle of antidepressants was officially recognized as a suicide attempt they'd be obliged to arrange a psychiatric review before he left. It would take days to get the psychiatrists to see him. Simmons would be on the ward for ages, regardless of the whites of his eyes.

Goldblatt took the pen out of the HO's hand. He turned to Simmons. 'Mr Simmons,' he asked, 'do you think you can manage by yourself at home?'

Simmons guffawed.

'Do you have anyone who can look after you at home?'

Simmons leered cynically. What kind of a stupid question was that? He began to think he had overestimated Goldblatt, who was turning out to be one of the most naive registrars he had ever faced.

'Don't be stupid,' he said.

'All right,' said Goldblatt, 'I won't be stupid. Instead of sending you home today, we'll send you home tomorrow.'

'But I won't have anyone at home tomorrow either,' he protested.

'Then make arrangements, Mr Simmons,' said Goldblatt reasonably. 'That's why we're letting you stay an extra day, remember?' Goldblatt turned to the HO and gave her pen back. 'Write that down,' he said.

'What?'

'That we discussed discharge plans. That Mr Simmons is going to make arrangements. That he's going to be discharged tomorrow.'

'Like fuck I am,' growled Simmons. 'I need a social worker!' he yelled, trying another old ploy to extend his stay. 'Write that down. Go on, write it down.'

'Don't,' said Goldblatt.

The HO didn't. She wasn't sure she knew what was going on, but she was fairly certain that when it came to taking orders, and she had to choose between her registrar and a patient, she should probably listen to her registrar. 'Malcolm,' she said, 'does he need any bloods?'

'No,' said Simmons quickly.

Goldblatt had been about to give the same answer. He looked at Simmons with interest. He glanced at Simmons's arms. Simmons hid them under the sheet.

'Hmm,' said Goldblatt portentously, taking the notes from the HO and pretending to read. He handed them to Ludo. 'What do you think, Dr Madic?'

'No!' shouted Simmons.

Ludo turned the pages. 'There's all kinds of tests we haven't done yet.'

'Rubbish!' yelled Simmons.

'And we haven't even been monitoring his liver function,' added Ludo.

'We really ought to monitor his liver function,' said Goldblatt.

'The other doctor said she didn't have to!'

'Really?' said Goldblatt. 'What did she say?'

'She said we could see how I felt and whether I was showing signs of getting better. I said I didn't want no bloods done and she said we'd try to manage without them.'

'Would that be Dr Burton?' asked Goldblatt.

'Yes.'

'Very sensible approach.'

'See!'

Goldblatt sighed. 'Regretfully, Mr Simmons, I'm not Dr Burton.'

'Which ones should we do, Malcolm?' asked the HO eagerly, pulling a piece of paper out of a pocket of her white coat.

'Let's see. LFT, U&E, FBC, CKMB, PT, APTT, Hep B and C, gamma GT, ALP, acid phosphatase.'

'No!' shouted Simmons, glancing frenziedly from Goldblatt to the HO, who was scribbling furiously. 'No no no!'

'He's right,' said Goldblatt. 'Cancel the acid phosphatase.'

'Why?'

'It doesn't rhyme.'

Simmons stared at Goldblatt with naked hatred. Goldblatt knew what the problem was, and Simmons knew that he knew. After years of self-injection, Simmons had no veins left. Nothing you could hit without doing a deep, penetrating and truly unpleasant puncture.

'Have you had much experience taking blood?' Goldblatt asked the HO, still staring back at Simmons.

'No,' said the HO.

'Good,' said Goldblatt, and he smiled.

'From his groin?' asked the HO in disbelief, when they had wheeled the notes trolley back into the doctors' office at the end of the round and Goldblatt told her what she was going to do. 'How do I take blood from there?'

'I'll show you,' said Goldblatt. 'It's an important technique. You need to be able to do it. When you can't get access to any other vein, you can always get into the femoral vein in the groin.'

'Don't worry, it's easy,' said Ludo.

'Of course it's easy,' said Goldblatt. 'Every technique is easy except swabbing the male urethra.'

'Rubbish. Swabbing the male urethra's easy,' said Ludo.

'Not if you're the male,' replied Goldblatt.

Taking blood from the femoral vein *is* easy. All it takes is a needle, a groin, and someone to slide one into the other to a depth of an inch or two. Oh, and get the needle in the right place. That's the twist. Like any medical procedure, no matter how easy, it takes time and practice to perfect the art. The HO needed the practice, and Simmons had the time. As Goldblatt watched, the HO slid her needle deep into the skin of Simmons's groin, moving it this way and that, poking about unsuccessfully in search of his femoral vein until she scraped along the underlying bone or twanged a fibre of his femoral nerve and made part of his thigh twitch like the leg of a frog in a physiology lab. Goldblatt encouraged her patiently. 'Try a little more medially,' he'd say, or, when that didn't work, 'try a little more laterally.' The HO, for her part, leaned over the bed, one hand holding Simmons's underpants away from his groin, the other hand wielding the needle, her nose almost thrust into the humid fold of Simmons's skin, and her face frowning in concentration. She refused to give in. Goldblatt admired her determination. Simmons squirmed and groaned and drew breath sharply each time the needle hit some particularly sensitive structure. Beads of sweat stood out on his forehead.

'Don't worry,' said Goldblatt to the HO with unwavering professionalism, 'concentrate on what you're doing. Usually it's much easier. This is a hard vein to hit. He's probably shot up there as well.'

Finally dark blood rushed into the nozzle of the syringe and flooded the cylinder as the HO drew back on the plunger. When it was full the HO pulled out the needle and turned around, beaming, holding the syringe up for everyone to see.

The HO was happy. Goldblatt was happy. Simmons, if possible, was even happier. It was such a happy moment that Goldblatt almost said yes when the HO, eager to practise her new skill, asked whether she should take another syringeful from his other groin in case they didn't have enough blood for all those tests they were ordering.

'Not yet,' said Goldblatt. 'But we'll need three sets of blood cultures to rule out infection.'

'If I'd known, I could have used some of this blood for the first set, couldn't I?' said the HO.

'Yes. Shame. We should have thought of that. Anyway, you can come back to do it this afternoon. And we'll need another set of liver function tests tomorrow,' added Goldblatt, 'and every day Mr Simmons is in here if he can't arrange to go home. And I think there'll be some other tests we'll require. Have you had a lumbar puncture yet, Mr Simmons?'

Simmons didn't last much longer. Goldblatt also stopped his order for codeine, which vastly lessened the attraction of staying in. It had been good while it lasted, but it was time to go. If he had to endure needles penetrating his almost impenetrable veins, he might as well be putting some kind of chemical cocktail into them rather than have a doctor taking blood out.

When Goldblatt came up to the ward on Monday morning, bed one was occupied by a new arrival. It was a good omen for the week ahead. Then Emma Burton came up to the ward to find out how her star patient's amazing recovery was progressing. Goldblatt told her that Simmons had left.

Emma looked at him with disbelief. After a moment her expression changed. It became hard and mistrustful.

'The Prof was very interested in Mr Simmons,' she said brusquely, and turned on her heel and walked off around the corner to her office.

Goldblatt listened to the sound of Emma's footsteps clattering out a warning tattoo. He was perplexed. The Prof was very interested in Mr Simmons? That didn't sound right. That didn't sound right at all. No, like the presence of Simmons in the first place it seemed to say a lot about Emma and almost nothing about anyone else. Goldblatt had the feeling that it was a very bad omen, more than enough to cancel out the good omen of Simmons disappearing from the ward.

But omens, as any necromancer will tell you, can't be undone. Once you slice the liver you have to read the signs.

'Emma's doing her round this afternoon, isn't she?' asked Ludo, as the sound of Emma's footsteps died away.

Goldblatt nodded. The specialist registrar ward round was scheduled for Monday afternoons.

'At two-thirty, isn't it?'

Goldblatt nodded again.

'Can't wait,' said Ludo.

6

AT THE BEST OF times, and even on the most harmonious of units, specialist registrar ward rounds are a source of friction.

The root of the problem is that, except in cases where the registrar is extremely inexperienced, they're unnecessary. With the registrar doing a round with the HO on a daily basis, and the consultant doing a round with the whole team on a weekly basis, do you really need the SR, who spends most of her time in clinics, to do a weekly round as well? The chief objective of most SRs on their rounds is to prove that the answer is soundly in the affirmative, while the chief objective of most registrars, not thinking ahead to imagine what their own futures might be like in one or two years, is to show the SRs that they're utterly superfluous. Thus, unless the SR or the reg happen to be of exceptionally pusillanimous character, the SR round is typically a miserable, grisly round of the most gruesome and vindictive variety. The SR spends it trying desperately to think of something new to add or, better yet, to contradict the previous instructions of the reg, while the reg invariably spends it fighting back tooth and nail, each side attempting to inflict maximal ridicule on the other in front of the more junior doctors.

Yet Goldblatt didn't resent it. It was one of many fine traditions of the profession and as such he thoroughly respected it. If Emma wanted to do her SR round by the book, naturally he was prepared to do his bit as well.

Emma did, it seemed.

Adopting a time-honoured ploy to establish supremacy from the off, she turned up a careful twenty minutes late for her first round. She rushed into the doctors' office at ten to three that Monday afternoon with a whole list of excuses designed to show how important and busy she was. No one was there to hear them. Getting into the spirit of things, Goldblatt had responded with an equally time-honoured counter-manoeuvre: he had waited ten minutes and then taken the rest of the team and started. Apart from the manoeuvring, there wasn't really any point in Goldblatt taking the rest of the team and starting, since he and the rest of the team had already seen the patients that morning. But then the whole exercise had no real point anyway, at least as far as the patients were concerned. And since he and the rest of the team had already seen the patients, it was turning out to be an exceptionally quick round, and if they were lucky they would finish the whole lot before Emma arrived, which would put her in the unusually fortunate position of having done her round without even having been there.

They didn't finish before Emma arrived. She discovered them halfway around the ward. Emma immediately pushed in front of the HO and seized hold of the notes trolley with both hands.

'Sorry I'm late,' she said authoritatively. 'Right, where are we up to?'

Goldblatt took a step back. It was a pleasure to welcome such a resolute captain aboard.

They went back to the start. Emma enjoyed a more leisurely pace to the round. She seemed to think she would be letting someone down if it lasted less than three hours. She wanted to know every trivial fact, read through the notes, review the result of every test, check every detail twice over, and demonstrate the thoroughness with which she examined each patient, commencing with a careful and far-reaching examination of those subtle indicators of health and disease: the fingernails.

Goldblatt got bored. A bleep came up and he used the opportunity to escape to the doctors' office where he answered the call and then lingered. Then he decided that he might as well use the opportunity to cancel one of the admissions that was booked for the next day and wasn't going to get in even if a cholera epidemic broke out overnight and carried off half the patients in the hospital. The cancellee cried on the phone, and Goldblatt listened sympathetically to her complaints and patiently explained the reasons for her cancellation, and then listened to her complaints again, and patiently explained once more, finding this a lot less tedious than watching Emma practise her examination technique, but finally the patient wanted to get off the phone, and although Goldblatt had been hoping to be asked to explain everything for a third time, he had no choice but to hang up. He went back to the round. They had inched their way two beds further along, and had drawn the screens around a patient who had a mild case of Fuertler's and was in for the work-up. Emma was stabbing her finger at an open page on the patient's notes.

'The Prof has written that he needs a colonoscopy while he's in,' she was saying violently to the HO. 'Why haven't you booked it?'

The HO glanced at Goldblatt. 'Because Malcolm told me not to when we went round this morning.'

'Did you tell her not to?' demanded Emma.

'Yes,' said Goldblatt. 'I told her not to.'

Emma turned away furiously. 'Mr Siepl, when you saw Professor Small in clinic, did she say you were going to have a colonoscopy?'

Mr Siepl hesitated. He was a chubby, bald man with a head like a cannonball, and his face had assumed a painful expression of confusion. Goldblatt felt sorry for him. They put you through such horrible ordeals in hospital. Yes or no? Which answer was he meant to give?

'That's the test where they put that huge long tube up your back passage to look at your bowel,' Goldblatt explained, in case this would help Mr Siepl decide.

'It's not huge!' said Emma indignantly.

'How big is it?' said Goldblatt.

'I don't know how big it is!' retorted Emma, not even glancing at him over her shoulder.

'It's about a metre long. Ludo, how long is a metre? Could you show us, please?'

Ludo measured a metre in the air between her two hands. Or maybe it was a metre and a half.

'I'd say that's huge,' said Goldblatt. 'Would you say that's huge?' he asked the HO.

'I'd say it's huge,' said the HO.

'Mr Siepl, would you say it's huge?'

'It's not huge!' snapped Emma, rudely interrupting before Mr Siepl had a chance to have his say.

'Well, it's pretty big, isn't it? Show us again, Ludo.'

Ludo showed them again. Like a fisherman telling the story about the one that got away, Ludo tended to exaggerate with repetition. She also had an impressive arm span. Mr Siepl stared at the gap between her two hands with silent terror.

'It doesn't matter if it is huge,' said Emma. 'If he needs it, he needs it.'

'True,' said Goldblatt. 'Emma, we explained to Mr Siepl that Professor Small was right to think about getting it done to make sure there was nothing serious going on, and to ask us to consider it when he came in. And now that he's here we can consider it. And that's what we've done, as we explained to Mr Siepl this morning.'

'Rubbish!' said Emma. 'The Prof wanted it!'

Goldblatt tried to suppress his exasperation. What more did Emma want? 'Yes,' he said between clenched teeth, 'but that was five months ago in clinic, and what she wanted us to do was *consider* it.'

'She did not. There's nothing about considering it here. She wanted him to have it.' Emma turned to the HO. 'I'm the SR. Book it!'

The HO glanced at Goldblatt. He reached for the notes. He was happy to save Emma's blushes in front of a patient – and the Prof's, if it came to that – but not at the price of putting that patient through an unnecessary colonoscopy.

'Professor Small wanted a colonoscopy to investigate altered bowel habit,' he said, reading the Prof's clinic entry. 'Mr Siepl, has your bowel habit altered?'

Mr Siepl looked a little abashed and possibly felt reluctant to talk about it. Maybe the audience wasn't big enough. There were only four doctors watching him, as well as Debbie, Sister Choy's second in charge, who kept putting her head in and out between the screens to see if they were finished. Discussion of something as personal as bowel habits would normally justify an audience of at least eight. On the other hand, there was also the family of three who had come to visit the old man in the next bed, but they were on the other side of the screen so it wasn't clear whether they really counted as part of the audience. They had lapsed into silence, anyway.

'I was a bit loose,' said Mr Siepl hesitantly.

'When?' asked Goldblatt.

'A few months back.'

'Before you saw Professor Small in clinic?'

'Yes.'

'And was there any reason you were a bit loose back then?' asked Goldblatt affably, having heard the answers to the exact same series of questions on his round that morning.

'Well, we'd been on holiday in Spain.'

'And?'

'Well,' said Mr Siepl, who was obviously getting to the really embarrassing bit, 'I ate a lot of fruit.'

'Fruit?'

Mr Siepl nodded glumly.

'And since then?' asked Goldblatt.

'Normal,' said Mr Siepl.

'Really?'

'Once a day. Regular as clockwork!'

Goldblatt handed the notes back to the HO. 'Book him a colonoscopy. Write that he had an increased frequency of bowel motions for a fortnight six months ago due to dietary factors, and that the symptoms have resolved.'

The HO pulled out a request form and began writing. 'Won't they query this?' she said, looking up for a moment.

'Yes. Better put down that it was specifically requested by Professor Small.'

The HO began to write again.

'Don't put that down,' said Emma.

The HO looked up.

'No,' said Goldblatt. 'Put down that it was specifically requested by Dr Burton.'

The HO looked down.

'Don't put that down,' said Emma.

The HO looked up.

'Give me the form,' said Emma. Her face had flushed pink, but her voice was cold.

The HO gave her the form. Emma put it in her pocket.

'I think we can afford to wait and watch how things develop,' Emma said to Mr Siepl, and avoided Goldblatt's gaze.

They moved on to the next patient. Once more Emma insisted on delving back into the patient's prehistory. Goldblatt found a pretext to drift away to do something useful. Like throwing scrunched-up balls of old results at the rubbish bin in the doctors' office. He had just about cleaned the whole place up by the time Emma, Ludo, and the HO came back from the round.

'Sorry, Emma,' he said, 'I got caught up. You know. Things.'

Emma looked at him with narrowed eyes. Goldblatt wasn't sure that she believed him.

'Everything all right?' he asked.

'Fine,' said Emma.

Goldblatt nodded. Fine. He still hadn't worked out what Emma meant when she used that word.

Emma looked suspiciously at the rubbish bin, which was brimming with scrunched-up results balls. A couple lay on the ground under one of the desks, where Goldblatt had neglected to retrieve them after missing the target.

Suddenly her eyes went wide. 'Who put those there?' she shrieked.

Goldblatt almost jumped out of his chair. 'What?'

'These!' cried Emma, already down on her knees and halfway under the desk. 'Who did it?' She backed out with the brown Manila folders that Goldblatt had tossed under there a few days previously. Emma stood up and clutched them protectively to her chest. 'Who put them there?'

Goldblatt, for one, was reluctant to answer. He looked at the HO. The HO looked back at him and glanced at Ludo. Ludo was watching him. Her mouth was expressionless, but her blue eyes, with their low and drooping lids, were smiling. It was a cold, unpleasant smile, malicious, cruel, and knowing, with a promise of excruciating pleasures to come.

'It must have been one of the cleaners,' said the HO.

'The *cleaners*!' hissed Emma, as if they were a clan against which she and the rest of the Burtons had been fighting a blood feud for generations.

'I'm sure it was a mistake,' said Goldblatt, tearing himself away from Ludo's gaze and the silent process of negotiation they had been conducting.

'A mistake! We can't have these sorts of mistakes. The Prof would go absolutely—' Emma stopped. Her eyes narrowed. 'Why didn't you pick them up?'

'Who?'

'You.'

'I don't pick things up off the floor!' retorted Goldblatt indignantly. He wrinkled his nose in disgust. 'I'm a doctor. And so is she. And so is she. And so are you. We're all doctors. I shouldn't have to tell you this. Didn't they teach you that in medical school? Things on the floor are dirty. Things on the floor give you disease.'

Goldblatt took one of the folders from Emma and held it up between two tentative fingers. 'What are these, anyway?' he asked, unable to keep the repugnance out of his voice.

'The Prof's Fuertler's files,' said Emma.

'Well,' said Goldblatt, 'she ought to take more care of them.'

Emma snatched the folder out of Goldblatt's hands and stormed off to her office to save the Prof the trouble.

Goldblatt glanced at Ludo, who hadn't taken her eyes off him for a second. He didn't know what bargain they had struck in return for her silence, but he knew she'd make him pay.

Five seconds later Emma stormed back in. 'Every patient on the ward has to have one of these filled in!' she announced vengefully.

'You should have told us before,' said Goldblatt.

'I'm telling you now.'

'Every patient?'

'Every patient with Fuertler's Syndrome!' retorted Emma, and stormed out again.

Goldblatt thought about that. 'She sounds serious.'

The HO nodded.

'Every patient needs a Fuertler's file filled,' murmured Goldblatt, warming to the alliteration of the rule.

'Every patient with Fuertler's Syndrome,' the HO corrected him.

'Every patient with Fuertler's Syndrome,' said Goldblatt, grateful for the HO's precision. 'And how many of our patients have Fuertler's Syndrome?' he enquired.

'Almost all our patients have Fuertler's Syndrome,' replied the HO cheerfully.

'Then they all need a Fuertler's file filled,' concluded Goldblatt, and settled back to wait.

There was a long silence, broken only by the sound of consciences creaking. Finally Goldblatt heard something snap.

'All right, I'll do it.'

Goldblatt looked at Ludo. 'You didn't move your lips,' he said in amazement. He turned to the HO. 'She didn't move her lips.'

'I'll do it,' repeated Ludo.

Goldblatt knew what that meant. 'Thanks anyway, Ludo. But we want someone to do the Fuertler's files.'

'I'll *do* it, Malcolm.'

'All of them?' asked the HO, scarcely daring to hope.

Ludo glanced at her dismissively. She was an SHO. She had her dignity. She wasn't about to start discussing work allocation with an HO.

'Well, that's...' Goldblatt stopped. He didn't know what it was. Surprising? Worrying? There were so many words he could have used. It was surreal, that was for sure. Ludo volunteering to do something...

'Malcolm?' said the HO.

Goldblatt looked around quickly, hoping the HO was going to say something to break the strange spell that seemed to have settled over the office.

'I still don't quite understand what we're going to do about Simmons.'

Goldblatt stared at her. This was getting *more* surreal. 'Simmons has gone,' he said, in case the HO had developed some form of acute amnesia. 'We don't treat patients who have gone. We treat patients who are here.'

'What about all those tests we were doing? What happens if one of them shows something significant?'

'I had a professor of Ophthalmology when I was a—'

'I know,' said the HO. 'If you don't want to see it, don't look.'

Goldblatt stared at the HO. 'Very good. And the other thing?'

'Beware the unilateral red eye.'

'Congratulations. You know as much Ophthalmology as I do.'

'I'm serious, Malcolm. What if something happens to him?'

Goldblatt shrugged regretfully. What *would* happen? But what could he do? Simmons had chosen to go. It was a free country.

'Maybe we should try to find him.'

Ah, the HO. So sweet, so charming, in her state of uncorrupted HOdom. Ludo laughed.

'What?' demanded the HO.

'Nothing,' said Ludo. 'Coffee?'

The HO came with them to the cafeteria. Ludo started to whine as they waited for the lift to arrive. The accommodation the hospital had provided for her was a decrepit, uriniferous room in a typically pestilential hospital accommodation block. Goldblatt had already heard about it twenty times.

'Complain,' he said.

'I have.'

'And?'

Ludo gave him a sour look.

'I moved into a new flat the week before I started work,' said the HO. 'It's brilliant.'

'Can I live there?' asked Ludo.

'No,' said the HO.

Ludo turned her back on her.

The lift arrived, but Ludo's whining didn't stop. She had no shame. There was a patient in a wheelchair with a nasogastric tube up his nose, for heaven's sake. He already had enough reason to be nauseated without Ludo making everyone's stomach churn. Goldblatt wasn't listening any more. Maybe the HO was. Or maybe some of the other people in the lift were. At least they hadn't heard it all before.

They got coffees and sat down at a table in the cafeteria. Goldblatt had no idea what Ludo was whining about now. He watched the HO, who was nodding, or shaking her head, or just frowning as she tried to keep up with Ludo's latest litany of victimization. The HO was small, and the white coat the hospital had provided was too big for her. She had rolled the sleeves up to her elbows.

Goldblatt was beginning to worry for the HO. She had landed in the middle of the most specialized unit he had ever seen. Pathologically specialized. If he hadn't seen it for himself, he wouldn't have believed such a unit could have existed.

It was full of Fuertler's patients admitted for the Prof's excruciating work-up of a thousand tests. While they were in, they all got a five-day infusion of a drug called Sorain, which was apparently supposed to help them. According to the product literature, Sorain had been shown to have some minimal effect on Fuertler's skin lesions. The Prof loved it. Everyone got Sorain no matter how mild or severe their Fuertler's was.

What kind of an introduction was this for the HO, dipping her toe for the first time into the surging seas of medicine? Wasn't there a risk that she'd mistake the overheated little inlet in which she found herself for the entire ocean? Sheltered in the foetid, tropical lagoon that the Prof had created, how would she learn to weather the storms that awaited her beyond the doors of the ward on the seventh floor? How would she prepare for the toll those storms would take on her?

Of course, there were the three beds that the Prof had allocated to Dr Morris when he joined the unit. With his passionate fascination for medicine, he filled them with the weirdest, most complicated and least diagnosable patients ever to step out of the pages of a medical textbook. Some of them were so weird that they were waiting to step into the pages of a medical textbook, and Dr Morris, who was planning to write one, was going to put them there. But they were no good for an HO. To learn her craft, an HO needs the meat and drink of medicine, the bread and butter of the trade: pneumonias, heart failures, myocardial infarctions, strokes, asthmas, diabetics, thromboses, overdoses, dehydrations, gastro-intestinal haemorrhages, and the exacerbations of any of a thousand chronic diseases. It was true that the HO would admit them when she was on call overnight, but under the arrangement Professor Small had reached in Fuertlerizing her unit, none of these patients went to her once they were admitted. The patients the HO admitted went to other consultants whose medical teams assumed responsibility for their ongoing care the following morning. If she was to learn her craft, the HO needed not just to see these patients when they came in, but to manage them on the ward over the ensuing days, learn the decision trees for their treatment, and see how these conditions evolved: their exacerbations, their complications, their resolutions. Snapshots at admission would teach her nothing.

Instead, she was going to see Fuertler's, a disease that evolved snail-like over months, or years, it if evolved at all. She would see every nuance, variant, and subtle manifestation that she was never going to need to know about again in the entire course of her career. Thirteen beds of more or less healthy Fuertler's patients, having the work-up, getting the wonder drug, and going out again. The only thing the HO was learning was how to get their endless tests done.

Admittedly, she was proving highly adept at this role. Goldblatt had already explained to her that the job of an HO is one part medicine, two parts blood-taking, three parts filling out forms, and forty-seven thousand, three hundred and twenty-two parts chasing other doctors and departments who promise to do things and don't. She had plenty of native cunning, and was well on the way to working out how to make sure the patients got as many of their tests as the opposition would allow. But if most of her life as an HO was to be spent chasing tests, it needed to be spent chasing tests on more than one rare and almost irrelevant condition.

Goldblatt watched the HO over his coffee as Ludo whined. How would she learn what life was like in the real world of medicine that teemed and boiled outside the Prof's hyper-specialized unit? How would she know what to expect when she was released into it?

'Have you been on call yet?' he asked suddenly.

Ludo stopped talking and looked at the HO with interest. She enjoyed whining, but nowhere near as much as she enjoyed *Schadenfreude*.

The HO nodded. 'On Friday. I'm on again tonight. It wasn't too bad. I got a couple of hours' sleep.'

'Let's hear you say that after you've been doing it for six months,' said Ludo. 'How many did you admit, anyway?'

'Eight,' replied the HO.

Ludo laughed.

'What?'

'Eight!' muttered Ludo contemptuously, as if the real work didn't begin until you admitted twice that number.

There was some truth in that, thought Goldblatt. Eight was light. If you had only admitted eight, you would have no idea what a night on call could be.

When she was on call, the HO was part of the team that did the medical 'Take', admitting and providing treatment for all the patients with acute non-surgical problems who turned up on the hospital's doorstep. She was teamed with a senior house officer and a registrar, with a strict hierarchy of personnel. The HO was 'first-on-call', the person to whom all the calls from the wards were directed. She fielded anything the nurses chose to throw at her, the steady stream of requests that go on all night, like the ticking heart of the hospital, to write up a drug, insert a drip, renew an intravenous order, take a blood test, review a patient, investigate a new symptom, declare a death. The senior house officer was 'second-on-call', taking the calls from other doctors in Casualty, and from GPs seeking advice or wanting to arrange an emergency admission, backing the HO up when she needed help, and ordering the HO off the wards and into Casualty to help with the clerking of new patients who had to be admitted. Finally, the registrar was 'third-on-call', the person to whom the second-on-call turned when he and the first-on couldn't manage, and who provided overall guidance for the team.

The HO was on call one night in every four, including one in four weekends. Ludo, as a senior house officer and second-on-call, would be on call one night in five. As registrar, Goldblatt would do medical Takes one night in nine. He was also on call for Dermatology and the Prof's unit one night in five, but this duty was carried out from home, and most queries, which were infrequent, were dealt with over the phone. When he was in the hospital for medical Takes on the weekends, he worked only one of the two nights. The HO and Ludo would both work both nights, starting Saturday morning and going through to Monday morning, following which they were expected to work a normal Monday on the Prof's ward, so that the whole period amounted to a fifty-six-hour shift.

Common sense, or even simple humanity, might have dictated that the doctors with the highest work intensity should have had the lowest on-call frequency. That would have meant the first-on-calls, or the HOs. In fact, they had the highest frequency. There were many carefully considered and fully justifiable reasons for this. For instance, HOs were the newest, weakest, and most vulnerable members of the profession, and thus the least likely to answer back when unreasonable demands were made of them. They were the least experienced, and thus the most likely to believe the old lie that the only way to learn how to practise medicine was to do it while too sleep-deprived to remember anything you saw. They were the most idealistic members of the profession, and thus the only ones still prone to believe that self-sacrifice was an important part of their vocation. And most importantly, HOs were the youngest and fittest of the species, and therefore the least likely to collapse and die embarrassingly of overwork.

The strict grading of the on-call hierarchy often blurred during the day, but in every hospital where Goldblatt had ever worked it invariably reasserted itself with a steel grip at night, when sleep was at a premium. There were certain rules that were never broken. The most important one was that you had no right to expect a more senior person in the hierarchy to look at a patient until you had already seen that patient. You had no right to expect a more senior person to try to perform a procedure, such as siting a drip, until you had tried and failed. In blunt terms, you had no right to be asleep when a more senior person was awake.

The intensity of the work, the physical toll taken by repetitive sleep deprivation, and the sheer number of years that a doctor was expected to go through it, combined to create an irresistible downward pressure that sent responsibilities lower and lower until they came to a halt at the very bottom, piled on the people who were least capable of carrying them out. An HO, having once or twice woken a registrar, soon learned that he was expected to assess patients and make decisions at night that no one would have dreamed of allowing him to make during the day. An SHO, who would have been instructed to refer even routine GP queries to her registrar during the day, would find herself giving advice over the phone to GPs when they rang about emergencies at night. In short, after the sun went down, the system ran on the fallacious but convenient assumption that just because someone was named to do the job, the job was being done by someone who knew how to do it.

And they would do that job, all through the night, all through the weekend, to the bitter end – no matter how exhausted, confused, uncertain, overburdened, and terrified they were of the barrage of demands that faced them.

Someone had to prepare the HO for the high-speed train of exhaustion and fear that was about to slam into her. It was better for her to know the things she would inevitably experience than leave her to face them alone when they first confronted her – as Goldblatt had been left alone after his encounter with BatesorBent – too frightened or ashamed or confused to talk about it. That was Goldblatt's reasoning, anyway, as they sat in the cafeteria.

Ludo's motivation was much simpler. She went straight for the jugular. 'We'll see how long it takes before she does it,' she said to Goldblatt, and laughed a dull, lazy, complicit laugh.

The HO glanced distrustfully at her, then turned to Goldblatt. 'Until I do what?'

Goldblatt sighed. He knew where Ludo was headed. Why on earth had he decided to have this conversation when she was with them? He wished he could stop.

But he couldn't. Once the lid of the box had been opened, even a fraction, it had to be opened all the way. He saw the anxiety deepening on the HO's face. Ludo laughed again.

'Don't worry about it,' said Goldblatt. 'It happens to all of us eventually. Don't feel guilty about it when it does, that's all.'

'What?' demanded the HO.

'Wishing your patients will die so you can sleep,' said Ludo.

'Malcolm!'

Goldblatt shrugged. Ludo had a certain way with words – or lack of a way – but that didn't alter the essential truth of what she was saying.

Ludo grinned at the HO.

'You're disgusting!' the HO shouted at her, jumping to her feet. Her small square face burned with outrage.

'She is disgusting,' said Goldblatt, 'but she's right.'

'No she isn't. She's a sour bitch who's pissed off because she can't find anywhere decent to live.'

'True again,' said Goldblatt, 'but she's still right.'

Ludo smirked.

The HO slumped back in her chair and stared at Goldblatt with terror

79

and confusion. Goldblatt felt for her. He knew she was feeling something that he too had once been capable of feeling. But like the innocence of that long-ago Goldblatt who had found himself saying a murderous goodbye to Three Hours of Work, the HO's ability to feel it would soon utterly disappear.

Ludo watched her avariciously. This was much more fun than whining.

'When will it happen?' whispered the HO.

Goldblatt shrugged, selecting a scenario at random. There were so many to choose from. 'Oh, it'll be in the morning some time.'

'The *morning*,' emphasized Ludo, like the voiceover in a trailer for a C-grade movie.

'Say about four o'clock. Let's say you're on call, and you're just about to leave Emergency after clerking your twentieth patient for the day.'

'You'll probably be going to one of the vending machines to get your supper,' Ludo added.

'No,' said Goldblatt. Once they had started, he thought, there was no point rose-tinting the reality. 'Not her supper, Ludo. Be realistic. Her lunch.'

The HO stared.

'So it's four in the morning and you're off to get your lunch. And you think – to the extent that you're still capable of thinking – that if nothing else happens you might just manage to get a couple of hours' sleep. And then some nurse who came on duty twelve hours after you started, and will go off duty twelve hours before you finish, stops you just before you can get out of the department. They've just had a call from the ambulance service to say some guy with a known gastric carcinoma is on the way in with a big haematemesis...'

'That's a bleed from his oesophagus,' said Ludo.

'I know that!' snapped the HO.

'... and he's got a BP of fifty over unrecordable, and he's still hosing. You hate that nurse. At that moment, you hate her like she's just sunk a knife into your mother's belly. This patient's going to take two, three hours to sort out. You're not going to get to bed. You're probably not even going to get your lunch. So what do you do?'

The HO had gone into some kind of trance and was staring at Goldblatt without breathing. Her glasses were hanging on against gravity at the very tip of her little nose.

'You could wait there,' said Goldblatt. 'The ambulance is only ten minutes away. Once that patient arrives, every second is going to count. You could wait, so you're on the scene to get to work as soon as they wheel him in. You could just nip into the nurses' room and steal a cup of coffee while you're waiting, maybe a biscuit...'

Goldblatt paused. He had an awful sense of déjà vu, which wasn't surprising because in fact the whole scene was déjà done, at least for him, over and over in countless variants, and like all moments of great drama it was nothing more than the barely veiled reconstruction of an event that had actually taken place.

'Or you could leave, go and have your lunch, and if they still haven't called you, go to bed, hoping...' Goldblatt paused, and he could sense Ludo watching with monstrous enjoyment, '... hoping the patient dies in the ambulance so you can get some sleep.'

The HO shot up from her chair. 'I'll never do that! Never!' she cried with zeal and repugnance.

Ludo laughed pitilessly

'You will,' said Goldblatt, as if unable to stop before he had finished painting the full Hogarthian sequence of the HO's inexorable moral demise. 'You'll rush off to bed wishing the patient dies in the ambulance and lets you sleep. Not only that, but when some nurse on a ward bleeps you at seven o'clock and you realize you actually got some sleep, which means no one called you from Casualty, which means the patient must have died – you'll be glad. You'll be happy. You'll punch the air.'

'I will not!' said the HO in disgust. 'Only Americans punch the air.'

'That's true, Malcolm,' said Ludo.

Goldblatt shrugged. 'Everyone punches the air if they're pushed far enough.'

'I won't,' said the HO, still resisting the truth. She pulled her white coat tighter around her, as if that were going to protect her.

'You will,' said Ludo.

'The reason I'm telling you,' said Goldblatt, 'is so you won't feel guilty about it. Everyone does it. More than once. You don't have to tell anyone when it happens, but if you think it would help, talk to someone. Don't feel you have to bottle it up. You can talk to me or...' he glanced at Ludo.

'Anyway, you can talk to me. Or not. It's up to you.' He paused. This was important. 'Everyone does it. Everyone ends up feeling like that at some point. Do you understand? It doesn't make you a bad doctor.' He watched to see if the HO understood. 'It's nothing to be ashamed of. It's reality. Don't repress it. Whether you tell anyone else or not, don't blame yourself.'

'You should tell me when it happens,' whispered Ludo.

The HO had decided to repress whatever she could. 'I didn't do medicine to do that to patients.'

'You're not *doing* anything to patients,' said Goldblatt. 'If they die before they get to you, they die. It's not your fault.'

'Well, I didn't do medicine to think about patients like that.'

'Neither did we,' Goldblatt pointed out.

'I'm going,' said the HO. 'You're both disgusting.'

The HO turned on her heel and walked away between the tables.

'Six weeks,' Ludo shouted after her. 'I give you six weeks.'

The HO kept going without turning around.

Goldblatt shook his head. Six weeks was too long. No one lasted six weeks.

'Four weeks,' he said quietly, as he watched the HO walk out of the cafeteria. 'If that.'

Ludo tossed her head dismissively. She was very conscious of the way she tossed her head, never tossing it without first pausing to visualize the effect it would achieve as her long dark hair swept romantically through the air.

Goldblatt noticed a team of doctors from another unit sitting down together at a table nearby. He thought about Emma and the round she had conducted that afternoon. He had the feeling that the round – or at least his part in it – hadn't been a raging success. For either of them.

Ludo started whining about the Prof, whom she hadn't even seen yet, even though she had just volunteered to fill out her Fuertler's files. She'd have to wait until Wednesday when the Prof did her round. And what if the Prof didn't come to her round on Wednesday, like last week? She wouldn't see her then, either.

Goldblatt shrugged. He had seen the Prof. He didn't think Ludo was missing much.

7

THIS IS WHAT HAPPENED at Professor Small's round on Wednesday mornings. The Prof would arrive, ten or fifteen minutes late, to find everyone crowded into the doctors' office, which was packed with chairs brought in from the much larger, empty, and perfectly usable nurses' tearoom next door. The HO would take up position behind the notes trolley. After five or ten minutes of confusion over the coffee that no one had made – *again* – and when one of the medical students had been volunteered to go and correct the omission, the Prof would nod her head as a signal that she was ready for the show to begin, and the HO would start to present the patients.

Presenting a patient is a standard medical skill, and consists of giving a history of the complaint and any other relevant past conditions and medications, a description of the examination findings, an overview of the test results, a rundown of current progress, and an outline of planned actions. Like most skills, it can be practised more or less skilfully. A presentation can be brief, well structured, purposeful, and strenuously relevant, or extensive, meandering, and tedious, depending on the abilities of the presenter and the interventions of the people to whom one is presenting.

The HO's audience on Wednesday mornings included not only the doctors on the team, but Sister Choy or her deputy Debbie, the ward physiotherapist, the ward occupational therapist, the ward dietician, two or three medical students, and a couple of student nurses. There was also a South African social worker called Jane who turned up late and left early, and in fact rarely spent more than ten minutes at the round. Was the office big enough for all these people? People shifted uncomfortably the way they do when their thighs and arms are touching other people with whom they are not in an intimate relationship. It wasn't until the physio and the occupational therapist had excused themselves and left – which they always did shortly after Jane had broken the ice by walking in and then walking out again – that thigh to thigh contact was broken off. The physio and the occupational therapist had better things to do than sit there and listen to searching and circular discussions of every test and symptom that had been recorded on every patient in the past seven days. So did the student nurses, who eventually left as well. So did everyone, in fact, but not everyone could leave.

It wasn't the HO's fault that every case she presented wandered off into thickets of confusion, and that they ended up spending never less than two hours in the doctors' office talking about the simplest set of patients Goldblatt had ever come across. Sometimes, after a night on call, the HO was too tired to remember what she had already said and she might start repeating sentences or falling asleep while other people were talking, but HOs always did that. No, the HO wasn't the problem. And Dr Morris wasn't the problem, either. When they got to the three patients that were allocated to him, they were presented, discussed, and disposed of in minutes. This was because Dr Morris actually knew what was going on with them, since he actually came to see them. But something happened when the discussion was of the Prof's patients. They were all straightforward Fuertler's cases admitted for the work-up, and they should have taken about thirty seconds each. Yet as soon as the HO started presenting them, some kind of chain reaction would begin, and the entire process imploded in chaos.

The HO would begin on a patient. After a minute or two Emma would interrupt, adding some trivial detail she thought the HO had forgotten. Instead of telling Emma to wait until the HO had finished, the Prof asked Emma if she was sure about the detail. As a matter of fact, Emma wasn't sure. She was never sure, but she did remember *something*. At least she thought she did. The Prof would ask for the notes. The HO would hand them over. The Prof would start looking through them.

'It says here she had a superficial venous thrombosis ten years ago,' the Prof might say, forgetting about whatever it was that Emma had claimed to remember, but discovering something equally irrelevant. 'Is this true?'

Who knew if it was true? When the patient's vein had clogged up ten years earlier – if indeed it had clogged up – Goldblatt, Emma, and Ludo had been at various stages at university, and the HO was still at high school. If anyone should have known it was the Prof – after all, it was her patient and the patient had been coming to her for years. And by now the Prof was holding the notes. What was the point in asking them?

'Yes,' Sister Choy would say, flipping through the nurses' cardex, which was the only source of information outside the Prof's clutches.

'Thank you, Sister Choy,' the Prof would say, throwing a pointed glance at the assembled doctors, before turning back to the notes to see if she could discover anything else of interest.

The Prof might then randomly decide she had to read through every discharge summary that had ever been written on the patient. Or see a particular X-ray and compare it with with all the others that had ever been taken, forcing the HO to rummage in the patient's X-ray folder and pull out film after film from various dates in the past. Or trace the evolution of a particular set of test results from the first recorded entry fifteen years earlier. It might go on for ten, fifteen, twenty minutes, a survey of a patient's entire life and times. Dr Morris would rest back and lean his head against the wall, a Zen-like look of detachment on his face, dreaming of the fascinating cases that were waiting for him all over the hospital.

Two things were obvious to anyone who had sat through more than a couple of these performances. First, Professor Small could never remember anything about her patients, although she insisted on behaving as if she did. She was always confusing them with somebody else, and attributing horrible deforming lesions to people who had barely a blotch of Fuertler's, and vice versa. Thus she was always looking for a pretext to grab the file so she could glance through the clinic notes she had made in her surprisingly curly, girlish writing. And the second thing was that the Prof hardly ever came right out and made a judgement or even expressed a firm opinion. Interpreting an equivocal test result or changing a patient's treatment, even something as simple as adjusting the dose of an antihyptensive, never passed without at least five minutes of questioning and cross-questioning. The Prof always wanted to hear what everyone else had to say first, especially Dr Morris. Only then would she pronounce in what she obviously hoped was a very thoughtful, professorial tone, no matter how simple or self-evident the issue.

So they would spend two hours on Wednesday mornings discussing the patients in a mind-blowing muddle, and it was only then that they staggered out of the doctors' office to see them. But the Prof had lost interest at this point and just wanted to get the rest of it over with as quickly as possible. She had already forgotten who was who and what issues had been discussed. She rarely did more by way of examination than stroking the back of one of her patient's hands, before standing back for Dr Morris, who was always ready to whip out his stethoscope and listen to a chest or to unsheathe his collapsible tendon hammer and tap out a set of reflexes, even when the chest and the reflexes in question belonged to the Prof's patients.

But this didn't mean that the Prof wasted the time she spent on the ward. On the contrary, the Prof used it expertly. She would drift regally towards a bed and stop a couple of paces away, while Emma discreetly whispered the patient's name in her ear, and then she would give the patient a very direct, very open look, as if to say 'I am yours. Yours! You have my total attention.' And after this communicative pause she would say, in the society hostess tone in which she had initially greeted Goldblatt, 'Mrs Edwards', or 'Mrs Patel', or 'Mr Lipkin', – or whatever name Emma had whispered to her – 'it's so *nice* to see you again'.

The Prof was good. When he saw her in action amongst the patients, Goldblatt had to admit it. He was in the presence of greatness.

It was all just a heap of appalling ritual and rubbish, of course, the Prof's majestic procession from bed to bed. It was empty performance, devoid of medical content, with no objective beyond its own existence, as far from Dr Morris's lean, lithe, and efficiently executed rounds as it was possible to be. But the patients lapped it up. It churned Goldblatt's stomach, but he realized that if he had been a patient and had seen Professor Small for only two minutes like that on one of her rounds, not knowing what kind of jamboree of inanity had gone before that two-minute snapshot, or what would follow later, he might have had the same response.

There was no doubting it, the patients absolutely loved her.

*

The first time Goldblatt experienced one of the Prof's rounds, a week after he had joined the unit, he sat through the interminable extravaganza in the doctors' office, going almost insane with boredom and frustration, desperately hoping, praying, that this particular round was an aberration. But in his heart of hearts, he already knew that it wasn't. It took only one glance at Dr Morris, lost in resigned, Zen-like contemplation, to see the truth.

Finally the last patient had been discussed. The HO was just about to start pulling the notes trolley towards the door, when the Prof, remembering a patient who had written her a letter to enquire about a cancelled admission, asked why a Mrs Hussein hadn't got a bed.

Goldblatt had no idea. In the week since he had started on the unit, he had cancelled a good dozen admissions. The least the Prof could have done was to have remembered Mrs Anderson, for whose cancellation she was directly responsible.

The Prof's question wasn't aimed at any of them in particular. Anyone sensible would have stayed quiet, and in another moment it would probably have been forgotten.

Emma started making up an excuse.

The Prof interrupted her. Emma started another excuse. The Prof cut her off. Emma backtracked to the first excuse. The Prof interrogated her. Emma flailed around for answers.

Goldblatt just wanted it to stop. He couldn't bear any more.

'It's the Broderip–Anderssen Principle,' he said.

The Prof looked at him. 'What did you say, Dr Goldblatt?'

He wasn't sure himself. The words had just come out. He said them again. 'It's the Broderip–Anderssen Principle.'

'What are you *talking* about?' demanded Emma precipitately.

'You haven't heard of it?'

Emma gazed at him with mistrust. Immediately, she regretted opening her mouth. She was dangerously exposed. And in front of the Prof! The Prof, Dr Morris, Sister Choy, two medical students, Ludo, and even the impudent HO, who had run away to complain to Goldblatt on her very first day when Emma had asked her to do one tiny little extra ward round, were all sitting there expectantly, waiting to find out what the

Broderip–Anderssen Principle was. None of them knew what this principle was, she realized, any more than she did. If only she had shut up
and thought for a moment before bursting out like that, she could have
been waiting as well. Yet somehow Goldblatt had managed to get her –
and only her – to admit her ignorance.

She wouldn't be surprised if he had made the whole thing up just to
put her on the spot.

But how could she be *sure* he had made it up? Maybe he was waiting
for her to allege that he had made it up, and then he would prove that it
was real.

Emma was flushing. She could feel it. Soon she would feel the warm
blood pounding inside her ears and she wouldn't be able to think at all.
By the time the warm blood started pounding in Emma's ears she was
always too flustered to think about anything.

'Is that *Broderip* and *Anderson*?' she said before the warm blood began
pounding, trying to sound knowing, in case there was such a principle,
and dubious, in case there wasn't.

'Yes,' said the Prof with polite interest. 'Is it, Dr Goldblatt?'

Goldblatt leaped to his feet. He had been sitting around for so long
listening to the Prof and Emma trawling shambolically through the
patients' notes without the production of anything even faintly meaningful, that some kind of spring inside him suddenly unsnapped and
launched him into the air. He grabbed a marker. BRODERIP–ANDERSSEN
PRINCIPLE he wrote in big blue capitals across the whiteboard on the
wall behind him.

'The Broderip–Anderssen Principle,' he proclaimed, turning back like
a lecturer to his class. 'First published in 1957 by Henrik Anderssen and
Walter Broderip of the Chicago School in one of the earliest examples of
applied queuing theory. Mrs Hussein didn't get in because of the Broderip–Anderssen Principle. She never had a chance.'

'Really, Dr Goldblatt?'

Goldblatt whipped around again. He seized the eraser and swept away
the big blue letters that he had written only a moment before, then filled
the empty board with maniacal speed.

$$r = \frac{Q}{2n-1} \left\{ \frac{E(f(p) - p') \, pdt}{t-1} \right\} (\Delta p)^2 \, dt$$

$r = $ *rate of admission*, he wrote underneath, scribbling frantically, $t = $ *duration of stay*, $E = $ *occupancy at equilibrium*, and so on, until each of the variables was defined. Then he scrawled *Broderip–Anderssen* across the top, and turned, slightly mad, slightly intoxicated, slightly believing that the random symbols on the board behind him actually meant something, slightly realizing that the danger was... Dr Morris.

'Is that delta p there?' asked Dr Morris with a look of intense concentration on his face.

'Where?' demanded Goldblatt, spinning back to examine the formula.

'There,' said Dr Morris.

'Here?'

'Yes.'

'No! God no!' Goldblatt slapped his forehead. 'Not delta p. You're right.' Goldblatt grabbed the eraser and obliterated the end of the formula with two brisk strokes. 'Not delta p squared dt – delta f p squared dt!' he hissed, berating himself and pressing the marker hard into the board as he added a new ending to the formula. 'There,' he said, collapsing into his chair.

The Prof peered at Goldblatt. 'So I take it,' she said very quietly, as if gingerly poking a finger into an open and unexplored wound, 'that Mrs Hussein didn't get in.'

Goldblatt gestured helplessly at the whiteboard. 'I can find you a copy of Broderip and Anderssen's paper, if you like.'

'No, thank you, I don't think that will be necessary.'

'I'd like to see it,' said Dr Morris, copying the formula on the back of one of the results forms that were lying around on the desk

Goldblatt should have known he was going to say that.

There was silence.

'Shall we go?' said the Prof.

She stood up and walked out of the office. Emma trooped loyally after her. Sister Choy followed, then the HO, pushing the notes trolley. Dr Morris got up, folded the piece of paper on which he had written the formula, and wandered out with a thoughtful look on his face. The medical students departed, having given way to the consultants. Only Ludo was left. She stood up and stared at Goldblatt, who was still lolling in his chair.

'There's a Broderip on the ward,' she remarked.

Goldblatt looked up at her.

'That's a coincidence, isn't it?'

Ludo, thought Goldblatt. Of all people!

Ludo turned to leave the office. Her woollen skirt clung to the outline of her generous bum. She moved slowly, taking her time about it.

A moment later he followed her out. The Prof had already sailed regally up to the first bed.

Emma glanced at him, eyes full of hostility.

And yet he hadn't intended to put her on the spot. Honestly. If anything, he had been trying to lead the Prof away from the self-excavated hole into which Emma had been sinking under the weight of the cancellation of the mysterious Mrs Hussein. And who asked her to say anything, anyway? If Emma had just kept her mouth closed, like everyone else, she would have had nothing to get all flushed about.

Even before the round, Goldblatt had the feeling that things weren't going well between him and Emma. Call it a hunch. Lesley always told him that he didn't see the effect he was having on people until it was too late, and there were plenty of occasions, he had to admit, that had proven Lesley right.

He knew that sometimes he said or did things that people misconstrued. He also knew that sometimes he said or did things that people didn't misconstrue. He couldn't help himself. He got impatient or frustrated or something would just seem so absurd that it demanded a response in kind. But who said Malcolm Goldblatt couldn't learn from experience? Reasoning that it might be helpful, for a change, to try the novel approach of working out what was happening before it was too late, he endeavoured to identify what was going wrong between him and Emma. There had been Simmons, of course, and Mr Siepl. But honestly, what alternatives did he have? Simmons needed to be kicked out for his own good before he overdosed on ward disinfectant, and Mr Siepl needed a colonoscopy about as much as Emma herself. When she had a chance to think about it, surely she'd see the sense in what he'd done. And there was her round, when he had spent all but about ten minutes in the doctors' office, but how could she know that most of the time he had been away from it he had been doing nothing? She might suspect it, but how would she *know*? All he wanted was to work harmoniously with her. It was probably his jokes that were the problem. They often were. That was what Lesley usually said. Emma didn't seem to get them. Maybe they confused her. Maybe she thought they were aimed at her. They weren't, or at least he didn't think they were.

He bleeped her later and arranged to meet in the doctors' mess, a kind of common room for the hospital doctors on the second floor. No jokes, he admonished himself seriously. Nothing that could be misconstrued. They just had to talk things through so they could work together. Surely it wasn't beyond them to do that if they could have a simple, straightforward conversation. Perhaps Emma's role in admitting the Broderip was a result of a misunderstanding that they could clear up.

It wasn't.

'Just don't do it,' he said.

'What am I meant to do?' Emma demanded angrily. 'The Prof rang me. What am I meant to say?'

'Say no. Then she won't ring you again.'

'It's easy for you to say.'

'I thought we agreed I was going to do the admissions,' said Goldblatt. 'You can do them if you like. Do you want to do them? I'm happy with that. Let's just say from now on you do the admissions.'

'I don't want to do the admissions. I'm the SR! What will she think if I'm doing the admissions?'

'Then don't do them. Emma, make things easy on yourself. What I'm saying is, I'll take responsibility for it. Let it be my problem. When she rings, say exactly what you just said to me. "I'm the SR. Malcolm's the registrar. He's doing the admissions." Tell her to talk to me.'

'I can't tell her to talk to you!'

'Why not?'

'Because she won't talk to you!'

'Because?'

'Because you won't do what she wants. You didn't do it with Mrs Broderip, did you?'

'Emma, if you won't do what she wants, she'll *have* to talk to me. I'll deal with it. Trust me. She's not the first professor I've had to deal with. I can manage.'

Emma breathed heavily.

'Look, she'll understand. Registrars do the admissions. The old SR didn't do them, did she? No. Exactly. See?'

Emma didn't reply.

'What happened to the old SR, anyway?'

'Nothing.'

Goldblatt found that hard to believe. 'Did she have a personal problem?'

Emma shrugged.

'Was there a problem with the Prof?'

'What difference does it make?' demanded Emma. 'She's gone, isn't she? I'm the SR now!'

There was silence. Emma threw a glance at Goldblatt, then looked away.

'All right,' said Goldblatt. 'Look, that's exactly what I'm saying. You're the SR. You said it to me – now you just have to say it to the Prof.' He paused. 'Just do it once, Emma. Tell the Prof to talk to me. Go on, give it a try.'

Emma considered for a long time, looking down at her shoes.

'You might be surprised,' said Goldblatt cajolingly. 'You might enjoy it.'

'Fine,' said Emma eventually. 'I'll try.'

'Fine,' said Goldblatt.

'Fine,' said Emma.

8

GOLDBLATT HAD MET LESLEY when he went back to university to do a law degree. She had been in the final year of a PhD in some arcane aspect of European law before taking up a pupillage, and was giving tutorials on torts to undergraduates. The other five students in his tutorial group were mere callow nineteen-year-olds whereas he was a callow twenty-seven-year-old, which was a year or so older than Lesley herself. He sensed there was something between them. Later on, she denied having felt it. She said she had never given him a second thought. Repression is an ugly thing, Goldblatt told her. It didn't make her change her story.

Anyway, falsely believing there was something between them, Goldblatt asked her out for a drink at the end of her course of tutorials, and for some reason that she could hardly recall later – *more* evidence of repression, Goldblatt told her – she said yes. That was almost six years ago. Since then, Lesley had become a barrister and now worked in chambers in Lincoln's Inn. Goldblatt didn't expect her to understand what it was like to work on Professor Small's unit. Her world had its own brand of driven, soul-crunching craziness, and was peopled with a range of creatures only marginally more likeable than the things you might find wriggling around in the droppings below the roof of a bat-infested cave. But she had never worked on a medical unit, even a normal one. What hope did she have of understanding one like the Prof's? He could barely understand it himself.

He tried to explain. But words failed.

'The place is just a basket case,' he said.

'What's wrong with it?'

'Everything! Name anything you like. The people, the patients...'

Lesley looked at him doubtfully. 'The patients?'

'Fuertler's Syndrome. I'm a reasonable man, Les. In small numbers, I have nothing against it.'

'Malcolm, you've only been there a week!'

True. But even during that week, there were things he hadn't mentioned to Lesley. Like the episode with the Broderip, for instance. And Simmons. And the way Emma kept using the word 'fine' as if it was a word from a language he didn't speak.

'Les, I've never seen anything like it. Of all the places I've been... this one takes the cake.' Goldblatt grinned. 'You know what my ex used to say.'

Lesley knew. Goldblatt had told her any number of times. 'If there's a hard way to do something, Malcolm, you'll find it.' From the way he always said it, you would almost have thought he was proud of it.

'Malcolm,' she said, 'you can't afford for this to go pear-shaped.'

Goldblatt looked at her pointedly. There were some things he was capable of working out for himself.

'All right,' said Lesley. 'Look, you are where you are. You're just going to have to find a way to make this work.'

He grinned again. 'I love it when you talk positive.'

'Seriously, Malcolm. Let's think about it systematically, one thing at a time. Maybe if you could deal with the worst thing, that might be a start. What is it? If you had to name one thing, the one thing that's worse than anything you've seen anywhere else before, what would it be?'

Worse than the surreal Fuertlerization of the unit? Worse than the Prof's unctuousness? Worse than Emma's intransigence?

'The admissions,' said Goldblatt, without needing to think twice.

'The admissions?'

'I've never seen anything like it. We have two or three cancellations every day. Every single day. And they cry.'

Lesley didn't understand.

'They cry, Les. On the phone. When I ring to tell them.'

Every morning, before he started his round, Goldblatt talked to Sister Choy or Debbie, the second in charge, to find out how many beds were going to become available that day, barring deaths and disappearances.

Armed with that knowledge, he then went to the doctors' office, sat down, opened one of the desk drawers, and took out a book that was kept there.

At first glance, the book looked like any one of millions of blue A4-size diaries that you would find in offices all over the world. But in reality it was nothing like them. Its bland, unremarkable appearance was just a cunning disguise for its enormous metaphysical power. The admissions book was a metaphor for life, for the relentless progress of time and the extinction of opportunity. When Goldblatt opened it, the past was on his left, page after page of names hopefully entered, and of which at least half had been mercilessly struck out with 'cancelled' written in the margins beside them. The future was on his right, page after page of as-yet-unobliterated names – four to a page – in Emma's handwriting, with a note saying 'cancelled x 1' or 'cancelled x 2!' or 'cancelled x 3!!' or 'cancelled x 4!!?!' written underneath. And in the middle, flat on the desk in front of him, was the page of the present, the Here-and-Now, the razor-sharp line separating the Will-Be from the Was, the Could-Be from the Wasn't, the soft underbelly of time palpitating in all its moist vulnerability beneath his poised pen. And with a stroke and a cursive 'cancelled', Goldblatt would perform the irreversible transmutation and send someone's future and its unlimited potential spinning irrecoverably away into the constricted past.

At that moment, as he sat with pen poised, he was the breaker of seals, the father of time. Sitting with the book of remembering and forgetting open in front of him, calculating the difference between the number of beds he had and the number of names on the page, deciding who would come in and who would be struck off, who would be chosen and who would be cast out... for that one moment each morning, Goldblatt was a god. A very minor god, barely a foot-washer to the major deities – but a god.

And then he was just a man again, picking up a phone and calling an Argentinian admissions clerk called Sofia to give her the names of the day's cancellees, and the dates, three or four months away, on which he was rescheduling them.

The names got into the book in the first place by coming to him on small blue cards, RSVPs to invitations he had never sent out. He would find them like a crop of blue fungus on his desk in the doctors' office on

Friday mornings, having been deposited there by the guardian angel who watches over all Fuertler's patients after the Prof's prodigious Thursday clinics.

The cards were filled out in the Prof's curly script or in the handwriting of the two clinical assistants who worked with her in the Thursday Fuertler's clinic. There were boxes on the cards to be filled in with important information, like the patient's name, age, hospital number, address, and reason for hospitalization. There were also boxes for unimportant information, like preferred dates of admission. Goldblatt wasn't sure if the Prof and her assistants filled that part out as a joke. Reservations at the Hotel Small, which rarely had room for all its guests, weren't allocated by preference. Sometimes the 'urgent' box on the card had been ticked, and then Goldblatt was in a real quandary. For about ten seconds. As far as he could work out, most of the 'urgent' patients were coming in for the usual Fuertler's work-up, and it wasn't immediately apparent what made one work-up more urgent than another. Besides, the Prof's performance with the Broderip had shown him that if a patient in clinic revealed the slightest sign of actually being ill enough to require admission, the Prof wouldn't be writing little blue cards with neat ticks in the boxes.

The card also had a box for Goldblatt to fill in, the putative date of admission. But the moment when he leafed forward in the book of time to find the next empty slot, then wrote the name in the diary, wrote the date in the box, and sent the card off to Sofia in the admissions office – that moment which should have been the end of the process – was only the beginning, the point at which each name took its place in the great, unending chain of cancellations that had wound itself like a python around the Prof's unit and was inexorably squeezing it to death. One day, he knew, he would come across that name again. When the future had turned into the present, and tranquillity had become confusion, his own hand, he knew, would strike it out once more.

He began to understand why Emma had said it was so stressful. Anyone who has ever been in charge of admissions will have found himself cancelling electives, but the sheer volume, density, and consistency of cancellations on the Prof's unit was something he had never come across before. They weren't an exception, they were the rule. Normally it was the admissions clerks who were supposed to ring patients to inform them that their admissions had been cancelled, but Sofia refused to ring anyone who had been cancelled already – which was just about everybody. Even if she had agreed to call them instead of leaving it to him, they would have rung him themselves. The Prof kindly instructed all her patients not to hesitate to contact her registrar, and even provided them with his bleep number in case switchboard lost it. Not only patients rang him, but mothers, husbands, cousins, GPs, MPs, and all sorts of do-gooders who should have butted out. They whimpered, ranted, threatened, pleaded, and tried every kind of emotional blackmail. And they cried, especially the patients. Goldblatt had already come across some whose next six-monthly infusions were due before the last ones had even been done. The anxiety this created was wrenching. Professor Small had convinced them that only six-monthly infusions of the wonder drug Sorain would keep them in one piece, and yet they couldn't get on to her ward to receive it.

It was like a cruel, horrible hoax, like some kind of endlessly recurring punishment out of a Greek myth, and Goldblatt, the liver-devouring eagle flying in every morning for the feast, found himself the agent of retribution through which the punishment was delivered.

He couldn't conjure beds out of thin air. There was simply no point asking him to do it, as if, by some exercise of *force majeure*, he could make it happen. Not only couldn't he do anything for those who rang him, he *shouldn't* have done anything for them even if he could. Was he meant to make exceptions for the people who complained most, wept longest, shouted loudest? Would that be fair? What about the others, the stoics who didn't ring? Or the lonely people who didn't have friend or families to campaign for them? The people on the phone grudgingly conceded the point when he put it to them, hoping to make them see his predicament. No, they said, it wouldn't be fair for him to make exceptions – meaning yes, he should, but only for them. Well, he wasn't running a discrimination programme against stoics and lonely people. Stoics and lonely people deserved to get in just as much as whingers and the socially successful. Whingers and the socially successful deserved to get in just as much as stoics and lonely people. And there was nothing Goldblatt could do to change the fact that so few of them did.

The unpalatable truth was that the numbers didn't add up. Professor Small didn't have the beds to give her patients the care she promised them. But she refused to face it.

She could have asked the hospital management for more beds. Given the income that the Prof's unit generated, they might have been agreeable. But the hospital management, she knew, had other demands to balance. The Prof's Seriousness Drive over the past year to secure an extra consultant and an SHO had been nothing less than heroic, fought tooth and nail against stiff opposition from consultants who felt that her unit was already too big for its Fuertlered boots. The very idea of starting all over again for extra beds frankly left her exhausted.

Alternatively, she could have extended the utterly arbitrary six-month interval that she had chosen for her patients' work-ups and Sorain infusions, reducing the frequency of admissions and solving the bed crisis at a stroke. But that was even less attractive, if possible, than going into battle for extra beds. Already the other consultants at the hospital didn't take Fuertler's Syndrome seriously enough. How much less seriously would they take it if her patients needed to come in less frequently, making it seem that Fuertler's was getting easier to treat, not harder?

At the very least, she could have cut down on the Broderipian 'emergency' admissions that came out of her Thursday clinic. There are patients in any clinic who, for murky reasons of their own, have an unwholesome desire to be admitted to hospital, and the doctor's role, as Goldblatt understood it to be traditionally defined, is to keep them out. But that wasn't how Professor Small operated. It was enough for one of her Thursday patients to say she had been feeling a bit under the weather and could do with a rest – and she was in. The Prof would be on the phone to Emma, who could be relied upon to manipulate beds, substitute names in the admissions book, and dance scantily clothed on the desk in the Prof's clinic room if required.

This was because of a deep need at the heart of Andrea Small's personality. Doctors are no different to anyone else. They have their fears, they have their desires. Constantly prickling with self-doubt, the Prof dreaded to discover that she wasn't respected. But not being respected was merely her fear. Her craving was to be loved.

Andrea Small's need to be loved controlled her behaviour with a complete lack of selectivity, and for precisely as long as the object of this need occupied one of her senses of physical perception. She wanted to be loved by whoever was in her field of vision or was speaking to her at the time, by friends and enemies alike, by secretaries, filing clerks, receptionists, doctors, nurses, physiotherapists, social workers, and the tea ladies in green smocks when she passed them on her rounds. Above all, she wanted to be loved by her patients, to whom she made promises of admissions she would never be able to keep, and who, perversely enough, were the only ones who did love her, blaming anyone but the Prof for the disappointment that inevitably followed her smiling reassurances. They didn't see the chaotic effects of her divisive and impossible quest for universal affection. The Prof walked around in a self-generated and self-validated haze of approval, while colleagues and subordinates shot spiteful glances in her direction that she interpreted as signs of warmth.

At some level, she must have known that what she gave with one hand to someone sitting in front of her, she was taking away with the other from someone who was absent. She must have known that when Emma manipulated the beds to get some grumbling non-coper in from clinic, she was bumping someone else who had been waiting patiently for months. In short, she must have understood the Broderip–Anderssen Principle, even if she didn't know it by that name.

But it made no difference, because at any given moment the Prof's concrete need to be loved outweighed any abstract understanding of the consequences to which this might lead. And the only person who could love her was the person physically sitting in front of her in the clinic, or the person physically lying in bed on the ward round whose name Emma had just whispered into her ear. Not the person who was just a name that was going to be bumped further along the Book of Time. The name that was going to be bumped further along the Book of Time would get its own chance, when it finally materialised in front of her as a person on the ward, to fulfil the Prof's need to be loved, and most were so pathetically grateful at having finally got hooked up to their Sorain drip that that was precisely what they did.

Goldblatt, who had been on the unit for barely more than a week, didn't know any of this about the Prof. But he knew what a few minutes of simple arithmetic could tell him.

'Rubbish,' said Emma, when Goldblatt pointed out the incontrovertibility of the numbers to her, having walked into the doctors' office and found her slyly leafing through the admissions book with a pen in her hand.

'Emma, there's no way we can get them in and out quickly enough.'

'Of course we can,' she snapped.

'We can't. Look, Emma, do we really have to book them at four a day?'

'The Prof told me to. That's the only way we can keep up.'

'But we're not keeping up. All we do is end up cancelling them.'

Emma stared at him.

'Emma, I'm not saying it's your fault. Okay, you've been told to book them like this, but it can't be done. Look at the cancellations. Look at them. Every day!'

'That's only recent.'

'How recent?'

'Recent.'

Goldblatt shook his head. He took the Book of Time from under Emma's hand and turned over the pages of the past, one after the other, page after page of cancellations. He flipped to the future, page after unrelenting page with quartets of names. 'We've got sixteen beds, Emma. Take Dr Morris's three beds away, that leaves thirteen. But we're booking four patients a day, and they're supposed to stay for five days.'

'So?'

Goldblatt clenched his fists in frustration. Emma wasn't stupid. She just refused to acknowledge the reality. He got up and wrote the figures on the whiteboard in the doctors' office. 'It's lumpy,' he said, turning around with the numbers on the board behind him. 'Monday or Tuesday? No problem. Beds empty out over the weekend. In steady state – theoretically – you could admit up to nine on one of those days and four on the other. Other days, with thirteen beds – none. If you want to bring in four consistently, even on those days – add four, and another four – you need twenty-one beds. And that's with a hundred per cent efficiency. Patients getting their last infusion on the morning they leave, going home, the new patients coming in and getting their first infusion that afternoon. Not a single overstay. Not a single emergency admission. In reality, you're probably going to need twenty-five beds. Maybe thirty.'

Emma was unimpressed.

'Emma!'

'What about weekends?' she demanded suddenly. 'Why don't we book them for weekends?'

'They're electives, Emma. We can't admit them on weekends. Besides, I looked at that. You'd still need sixteen beds – that's at maximum efficiency, no emergencies. Make it twenty.'

'The Prof says we can always sneak a couple in,' murmured Emma.

'Does she? And is the Prof going to come in and clerk them?'

'The house officers will clerk them.'

'Which house officers?' enquired Goldblatt.

'The ones on call,' said Emma.

'Oh,' said Goldblatt. '*Those* house officers. You mean the ones who have to manage fifty emergency admissions already. Well, I suppose the Prof's right. What's another couple of patients if you're going to be up all night anyway?'

Emma stared at Goldblatt intransigently.

'Emma, please, I'm not trying to be difficult. I'm just pointing out the reality. Look at the numbers. Booking them like this, you're going to be cancelling two fifths of your patients routinely. Routinely. That's *before* you take into account the work-ups that take longer than normal, or someone who gets ill, or one of the emergencies our leader brings in from clinic.' Or clinical coups of your own, Goldblatt added silently, like Simmons.

Emma looked.

'That's why we're actually cancelling half. In fact more than half. And it's going to get worse.' As more cancellations piled up, they would occupy more of the slots for new admissions, creating even more cancellations, which in turn would occupy more of the slots... Suddenly Goldblatt realized what he was really saying. They were sitting on a gigantic juggernaut of cancellations that was picking up speed under the momentum of its own ever-expanding mass until, burning white hot, it would eventually overtake itself and explode in one final luminescent cataclysm through the logical impossibility of its continuing existence before collapsing into a black hole that would suck them all irrecoverably into its fathomless depths.

'Rubbish,' said Emma

Goldblatt hugged his arms around his shoulders and hunched over in pain. He thought he was going to start hyperventilating. 'What do you mean "rubbish"? I haven't made this up. Look at the book! The book doesn't lie.'

'People cancel,' said Emma.

'They *what?*'

'They cancel.'

'On *this* unit?'

'You have to book in enough people so you never waste a bed when one of them cancels.'

'What are we running? An airline?' Goldblatt gave her the book. 'Find me a patient who cancelled. Find me *one*.'

Emma began to leaf through the pages. Page after page after page.

'Here,' she cried at last, thrusting the book at Goldblatt.

'Where?' said Goldblatt.

'There!'

'Here? The fifth of January?'

'Can't you read? Robbins. "Husband rang to cancel."'

Goldblatt read. 'She died, Emma. He cancelled because she died.'

'So? She still cancelled.'

'For fuck's sake, Emma! The woman died!'

'We can't keep beds free for dead patients, Malcolm,' retorted Emma primly. 'Perhaps you've done that in other jobs, but we can't afford those sorts of luxuries here.'

Goldblatt took a deep breath. 'We should talk to the Prof. Let's go to her. Both of us.'

Emma looked at him as if he was out of his mind.

'I'll go myself.'

'No!'

Goldblatt gazed at her quizzically.

'She knows. She doesn't need you to tell her.'

Goldblatt took another deep breath, 'All right. Listen, let's at least agree to stop booking people on Fridays. Look at the book. No one's got in on a Friday for the last month. The Prof floods the place from her clinic on Thursdays, and we're way over our bed count until Monday at the earliest. Let's leave Friday open, all right? Let's start with that.'

Emma looked at him suspiciously. 'The Prof wouldn't agree.'

'Then let's do it *for* her. That's our job. To do the little things the Prof doesn't want to do for herself.'

Emma shook her head.

'Why are you always defending her?'

'Who? Who am I defending?'

Goldblatt didn't answer.

Emma got up. 'I'm not defending anyone,' she said angrily, and walked off to her office.

Why Emma defended the Prof was her business, but she not only defended her, she aided and abetted her, and that made it Goldblatt's business as well. If he left a day in the Book of Time with fewer than four names, the page would miraculously fill up with the extra names in Emma's hand-writing. And every Friday morning he would arrive to find a Broderip or two from the Prof's clinic who had arrived courtesy of Emma's under-ground railway, occupying beds that had been earmarked for people who would shortly, as a result, be receiving one of the dreaded phone calls from Professor Small's registrar.

And in order that the Prof could play the darling nymph to her adoring patients, Goldblatt continued in his unwanted role as the wrathful god. Each morning, as the mountain of cancellations grew steadily higher, he sat down with the Book of Time and made his selection.

He didn't want to be a god. He had never wanted to be one. Even when he saved someone's life by pumping on their chest and sending just the right dose of electricity through their fibrillating heart – those times when you step out from behind the screens in front of the terrified relatives, and you are, you just *are* a god – even then, he never wanted to be one. How did you know what was going to happen next? How could you know what was happening behind you? What if the same heart started fibrillating once more as soon as your back was turned, only this time it wasn't going to be persuaded so easily to get working again. Before you knew it, you would be back in front of the same expectant crowd, but this time it was with a different speech. 'I'm sorry but it was quick and painless and would you mind signing a form so we can do an autopsy please?' That one never got quite the same reception.

But people wouldn't let you do it. They wouldn't let you get away without the halo. When you tried to turn it down they thought it was false modesty and added it to their catalogue of medical arrogance, merely proving, as everyone already knew, that all doctors think they're gods. Like the ancients chipping statues to Augustus, when people want divinity, they find it.

It was just one of the things medicine did to you, just one of the ways it devised to make you both more and less than a normal person. It was like the stony, bleary trudge through the nights on call that brought you to the lowest level of snarling humanity and showed you how low you could sink, while simultaneously setting you apart, so that afterwards you would always think of yourself as special, different, just for the fact that you'd been through it and survived, as if your soul had been forged in a white heat that was reserved for you and your profession alone. Or like the dealing with death, the dreadful familiarity that robbed you of something soft, fragile, and precious, and put in its place an equally precious hardness and strength. The being a god was one of these things. Like the others, it gave with one hand and took away with the other.

And here it was once more, in a new manifestation, a different guise. Old Mother Medicine was doing it to him again, finding a new way to get to him, just when he thought he had seen it all.

Because when push came to shove, he was no better than any other deity. He was fickle, and his whims were inscrutable, most of all to himself. Compassionate one moment, impassive the next, stern then yielding, sympathetic then unrelenting, his moods swung from hour to hour and day to day. The phone calls were endless, the pleas, the tears. With one weeping cancelee he would be gentle, understanding, reassuring, and helpful, listening with infinite patience to the story of the week taken off work, or the arrangements made with the mother to look after the kids in preparation for this admission that, he had rung to say, wasn't going to happen. And with the next one –having already spoken to one too many that day, or having been interrupted in the middle of a busy clinic that was already running an hour late with a benchful of patients still waiting for his attention – he would be brisk and unwavering, repeating bureaucratically that the hospital was very clear in its communications that it couldn't guarantee a proposed admission date, as the pleas of the patient on the other end of the phone became increasingly tearful. He would put the phone down and feel sick at what he had just done. Why had he done it? At those moments, he hated himself. He hated being put in that position, and he hated not being able to change it. Most of all, he hated what it did to him.

There was no real mystery about it. He was human. Not a god at all.

9

JUST BEFORE NINE A.M. on the fourth Sunday after he had started on the unit, Goldblatt walked into the hospital carrying a bag. He went to the doctors' mess, bleeped the registrar who had covered the Saturday, and sat down to wait.

The mess was strewn with plates covered in coagulated gravy, soft-drink cans, coffee cups, torn newspapers, take-away pizza containers, and other debris indicative of the forced incarceration of desperate people. It had a stale smell, and Goldblatt opened a window on to the cold, grey air of a late February morning. The HO, he knew, was already somewhere in the hospital. It was her first weekend on call. Since she and Goldblatt worked different Take cycles, and since she was required to cover both days of the weekend, and he did only one, it was purely a matter of chance that he was rostered on this particular Sunday as her medical registrar.

The Saturday reg arrived in the mess with a senior house officer called Steve. They had just finished a quick round of the patients who had come in the day before. Like the HO, Steve had to cover the Takes on both days of the weekend. The HO had been with them on the round, but they had sent her straight back to the wards, hoping to get the Sunday morning bloods taken before the emergencies started coming in. On busy Sundays it wasn't unusual for house officers still to be taking Sunday morning bloods at midnight.

'I usually handle things myself with the house officer,' said Steve after the other registrar had told Goldblatt about the patients who needed review, handed over the key to the on-call room, and gone. Steve soon let it drop that he had just passed the second part of the Royal College exam, and it was obvious that he felt he knew enough to do without anyone else's advice unless he asked for it. That suited Goldblatt. There was nothing worse than an SHO who was always pestering you for confirmation of his decisions. With someone like Steve you could be sure that after midnight only a major catastrophe with casualties numbering in the hundreds would induce him to call his registrar and admit that he couldn't cope. This was a highly desirable situation that considerably boosted Goldblatt's chances of getting some sleep overnight, which was the main concern of just about any registrar.

'OK,' said Goldblatt.

'The way we do things here is pretty standard. I take the calls from the GPs and divide the admissions between myself and the house officer. I'll have a look at the patients she sees as well. If there's a medical student around, I'll see the patients he clerks too. I'll probably be in Casualty all day. If the house officer gets into trouble on the wards I'd appreciate it if you could help her out.'

'OK,' said Goldblatt.

'Can I tell her to ring you direct? Not after midnight, of course,' added Steve quickly. 'I didn't mean that.'

'OK,' said Goldblatt.

'And we'll call you if the numbers start building up in Casualty. Is that all right?'

'Sure,' said Goldblatt.

'Well, that's about it, then,' said Steve. 'The bed numbers are pretty tight, but that's always the way. Takes are busy here, but they're great experience.'

Goldblatt nodded. He was sure they were, and he hoped Steve would find the experience just as great as he hoped. Personally, Goldblatt had never found that the great experience of busy Takes was enough to compensate for the fact that they were busy.

Steve finished his coffee. He had a narrow face with a sharp nose, and receding blond hair. He did everything very deliberately, as if each movement of his body was designed to give the impression that he was in control. He was wearing his white coat, and his tie was tightly knotted at the throat. Goldblatt was in jeans and an open-necked shirt, and he had no idea where his white coat was. Steve looked good for a guy starting his second day on call. It was probably the morning blush. If you got a couple of hours' sleep you were usually all right until midday.

Steve glanced at his watch and got up. 'I'd better go,' he said, 'they rang me half an hour ago about some old lady who's been brought in with a stroke.'

'Expecting anything else?' asked Goldblatt.

'A couple. There's a known epileptic who's been fitting all night. And a GP rang me at six about someone with severe Crohn's disease, but he hasn't turned up yet.' Steve shrugged. 'Nothing we can't handle.'

Steve left. Goldblatt looked around the battlefield of the mess. He picked up the shreds of one of the Saturday papers and read an article about celibate priests. Priests apparently didn't want to be celibate any more, and frankly Goldblatt couldn't blame them. A woman arrived to clean away the detritus that had been deposited overnight. Goldblatt bleeped the HO to find out if she was still alive. The HO said she was, but there was something in her voice that made him wonder whether she was lying. During the week she had been strangely excited about her first weekend on call, but it sounded as if that was a long time ago now. She hadn't finished the bloods, but Steve had just bleeped her to come down and help out with a man in cardiac failure who had turned up hard on the heels of the stroke.

'OK,' said Goldblatt, 'let me know if you're in trouble.'

'I'm in trouble,' said the HO.

'No, you're not,' said Goldblatt. 'This isn't trouble.'

'It feels like trouble.'

'It isn't trouble.'

'Then how will I know when I am in trouble?' said the HO.

'I'll tell you.'

He put the phone down. A man from the hospital shop brought the Sunday newspapers into the mess. Goldblatt picked up one of the broadsheets and started reading. He wasn't really interested in most of the pap that padded it, but once you left and started to get involved with what was happening outside the door of the doctors' mess, it didn't stop.

But there was only so long you could stay there. Eventually he went to the accommodation block behind the hospital and dropped his bag off in the on-call room, and then came back to see a patient on the Coronary

Care Unit the previous day's reg had asked him to review. Then there were another couple of patients he had to see on other wards. One of them needed a blood test. Goldblatt magnanimously did it himself even though he could legitimately have demanded that the HO come up to do it. Who said he didn't pitch in with both hands?

Once he got going, the rest of the morning passed in a grey stream of patients on the wards whom the HO kept ringing him to go and review. She was never there when he arrived, always having been called back down to Casualty, where Steve was ploughing through the growing crowd of hopeful applicants queuing for admission. At one o'clock he snatched a quick lunch, and then went down to review what Steve had done and help out.

Over the next few hours he saw a succession of patients. At around four in the afternoon there was a brief lull before the Sunday-night rush began. Goldblatt grabbed a coffee. The HO went off to the wards to take the rest of the morning bloods.

The Sunday-night rush was the last great hurdle of a weekend on call. It could start as early as midday and go on, in some cases, right through to the next morning. A rush developed when a critical mass of GPs suddenly decided they couldn't cope any more with various patients who had been gradually deteriorating at home over the weekend. The Rushed – as the patients were technically known – weren't necessarily all that ill. Some would be close to death and should have been admitted days before, but others would end up being sent home from Casualty after a five-hour wait. There was something about Sunday nights, maybe just the loneliness at the end of two days of house calls, that induced a collective madness in GPs and made them unable to tolerate uncertainty for one second longer.

Early in the evening a patient on the Haematology ward developed chest pain that turned out to be a full-blown myocardial infarction, and by the time Goldblatt had dealt with that, transferred the patient to the Coronary Care Unit, organized treatment, and got back down to the Casualty bear pit, it was eight o'clock and the department was awash with the Rushed. Virtually all the SHOs in the hospital were down there masquerading as gynaecologists, ophthalmologists, paediatricians, surgeons, psychiatrists, and any other specialist who happened to be required.

Goldblatt hadn't heard from Steve since he had gone up to the Haematology ward to deal with the infarct. He wondered just how much trouble Steve was in.

Lots. Steve came out from behind the screens around one of the cubicles, glancing around apprehensively like someone who knows he's under attack but doesn't know where the next blow is coming from. He'd loosened his tie. His face was pale, his eyes were sunken deep into dark sockets, and he looked as if he needed intravenous rehydration a lot more urgently than the various patients lying around the department with drips in their arms. He saw Goldblatt and glanced at him grimly in recognition.

'All right?' said Goldblatt.

Steve managed a despairing grin.

'What have you got?'

Steve pulled a piece of paper out of his pocket. 'There was the haemophiliac with a haemarthrosis because he couldn't find his factor VIII.'

'You already told me about him. I saw him before,' said Goldblatt. 'What else?'

'The stroke.'

'Which stroke?'

'The second stroke. The old guy.'

'You told me about him as well. Do I need to see him?'

Steve shook his head. 'Just a normal stroke,' he murmured, studying his list. 'What about the myocardial infarct? Did I mention him to you?'

'Which one? I just saw one on the Haematology unit.'

'No, the one who came in. Sixty-three-year-old male.'

'No, I haven't seen him.'

'He's OK. Straightforward anterior.' Steve glanced at one of the high-dependency cubicles, which was temporarily empty. 'Looks like they've just taken him up to CCU.'

'Did you strep him?'

Steve nodded.

'Any failure?'

'No problems. He's fine.'

'I'll look at him later,' said Goldblatt.

'Don't worry about him. First MI. Smoker. Overweight. We'll hear if anything happens.' Steve paused to peruse the piece of paper, which was covered in hastily scribbled notes. 'Let's see. There's a pyelonephritis one of the medical students is seeing, and I'll have to see her afterwards. I've got an asthmatic having a nebulizer. He'll probably go home. That bleeder we had earlier stabilized. Oh, you remember that patient with bronchial carcinoma? He died.'

'Down here?'

Steve nodded.

'Died in a Casualty department.' Goldblatt shook his head. 'Imagine doing that. Idiot GP. What the fuck did he send him in for?'

Steve looked over his list, possibly not even hearing the question. 'There's a thrombophlebitis. I've got a severe diarrhoea coming in, a swollen leg...'

'What about the one you were seeing in there?' asked Goldblatt. 'Who's that?'

'Some old guy with Parkinson's who's had a fall.'

'Bringing him in?'

'The wife says she can't manage. We've only got two male beds left in the hospital.'

'The guy with the Parkinson's, can he walk?'

Steve shrugged. 'Kind of.'

'Any acute problems?'

Steve shook his head.

'Well, if he can walk... he can walk,' said Goldblatt, citing an age-old adage of med regs everywhere struggling with bed shortages. 'Get him back for an early review.'

Steve nodded.

'All right,' said Goldblatt. 'Now, where's the house officer?'

Steve looked at his list again. 'I think she's with the headache.'

'Which headache?'

'Didn't I tell you about the headache?'

The headache was around the corner in one of the treatment rooms. Goldblatt pushed the door open quietly and saw an obese man in his forties lying curled up on his side with his spine exposed under a bright yellow light. On one side of him was a student nurse, and on the other was the HO, seated under the light with an instruments trolley at her elbow, gloves on her hands, and a long needle poised between her fingers. If Goldblatt hadn't known any better, he would have said she was about to try a lumbar puncture.

'I don't think you want to do it *exactly* like that.'

The HO jumped. 'Malcolm!'

'Do you think you want to come outside for a second?'

'Why?' asked the HO.

'I think you should.'

The HO told the patient she'd be back, and stepped into the corridor with Goldblatt.

'Does Steve know what you're doing?' asked Goldblatt.

The HO nodded.

'Have you ever done a lumbar puncture?'

'I saw one yesterday.'

'And does Steve know that?'

'Steve did the one I saw.'

'I see,' said Goldblatt. 'And you feel confident doing it by yourself?'

'He didn't have time to show me again. He told me to do it. "See one, do one, teach one." Isn't that what they say?'

'Who? All the doctors who have been struck off for malpractice?'

Goldblatt gazed at the HO. She was on automatic. She had big black bags under her eyes and greasy smudges on her glasses. She was still holding the needle even though she had desterilized her gloves by touching the door when she followed Goldblatt out.

'I've got two patients to see after him,' pleaded the HO. 'And I don't know what else after that. And the wards keep calling me. Can't I go back and get this finished? Please? Can't I?'

'Sure. But let's see if we can get the needle in the right place.'

Goldblatt went back in with the HO and guided her through the procedure. As anyone who had done a lumbar puncture before would have known, the obesity of the guy with the headache made him a nightmare LP candidate. After the HO had had two tries, Goldblatt put on a pair of gloves and did the job himself. He left her labelling the specimen tubes for the lab, and went back to Casualty. The Rush was in full swing. There was no standing on ceremony now. Steve was drowning. Goldblatt plunged in. He saw a woman with inflammation of the superficial veins in one of her legs and sent her home. He saw a diabetic with raging cellulitis of the foot and welcomed him to the hospital. He dealt with another six patients, none of whom required admission, and reviewed a couple of others that Steve was bringing in. The next one he saw should have been sent in twenty-four hours earlier. He had a past history of a heart attack, and a malignancy known as a VIPoma – not a tumour reserved for celebrities, but one that secretes large amounts of a hormone called Vasoactive Intestinal Peptide, causing profuse and watery diarrhoea – and his bowel had been pouring out fluid a lot faster than he could replace it by drinking. Goldblatt examined him. He was anxious and severely dehydrated. Goldblatt took bloods and inserted a drip to start rehydrating him intravenously.

The VIPoma was a big man in his sixties, with a barrel chest and a ruddy face.

'Will it stop?' he said anxiously once Goldblatt had put the drip in. 'I've never had the diarrhoea so bad.'

Goldblatt nodded. 'It'll stop. If it doesn't, there are things we can use. The first thing is to get the fluid back into you. That's what's urgent. Let's worry about that right now.'

The VIPoma nodded.

'Where's your wife?'

'She went. Had to get home. I was waiting so long.'

Goldblatt smiled. 'Sunday nights are bad.'

'It's all right, doc.' The VIPoma looked down at the drip in his arm. 'I feel better already. Can you just... Oh, can you get me a nurse? Quick!'

Goldblatt couldn't find a nurse. He got him a bedpan and helped him on to it.

Goldblatt left the cubicle. It was after one in the morning now. The Emergency department was quieter. Some of the cubicles were vacant. The Rush was waning. Goldblatt found Steve and the HO sitting opposite each other across a desk in the doctors' area, writing notes. Each of them still had one patient left to see. If no one else came in, and if the wards stayed quiet, there was even a chance they might get some sleep. The medical student who had been hanging around for most of the day had disappeared. Goldblatt sat down and wrote up his notes about the VIPoma. Only the blood results were missing. The potassium would probably be low as a result of the VIPoma's diarrhoea. Goldblatt had included extra potassium on the intravenous orders, but more might have to be added. He told Steve about the patient, and Steve muttered something unhopeful about finding him a bed. Goldblatt told the HO to check the blood results and add more potassium to the VIPoma's intravenous fluid if necessary. He wrote down the amounts she should add, depending on the blood result. The HO nodded, without looking up.

Goldblatt stood up. 'Looks like you can handle it now,' he said, glancing around the department.

Steve nodded.

Suddenly he was aware of his own tiredness. 'Call me if you need me.'

'I'm sure we'll be OK,' said Steve, reasserting the autonomy that made him such a great second-on-call for a registrar to work with.

Steve's bleep went off. He called through to switchboard. 'Medical SHO,' he said. He waited. 'This is the medical SHO,' he said again, then listened for a long time. Goldblatt watched him. Suddenly the exhaustion and helplessness that Steve had managed to suppress when the Rush ended were visible again. His face collapsed. Even after all the years he had done it himself, Goldblatt still didn't know how anyone coped with two consecutive nights on call.

He glanced at the HO. She was watching Steve anxiously.

'OK, send him in,' Steve said eventually in a toneless voice. 'Let me just write down his name.'

Steve listened and wrote something on a piece of paper. He put the phone down and looked at the HO.

'We've got a patient with end-stage alcoholic cirrhosis coming in. He's got a depressed conscious state and a low BP. GP thinks he's got pneumonia and he might be bleeding internally.'

'Sounds like a mess,' said Goldblatt.

The HO closed her eyes in despair. Her face screwed up until all that was left was her little button of a nose, and the glasses balancing in front of it, and her tousled red hair on top of it.

'Call me if you need me.' Goldblatt looked at the HO. 'Make sure you get the results on that lumbar puncture and the potassium level on the man with the VIPoma.'

The HO's eyes were still closed. She nodded.

Goldblatt left them.

He joined them again two hours later, the high-pitched *ping ping ping* of the cardiac arrest bleep ringing in his ears.

A big, pale mound of a belly was the first thing he registered as he ran into the room. And doctors and nurses all around it. Steve was pumping on a broad pink chest. The belly rolled and rippled with each of Steve's compressions. Another doctor, presumably the anaesthetics SHO, was standing at the patient's head, squeezing on a bag that was connected to a tube that had been put down his throat. The HO was trying to get blood from a groin. Goldblatt looked at the ECG monitor on the emergency trolley beside the bed, trying to assess the situation, still partly asleep after having been woken by the bleep three minutes before, clammy, disorientated, still breathless after running from his on-call room, his body still recalibrating from the shock of dashing out of the accommodation block into the freezing night air and then back inside.

The ECG was showing a dead flat line.

'Have you shocked him?' asked Goldblatt.

Steve shook his head.

'Drugs?'

'Adrenaline. Twice.'

'Who is he?' said Goldblatt as he made his way around Steve towards the patient's head. 'Anyone know anything about him?'

'He's the patient with a VIPoma you admitted before.'

Goldblatt looked down at his face. 'What was his potassium?' he asked as he pulled back on one of the VIPoma's eyelids and shone a torch into his eye.

The pupil was dilated, but there was a flicker of contraction.

Goldblatt let go of the eyelid and put the torch back in his pocket. He looked around to find the HO staring at him. Frozen. Her needle was still stuck in the VIPoma's groin.

'What was the potassium?' Goldblatt asked again.

'I don't know,' the HO whispered.

'Go and find out.'

The potassium was 1.6. Less than half the lower limit of normal.

They worked on the VIPoma. They poured drugs and potassium into him, and Goldblatt tried to shock his heart back into action with the electrified paddles of the defibrillator machine, progressively turning the power up and leaving big red rectangular burn marks on the VIPoma's skin. Steve kept pumping on his chest until the sternum under his hand started to make a sickening, crunching sound with each compression. The HO stood there transfixed, watching. Eventually Goldblatt checked the VIPoma's pupils again. Dilated and fixed.

'OK,' said Goldblatt. 'That's it. Stop.'

Steve stopped pumping and stepped back. The big pale belly lay still now, lifeless.

Goldblatt looked at the HO. 'Do you want to call his wife?'

The HO stared at him.

'No? Then I suppose I'll have to do it.'

10

THIS WAS HOW IT happened. People didn't realize it. When you listened to them, you just had to laugh. They missed the point. Long hours meant tired doctors, they'd say, and tired doctors made mistakes. They prescribed the wrong drugs, gave the wrong doses, made the wrong incisions – and people died.

No, tired doctors hardly ever made mistakes. No matter how tired you were, it was almost always possible to summon up enough brain-power for twenty seconds in order to check the name and dose of a drug. Your adrenaline would see to that. In his entire career, Goldblatt had seen only one serious mistake that he could attribute to simple fatigue, when one of his SHOs calculated the wrong rate for an insulin infusion at three in the morning. Even then, the monitoring regimen the SHO had scheduled ensured that the mistake was discovered before any harm ensued. The truth was different. Tired doctors didn't make mistakes – tired doctors weren't there. Doctors have discretion. That's what people didn't understand. They have discretion, and tired doctors use that discretion differently than fresh doctors.

Say you had a patient who'd been deteriorating through the night. In between seeing new emergencies in Casualty, you got him stabilized, and finally managed to get to bed at four a.m., desperate for sleep. You knew your bleeper might go off any second. On the other hand, you might just get three hours' sleep before the full day of work that faced you. There weren't going to be any concessions for what you'd been through overnight. Maybe a jokey 'Two hours' sleep, eh? Lucky you!' from some consultant. No one cared. No one wanted to know. New day, new patients, new clinic, new life. Any sleep you got between now and then was precious. So you got to bed at four, and you had this sick patient who, you knew, should be assessed again in an hour or so. That's what you'd do during the day – no question. After all, they taught you at medical school that you're meant to identify problems early, not wait until they've had a chance to progress and develop their own complications.

So what were you going to do? Were you going to get up again in an hour and review the patient, or were you going to let the nursing staff call you if they thought he needed to be seen? If you were going to wait for a call from the nurses, were you going to give them explicit instructions about when you should be called, or were you going to leave it up to them to decide, knowing that most nurses, having been intimidated by doctors they'd woken in the past, wouldn't call unless they judged the situation to be extreme? And if they did call you, would you get out of bed to assess the patient in person, or would you try to deal with it over the phone? And if you did go to assess the patient, and if you were an HO out of your depth, did you dare to wake a more senior colleague, or would you try to muddle through it tragicomically on your own?

Welcome to the grey realm of the doctor's discretion. There were no right answers to these questions. Sometimes it was one, sometimes another, depending on the case. There were no rules here, no certainties. Only judgements. The chances were that no one would ever know anything about the decision you made except what you chose to write in the notes. And there weren't any fixed standards by which to measure your decision anyway. No one was there, looking over your shoulder from the shadows of the darkened ward, when you made it. How could anyone else know how ill the patient really was when you saw him before you went to bed? How could anyone really know what your true assessment had been? No one would ever know but you.

It was all in the realm of discretion, guided by how exhausted you were, how frustrated you were, how desperate you were. Yes, people died because of tired doctors, and that was how.

But what could you do? A system that institutionalized exhaustion as a mode of operation just had to accept that sooner or later it would kill off its agents' altruism. In its place would appear the survival strategies to which exhausted individuals resort.

Was this a good thing to do to medical practitioners? It was going to turn people who started off as carers into survivors. It was going to turn their patients into their adversaries. And at least a residue of this – so scarring, so indelible – was going to remain in the soul of each one even after the hard years were over.

But people didn't understand – or refused to. 'Fifty-six hours?' they would say when Goldblatt told them. 'That must be hard.' No, not hard. Hard wasn't the word for it. They didn't have the word for it because they had never gone through it. If you have never worked more than eight or ten or fifteen or even twenty hours in a row you have no idea. You can't understand the irresistible power of the urge to sleep, its necessity, after thirty, forty, fifty hours without it, and what you will do for just an hour's respite. It's not merely tiredness, but a deep dragging fatigue that eats you from the inside like a cornered beast, clawing and cleaning out your abdominal cavity as the demands come unstoppably, incessantly, uninterruptedly, until there's nothing left inside you but the dumb, brute desire to survive. It's one of those experiences you can't understand unless you've been through it, like being a soldier under fire.

And it wasn't just once. It was the steady grind of the nights, every third or fourth night, and every third or fourth day after, pretending still to be alive while you walked around the hospital. It was week after week, month after month, year after year. 'But you get some sleep, don't you?' people would ask, and how could they know what it was finally to lie down in a strange little bed in a strange little room at three or four or five in the morning with a bleeper lying beside your head, knowing that the sleep wasn't yours, it was borrowed, and that all over the hospital there were a hundred hands hovering over a hundred phones just waiting for oblivion to descend on you so they could dial your number and bring you sharply and sickeningly back to consciousness. You didn't understand it yourself until you had been woken five minutes after collapsing in exhaustion and found yourself half-running, half-stumbling in a cold sweat out into cold or rain or even snow, and then through corridors to a ward where you found yourself pumping on an arrested heart and wiping away the slime of blood, mucus, and vomit coming out of the orifices of a person already dead. Then you understood. And there was nothing unusual about this, or heroic, or exciting, or even interesting.

It just happened, over and over and over and over and over.

And now there was one more tombstone to be added to the tally. Because a doctor who had been a doctor for all of three weeks, burning in the flaming crucible of her first weekend on call, undergoing an intensity of exhaustion that she had never in her life experienced before, used her discretion to delay checking a test result. One result among literally hundreds that she had screened that day.

Without even knowing it, the HO had been using her discretion all night. And all of the night before. She had missed other results as well. But as it happened, those didn't matter. And there were lots of results that she had checked which didn't matter either. In fact, of all the results of all the tests she had to check over the course of that long day, this was the only one that would have made a meaningful difference to the treatment of any of her patients. Funny. This was the only one she *really* needed to know.

Bad luck. What are the odds?

Goldblatt rang the VIPoma's wife. The HO sat nearby at the nurses' station, watching silently, listening as he gave the news. He stood up. 'Come on,' he said, and left the ward. The HO followed him.

They were on the seventh floor, across the lobby from their own ward. They walked past the lifts and through the doors. They didn't need to go there, but they went instinctively. Like going to their own territory.

The ward was dark. A patient was coughing somewhere. A couple of nurses were sitting in the subdued light of the nurses' station. Another nurse walked down the corridor and turned into one of the rooms, carrying an injection tray.

A ward at night. Lights glowing behind screens, the sound of people sleeping, nurses murmuring, your own footsteps on the lino as you go about your work.

They went to the doctors' office.

'Have you been to bed?' Goldblatt asked.

The HO perched on the edge of one of the desks in the office. She shook her head.

'Did you get the lumbar puncture result?'

The HO nodded. She dug around in the pockets of her white coat, pulled out a piece of paper, unfolded it, and examined it. She threw it down on the desk. She pulled out another piece of paper, looked at it, and threw it down. She dug around in the pocket. More pieces of paper came out.

'Have you thought of getting a notebook?' asked Goldblatt.

She went on digging. Finally she found the one she wanted.

'No organisms,' she read. 'Four white cells. Three hundred red cells.'

'Good,' said Goldblatt.

The HO didn't look pleased. She looked crushed. She looked pulverized. She looked like a piece of pale, red-headed skin that had once had a human being inside it.

Goldblatt watched her. The HO was waiting for him to say it, he knew.

'You didn't check the potassium.'

'I...' the HO shook her head helplessly.

'You forgot.'

'I didn't forget. I just didn't... I was going to check it. I was going to! But things kept coming up. They kept ringing me. Drips and blood cultures and people with chest pain and sleeping tablets. I didn't get around to it. I never got time to sit down at a computer.'

'It's not good enough,' said Goldblatt.

'I know it's not good enough. But they should have rung me. They should have rung me! They're meant to do that. They should have rung me with a result that was so low.'

'True,' said Goldblatt. 'Are you sure they didn't?'

'I would have got the fucking result!'

'Are you sure you answered all your bleeps?'

The HO stared at him. She had that frozen look on her face again, the one she had had when Goldblatt had shone the torch in the VIPoma's eyes and asked what his potassium was.

'Listen,' said Goldblatt quietly. 'Tests are dangerous. They give you a false sense of security. They make you think you've done something. A test isn't worth anything until you know the result and you've acted on it. You *have* to get the result. You can't rely on anyone to make sure you're informed of it. It's your responsibility. You *have* to check it yourself.'

'What will they do to me? What's going to happen, Malcolm?'

'To you?'

The HO nodded.

'Well,' said Goldblatt. 'I'm going to have to report you, of course. I'll have to say that you forgot to check the potassium result despite my explicit instructions, and therefore the patient died.'

The HO stared at Goldblatt again. Her eyes were wide. They weren't just wide, they were two enormous, pupil-pierced balls staring at him in naked terror.

Goldblatt shook his head wearily. 'Nothing's going to happen to you.'

'But I just killed someone!'

'I don't know if I'd shout about it if I were you.' Goldblatt paused. 'Look, you didn't *kill* him. He had a malignancy, didn't he? And he had heart disease. Hadn't he had an infarct in the past? It was waiting to happen. You just... helped.'

'Malcolm, they'll strike me off!'

'They can't strike you off. You're a House Officer. They haven't struck you on yet.'

The HO didn't look reassured.

Goldblatt sighed. 'Nothing will happen to you. The patient died of a cardiac arrest secondary to coronary vessel disease and hypokalemia, which was secondary to his underlying malignancy. He wouldn't have had the hypokalemia at all if his GP hadn't sat on him all weekend. Nothing's going to happen to you.'

'But we didn't treat his hypokalemia!'

'We did – but not vigorously enough.'

'What about Steve. What will Steve say?'

'I'll talk to Steve.'

The HO frowned. Goldblatt watched her. The HO's lips were compressed in concentration. She glanced at him furtively.

He could report her. He had given the orders. He had written them in the notes before he left the Casualty department. He had written 'HO to check K urgently.' He had even written the doses of potassium to be added to the VIPoma's fluids if the levels were found to be low. And he had told her as well. Verbally. Twice. But the HO hadn't done it. None of it.

But what good would it do? He would be reporting the wrong thing. He would be reporting the symptom and letting the disease walk scot-free. As a doctor, that was something he had been trained never to do. Right?

'I'll talk to Steve,' he repeated. 'Now, what are *you* going to do?'

The HO gazed at him, uncomprehendingly.

'This isn't trivial,' said Goldblatt. 'A man has died. I've just had to wake his wife to tell her. Learn! Learn from this. For God's sake, tell me you've learned something from this.'

'Of course I've learned something!'

'Well, don't forget it. That's what matters now. Remember this for the rest of your life. Teach it to others. Do that, at least, and that man's death won't be entirely in vain.'

The HO frowned.

Goldblatt sighed. 'If we got rid of every doctor who killed someone when they were a house officer, we'd have no one left. Everyone kills someone. You're lucky if it's just one.'

The HO looked at him. 'What about you?'

'What about me?'

'Did you kill someone?'

Goldblatt gazed at her earnestly. 'What do you think?'

'When?'

Goldblatt took a deep breath. 'There are some questions you don't ask.'

The HO let her head drop back against the wall. She closed her eyes and took her glasses off. There were deep red marks on her nose from her glasses, and black bags under her eyes.

'Have you still got a lot of stuff to do?' asked Goldblatt.

The HO nodded. 'That patient with the end-stage cirrhosis they rang Steve about still hasn't got here.' She took a deep breath and let it out slowly.

Her bleep went off. She picked up the phone and dialled.

Goldblatt watched her as she listened to whatever was being said to her. Suddenly she said '*Yes!*' and clenched her fist at her side.

Goldblatt raised an eyebrow. It wasn't exactly punching the air, but it was close.

'What was that?' he asked, when she put the phone down.

'That was Steve. The guy with the cirrhosis won't be coming in after all. He—'

The HO stopped.

'Died?' said Goldblatt.

'In the ambulance,' she whispered.

Goldblatt nodded.

The HO stared at him. Slowly, she unfolded the fingers of her clenched fist. Her eyes were wide, uncertain, scared, shocked.

She was lost, her markers were gone. Was she sinking into corruption, or climbing out of naivety? She found herself in a new landscape, and she wanted someone to tell her what was right and what was wrong, which way was up and which way down, but she didn't know who she could trust to tell her. Goldblatt? Something in her, perhaps just the lack of any other guide, made her want to follow him. But how could she know that Goldblatt wouldn't lead her further into confusion, that it wasn't because of him that she found herself here in the first place?

Goldblatt watched the HO pupating, tearing blindly at the cocoon of innocence that enshrouded her. There was only so much he could do. She had to do the rest herself.

Suddenly he felt very protective towards this slight, small person who had been given to him as his HO, with her square face and her pinched nostrils and her glasses that were always slipping halfway down her nose.

'Listen,' he said quietly, 'I know I must seem like a cynical old crate to you...'

'No, you don't,' said the HO.

'Don't I?' asked Goldblatt, genuinely surprised.

'You seem... I don't know what to make of you, Malcolm. Sometimes you're really kind... and sometimes you seem angry. Under the jokes, I mean.'

'Are they that transparent?'

'Only the bad ones.'

Goldblatt shrugged. Fair enough.

'I'm not angry with you,' he said.

'I know you're not. I don't know why, but you're not.'

Goldblatt frowned. Heart-to-hearts with colleagues at four o'clock in the doctors' office were never a good idea. You were all too likely to say what you actually felt. About all kinds of things.

'Well, I just wanted to say... I know it's tough being a house officer. Even if I don't seem to sometimes. I know what you're going through.'

The HO nodded.

'And if you ever need to...' Goldblatt looked at her. He shrugged. 'You know... talk or whatever. I'm here.'

'Thanks,' said the HO.

Goldblatt nodded. 'I mean it. Don't hesitate.'

'Malcolm?'

'What?'

'You won't tell Ludo, will you?'

'About the man with the VIPoma?'

'No. I mean yes, about him, but also about *that*... Just now.'

Goldblatt smiled. 'No, I won't tell Ludo.'

'I'll never hear the end of it, Malcolm. Honestly. Please.'

'I won't tell her. But remember what I told you that time in the cafeteria. Don't blame yourself.'

The HO watched him.

'Now do what you have to do and try to get to bed,' he said, and he left to go back to his own on-call room.

He didn't see the HO again until nine o'clock, when he came back up to the ward to start the day's work with the morning round. Another medical team was starting their round on the ward as well. The HO was in the doctors' office.

'How was the rest of the night?' he asked.

The HO shrugged. 'OK.'

There was a silence between them then. It was a little awkward. But only a little.

Goldblatt opened the admissions book and counted up the cancellations he would be making. They heard footsteps outside. Ludo walked in. She observed the HO's bedraggled appearance with satisfaction.

'You were on this weekend, weren't you?' she said. 'How many patients did you admit?'

The HO unfolded one of her crumpled pieces of paper and counted the names. 'Thirty-two.'

'Thirty-two!' retorted Ludo contemptuously, hanging up her coat. Her woollen skirt strained over her behind. 'You're lucky. My record's forty-six.'

Goldblatt looked at the HO to see how she was going to respond.

'Thirty-two's enough!' said the HO stoutly.

Goldblatt nodded to himself in approval.

Ludo sat down. She turned to Goldblatt. 'I had a terrible weekend.'

'Really?' asked Goldblatt.

'You know I was moving into that new flat? My flatmate! Malcolm, she's a nightmare. Just listen to this...'

A new week was beginning. All was as it should be on the ward on the seventh floor. Rounds were starting. Ludo was whining. Cancellations were waiting.

Goldblatt glanced at the HO.

The HO stared at her piece of paper, thinking.

11

THE BRODERIP–ANDERSSEN PRINCIPLE, LIKE so many fundamental truths of existence, was soon forgotten. Or so Goldblatt assumed, until the day Dr Morris knocked on the door at the end of his clinic.

Dr Morris sat in the chair on the other side of Goldblatt's desk, which had been occupied until two minutes earlier by a large, sweaty electrician with unusual shooting pains in his fingers, and waited for Goldblatt to finish dictating his letter to the patient's GP. Having absolutely no idea what was causing the pains, Goldblatt had ordered blood tests, X-rays, and a complicated neurophysiological investigation for which there was probably a waiting list of four months. By then, with any luck, the pain would have gone away by itself.

'All right,' said Dr Morris when Goldblatt was finished. He pulled a piece of paper out of his pocket, unfolded it, and tossed it on the desk. 'Explain it.'

'Explain what?' said Goldblatt, hoping that Dr Morris wasn't going to ask him to justify all the tests he'd just ordered. That kind of thing was always tedious, if not downright embarrassing.

'I can't work it out. It doesn't seem to make sense.'

'What?' asked Goldblatt suspiciously.

Dr Morris nudged the paper towards him. 'This.'

Goldblatt looked at the paper. A strange formula was written on it. He stared at the mysterious symbols. 'What is it?' he asked.

'What are you talking about?' Dr Morris grabbed the piece of paper, looked at it, and threw it down in front of Goldblatt again. 'It's your formula. Broderip–Anderssen. I searched for their paper. 1957, isn't that when you said it was published? We have an excellent librarian here, but she couldn't find it either.'

'Really?'

Dr Morris nodded.

'Did she spend a lot of time trying?'

'Quite a lot.'

Goldblatt was silent for a moment. 'Do you really want to see the paper?'

Dr Morris nodded again. 'It sounded fascinating.'

'Well, it's just that it's a very old piece of work...' Goldblatt stopped. Normally he would get out of a spot like this with more of the type of confabulation that had got him into it. Something like Broderip having retained copyright of the paper, for instance, and in a fit of pique at Anderssen, having withdrawn it from circulation. But he had a feeling that with Dr Morris, the more he went on, the worse it was going to be. 'It's just that it's so old that...' he said instead, 'you know... it hardly even exists.'

Dr Morris peered at him. 'I don't understand.'

'No,' said Goldblatt. He picked up the piece of paper Dr Morris had thrown down on the desk. 'This isn't really the Broderip–Anderssen formula.'

'But that's what you wrote. I copied it exactly.'

'Dr Morris, there is no formula.' Goldblatt broke the news as gently as he could. 'There is no paper. The truth is, there was no Olaf Anderssen and Andrew Broderip.'

'Henrik Anderssen and Walter Broderip.'

'Them neither.'

Dr Morris picked up the piece of paper and gazed at it almost wistfully. 'But you wrote it. This formula.'

'True,' said Goldblatt.

'Then what is it if it isn't the Broderip–Anderssen formula?'

'No idea,' said Goldblatt.

Dr Morris stared at him.

'I made it up.'

'You made it up?'

Goldblatt shrugged.

Dr Morris stared at him for a second longer. Then he grinned. His mouth puckered as if he had a slice of lemon inside it. It was a strange but convivial grin, and Goldblatt couldn't help responding in kind.

'You made it up?' asked Dr Morris again, chortling with childish pleasure.

'So it seems.'

'Why?'

'I don't know. I do things like that. I mean, not all the time, ... ' Goldblatt added quickly, realizing that if he wasn't careful he wouldn't be playing Bluff the Journal again any time soon, at least not with Dr Morris, who provided him with easily the most challenging and enjoyable games he had ever played. 'Don't you ever just feel the need to...'

'What?'

Goldblatt shook his head.

'I heard you don't manipulate beds, either,' said Dr Morris.

'Very rarely.'

'So what about this principle?' enquired Dr Morris.

'The Broderip–Anderssen Principle?' Goldblatt sighed. Suddenly he felt weary. There was no reason for all this laughter and bonhomie. If there was such a principle, it embodied a hopeless, churning endlessness. 'The Broderip–Anderssen Principle, broadly speaking, states that for every patient sitting in a bed there's at least one equally if not more deserving patient lacking a bed.'

Dr Morris nodded. Then he frowned slightly. 'By the way, did I see you with a squash racket the other day?'

'Possibly.' The hospital had a pair of courts, and a couple of evenings previously Goldblatt had played with an SHO he knew from an earlier job.

'We should have a game one day.'

Goldblatt smiled. When would Dr Morris conceivably have the time for a game of squash?

'Thursday afternoons,' said Dr Morris, as if he could tell what Goldblatt was thinking. 'I can make an hour on Thursday afternoons. Not this Thursday, though.' He got up. 'Let me check, and I'll let you know which Thursday I can do it.'

'I'll be ready.'

'I'm serious. I'll let you know.' Dr Morris went to the door. 'And your Broderip–Anderssen Principle, by the way, it's not true.'

'It is true.'

'It isn't.'

'It is,' said Goldblatt, who couldn't bear these optimistic medical types who obstinately refused to succumb to the overwhelming inadequacy of the system in which they worked.

'It isn't. For every patient sitting in a bed there isn't at least one equally deserving patient lacking a bed.' Dr Morris opened the door. 'There's two.'

Dr Morris was a new consultant. Only five months earlier he had been a specialist registrar, and most of the time he still acted like one. He wrote orders on drug charts, and came up to the ward to see patients without organizing an entourage, and made appointments to see relatives, and actually kept the appointments he made. He also took blood in clinic from patients who were too frail or elderly to go to the second floor and wait three hours to have their blood taken in the Pathology department. The last of these activities was a step too far for Rosa, the gargantuan West Indian nurse who ran the clinic, and whose great speciality, until Dr Morris came along, had been taking blood from the frail and elderly patients. Rosa still got to take blood from ninety per cent of them, since none of the other doctors had any interest in doing it, but it didn't seem so special after Dr Morris turned up and started sticking his needles in where they weren't wanted.

Dr Morris was a *very* new consultant, Rosa told everyone knowingly. Soon enough he'd be too high and mighty to be taking blood from little old ladies, and then they'd all come back to Rosa. Oh, yes, they'd all come running back to Rosa, and Rosa would take them back, like the big-hearted fool she was, even though they'd lost their heads and gone running off the minute a consultant beckoned.

Goldblatt wasn't so sure that Dr Morris would ever be too high and mighty to take blood from little old ladies. True, Dr Morris was only five months old as a consultant, and there was still bound to be some moisture behind his ears, but there was something different about him, something slightly odd. Dr Morris loved medicine.

Medicine. Not the prestige, the power, the academic kick, the money to be made from private practice, the fawning gratitude to be had from patients, the sexual favours to be sampled from nurses, the harrowing stories to be told at parties, or any of the other things that usually masquerade as a love of medicine – but medicine itself. Wherever he went he was always shooting off curious and investigatory glances, as if searching for new medical challenges inside sluice rooms, under desks, behind computers, in notes trolleys, and anywhere else they could conceivably be hiding. Dr Morris just loved medicine. He loved everything about it.

He loved the patients who were the substrate on which medicine thrived. He loved talking to them, listening to them, reassuring them, and smiling at them. He loved having his finger on the pulse. Literally. He loved to apply his stethoscope to a neck and hear the turbulent whoosh of blood being forced through a narrowed carotid artery, to tap a tendon and watch a limb jerk with pathological briskness, to press probingly under the lip of a ribcage and feel the shy tip of an enlarged spleen nuzzle into his fingers. He loved making diagnoses and ordering tests that confirmed them and prescribing drugs that alleviated them and reviewing patients who had them. He even loved the side effects of these drugs, which engendered new clinical signs for him to elicit, new diagnoses for him to make and new drugs for him to prescribe.

To Dr Morris, there was nothing more enjoyable than the diagnostic conundrums posed by sick, complicated patients in whom a hundred different investigations had already been done without turning up a single abnormality. The motor of his formidable mind roared into life, and he dragged the seafloor of medical rarity like a curtain-net, reeling off long lists of unimaginable diagnoses, and thinking up another hundred tests to try. His face beamed with intellectual pleasure, and his eyes sparkled with boyish delight. Nothing, in his opinion, was beyond diagnosis, and no condition, in principle, could not be elucidated.

In reality, plenty of conditions can't be elucidated, and there was nothing more depressing, in Goldblatt's view, than a blind refusal to recognize this reality. He didn't think that the patients who obsessed Dr Morris with their Byzantine conditions were necessarily the most interesting. Frustrating, maybe. Tormenting, possibly. Tedious, certainly. But interesting? Goldblatt wasn't so sure. More interesting to him were conditions that you diagnosed at a glance, treated at a stroke, and reviewed once a year. But not to Dr Morris, for whom even the whiff of a gangrenous toe was interesting, the cue for a thousand fascinating conjectures.

Fascinating was a word Dr Morris used a lot. He used it so much that Goldblatt suspected it had lost virtually all meaning for him and had become nothing more than an undifferentiated positive signifier in his vocabulary. Whenever you got hold of Dr Morris he was with a fascinating patient, or he had just come from a fascinating patient, or he was just on his way to see a fascinating patient. Fascinating patients sprouted like toadstools wherever he went or wherever there was even a rumour that he was going to appear. Yet by the time Goldblatt arrived, the fascinating patient had invariably disappeared, replaced in the bed by just another sick, elderly person whose body systems were falling apart at unsynchronized rates.

Needless to say, all this clinical hyperactivity didn't leave Dr Morris with a lot of time, and in case it did, there were plenty of other things to do. He loved research, and was collaborating on projects with professors in three other hospitals. He loved teaching medical students, and made irrational arrangements to come in early or stay back late to give them extra tutorials. He loved the warp and weft of the very organizational fabric of hospitals, and in the five months since becoming a consultant he had already volunteered for the Dean's Committee for Undergraduate Education, the Interdisciplinary Committee for Ancillary Services, the Medical Department Audit Committee, and the Consultants' Dining Room Committee.

Curiously, Dr Morris was reputed to have a wife and two small children, and mathematically, subtracting the number of hours he worked from the number of hours in the week, it was possible that he actually glimpsed them from time to time. Whether they suffered as a result of this was a matter of conjecture. But that someone else suffered from the effects of Dr Morris's unmanageable energy and his insatiable appetite for work, perhaps even more than his wife or his occasionally glimpsed children, was beyond dispute. And the bitter irony of it was that Professor Small was utterly responsible for bringing it all upon herself.

*

As part of the Prof's Seriousness Drive, the appointment of Dr Morris had been nothing short of a coup. Not only did the Prof now have a junior consultant on her unit, but what a consultant she had! Her colleagues couldn't fail to take her seriously when they saw what a brilliant young man she had recruited. Or to put it more accurately – or at least as the Prof preferred to put it – what a brilliant young man had sought her out as a mentor.

At first, the Prof found it wonderfully comforting to have Dr Morris around. More comforting, if she was to be completely honest with herself – which was something the Prof never did lightly – than a mentor should find it. Patients are allowed to have more than one disease, even patients with Fuertler's Syndrome, and the Prof couldn't very well refer every swing of blood pressure or incident of indigestion to one of her specialist colleagues. In theory, at least, she was supposed to be able to treat those things herself. Now all these difficult decisions on ward rounds, which she had been forced to validate in the past by surreptitious glances at her SR or Sister Choy, could be put openly for erudite discussion with Dr Morris as a fellow consultant without fear of humiliation. And problems that came up in clinic could be explored in passing when the Prof called Dr Morris into her room on the pretext of conferring on some organizational matter. With his encyclopaedic grasp of medicine, Dr Morris was brimming with knowledge, and all the years that had gone by before he arrived now seemed unbearably lonely in retrospect.

In short, when Dr Morris first joined the Professor's unit, it had been a delight to have him around.

Yet all this knowledge and energy came at a price. The Prof soon discovered Dr Morris's nasty habit of sniffing around the hospital and returning with news of horrendously complicated patients sequestered in wards and recovery rooms all over the place. The three beds that she had given him, the Prof began to suspect, and the endless parade of Fuertler's patients in the other beds, wouldn't satisfy him for long. A couple of months after Dr Morris arrived, on one horrible day that would long live in infamy, the suspicion turned to grim conviction. Dr Morris suggested the unit should do Takes.

Professor Small stared at him.

T- T- Takes? Was that what the boy had said? Takes?

It had taken the Prof five years of fiendish plotting to free her unit from medical Takes, and now this overeducated prodigy with his fetishistic medical infatuation was suggesting that they should start doing them again.

Professor Small's head shook tremulously. 'Takes?' She managed a weak and vulnerable smile, desperately trying to think of a way to get Dr Morris out of her office so she could be alone with the Scale to recover her poise.

Tom de Witte had laughed when she told him of Dr Morris's appointment. It had flattered her to think that she would have someone like that working under her, he said, and he laughed his big, booming laugh again. The Prof denied the accusation, and treated it with complete disdain. But Tom was right. Normally he showed absolutely no insight into anything but the bronchoscope with which he habitually peered down the airways of diseased lungs, and this lack of awareness was one of the most satisfying things about having a liaison with him. His decision to be right in this one specific case felt like a terrible betrayal.

In so many ways, thought the Prof bitterly, Tom de Witte was just like all the others.

Yet the truth had to be faced. Had she not overreached herself by appointing Dr Morris? Andrea, she was forced to ask in a moment of searing but cathartic honesty in front of the Scale, was your unit really ever going to be able to satisfy a medical dynamo like him? The irony was almost unbearable. She could have chosen one of any number of compliant mediocrities who had applied for the post without fear of being dragged back down into the dreadful morass of general medicine that she had struggled so hard to escape. Any one of them would have counted themselves lucky to have their three beds and their three clinic sessions, and would happily have spent the rest of the time surreptitiously building their private practice, like any sensible person. But no, she had thrown it all away by impulsively choosing the brightest, the most energetic, the most intelligent, and the most promising candidate she had ever seen in any interview anywhere, just like a flighty girl sacrificing everything for one mad moment of romance.

Yet hindsight, Andrea knew, solves no problems. She had appointed Dr Morris, and she couldn't just unappoint him. Even if she could, imagine how her fellow consultants would laugh at her then. No, something special was needed, a solution, a plan, one of the brilliant evasions that were the foundations of all her truly great strategies.

In the end, the Prof fabricated a counter-manoeuvre of genuinely Napoleonic proportions. Dr Sutherland, one of the other physicians in the hospital, had just gone on sabbatical, and no one had been found to cover his duties. The hospital management was desperately looking for a solution, preferably one that would cost them nothing. Here it was! Dr Morris could cover Dr Sutherland's Takes. He could also do Dr Sutherland's rounds, and look after Dr Sutherland's patients, and do Dr Sutherland's clinics. And he could do all of that while still doing the work on the Prof's own unit, which was meant to be a full-time job in itself. There! If that didn't knock the stuffing out of him, the Prof thought, and make him yearn for a nice quiet life on her unit, she didn't know what would.

Dr Sutherland wasn't there to object. In any event, it was unlikely that he would have. He was a suave, ingratiating man who had spent the last twenty years building a booming private practice, and retained his public appointment primarily and almost solely because it was good for business. He spent far more time at his rooms in Harley Street than at the hospital. In fact, by a freak of physics, even when Dr Sutherland was in the hospital he was often in Harley Street. One of his clinic slots was mysteriously cancelled every week right up to the expected date of his retirement in eight years' time, and no one expected him to appear even for the other clinics that hadn't been cancelled.

None of this was a secret. The Director of the Department of Medicine and the hospital Chief Executive both knew that Dr Sutherland treated the place as a front for his private activities. But they also knew that at any one time twenty per cent of the patients on the hospital's private floor belonged to him, and that he was responsible for perhaps another third of the patients there through his extensive contacts and his indefatigable efforts on behalf of private medicine, which created a certain financial argument in favour of turning a blind eye to his idiosyncratic way of doing business.

Much of what Dr Sutherland did was idiosyncratic, and not only his invisible approach to clinics. When it came to his medical Takes, he saw himself as more of a middleman than an executive, his unit more of a clearing house than a depot. Unlike other consultants, who generally saw their patients first thing in the morning after a Take, Dr Sutherland insisted on scheduling his post-Take rounds for late in the afternoon. Occasionally he turned up for them. By then, he expected his registrar to have distributed or otherwise disposed of the majority of the admissions. The reg was under strict instructions to enquire of each patient whether he or she was privately insured, and, if so, to recommend immediate transfer to more conducive surroundings. The name of a physician practising privately in the appropriate speciality could be obtained from Dr Sutherland's secretary, who would also make the necessary arrangements.

For the rest, other measures were available within the public facilities of the hospital. Heart failures went to Cardiology, diabetics to Endocrinology, peptic ulcers to Gastroenterology, and strokes to Neurology. The beds on these specialist units were usually reserved for complicated cases, and their registrars would have laughed in the face of anyone else from a general medical unit who tried to flick such straightforward patients at them, but they too were under strict instructions. When Dr Sutherland's registrar called them to ask for a transfer, their consultants instructed them, they said yes. No arguments, just yes.

The amazing power of Dr Sutherland's registrar to flick patients to other units originated in nothing more mysterious than the amazing power of his boss's list of preferred private physicians. No one could afford to be left off this legendary list – which was exactly what would happen to a consultant who refused referrals from Dr Sutherland's registrar. The list was kept in a locked drawer, and Dr Sutherland's secretary was under strict instructions not to release it to anyone. The entire hospital bristled with strict instructions attached to Dr Sutherland's name. The world he had created for himself within it was like a serene, exclusive, and strongly gated community, and it would have taken a consultant who was new, young, bright, with no interest in private practice, and almost unbelievably idealistic to have blundered into this genteel microcosm without even being aware that it existed...

'Where have they gone?' Dr Morris demanded in astonishment when he turned up for his first post-Take round in charge of the unit, and the registrar informed him that there were only three left to see of the fourteen who had been admitted.

He soon discovered the truth. Well, Dr Morris didn't flick patients. He had never knowingly flicked a patient in his life.

A change came over the Sutherland unit, which had a nominal allocation of twenty beds and normally had trouble filling a quarter of them. Two weeks and three Takes later it had thirty patients groaning and moaning all over the hospital. The Sutherland doctors, who had signed up for the cushiest little number in London, found themselves dancing to the tune of their bleeps from the minute they arrived at nine in the morning until they finally stopped running dementedly between wards at ten o'clock at night. The ward rounds, which used to take twenty minutes, became three-hour slogs through the thickest, densest marshes of medicine. The customary haemorrhage of private patients out of the Sutherland unit slowed to a trickle, and the number on the unit kept rising. One horrible Friday afternoon it topped forty, and the reg went off sick. The SR, who had gone to the States on holiday, rang to say she wouldn't be coming back. The house officer was off for two days during the following week, and then had to take emergency leave because of the death of a grandmother in Iceland. He refused to say whose grandmother it was.

To the pseudo-Sutherland, absenteeism was a challenge. He refused to read the message that lay behind it, and lurched exultantly from one Take to the next with half a team, a clapped-out locum SR who was older than himself, and an irrepressible desire to see more, do more, and treat more.

The Prof observed him with growing terror. If her Sutherland manoeuvre was designed to knock the stuffing out of Dr Morris, it had failed miserably, or worse, it had merely replaced the stuffing with brimming reserves of energy that even Dr Morris hadn't known were in him. He drank deep and lustily from the supposedly poisoned chalice she had thrust at him and then held it out for more. What kind of a monster had she created? One day, the Prof knew, Dr Sutherland would come back to reclaim his rightful place, and then Dr Morris would be stalking her again, fizzing with even more unexpended energy than he had at the start. How long then until the terrible T-word was uttered once more?

But other consultants came to value him. For a time, while Dr Sutherland was away, one of their principal flows of private patients might be choked off at the source, but in the longer term, Dr Morris would be a useful colleague to have. The reason was simple: Dr Morris had an interest in seeing any case that was complicated or difficult, and sometimes arrived, even without being invited, to examine a patient for his own education. There's nothing the average consultant values more than someone who's interested in their difficult and drawn-out cases because, with a bit of luck, he might be persuaded to take these hopeless cases off their hands – which as far as Goldblatt was concerned, meant on to his hands. Because when Dr Morris wasn't running around the hospital as the pseudo-Sutherland, he was back on the Prof's unit as Dr Morris, and as the numbers on the Sutherland unit doubled and then threatened to triple their nominal bed allocation, Dr Morris had decided that he was going to use his three beds on the Prof's unit for the most fiendishly difficult of the difficult referrals that were starting to come in to him from all his new friends.

Goldblatt regularly got calls from other registrars in the hospital asking him to bring Dr Morris along to see the latest fascinating medical conundrum that was going to rewrite the textbooks. According to the etiquette of the profession, a registrar is obliged to see any patient referred to a consultant before daring to mention the patient to that consultant. Since it was perfectly obvious that neither he nor Dr Morris would have anything new to suggest about these patients, who had already had every test under the sun and were being referred only to see whether Dr Morris would transfer them to his unit, the whole exercise amounted to a double waste of time and effort. Besides, it soon became painfully clear to Goldblatt that Dr Morris would readily agree to transfer these patients as soon as one of his beds became available, or even sooner. In short, Dr Morris was being exploited. He had to be protected from himself. As his registrar, the responsibility fell to Goldblatt, and Goldblatt was never one to shirk his duty.

He employed a variety of techniques. Simply failing to answer his bleep was surprisingly effective at warding off the most speculative advances.

In other cases, the referring registrar could be persuaded that unless a cleaner went postal and cleared twenty beds on the seventh floor with a shotgun, there was no hope of their patient being transferred. Others didn't call back to find out when Dr Morris was going to see the patient after Goldblatt conveniently forgot about the referral for a day or two. By one means or another, Goldblatt was able to shield Dr Morris from many fruitless referrals that would otherwise have occupied him. But he couldn't be in all places at once, and without putting a tap on Dr Morris's phone it was impossible to prevent unscrupulous characters calling directly and taking advantage of him.

A woman with recurrent neuropsychiatric episodes and a fleeting rash on her neck? A man with hypertrophy of his left tibia and a renal bruit? A woman with cystic lesions in her metatarsals and intermittent abdominal pain? Send them across, send one, send all! Fascinating!

12

A MONTH HAD PASSED since Goldblatt had started on the unit. He still hadn't worked out what Ludo was supposed to be doing.

Every day he did a round with the HO, which is the time-honoured way for registrars to thwart the well-meaning attempts of house officers to harm their patients. Ludo was supposed to be on the rounds as well. Sometimes she was. Goldblatt spent a lot of time trying to define the pattern of her attendance until he realized it was a trick question. There was no pattern. After a while he understood that a tacit agreement had developed between them. The only problem was that he couldn't say for certain what he had agreed to.

The Prof had never had an SHO before she set out on her Seriousness Drive, of which this was the latest achievement. It wasn't an unalloyed triumph, it had to be admitted, because she had been forced to agree to share the new half-and-half SHO with the Dermatologists, who were her bitterest rivals. Dr Mowbray, in particular, was always trying to get hold of Fuertler's patients on the laughable grounds that Dermatologists were best able to treat their skin lesions. But the Dermatologists had previously had a whole SHO, and now they only had a half, whereas she now had half an SHO, and previously she hadn't had one at all, so that was the same as the gain of a whole SHO if you took into account the Dermatologists' loss. This surely must have removed the last shred of credibility from their claim to be able to treat any aspect of a disease as serious as Fuertler's. And the Prof realized that, from her own perspective, it wasn't necessarily a bad thing to have only half an SHO, because apart from raising the seriousness level of her unit, it wasn't clear that there was actually anything for an SHO to do.

If the Prof did know what the SHO was supposed to do, she was staying decidedly quiet on the matter.

Emma, following her Fuehrer's lead, was staying silent on the matter as well. It was therefore Goldblatt who had to cope with Ludo moping around the ward every day, whining about not having anything to do, and then disappearing as soon as a solution to her complaint seemed likely to appear. Naturally, Ludo wasn't the innocent whiner that she appeared. She perceived perfectly well the unique power of her position on the Prof's unit. As its first SHO, there was no precedent for her role, and the absence of instructions from the Prof left open both of the two possible routes for an SHO on a unit that also has a house officer: dividing the patients with the HO and slaving away as a pseudo-HO, or floating along as a kind of pseudo-registrar providing an extra level of supervision to the HO.

Ludo knew *exactly* which role she wanted.

She laughed in Goldblatt's face.

After a week of watching Ludo do absolutely nothing except drink the coffee that she coerced him to buy for her, and promise to fill out the Prof's Fuertler's files, Goldblatt had suggested that she should divide the patients with the HO. When she had finished laughing in Goldblatt's face, Ludo fixed him with an expression of superb Balkan haughtiness. She was senior enough, she reminded him with disdain, to have failed the first part of the Royal College exam five times. She was senior enough, she continued, to have passed it on her sixth attempt. And she was senior enough, he shouldn't forget, to be preparing, even now, for her first attempt on the second part. Divide the patients with the HO? He must be joking!

Ludo's response to Dr Morris was identical in intent but different in presentation, demonstrating a finely honed ability to tailor her tactics to her audience. When Dr Morris suggested that she divide the patients with the HO, Ludo gazed at him with an expression of abject Balkan imprecation. She had failed the first part exam five times, she reminded him tearfully. She had only barely scraped by on her sixth attempt, she continued. And now, she wailed, she felt her chances of passing the second part, which was so much harder than the first part, were slim. What was to become of her if the job left her no time to study for the exam? What, oh what would become of her?

Eventually Dr Morris sued for peace and agreed to speak to the Prof and let her decide. Ludo may have thought she had already won. Apart from a couple of ambiguous remarks on her rounds, the Prof hadn't actually addressed a single word to her. No one could say for certain whether the Prof knew she existed. The Prof laid that mystery to rest when she called Ludo down to her office and suggested that she divide the patients with the HO.

Ludo slumped, broke into tears, swore that both Goldblatt and Dr Morris had promised she wouldn't have to do it, alleged that the HO wouldn't let her do it, and told any number of other lies until the Prof relented. In the cafeteria afterwards she laughed about it. She confessed shamelessly to having told the Prof that Goldblatt made incessant demands on both her and the HO and treated them severely when they failed to meet his expectations, while tearfully emphasizing the unhappiness this caused.

Goldblatt stared at her in disbelief. 'I do not make excessive demands!'

'I had to make her feel sorry for me, Malcolm.'

'So you lied to the Prof about me? You don't think I've already got enough trouble with her?'

'And whose fault is that?' retorted Ludo. 'Who decided that he doesn't manipulate beds? Well? Was it me? I don't think so.'

'How do you know about that?'

Ludo raised an eyebrow.

Goldblatt shook his head. Then he put his head in his hands. 'Ludo! What have you done?'

'I didn't lie about you, Malcolm. You do make excessive demands. What about yesterday when I was late for the round?'

'You were late for the round!'

'At least I came.'

'I don't know why you bothered.'

'That's not very nice,' said Ludo, and pretended to be hurt.

'Ludo, if you're going to be there, you should be there on time.'

'See? That's exactly what I mean.'

'We said we'd start at nine. Do you call that an excessive demand? You didn't turn up until a quarter to ten. We'd finished! And what exactly did I do to you? What was it that was so severe? I told you to be on time next time.'

'It was the tone, Malcolm. You're not very sensitive.'

'I suppose you said that to the Prof as well.'

Ludo didn't reply.

Goldblatt groaned. He had already deduced that Ludo wouldn't hesitate to use anything he had said, in or out of context, if she thought it could help her. Now he realized she was prepared to use anything he hadn't said as well.

'I had a good reason for being late.'

'What? A Dermatology round?'

Ludo tossed her head scornfully. 'Buy me a cup of coffee.'

'Why should I?' demanded Goldblatt angrily.

'Oh, go on, Malcolm,' Ludo whined.

Goldblatt stared at her. He almost had to suppress a smile at the slovenly, shameless appeal in Ludo's voice. Ludo! When she agreed to do something, she dumped it on the HO as soon as he left the room and brazenly blamed the HO later if it wasn't done. She flung excuses around without concern for decency, probability or even the flimsiest appearance of consistency. Ludo seemed to think that her role as the Dermatology SHO provided her with a justification for any level of absenteeism from the Prof's ward. Either she wasn't very inventive or she was too lazy to think of any other reason. Probably both. To judge by Ludo's excuses, there was a tremendous epidemic of skin disease gripping London, and the Dermatology service was stretched well beyond breaking point. Apparently there were two, three, four, or even five rounds each day on the two patients that the Dermatologists had in the hospital, and outpatients' clinics that sprang up randomly across the week, coinciding uncannily with the periods when the workload on the Prof's unit was at its peak.

It didn't seem to worry Ludo that a single call to the Derm reg would have exposed her. Goldblatt didn't even need to make the call. He knew that most of Ludo's Dermatology clinics didn't exist. Ludo knew that he knew, and took no special steps to hide the fact. If Goldblatt offered to buy her a coffee, she cancelled her Dermatology clinic with a snap of her fingers. Her brazenness would have been insulting had there not been a certain magnificent, imperturbable insouciance about it.

'How many Dermatology clinics *do* you have?' Goldblatt enquired with genuine interest after he had bought Ludo another coffee.

Ludo sipped the coffee defensively. Information was power, she knew. 'Millions.'

'Millions?'

'I know, Malcolm. It's awful. And they want me there for all of them, if I possibly can be.'

Why did they want her there for all of them, if she possibly could be? The amount of Dermatology that Ludo knew could have been scratched in capital letters across the back of an eczematous hand, and she herself had told him that the whole business was so boring that she still hadn't succeeded, after a month, in memorizing whether you gave steroid cream for eczema and tar cream for psoriasis, or vice versa. Whichever it was, she had managed to give tar cream for the wrong condition on her first day, and the lucky recipient of her prescription, who had smeared himself head to foot in the wonderful new cream that no one had even suggested to him before, now composed half of her inpatient caseload in the hospital. After that Ludo was too scared to prescribe anything but an antifungal for athlete's foot.

'What do you do there?' asked Goldblatt, thinking about the tar cream debacle.

Ludo frowned. She had backed herself into a corner. 'I need a good reference,' she said at last.

'And what about the Prof? Don't you need a good reference from her?'

'The Prof doesn't know I exist!'

'Yes she does. She called you into her office today. Remember? So you could complain about the incessant demands I make on you.'

Ludo sipped her coffee. She gave Goldblatt a sidelong glance. 'Oh, Malcolm, I didn't really mean it. The Prof knew that.'

Goldblatt gazed at her sceptically. What *did* Ludo do all day, apart from thinking of lies to tell about him? Not that he wanted to stop her doing whatever it was that she did. It would have been nice just to... know.

She was always in the cafeteria, it seemed, or always trying to get there. As each species has its natural habitat, so the yellow Formica tables, green vinyl chairs and cheap blue carpet tiles of the cafeteria constituted Ludo's. 'Coffee?' was her inevitable suggestion when anyone made the mistake of admitting they had five minutes to spare. And once she had inveigled Goldblatt down there, she never seemed to leave. She always said she'd stay for just a few minutes more when he had to go. Five minutes stretched with miraculous elasticity into fifteen minutes, thirty minutes, an hour, or even longer once Ludo arrived in the cafeteria and the limit-less, Formica-lined vista of the time-space continuum opened before her.

The cafeteria was the nerve centre of whatever operation Ludo thought she was running. It was there, while she was sitting with Goldblatt, that she would receive the incoming bleep of the Dermatology registrar who was looking for her so they could start the round that was supposed to have started fifteen minutes earlier. Goldblatt would watch her answer the bleep from one of the phones on the cafeteria wall. And where was she when she received Goldblatt's bleep when *he* was looking for her to start a round that should have started fifteen minutes before? With a Derma-tology patient, of course, Ludo would reply, over a hum of conversation and a certain familiar clinking of crockery in the background.

And suddenly Goldblatt understood. After four weeks, it came to him in a moment of blinding clarity. When you boiled it down, when you reduced it to its essentials, when you stripped away the flimflam and glitter... Ludo's role on the unit was to hang around in the hope of persuading someone to go down to the cafeteria and buy her a cup of coffee.

Ludo Madic was running the risk of being left with nothing. Or very little. It happens to lots of people in the system. They get their first part exam and they do their SHO jobs and then they just don't progress any further, and end up as clinical assistants like the ones who worked in Professor Small's Fuertler's clinic, piece-workers who don't have any ongoing care of patients of their own, which in the medical profession is the crucial test of a doctor's dignity, and are therefore secretly, or not so secretly, looked down upon by everybody else.

Having passed her first part, to have any hope of getting a foot on the ladder of specialist training, Ludo still had the second part to pass, which was an even tougher set of exams consisting of written papers, oral questioning, and examination of patients live in front of examiners, all of which tests a vast range of knowledge and is designed to put the candidate through the most pants-wettingly pressurized experience of his or her life. Even outstanding candidates are known to fail the second part. Ludo wasn't an outstanding candidate. Failing the first part five times was outstanding, in a sense, but not in the sense that made her an outstanding candidate.

Ludo had spent so long in passing the first part that she couldn't afford the same repetitive head-banging run of failures this time around. By now, bright young things one or even two years behind her would be getting their second part, and soon she'd appear too old or too ordinary to compete with them for jobs. Three or four attempts at the second part stretching over the next couple of years would be the end of her. Passing it like that would mean consigning herself to the worst registrar jobs in the most dishevelled hospitals in the country, the sort of jobs that are usually occupied by graduates from the developing world who do a year as a registrar in England and go home in glory to practise as full-blown experts. Yet there was no evidence that Ludo was planning a future as a specialist in Nairobi, even assuming anyone there was desparate enough to give her a job.

There was no evidence that Ludo was planning anything. She was burned out after years as an overworked SHO in a succession of drab jobs in undistinguished hospitals, and had reached the point where the most important consideration in her choice of posts was the amount of sleep she would get. Yet the job on the Prof's unit should have been a gift to her. It's a time-honoured practice for SHOs preparing for the second part exam to find themselves jobs on overstaffed units like the Prof's and spend half their time studying, and it's a time-honoured practice for consultants to create overstaffed jobs precisely to enable them to do this. Ludo should have been studying her oversized butt off. Goldblatt could have understood it if she was bunking off the ward to bury herself in the library or practise her examination technique on complicated patients around the hospital. He would have helped her bunk off even more.

Goldblatt and Dr Morris both did what they could, practising the traditional method of medical teaching intensified with the second part examination in mind: hurling barrages of difficult questions on subjects drawn from the footnotes of medical literature in the most embarrassing circumstances possible.

The aim of these Teaching Attacks was for the victim to develop the ability to regurgitate vast amounts of obscure information under incredible pressure, with the prospect of belly-laughing, thigh-slapping derision hanging constantly over her head, which is what you have to be able to do in order to pass the second part. They were launched in front of patients, nurses, orderlies, cleaners, radiographers, visitors, and anyone else who might get a laugh out of watching a doctor squirm. Ludo was ordered to reel off lists of symptoms, signs, causes, diagnoses, prognoses, investigations, medications, and treatments, just as she would be asked to do in the exam. She had to put up some kind of effort for Dr Morris, who was a consultant and therefore a potential source of a reference, but she felt free to treat Goldblatt with as much contempt as was necessary to cover up her ignorance. She shrugged, or said she couldn't think, or she was just about to study that topic, or simply lapsed into sullen silence while Goldblatt's hand, with clenched fingers ready to snap out at each item on the list, stayed thrust in front of her nose. The HO was always champing at the bit to give her answers, most of which were wrong, and Goldblatt almost had to restrain her physically so that Ludo could try. Ludo never tried, or at best gave one desultory response and listened sourly while Goldblatt reeled off the remainder of the list.

Lists were good for you. This was what Ludo refused to understand. Hadn't she ever been to medical school? Medical exams at any level, undergraduate or specialist, are largely great brainless tests of recollection, and no one can pass them without memorizing millions of lists. There were whole books of medical lists. What was her problem? Lists are the magic charms of the profession. Lists are the entry ticket. Lists are power.

'Lists are good,' Goldblatt cried in exasperation in the doctors' office one afternoon, when Ludo had refused to give the six chief causes of combined enlargement of the liver and spleen, one of the most basic lists in medicine, which even an undergraduate might be expected to know. 'Get it into your head, Ludo. Lists are good! Lists are your friend! Say it. Lists are good.'

Ludo grimaced. Of course lists were good. She knew that. That's why everything was so easy for people like Goldblatt, who could remember them.

'If we were bats,' Goldblatt said suddenly, 'what would our CT scans look like?'

'What sort of a question is that?' demanded Ludo.

'One that has an answer. Well?'

'Rorschach blots!' said the HO. 'They look like bats.'

'They look like bats to *you*,' Goldblatt said.

The HO frowned, pondering Goldblatt's obvious but strangely troubling remark. She was sitting at the computer, where she had been transcribing lab results into the patients' notes. The hospital had invested a huge sum of money in a computer system that could flash up a patient's latest results at the click of a mouse, and had invested nothing in printers for the doctors' offices, or a porterage system that could deliver a hard copy of the results quickly enough for them to be of any use. Consequently, every HO in the hospital had to spend an hour at the end of each day sitting in front of a computer terminal manually transcribing the results from this space-age system with the medieval implements of pen and paper.

'Well?' said Goldblatt, turning to Ludo again.

Ludo stared at him for a moment. Then she shrugged combatively.

Goldblatt shook his head. Ludo didn't want to think. She didn't even want to try. That was half her problem.

There was no evidence at all of any knowledge seeping into her brain. She kept saying the same dumb things on ward rounds, and if she was learning anything at all, if she was steadily accumulating the huge amount of knowledge you need in order to pass the second part, she was nothing short of brilliant at hiding it.

And she knew the risk she was running. That was the most frustrating thing about her. She knew it, and yet all she could bring herself to do about it was whine. Admittedly, she whined very competently, subjecting Goldblatt to many exquisitely honed laments over cups of coffee at headquarters. Yet whining, in Goldblatt's view, was unlikely to improve the situation.

She needed to take control of her life. She needed to vault the hurdle of the second part with one staggering leap and get out into the field where the race for meaningful jobs began. She needed to study. She needed to build her knowledge. She needed to find other doctors who were preparing for the second part and practise her examination technique with them so she could reproduce it flawlessly when the time came in front of two eagle-eyed examiners who wanted her to fail. Goldblatt told her all these things just about every time he ended up in the cafeteria with her, building up a real head of motivating steam in an attempt to drag both himself and her out of the apathy and depression that she insisted on sharing with him. And for a moment, he would see Ludo's back stiffen and her chin tilt with determination. Yet soon her back had sagged and her chin had dropped again, and Goldblatt would find himself back in the cafeteria saying the same things once more. She needed to work out a programme of revision and she needed to construct a schedule and she needed to allocate her time and she needed to stick to it obsessively...

And she needed a fuck.

Or to put it less bluntly, intimacy. A pair of eyes looking into her own, the touch of a hand on her skin, the sense of wholeness that comes from being wanted.

Everything about her cried it out. Nothing was right. The flat she had rented was too expensive, the girl she was sharing it with was awful. The books she had to study were boring, the other SHOs who said they'd study with her never turned up. Ludo's whole despondent demeanour, her sad, slow and defeated posture, her lack of energy and self-motivation, her hopeless conviction that she'd fail her second part at least three times in a row, cried it out like a howling Greek chorus in a play that couldn't decide if it was tragedy or comedy.

They were in the cafeteria, inevitably, when the thought came into Goldblatt's mind. Just as it did, Ludo turned and looked at him with those half-closed lids low over her blue, drowsy irises, as if she could tell exactly what he was thinking.

Goldblatt looked back at her. There were moments, he had to admit, when there was a smoky, seductive salaciousness about Ludo. Most of the time she just looked heavy, slovenly, and slow. And yet there were these moments... moments of extreme haughtiness and egotism, a degree of naked, unabashed selfishness, which was so naked, so unabashed, that it was magnificent, voluptuous, sexy. Her slovenliness just made it all the more sexy.

'What are you thinking about, Malcolm?' The words came out of Ludo's mouth like smoke curling into the air, sluggishly, sinuously.

'Nothing,' he said. His mouth had gone dry. He stood up. 'I've got to go.'

The Fuertler's files were the answer to Ludo's problem. Not all her problems, and not even the most important one. Just the one about not being appreciated by the Prof, who had shown no recognition of her existence except for that one conversation in which Ludo had cried and lied to avoid being an HO.

Volunteering to fill in the Fuertler's files was therefore a strangely smart move on Ludo's part. It was so smart that Goldblatt thought she must have made it by mistake, and was expecting the HO to come and tell him that Ludo was making her do the work. But the HO didn't tell him anything, and Goldblatt was finally forced to conclude that, hard as it may have been to believe, Ludo had known exactly what she was doing and actually intended to carry out her promise.

Perhaps he shouldn't have been so surprised. If there was one thing Ludo would know, having practised the art of evading responsibility in at least five different hospitals, it was how to do just enough work to appear occupied and, if possible, overworked. The Fuertler's files were perfect. For the price of spending half an hour filling in a file on each patient, Ludo could claim to be involved in the care of every patient on the ward – and in a way the Prof couldn't help but notice.

Anyone who has ever worked for a professor with a special interest in an uncommon disease knows that filling in research records is just as important as providing their patients with care. And since it's much easier to get a patient out of hospital alive than to get medical staff to keep accurate records on them, and since records live a lot longer than patients, most professors spend a lot more time worrying about their records than about their patients. It was a dead certainty that any professor who kept something called Fuertler's files would let the SHO just about write her own reference if only she could keep the files up to date. In comparison with this service, the HO's Sisyphean labours in clerking the patients in, guiding their stay through the endless delays imposed by human physiology and hospital bureaucracy, and sending them out again, would count for nothing. In short, Ludo's move had all the makings of a step towards stardom.

On the other hand, it also had the makings of a step towards oblivion. Just as the Prof would swoon and salivate in ecstasy over Ludo if she kept the files up to date, she would decapitate her with her bare hands if she failed to complete them.

And this was where Ludo's strangely smart plan was falling apart. Something had gone wrong. For once, not because of anything she had done. Much as she wanted to fill in the files, Ludo was finding it impossible to do so. Funny how something as simple as taking responsibility for a set of brown Manila folders can push you into a war zone. Without knowing it, Ludo had positioned herself dead centre in the crossfire.

It was Ludo herself who realized that something more than mere co-incidence was at work. Being naturally trusting, Goldblatt was reluctant to believe it. But Ludo whined and whined, and eventually Goldblatt was forced to listen to her allegations.

'Emma keeps telling me she'll show me how to fill them in,' Ludo whined, 'but she hasn't done it yet. She always says she's busy. Last week she told me she'd do it on Monday and it's already Thursday.'

Goldblatt knew what day it was. 'I'm sure she'll show you,' he said impassively.

'I don't think she will,' replied Ludo.

'What do you mean?'

'I just don't think she will.'

She didn't.

'How hard can it be to fill in a Fuertler's file?' demanded Goldblatt a week later, as a troubling sense of déjà vu settled over him in the cafeteria.

'I don't know,' said Ludo. 'I've never done one.'

'You've never done one? What have you been doing for the last month? Who's been filling out the files?'

'Who do you think?' retorted Ludo venomously.

Goldblatt frowned. It was starting to look as if Ludo's sense of victim-ization, for once, had a basis in reality.

'Emma said she had to show me. She said if everyone doesn't fill them out in exactly the same way they'll lose consistency.'

'Ludo, have you even looked at one of the files?'

'No.'

'What do you think will happen if you just take a peek?'

They went up to the ward. Goldblatt opened one of the brown folders that were lying around on the desks in the doctors' office. Ludo half cowered behind him.

Nothing. No one was vaporized. No explosion ripped through the room, no demonic apparition leaped off the page.

The first sheet in the file gave the patient's personal details, then there was a page with an account of the patient's medical history, followed by the record of the examination and tests taken the first time the patient was seen by the Prof. After that there was a standardized page for every subsequent visit to the Prof's Thursday clinic. Finally there was a series of stapled three-page entries for each ward admission. According to these, when the patient came into the ward, Ludo was meant to go through a set of questions about specified symptoms, do an examination, and record the results of certain tests that the HO was supposed to order as part of the Fuertler's work-up. No big deal. There were even pre-printed outlines of the human body – front, back, face, and hands – to make it easier to record the patient's skin lesions. The only part they couldn't decipher was a series of tests of skin laxity that Goldblatt had never heard of, with names like 'Dorsal Hand Stretch' and 'Sternal Pinch', which Ludo was supposed to score. Ludo followed Goldblatt into the hospital library to find out what they were. From the way she looked around, you would have thought she'd never been in there before. They couldn't find the tests described in any textbooks. Goldblatt deduced that the Prof had probably made them up herself. No problem.

'No problem?' repeated Ludo incredulously. 'I told you, Emma refuses to—'

'Ludo, when you're with the patient, you're going to be with someone who's seen the tests done hundreds of times before.'

'Am I?'

'Yes.'

'Who?'

'The patient! On themselves!' Goldblatt rolled his eyes in exasperation.

'If you can't figure out a way to get them to show you what the tests are, you don't deserve to call yourself a doctor.'

Ludo gave Goldblatt a disdainful glance. But he was right, of course. Suddenly Ludo frowned. 'Malcolm, what if the Prof asks who showed me? What if she asks me to show her how I do them?'

Ludo should be so lucky, thought Goldblatt, that the Prof would ask her anything.

The answer was simple. 'Tell her Emma showed you.'

'But Emma didn't show me.'

'Exactly,' said Goldblatt. 'And we'll let Emma say why.'

Ludo laughed. She liked that idea. Goldblatt had known she would.

But Emma wasn't beaten yet. Next, the folders disappeared from the ward.

'They're gone,' said Ludo.

'Where?'

'I don't know.'

'Have you looked under the desks?'

'Malcolm, please. They're gone!'

'Where?'

'Don't, Malcolm,' Ludo pleaded. 'Not today. It's the wrong time of the month.'

And *that* was more information than he needed.

'I'm not joking, Malcolm. We've got to do something.'

'We', thought Goldblatt. How rarely Ludo used the word – how telling when she did.

The folders had gone, but that didn't necessarily implicate Emma. There was one other place to look.

They went down to the Prof's secretary on the first floor, who sat in front of a wall of shelves on which the Fuertler's files stood in long, brown, dusty ranks. The Prof's secretary hated the files, which made her room look like some kind of archive. None of the folders for the patients on the ward was there. Those for the patients who were booked to come in during the next week were gone as well. When Goldblatt asked to see the book where people signed the files out, the Prof's secretary looked at him as if he came from another planet. Or at least from a medical unit where people knew how to do things.

Of course, thought, Goldblatt. Why *would* you want a book? Why on earth would you want to be able to trace the whereabouts of a set of files containing unique information that had never been copied, catalogued, or entered on to a computerized database, and therefore could never be retrieved if the hard copies were lost? Why would you want to do anything to discourage people from just walking off with them and never putting them back? And why would you worry about people never putting them back, when even a few small gaps could render the whole lot useless for the purpose of drawing statistically reliable conclusions?

Goldblatt asked the Prof's secretary who had taken the missing files. She gave him another look. The meaning of this one was even clearer.

Goldblatt felt a new respect for the Prof's secretary. She was surly, dismissive, and unhelpful, but she had a real knack for communicating without saying a word.

Hiding the Fuertler's files was crude, thought Goldblatt, but effective. He couldn't resist the challenge.

'They're in her office,' said Ludo when they retreated to the cafeteria to think the problem over. 'They have to be.' Ludo's shoulders were hunched and she was leaning forward conspiratorially with a desperate gleam in her eye. She looked as if she was capable of anything – absolutely anything – except thinking of a way to get the files back from Emma.

Goldblatt nodded.

'The Prof will forget I even exist if Emma doesn't let me fill them in.'

Goldblatt shook his head. The Prof wouldn't forget she existed. She would remember, only too well.

Ludo stared at him in despair.

'We'll just have to go in there and get them,' said Goldblatt at last.

'How? Emma always keeps her door locked.'

Goldblatt thought about that. 'Then we'll need a little bit of guile.'

'What's that?'

'Trickery.'

'Ooh, Malcolm! I love it when you talk dirty.'

Guileful plans, Goldblatt had learned, always work best when fronted by the least guileful person you can find.

'But why do I have to tell Emma the Prof's looking for her?' asked the HO, looking back apologetically at the patient they had dragged her away from.

'Don't worry about that,' said Goldblatt.

'It's for your own sake,' added Ludo. 'The less you know the better.'

The HO peered suspiciously at Ludo. Then she turned back to Goldblatt. 'Malcolm, what's going on?'

'Don't worry. If Emma asks later, just say I was the one who told you the Prof wanted her.'

'What if she asks when I tell her?'

'She won't. Trust me.'

The HO did trust him. The trouble was, the HO didn't trust Ludo, and for the first time she could remember, Goldblatt and Ludo seemed to be telling her to do the same thing.

'Wait one minute after I go into her office,' said Goldblatt. 'No more. Then come running in and say the Prof's in clinic and she's been looking for her everywhere.'

'*Everywhere!*' shouted Ludo, demonstrating what was required. '*She's been looking all over—*'

'Thanks, Ludo. We get the picture.'

'What if she asks why the Prof didn't bleep her?' said the HO.

'She won't. Trust me. Just come running in and make it look real. And then stand back.'

'Stand back?'

'We don't want you getting hurt.'

An enraged bull elephant would be as nothing to Emma Burton once she thought the Prof was looking for her.

The HO hesitated.

'All right?' said Goldblatt.

'All right,' said the HO.

'Good.' Goldblatt turned to go to the SR's office, which was on the other side of the nurses' tearoom. He looked back at the HO. '*One* minute.'

He knocked on the door.

'Who is it?' said Emma.

Goldblatt went in.

A minute later, the HO came tearing into the room. 'The Prof!' she cried. 'The Prof!'

'What? What?' demanded Emma, jumping to her feet.

'She wants you! In clinic! Now! She's been—'

The HO jumped out of the way, just in time. And Emma was gone, flying out of the room in a flurry of white coat.

Goldblatt gazed at the HO with genuine admiration. 'That was excellent.'

'I did some acting at university,' said the HO. 'Ibsen, Chekhov. My Portia in the *Merchant of Venice* was...' The HO stopped. She shook her head, mirroring Goldblatt's own gesture. 'No? Well. There we are. Um... Anything else, Malcolm?'

'No. Thanks.'

The HO left. Goldblatt looked around the SR's office. It was a dank, windowless little room with a desk and a set of shelves. It must originally have been intended as a bathroom. There was a small sink against the wall with two stoppered pipes sticking out of the plaster. The room was a terrific mess, with papers and files and patient records that Emma had taken with her because she never managed to dictate her letters in time, despite the fact that you weren't supposed to remove patient notes from clinic. Suddenly Goldblatt understood why the spotty youth from Medical Records was always hanging around the ward looking for missing notes. There were mugs of cold, scummy tea. Funny that the nurses were always complaining that their tearoom next door was chronically short of mugs.

And there, in a pile on the floor, was a stack of brown Manila folders.

Goldblatt picked them up.

Ludo appeared in the doorway.

'Here,' he said, putting the Fuertler's files in Ludo's arms. 'Enjoy.'

13

'DO YOU THINK THAT's normal, Malcolm?' asked Lesley, when Goldblatt regaled her with the tale of Emma's concealment of the Fuertler's files and the improvisatory piece of street theatre he had staged with the HO in order to recover them.

Goldblatt frowned. Normal? What kind of a question was that? Nothing was normal on the Prof's unit, and by now Lesley knew it. But he was quite proud of the street theatre, and all he really wanted from Lesley was for her to tell him how clever he was. He had already told himself how clever he was, a number of times, but it wasn't the same as hearing it from someone else.

But Lesley wasn't in a congratulatory mood. He could already hear it in her voice.

'I'd be worried if someone I worked with did that to me.'

'Really?' he said.

'I'd be worried about what she was going to do next.'

Goldblatt sighed. 'What can she do, Les?'

'Don't laugh, Malcolm.'

Goldblatt laughed.

'That's all you ever say. "What can they do?" You're hopeless! It's not the first time. You never see it coming. People *do* things, Malcolm. Haven't you learned that by now?' Lesley stared at him in despair. 'You're blind to it. You know what your problem is? You think it's a joke. You think everything's a joke. You can't believe anyone's going to take anything seriously – and then they do. And they stab you in the back. You never believe they're going to do it, and they do.'

'Like who?' demanded Goldblatt. 'Just give me one example.'

'Dr Oakley.'

Good example. 'Well he was just... he was just...'

'He was what? "He'll support me, Les. Dr Oakley will back me up, Les. Dr Oakley will stand up for me, Les." Do you remember that, Malcolm? Do you remember what you said? And then what did he do?'

Dr Oakley was a consultant on the unit where Goldblatt had held his last substantive post. They both knew perfectly well what Dr Oakley had done, and the impact it had had on Goldblatt's career. Goldblatt was still feeling the effect. Was there really any need to drag it all up again?

'You're the one who asked for an example, Malcolm.' Lesley shook her head. 'How do you keep getting yourself into these situations?'

'What situations?'

'*These* situations.'

Goldblatt was silent. Lesley gazed at him.

'It's not so bad, Les.'

Lesley held up her hands, as if she wasn't going to say anything else.

Goldblatt knew she would. In another minute or two. She could never stop until she had said everything she wanted to say. And she hadn't said everything yet, he could tell. Not by a long shot.

He smiled to himself, watching her as she finished off her salad with sharp, jabbing thrusts of her fork. That was one of the things he loved about her. The way she couldn't help herself when there was something to say.

She put the fork down. She was staring at her plate. It was coming. He could see it. Another moment... Another moment...

'I'm sorry, Malcolm, but do you know what I see? I see a professor who can't cope with what's going on in her own unit and doesn't even want to know. I see a locum specialist registrar who's got some kind of a complex and seems to be sabotaging what everyone else is supposed to be doing. And then I see you, Malcolm.'

'At least there's a bright spot somewhere.'

'You see? There you are! A joke! This is the weirdest, most dysfunctional, most...' Lesley shook her head impatiently, searching for the words, '... *fucked-up* unit you've ever worked on. And now you do this thing with these... *files*. You just keep waving the red rag, don't you? You can't help yourself. Why didn't you let this SHO sort things out for herself? Why do you have to get involved?'

Goldblatt didn't say anything.

'I thought the last place was bad, but this one? Malcolm, honestly, what do you think is going to happen if you keep going like this?'

Goldblatt sighed. 'What do you want me to do?'

'Be smarter.'

'You usually tell me that's my problem.'

Lesley rolled her eyes.

'Look, what difference does it make? I'm on a fucked-up unit, you said it yourself.'

'It isn't the first.'

'Thank you. Is it my fault?' Suddenly it was all coming out of him, as well. 'What do I do about it? Another fucked-up unit! That's what you get as a locum, Les. You get fucked-up units, all right? And then you end up getting another locum job on another fucked-up unit. And another one. And another one. And it never fucking ends!' He was breathing heavily. 'Thank Andrew Oakley!'

'Of course. Blame him, as always.'

'Why not?'

'Don't you think you might have had something to do with it? Don't you think you might have contributed?'

'I'm not going to go into it again. It's ridiculous!'

Lesley stared at him. 'Look how angry you are.'

'*I'm* angry?'

'No, of course not. Not you. Not Malcolm Goldblatt. He's always in control.'

Goldblatt was silent for a minute. 'The other day my house officer said she thought I was angry,' he said quietly. He looked at Lesley and smiled disbelievingly.

'Malcolm,' said Lesley, 'have you taken a look at yourself recently?'

'What?'

'I don't believe you. I just don't believe you any more.' Lesley got up from the table. She leaned against the wall, arms folded, her head shaking in exasperation. 'And don't tell me about the old Jewish lady, all right? Just don't tell me about her.'

'Which old Jewish lady?'

Lesley looked at him with astonishment. 'What do you mean, which old Jewish lady?'

'Which old Jewish lady?'

'The one you're always talking about.'

Goldblatt looked at her uncomprehendingly.

'The one who was *vhizzy*, Malcolm.'

Goldblatt smiled incredulously. 'Have I told you about her?'

'Malcolm, are you serious?'

Goldblatt preferred not to answer questions like that.

'You've told me about her.'

'No.'

'Yes.'

'No.'

'Yes. The orange tablets? The Helmstedt accent?'

'The Helmstedt accent... the orange tablets...' repeated Goldblatt slowly 'I *have* told you about her, haven't I?'

'Yes, Malcolm. You have.'

'When?'

Lesley laughed.

'How many times?'

Lesley shook her head in amazement. 'How many times? She's in your head, Malcolm.'

'No. She's dead.'

'Exactly. She's dead and she's gone to live inside your head.'

Goldblatt frowned, wondering. *Had* he told Lesley about the old Jewish lady? He must have, but he couldn't remember. He looked back at Lesley. 'I wasn't going to mention her, anyway.'

'Well, don't!'

'I won't.'

'Good. Because I never want to hear about her again.'

Goldblatt shrugged. Since it seemed that she knew about her, what did Lesley have against the old Jewish lady? It didn't hurt to hear about her now and then.

But maybe this wasn't the moment. Lesley was gazing at the floor, arms folded tightly across her chest. She looked angry. Why was she angry?

Hadn't she just said that he was the one who was angry? He wasn't angry. Not until now, anyway. Maybe now he was angry.

He wondered how angry Lesley really was. He wondered if she was so angry that she wasn't going to want to have sex with him that night. But if she was angry and then they made up, they'd have even better sex. Make-up sex with Lesley was awesome, easily the best make-up sex he'd ever had. The best sex he'd ever had, make-up or not.

He glanced at her again, wondering.

Lesley noticed him. For a moment, her glance was unrelenting.

Then she smiled. She couldn't help it.

Goldblatt grinned. She probably knew exactly what he was thinking.

Suddenly her gaze was serious again. 'Be careful of that SR, Malcolm. All right? Watch out for her. People do things. You never see it until it's too late.'

Goldblatt laughed. 'What's she going to do, Les? Bite me?'

It really hadn't occurred to Goldblatt that he had to be careful of Emma.

He had managed to figure out that things weren't going well between them, and he had even had a conversation with her to try to smooth things over, which had turned out to be fine, which was worrying. But that Emma would actually do something, that was another thought altogether. Lesley was right. He never saw it coming. Life had poked him in the eye with so many sharpened sticks – some of which, he had to admit, he had wielded himself – that when each new poke came he tended to blink, wipe away the blood, pick up any stray scraps of retina, and keep going. Even when he hadn't done it himself, he just never seemed to respond by figuring out how he could poke the poker back. Sometimes, he wished that he was the kind of person who did. But whenever he set out to do it, he just couldn't motivate himself to bother. It seemed ridiculous. But other people did bother, apparently thinking he had poked them in the first place. They poked him even when he didn't see how they could possibly believe he had poked them to start with.

If Lesley was right, Emma was the kind of person who bothered. It was obvious that Emma and he were spectacularly ill-suited to be working together. It was madness that she had been positioned as his SR and he as her junior. It wasn't that Goldblatt thought Emma lacked competence – she just lacked experience. And inevitably there were going to be incidents where inexperience showed.

As when Emma tried to get a colonoscope shoved up Mr Siepl's rectum just because the Prof had requested it. Goldblatt didn't believe for a second that Emma, without the Prof's prompting, would have ordered that test, given the story that Mr Siepl told. But a more experienced registrar would have known that the Prof had requested it because she couldn't be bothered taking a proper medical history in clinic, which in turn was because the Prof was a terrible clinician, ten times worse as a clinician than Emma herself. You only had to sit through one of those head-banging corroborees the Prof called a ward round to see that. All those desperate scufflings through the notes, those hesitations that were disguised to sound like thoughtful speculation, those furtive glances at Dr Morris...

An experienced registrar would have known that this isn't an unusual phenomenon in a major teaching hospital, where a proportion of appointments to consultant posts are made largely on the basis of academic achievement. Academic achievement bears no relationship to clinical skill, and consequently, teaching hospitals teem with academically inclined consultants who are fine researchers and terrible clinicians. Goldblatt had worked with some who were truly appalling. In Professor Small, Goldblatt recognized the signs – not the academic achievement, but the lack of clinical acumen. Like all terrible clinicians, she relied on tests to make up for her deficiency, ordering investigations that would have been unnecessary if she were able to practise the art of taking a history and examining her patients properly. Emma, apparently, defined her role in life as ensuring that every one of these tests was done. An experienced registrar would have done the opposite. She would have known that terrible clinicians like the Prof secretly know how terrible they are and will turn a blind eye to reasonable revision of their tests by competent subordinates. In fact, they more or less expect it to happen and come to rely on it.

The problem as Goldblatt saw it was simple. Emma had risen too far too fast.

But he was wrong. Or not entirely right. Emma had risen too far too fast, that was true, but that was barely the half of it. The other half of it lay in the nature of the relationship that had developed between Emma and Professor Small before he had even arrived on the unit. Goldblatt hadn't yet recognized the intensity of the Prof's fear of disrespect and her craving to be loved – his understanding of the relationship between the Prof and her locum SR was even murkier.

And yet there were really only two things he needed to know to understand this relationship. The first thing was that the Prof gave Emma concert tickets. The second was that Emma took them.

No one had been more surprised than Emma Burton herself when she got the job as registrar on Professor Small's unit.

After eighteen months of drudging SHO jobs in district hospitals in the Midlands, she passed her second part and decided to try for a registrar post in London. Suddenly she found herself competing with people who had done two or even three years as SHOs in London teaching hospitals, and who seemed to project an air of vastly more confidence, knowledge, and capability than she had. Job after job slipped past her. Following each abortive interview she was advised to come back after another year as an SHO, but she had begun to wonder whether that was just another way of saying that she needn't bother coming back for a job in London at all. She had almost resigned herself to looking for a reg post elsewhere, when she was notified that she was shortlisted for the registrar job on Professor Small's unit, for which she had applied a couple of months earlier. She almost didn't bother coming for the interview, but at the last minute decided to... and got the job!

She still didn't understand why. She couldn't see her advantages over the other candidates, who all came from well-known teaching hospitals in London. They had all seemed much cleverer and more experienced than her when they had been speaking to each other while waiting for the interviews to start. She had barely opened her mouth.

The reg job on Professor Small's unit was a big step up for Emma. It wasn't only her first registrar job, it was her first job in a major teaching hospital. She found it difficult. She had never supervised her own HO, and found it hard to be decisive. People expected her to know more than she did, and she worried about her want of medical experience. The administrative demands often seemed overwhelming, and she feared that Professor Small would think she lacked organizational ability. The competitiveness of the academic environment was confronting, and she didn't know what to say when other doctors asked about her non-existent research interests.

Emma felt uncomfortable about other things as well. She had moved in with her sister, who was an accountant with a firm in the City, and was embarrassed that she didn't live independently. Or with a boyfriend. She didn't even have a boyfriend, and that embarrassed her too. In reality she didn't have any friends at all, at least not in London, and that wasn't only embarrassing but created real difficulties whenever the Prof gave her a pair of concert tickets and she had to find someone to take.

None of these things was a surprise to the Prof. She recognized in Emma a version of herself – shorter and plumper, but still in many ways a version of herself – as she had been in her own early days, before her Fuertler-fuelled rise to power. Wasn't that, after all, the reason she had chosen to give her the job?

The Prof soon had good reason to be satisfied with her choice. Her new registrar wasn't at all like the snippety, uppity London-trained registrars she had had before. Emma was desperate to please. She had never worked within shouting distance of a professor, and in her uncorrupted mind a professor, any professor, was only one step lower on the ladder of infallibility than a god. She listened seriously to the Prof's medical prognostications, and paid her more homage and attention than the Prof could remember having been paid by another doctor in years. Every wish of the Prof was her command, and she would stay back until all hours of the night or come in on weekends to fulfil them, even though she was hopelessly disorganized and committed herself to do so much that she rarely managed to achieve half of what she promised to do. She was like moist, malleable putty in the Prof's hands and the Prof was going to mould, fashion, and shape her. She had every intention of holding on to Emma for as long as she could – she just wasn't going to let her know that.

Emma, for her part, began to see a golden vista of a career opening up for her under the aegis of Professor Small, if only she could hang on to her job. First the reg post, then a research degree in the Prof's lab, then the SR job on the Prof's unit, then a consultancy. Why not? Was it too much of a dream?

Unaware of the degree to which the Prof valued her pliant ineptitude, Emma lived in terror of this vista suddenly being snatched away in some cataclysmic act of punishment. She was petrified that the Prof would discover that she had little confidence, and hardly ever managed to get any of her work finished on time. Consequently, she drove herself into a frenzy, falling behind in her work and pretending to be confident. If only she had realized that it was precisely these qualities that the Prof had already discerned and most cherished in her, she could have relaxed and enjoyed the natural defects of her ways. Instead, her anxiety grew, and with it her obsequiousness, making her ever more attractive to the Prof, who, as a result, was ever more careful to do nothing to let Emma see that she knew all about her, staging carefully managed displays of anger at some administrative folly once every fortnight, and driving her into further agonies of self-doubt.

They were in a circle, Emma and the Prof. Whether it was vicious or virtuous, they were chasing each other around it at ever increasing speeds.

The relationship grew closer, warmer, stickier. They became a familiar sight in the hospital corridors – bony, hair-sprayed Andrea Small, dressed in one of her chic grey or brown suits with an orange or yellow Liberty's scarf thrown elegantly over her shoulders, and chubby, pink Emma Burton trundling along beside her in her white coat. The Prof never went to see a patient without Emma in tow, not even her patients in the private wards of the hospital on the ninth floor. Emma soon started including the private patients on her daily rounds with the house officer, sensing that the Prof would appreciate it if she did. By way of reward, the Prof bleeped Emma every Monday afternoon and asked her to come and help out in her private Fuertler's clinic.

While the SR routinely went to the Prof's NHS clinic on Thursdays, it was a great compliment for the registrar to be asked to come and help out in her private clinic on Mondays. But it was also a great disruption, because that just happened to be when the SR did her ward round. At the clinic, Emma invariably found herself doing nothing more useful than sitting in the Prof's consulting room and observing the technique of the great Fuertlerologist. Had one been less terrified by the prospect of one's golden vista turning into an ashen apocalypse, one might have wondered whether the Prof wasn't merely trying to get one away from the SR, like a jealous mother who can't stand her daughter having her own friends. One might even have been quite ambivalent about the apparent indispensability one had suddenly acquired.

There were a lot of things in the relationship that developed between Emma Burton and Professor Small that one might have been ambivalent about. An intricate array of rewards and punishments was woven into its fabric to which only the Prof held the code. Emma's mood oscillated from euphoria to black despair, and it was the Prof who pushed the pendulum. As registrar, Emma was required to dictate summaries on patients who had been discharged, which were sent to their GPs. The Prof made a point of reading them before they went out. It took Emma agonies of procrastination and uncertainty to dictate each summary, and she was soon a long way behind. For week after week the Prof would just read the trickle of summaries, not saying a word. The tension built. Emma became frantic with the knowledge that she was falling further behind and with the fear that the Prof must be growing increasingly unhappy. The Prof's silence made it worse. By the time the Prof asked her into her office to enquire about the backlog in discharge summaries it was almost a relief. The Prof would look at Emma and shake her head in mute disappointment. Emma tried to explain. The Prof shook her head some more. Emma started crying. Crying wasn't going to help. The Prof told her that it wasn't good enough. Emma left. Ten minutes later the Prof bleeped her to tell her not to worry, that she, the Prof herself, would come in on the weekend and do some of the summaries. Herself? Yes, the Prof said, herself. On the weekend? Yes, the Prof said, on the weekend. Emma told her that she'd come in on the weekend as well.

They would both be there on the weekend. But they wouldn't do any discharge summaries, or one or two at the most. The Prof would take Emma out to lunch in one of the cafes nearby, and give her two tickets for a concert that night. Knowing perfectly well that Emma had no one to take but her sister, the Prof would tell her to let her know who she went with. Discharge summaries weren't mentioned again for another month, when the Prof suddenly discovered that it still wasn't good enough.

The Prof soon began hinting that she might be able to extend Emma's registrar year until Emma could find a place to do her research degree. Then she started hinting that the Fuertler's Foundation might come up with the money for an MD for Emma in the Prof's lab, side by side with the foul-mouthed Russian post-doc Bolkovsky, who could supervise her.

Occasionally, the Prof hinted that the Fuertler's Foundation money might fall through.

All of this had been going on for months by the time Goldblatt arrived. It was so far outside what he understood as a relationship one has with one's boss that he probably wouldn't have known how to deal with it even if he had recognized it from the start. Which he didn't. He simply fell into the middle of it, as if out of the sky.

Because one day the SR walked out.

The Prof didn't like the SR. She had never really liked her, but at the time there had been complicated political reasons involving favours owed and obligations to be created that had made it prudent to appoint her. The SR had all sorts of ideas and criticisms, and didn't approve of the way the Prof did anything. In the Prof's opinion, she was haughty, uppity, and opinionated, and the Prof was glad to see the back of her. In fact, looked at from a certain perspective – or from almost any perspective – it might even have been said that the Prof had helped her on her way.

But losing the SR, however welcome, did create a problem. The SR's contract was supposed to have run for another eight months. After that – although there would be the tedious charade of interviews to go through – the position was spoken for. It had long been promised to a registrar who was finishing his MD on Fuertler's of the lungs in Tom de Witte's lab. Tom de Witte claimed that the heir apparent couldn't possibly finish his research in under eight months, as he and the Prof had originally agreed. The Prof said she needed an SR now, and hinted that she might advertise the post as a substantive job, which had to be for a minimum of a year, and dump the heir apparent. Tom de Witte was outraged. The heir apparent had come to him from a cardiologist friend who used him as the respiratory consultant for all his private patients, so there was a lot to play for. Six months, said Tom de Witte, mentally turning the screws on the heir apparent, who was a lazy dog and should have finished his research by now anyway. Done, said the Prof.

Six months. Who could fill the gap for six months?

Emma Burton hadn't even been a registrar for that long. She was still finding her feet, and the feet she had found were decidedly wobbly.

But the Prof couldn't face another bout with someone like the old SR, and impulsively reached for the one person she knew who would never give her that kind of aggravation.

'Emma,' asked the Prof, having summoned her to her office, 'how would you feel about taking over as the SR?'

'As SR?' replied Emma weakly.

'Yes,' said the Prof, 'for the next five or six months.'

Emma looked towards the Prof uncertainly, fixing her gaze on the flaming, red-hot diadem that the Prof was holding out invisibly for her to don.

'It will be good for you,' said the Prof.

'All right,' said Emma.

'Just all right?'

'No. Thank you, Prof.'

The Prof gave her a pair of tickets she just happened to have for a concert that evening so that Emma could go out and celebrate her temporary promotion.

But that only created another vacancy. The Prof eventually realized that she should have waited to see the quality of the applications she got before choosing to make Emma the locum SR. The usual morass of clapped-out locums with experience in obscure and unsavoury hospitals sent in their names, but then the Prof came across Goldblatt's CV and suddenly discovered that she had turned up an outstanding – or at least not heartsinkingly mediocre – candidate. She selected him immediately. Perhaps she felt, deep down, that if Emma was the SR, someone on the team actually needed to know what they were doing. Yet the consequences shouldn't have been too hard to predict. Emma barely had the self-confidence to tell an HO what to do. What the Prof thought she was going to do when it came to managing Goldblatt was something that Goldblatt, for one, never managed to figure out.

At the precise moment when all of Emma's self-doubt had been brought to an exquisite height of sensitivity by her premature promotion, here came Malcolm Goldblatt, swaggering on to the ward like a walking magnifying glass to amplify her insecurity.

And to add insult to injury – or injury to injury, from Emma's perspective – as registrar, Goldblatt got the running of the ward, and with it the lion's share of chances to fulfil the Prof's bidding. In one fell swoop, the care of the patients, the arrangement of the admissions, the dictation of the discharge summaries, and, most crucially, the filling of the Fuertler's files, had been taken out of her hands. In the careering rollercoaster ride of favour and emotion on which Professor Small was taking her, the one certainty Emma had fashioned for herself was that her capacity to stay aboard depended on her ability to demonstrate, continuously and convincingly, her unwavering loyalty, indispensability, and adulation to the Prof. In order to do this Emma needed ward patients. She needed Fuertler's files. She needed some incompetent turtle of a registrar so she could come riding back on to the ward and save the day, restoring order to the unit, hope to the sick, and the light to Professor Small's eyes. Instead, she got Malcolm Goldblatt, who was five times as experienced as she was.

Of course, complained Emma bitterly to her sister – who heard every excruciating detail of Emma's travails each night when she came home from her accountancy job, and often on the phone during the day as well – Goldblatt had offered to let her keep any of the registrar functions she wanted. Very magnanimous! She knew that offer for what it was, a cynical ploy to steal the SR role from under her nose. Well, the Prof had made *her* SR, and she had made her SR for a reason. The registrar could do the registrar jobs!

Yet those were the jobs she craved. Without them, all Emma had were the Prof's ward round and Thursday clinic to serve her. And Goldblatt, of course, was at the Prof's round as well.

Emma was choking. Already she could feel herself gasping for the oxygen that flowed in the form of the Prof's approval. If it hadn't been for

Goldblatt's suicidal refusal to manipulate beds she might have gone out of her mind with anxiety. But that was nothing but the barest lifeline, a mere trickle of opportunities to demonstrate her reliability and loyalty, and what a villain Goldblatt was by comparison. And the only reason she got even that was because Goldblatt, the lilywhite, had turned it down. Goldblatt, with his big announcement that he didn't 'manipulate' beds.

Before she had heard Goldblatt say that, Emma had always thought it was a privilege to help the Prof when there was a patient she wanted to admit. Somehow Goldblatt had managed to make her feel dirty for doing it. Yet she couldn't just stop. Someone had to do it, she said bitterly to her sister. It was all very well for Goldblatt to tell her that she should tell the Prof to talk to him. You couldn't tell the Prof who to talk to. She couldn't, anyway. And you couldn't just tell the Prof she couldn't admit somebody she wanted to admit. Did Goldblatt think that just because he had made his big announcement, anything had actually changed? The Prof still expected beds to be manipulated, and Emma was still manipulating them, doing Goldblatt's dirty work because he was too pure and high-minded to do it himself. Just because he thought he was the only one who was allowed to have principles.

Well, she had principles too! Plenty of them, she told her sister. Only she didn't necessarily shout about them all the time. She had better manners. She didn't necessarily want to humiliate other people by sticking to them.

And what about that other ridiculous principle of his? He had humiliated her then, too. No one could know every principle in the world. She didn't know the Broderip–Anderssen Principle. So what? It didn't mean he had to make a fool of her in front of the Prof. He could have said: 'This is a very obscure principle that very few people know.' Or he could have said: 'I'm sorry, I've forgotten it.' That's what she would have done. She wouldn't have gone ahead and given a lecture on it.

And there were all the other things. There was the way he had got rid of Simmons, for instance, as if Simmons wasn't even sick enough to be in hospital. He could have waited for her round. She would almost certainly have sent Simmons home, wouldn't she? He could have let her make the decision.

Emma hated him. Slowly, surely, her hatred grew.

Lesley knew. Instinctively, without even having met her, without having heard about half the things that had happened, Lesley knew what was going on in Emma's mind. Even if Lesley had heard about nothing else, the story about the hiding of the Fuertler's files, alone, would have been enough to alert her.

But Goldblatt laughed it off, as he always did. Even after Lesley told him to be careful, he couldn't take it seriously. So Emma and he didn't get on. So she disliked him. What could she do? Talk behind his back? What could she say? She was the one who had admitted Simmons, she was the one hiding Fuertler's files amidst the mounds of illicitly purloined notes in her office. Who was the one behaving reasonably, and who was the one flailing around out of her depth? Surely anyone looking at the situation fairly and objectively would see that at once.

Besides, even if she wanted to talk behind his back, who would she talk to?

14

IF EMMA DID TALK to somebody, it wasn't Goldblatt. In fact, she did the opposite. She stopped talking to him altogether.

She didn't inform him that this was what she was going to do. That, after all, would have required talking to him. No, Goldblatt worked it out for himself.

The most surprising thing about it was how little difference it seemed to make. Emma still ran around behind his back, manipulating beds to get favoured patients on to the ward and whispering orders to the HO, and Goldblatt still reacted, cancelling admissions from beds that he no longer had and countermanding the orders Emma had given. They just didn't talk to each other about it and pretend they were never going to do it again. Looked at from a certain point of view, not talking to each other removed a lot of inefficiency.

But it did create some difficulties. The unit's monthly meeting was coming up, when they would have an invited speaker and be expected to present an interesting case. Normally, an SR and registrar would discuss the patient they were going to present. That wasn't so easy now. And it did create some moments that were not only difficult, but downright awkward.

For instance, Emma still brought her lunchtime sandwich up to the doctors' office to read someone else's newspaper while she ate. Usually Goldblatt's, since no one else brought a newspaper each day. Normally she waited until she knew that Goldblatt was gone and it was safe to enter. On the Friday before the unit meeting, Goldblatt walked in to find her munching contentedly over his copy of the *Guardian*. Being naturally respectful of other people's need for rest and relaxation, even if it was with his newspaper, he sat down at the other desk to start dictating discharge summaries. Emma stopped chewing for a moment, then kept eating, pretending not to have noticed him. This was pretty hard to believe, given the size of the doctors' office. Goldblatt opened a set of notes and picked up the Dictaphone. He caught Emma glancing at him out of the corner of her eye. Emma looked away quickly. He started dictating a summary. When he caught Emma glancing at him again, she started to flush.

Goldblatt looked at her as she went redder and redder. The colour change was extraordinary in intensity, and made Goldblatt speculate about histamine release and bradykinin cascades and other chemical triggers in the human body that he hadn't bothered to think about since he sat his physiology finals. He put down his Dictaphone and watched. Emma flushed even more. Even her chubby forearms flushed. Not only did they flush, they went blotchy. This led to another series of interesting questions. Why does a person blotch in one place and not in another? Does a person blotch in the same place each time, or are the blotches migratory? Does the intensity of the blotching vary with the location? These were only some of the questions that Emma's blotches raised in Goldblatt's mind. He longed to stroke her forearm and find out whether the long, raised, red and intensely itchy tracks of dermatographism would appear, as the textbooks predicted.

'Can I stroke your forearm?' he asked suddenly.

Emma didn't say anything. She had frozen, mouth in mid-chew, as if she thought Goldblatt was about to molest her. Goldblatt resented the insinuation. But he tried to see the situation from her point of view. It must have been a difficult predicament, considering that she had taken a vow not to talk to the person who was interested in stroking her.

'I just want to see if there's any dermatographism,' he explained in a friendly, professional tone, hoping to dispel any misconceptions about his intentions. 'When you flush, you know. I'm just curious.'

Emma swallowed. She flushed deeper. Her blotches intensified.

Goldblatt felt sorry for her. It must be hard to have skin that betrayed you so comprehensively every time you felt guilty or embarrassed. If he had skin like that he'd be continuously blazing like a beetroot. He wondered if he'd faint. With all that blood going to his skin, he reasoned, his central circulation would be volume-depleted.

'Do you faint a lot?' he asked.

Emma took another bite of her sandwich, still staring fixedly at the newspaper as if he weren't there.

But that wasn't going to work. Goldblatt didn't really believe she wasn't aware that he was there. Not really.

'I just wonder,' Goldblatt explained, 'physiologically, if you flush a lot you must deplete your central circulation.'

Emma was flushing even deeper, if that was possible. What was happening to her central circulatory volume? Goldblatt was dying to know. He wished he could slip a Swan-Ganz catheter into her jugular vein, a relatively straightforward procedure that he had performed a number of times, so he could measure her pulmonary artery pressure. By now his curiosity far outweighed his natural desire to respect Emma's wish to stop talking to him.

'That's the mechanism in soldiers who faint on parade,' continued Goldblatt. 'Depleted central circulation.'

'The blood's in their legs!' hissed Emma suddenly. 'Not in their skin.'

'True,' said Goldblatt, tactfully refraining from pointing out that she had just spoken to him. 'But the mechanism's the same. Whether your blood pools in the veins of your legs or in the capillaries of your skin, it's still going to deplete your central circulation.'

Emma didn't reply. She took another bite of her sandwich, but she didn't really look as if she was enjoying it. Her breathing had become laboured. And she was so red! Her ears, especially. They were like two boiling red barnacles stuck on either side of her red face. If he hadn't known about histamine release and bradykinin cascades – or at least if he hadn't know that he had once known about them – he would have thought there was something seriously wrong with her.

She shot a malevolent glance at him.

'Do you remember much about bradykinin?' he said.

Emma shook her head in disgust.

Emma didn't seem to be curious to delve into the physiological depths of her extraordinary redness. In fact, now that he thought about it, he had never seen Emma show much curiosity about physiology in general, or about biochemistry, or pharmacology, or any other of the arcane medical sciences. Her lack of curiosity about these matters was disappointing. Goldblatt simply could not see the point in having undergone the brain-stuntingly dementing experience that people call a medical education if you derived no pleasure from idle speculation in these areas. May as well have done a law degree.

It wasn't only natural curiosity that Emma didn't have. She didn't have a sense of humour, either. Or it would have been more accurate to say that as far as Goldblatt could tell she had a very selective sense of humour. She laughed heartily at any jokes the Prof made, and tittered politely at Dr Morris's witticisms, not being sure whether Dr Morris was important enough to justify full-blown laughter, but she refused even to smile when Goldblatt said something funny, although Goldblatt was much funnier than the Prof, even if he said so himself. The Prof rarely came up with anything more than a tame little quip at which she would laugh, shaking her head with its wavy helmet of hair, as a sign for everyone else to join in. On the other hand, Emma did laugh at Goldblatt's jokes if the Prof laughed first. You would then be sure to hear her joining in a fraction of a second later, searching for the Prof's eyes with her own submissive glance to be certain the Prof could see that she had got the joke.

But it was a shame Emma didn't have a sense of humour, for she had a lovely smile. When Emma smiled her whole pink face lit up, and she looked genuinely and ingenuously happy, like a little girl who has just been given a pony for her birthday. Honestly, Goldblatt thought there was really something about her at those moments. But there wasn't much chance of a smile now. Not unless Emma had contracted the world's fastest case of tetanus and developed end-stage rictus at record speed.

'Listen, Emma,' said Goldblatt, 'can't we talk to each other? This is silly. Let's at least start talking to each other again.'

'I am talking to you! Did I ever say I wasn't talking to you?'

Goldblatt sighed. 'Then let's talk about the unit meeting.'

'Why? It's all organized. I've spoken to the Prof.'

Naturally, thought Goldblatt.

'We're going to show Mr Gust.'

'The man with bruises on his back?' Goldblatt frowned. 'He only came in yesterday. We haven't got any of the tests—'

'We're showing him. The Prof's decided.'

'Are you sure that's wise?' said Goldblatt.

Emma didn't reply. She had already said enough. Too much, in fact.

Unit meetings in hospitals are like cocktail parties on the diplomatic circuit. The location and the personnel may vary, but the scene is always the same.

Imagine a seminar room. On a table in one corner are packets of crisps, cartons of orange juice, and Marks and Spencer finger food supplied by a drug company. A makeshift advertising stand is set up in another corner, with glossy brochures and drug samples and mugs or pens with the appropriate drug names. A drug company rep hands around a sheet for everyone to sign so she can claim expenses from her marketing manager. Everyone licks mayonnaise and crisp crumbs off their fingers before they reach for their pens. Then, after the preliminaries, which are also the finalities for those who are shameless enough to come solely for the food and leave as soon as the samosas run out, everyone sits down, and an invited speaker from another department or from a neighbouring hospital gives a talk on a topic in which he or she has established a reputation as a Wise Sage. These reputations are often hospital-specific. The Wise Sage in one hospital might actually turn out to be the Dumb Ignoramus in another hospital if they were magically transported there.

In a teaching hospital of any size there's a whole circuit of weekly or monthly unit meetings, in addition to the Grand Round organized by the Department of Medicine, which is a regular meeting at which a unit presents a case to the entire medical body – or at least as many members of the body as choose to turn up. A unit will generally present once or at most twice a year at a Grand Round, but in the meantime the consultants are all expected to do their share for each other's meetings, visiting each other's units and giving a talk on their area of speciality. Generally it's the same prepared talk on each occasion, and if you hang around in one hospital you'll start to hear the talks over again. The consultants are prepared to tolerate this because they're all in it together, and none of them wants to have to go to the trouble of thinking up a new talk every two years. The junior doctors tolerate it because junior doctors tolerate anything consultants tolerate. Besides, it's rare for juniors to be in the same hospital long enough to realize what's happening.

Hoping to attract spectators from other units, most consultants like to present interesting patients at their meeting in addition to the traditional after-finger-food talk. The Prof's meeting was held on the last Monday of the month at five o'clock in the seminar room behind the Physiotherapy department on the ground floor, and was supposed to feature a speaker for thirty minutes, followed by a case presentation and discussion. The case could be a patient who had been seen in clinic and had been asked to return specifically for the occasion, or it could be a patient from the ward. In the case of the Prof's unit, often it was nobody. The plain truth was that no one could be bothered going to all the trouble of arranging for an outpatient to come in on a Monday evening for just twenty minutes, and there was always the difficult and potentially embarrassing question of whether the hospital offered to pay for their taxi. As for the ward patients, it was possible to pretend for only so long that any of the ordinary Fuertler's patients on the ward upstairs were interesting enough to justify being brought down for discussion. Dr Morris's patients, of course, would have been interesting enough for a whole fistful of meetings, but the Prof wasn't going to start having non-Fuertler's patients appear. That would be the start of a slippery slope, and the dreaded T word wouldn't be far behind. Anyway, since no one ever came to the Prof's monthly meeting except the doctors on the Prof's own unit and the invited speaker, there was no point bringing a patient down from the ward whom everyone but the speaker had already seen.

But not this time. This time, the Prof was determined to have a patient. The invited speaker just happened to be Elizabeth Mowbray, the Dermatology consultant who stubbornly claimed that Dermatologists were capable of treating Fuertler's Syndrome, which the Prof found such an absurd idea that she laughed out loud each time she heard it. Well, Dr Mowbray was going to see that the Prof could easily produce an interesting patient when it suited her. And for once, the Prof could. She had the perfect candidate sitting on her ward. Mr Gust, the man with bruises on his back.

The lesions in question weren't technically bruises, not in the sense of being haematomas, but they looked like them. Or a bit like them, anyway. They were big areas of thickened, darkened, brawny skin. And they weren't only on his back. There were a few smaller patches on his chest, and even some on his hands.

The man with bruises on his back had turned up at the Prof's Thursday clinic, having been referred by his GP, who wondered whether he had an unusual case of Fuertler's Syndrome. Whether or not he had Fuertler's Syndrome, the case was certainly an unusual one, since the existence of a GP who not only knew what Fuertler's Syndrome was but thought he could actually recognize it was an extraordinary phenomenon in itself. As for the Prof, she had no idea whether the man with bruises on his back had Fuertler's. The patches on his back had developed over the past eight or nine months, and the patches on his hands had been there for even longer. The Prof had never seen anything like them. She threw him into hospital as an emergency, indirectly bumping a tearful multi-cancellee, ordered a full Fuertler's work-up, and hoped that this swift and decisive action would help to make the diagnosis obvious.

But the Fuertler's work-up wasn't finished, and hardly any of the results were back. Nor were the results of the other tests Goldblatt had ordered on the strong suspicion that this would turn out not to be a case of Fuertler's at all. He had a diagnosis in mind, and was waiting for an opportunity to talk to Dr Morris about it. Personally, Goldblatt wouldn't have chosen to show the man with bruises on his back at a meeting. Not yet. If there was one big lesson Goldblatt remembered from law school, it was that you don't put a witness on the stand unless you already know what he's going to say.

He would have shared this lesson with Emma, but Emma didn't seem in the mood for sharing.

Dr Mowbray's talk was on the diagnosis and treatment of Sezary's Syndrome, an uncommon malignancy of blood cells in the skin that eventually progresses to involve the internal organs. This talk was one of her two prepared lectures, which could be shortened or lengthened to measure, and was the one she always gave when her turn came up, every couple of years, to go to Andrea Small's monthly meeting, as a way of driving home the message that Dermatologists deal with some very serious diseases and are certainly capable of taking on something as simple as Fuertler's Syndrome. There was much that Dermatologists were able to do for Sezary's Syndrome using topical treatment to delay internal spread, and Dr Mowbray went through it all, complete with a series of truly nauseating photos showing an abundance of tumour deposits in the skin in various stages of breakdown and ulceration.

At the end there was an awkward minute when no one could think of a question to ask. Dr Morris came to the rescue, dredging his bottomless memory and asking Dr Mowbray's opinion of the findings in a recent journal article on Sezary's Syndrome that no one else in the room, including Dr Mowbray, had ever heard of. Goldblatt wondered if Dr Morris was playing a particularly high stakes game of Bluff the Journal – but immediately rejected the idea. Dr Morris was the one person who wouldn't need to do that. Dr Mowbray asked for the reference so she could look it up.

There was another silence.

The Prof, as the hostess, stood up.

'Elizabeth,' she said, after waiting another minute to be absolutely sure that no one else amongst her brilliant staff had a further question. 'This is fascinating, as always. It's wonderful to hear about the treatment of Sezary's Syndrome. Again. The topical treatments for the cutaneous disease are very impressive. But I can't help wondering what it's like to have to hand over your patients to the Haematologists when the malignancy eventually spreads. It must be terribly difficult for you to lose the care of these patients during the most difficult and challenging phase of the illness.'

'I wouldn't say we lose them,' said Dr Mowbray, squaring her shoulders at the Prof, who was standing no more than two yards away, 'any more than you lose your Fuertler's patient with pulmonary fibrosis to Dr de Witte.'

The Prof smiled indulgently. 'No, Elizabeth. It's not the same at all with my Fuertler's patients. Dr de Witte looks after one particular aspect of the illness when there's a need, supporting my treatment. And even that's only necessary in a tiny proportion of cases. But with Sezary's Syndrome, the Haematologists really are taking over the patient's entire care. After all, it's fundamentally a haematological condition, not just one aspect of the illness.'

'No, Andrea,' replied Dr Mowbray with her own icy smile. 'You misunderstand. It's shared care. There's still dermatological input. You understand the theory of shared care, don't you?'

'Of course,' said the Prof, oozing condescension. 'It works very well in theory. But in practice one partner is always more senior than the other. Surely the Haematologists are very much the senior partners for your Sezary's patients.'

'Well, Andrea, if you put it like that, who is generally on top when it comes to you and Dr de Witte?'

The Prof blinked. Her head shook slightly, moving her hair with it en bloc.

Dr Mowbray gazed at her expectantly.

'Well, thank you, Elizabeth,' said the Prof after a moment in a strained voice. She put her hands together. There were only six people in the audience and it wasn't much of a round of applause.

Dr Mowbray nodded and sat down.

'And now we have a truly fascinating patient!' announced the Prof, recovering her aplomb. 'A real treat. One of the most atypical cases of Fuertler's Syndrome I've ever seen.'

The man with bruises on his back had already been brought down from the ward and was waiting outside the seminar room in his pyjamas and dressing gown. He was a big, ruddy, jovial bricklayer, and he didn't mind waiting outside for as long as the doctors needed him, just as he hadn't minded sitting on a bench in the Prof's clinic from ten in the morning until six-thirty in the evening while Emma had manipulated beds to get him in.

But before he was brought in, the HO was supposed to present his case.

The HO stood up. She described the development of the patches on his skin, or tried to, until she forgot how long the skin on one of his fingers had been inflamed, which was the opening Emma had been waiting for. She jumped up, muscled the HO aside, and took over. Emma finished the story, which she had spent three hours perfecting in her office, and went out to call the man with bruises on his back. He came in and sat down on a chair that had been placed at the front of the room. Emma introduced Dr Morris and Dr Mowbray. The patient looked around and grinned at Goldblatt, folding his arms across his chest. Emma asked him to take off his top. He removed his dressing gown and pyjama top, revealing the outline of a powerful workman's torso softened by fat, with the thickened, discoloured patches that were the cause of all the excitement. Dr Morris got up, stood in front of him for a moment, and then examined his back. Dr Mowbray went over to him as well. She knelt and examined the backs of his hands. She looked at his chest, running a finger over a patch of discoloured skin.

'It's the most unusual case of Fuertler's Syndrome I've ever seen,' said the Prof, who had got up as well and was stroking an area of the man's back with her finger.

The three consultants circled the man with bruises on his back like three lions around a kill. He glanced from one to the other and grinned.

'Of course, Fuertler's Syndrome is so rare and complex that one can never—'

'It's Porphyria Cutanea Tarda,' said Dr Mowbray, straightening up.

The Prof stared at her.

'Pathognomonic. Couldn't be anything else. I saw a case that was almost identical... must be eight years ago. What do you think, Anthony?'

Dr Morris nodded thoughtfully, gazing intently at an area of skin on the man's back. 'That *was* going through my mind, although I've never actually seen a case.' He leaned closer and examined the man's back again. 'Fascinating!'

The Prof stared at him, aghast. Going through his mind? Fascinating? Where was his loyalty?

'Pathognomonic,' repeated Dr Mowbray crisply. She knelt in front of the man with bruises on his back. 'Sir,' she said, 'how much do you drink?'

'On weekdays or weekends?' he asked, grinning broadly.

'There you are,' said Dr Mowbray. She stood up and turned to the Prof. 'Shall we take him over for you, Andrea?'

Professor Small stared at Dr Mowbray, her face frozen in a contrived smile of appreciation. Or disbelief.

She tottered a couple of steps backwards and sat down.

'Yes,' she whispered. 'That would probably be best.'

Dr Mowbray knelt down again and began to speak to the man with bruises on his back, explaining the rarity of his condition and its relationship to alcohol consumption. Dr Morris continued to examine the fascinating lesions on his hands.

The Prof watched them silently. She looked at Emma, who was staring at her with fear and confusion. And then, the Prof's head turned further. Towards Goldblatt.

It was a pained glance that she gave him, searching, vulnerable, bruised. A glance that rose up with a silent cry out of the depth of her humiliation and involuntarily sought the object it feared most to see. It lasted only a moment, but a moment was enough.

Goldblatt frowned. There was something troubling about the glance that Prof had just given him. He wished she hadn't done it. It wasn't going to help anyone that the Prof had been embarrassed in front of an audience, much less that she had brought it upon herself. But worse still was the fact that she had felt impelled to look in his direction at the exact moment when her humiliation was most acute.

Goldblatt couldn't help feeling that something about that was particularly bad. Not for everyone. For him.

15

THE MORNING AFTER THE unit meeting started for Goldblatt as a perfectly blameless Tuesday and continued in that vein for about two minutes, which was the time it took for him to walk into the doctors' office, take off his coat, glance at the Book of Time, feel his heart sink at the sight of four names vying for a maximum of two available beds, come out again and walk past the occupant of bed eight on his way to his morning admissions colloquy with Sister Choy.

'Doctor!' shouted the man from bed eight. 'Doctor! Doctor!'

Goldblatt stopped.

'Doctor!' shouted the man again.

'What?' said Goldblatt, unwillingly taking a very small step towards him.

Even as he did it, he knew it was a mistake. Patients who shouted 'Doctor!' across the ward were usually asking for a bedpan. If not, they were wondering what had happened to the tablets they were supposed to have been given an hour ago. Or when they were going for the test that had been booked for them. Or what had happened to the breakfast they were supposed to have been given. Or they had some other question concerning one of the thousand omissions, substitutions, and alterations that occur on a ward every day, and which only the most naive patient could genuinely imagine that a doctor would be able to answer. As anyone ought to know who has been in hospital for more than ten minutes, nurses run their wards in accordance with secret and impenetrable cultic rites that are as much a mystery to doctors as they are to patients. It follows, therefore, that any doctor who is foolish enough to give in to a patient's request for assistance will have to spend ten minutes finding, interrupting, and irritating a nurse. Or to put it another way, patients who call out to doctors are shamelessly exploiting the supposed helplessness of their situation in order to substitute the doctor for their bedside buzzer, which as everyone knows serves a largely ornamental purpose.

But Goldblatt had stopped now, and responded.

'Are you a doctor or not?' demanded the man who had yelled 'Doctor!', as if he had some kind of a right to know.

Goldblatt gazed at the man. He had sallow skin, a black moustache, and a few long strands of dyed black hair plastered unconvincingly across his skull from a parting half an inch above his left ear. To top it off, he was wearing purple mock-satin pyjamas.

'That depends,' said Goldblatt at last, adjusting the stethoscope that was hanging around his neck.

'On what?' demanded the man sarcastically.

'On who's asking,' Goldblatt took the chart off the end of the man's bed, glanced at the unfamiliar name, and said: 'No, I don't believe I am.'

'What's your name?' demanded the man.

'Dr Goldblatt,' replied Goldblatt.

'But you said you're not a doctor!'

'My parents had high hopes for their children and thought they'd give us a head start. You should hear what they called my brother.'

'You *are* a doctor,' said the man.

'True,' said Goldblatt. 'But there's one important fact you have to consider.'

'What's that?'

'I'm not your doctor.'

But Goldblatt was his doctor, as he predictably discovered fifty-four seconds later when he found Sister Choy and she informed him that Dr Morris had admitted a new patient overnight. Sister Choy needn't have bothered even telling him the name. After his conversation with the man who yelled 'Doctor!', there was only one possibility. Fate works like that.

Mr Lister was a short, surly fifty-six-year-old who claimed never to have had an ill day in his life. He did some kind of manual labour in a mattress factory, smoked twenty-five cigarettes a day, and drank a minimum of two pints a night. Three months earlier he had started to have sweats. At first the sweats came on at night and he drenched the bed, which upset his wife. Then they started coming on when he was at work, which upset his boss. He felt tired, drained, washed-out, and irritable, and his desire for cigarettes diminished. That upset Mr Lister, and he finally decided to go to a GP. The GP gave him a course of antibiotics and told Mr Lister he'd be smoking again in no time. He lied. He gave Mr Lister another course of antibiotics and ordered a chest X-ray. Nothing happened. The antibiotics didn't cure him, and neither did the X-ray. Mr Lister was still having sweats. The GP sent him to his local hospital.

At this stage, having had a fever regularly for more than six weeks, Mr Lister had officially become a Pyrexia of Unknown Origin, or PUO. Infections and inflammatory illnesses are two of the main causes of PUOs. Cancer is the third.

Everyone at the hospital expected Mr Lister to have a nice straight-forward lung cancer. His smoking history made the odds ten to one on. It was just a matter of finding the tumour, and in no time at all he'd be on his way out again with a diagnosis, an appointment at the Radiotherapy clinic, and six months to live. The chest X-ray that was ordered, however, was normal. Then everyone remembered his GP had already done a chest X-ray, and that had been normal as well. Unwilling to give up on the prospect of a neat conclusion to the affair, the consultant ordered a CT of the chest, looking for a tiny little cancer hiding in some out-of-the-way bronchus behind the heart. No luck. Things were starting to look complicated.

By now, the results of various blood tests were coming back without giving any clues to the cause. Nonspecific changes, nothing more definite. Blood cultures didn't grow any bacteria. The consultant told his registrar to try another chest X-ray, perhaps hoping that the radiation from the earlier X-rays might have produced the cancer that was supposed to be there. Still no luck. They tried an ultrasound of the liver and gallbladder without having any definite idea what they were looking for. Nothing. More blood cultures: negative. Echocardiogram: normal. Abdo CT: unremarkable. Lumbar puncture: clear.

Over a week had passed. Mr Lister was growing restless and increasingly irascible with his fever. At ten o'clock every morning he started to shiver, his temperature rose towards forty degrees, and by eleven-thirty he was drenching the bed as his temperature fell again. Another week of unrevealing tests went by. This was getting beyond the competence of the consultant, his fellow consultants, and of the investigations that the labs in the peripheral hospital could run. In fact, it had already got beyond them. At the end of the second week, Mr Lister told the consultant he was going to leave. The consultant thought this was an excellent idea and told him that he had heard of a very clever new doctor who was especially interested in cases like his.

'And what kind of cases is that?' asked Mr Lister sceptically.

'Difficult cases,' said the consultant, speaking with many layers of meaning.

'Is he here?' asked Mr Lister.

'No, he's at another hospital.'

'When can I go there?'

'Tonight,' said the consultant. 'I hope.' And he walked off to call Dr Morris, whose fame as the local sink of all medical conundrums, like a ripple on a pond, was relentlessly spreading.

Dr Morris's response to the consultant's description of the case consisted of one word. Fascinating! His three beds on Professor Small's unit were full, with the earliest discharge set to take place in three days, but Dr Morris wasn't going to let that get in the way of a prize as delectable as a PUO that defied diagnosis. His alternate existence as the pseudo-Sutherland gave him opportunities of which other consultants could only dream. The Sutherland unit was on call that night, so every empty bed in the hospital, theoretically, was his. But only for emergencies, not for elective admissions from other hospitals. Dr Morris's incurable inventiveness found a way. First, slyly adopting the guise of the pseudo-Sutherland, Dr Morris rang the bed coordinator to find out where he could get a bed. Second, having reserved the bed for a Sutherland unit patient, he rang his latest locum Sutherland registrar to arrange a transfer into it of his patient on the Prof's unit who was going to be discharged in three days. This was the key step in the chain. Utterly illicit, but difficult to detect, and sparklingly brilliant. The last step was easy. Having freed a bed on the Prof's unit, the pseudo-Sutherland turned back into Dr Morris and rang the consultant at the other hospital to let him know that he could send Mr Lister in to the bed that was being vacated. The whole procedure ran like clockwork, and by nine o'clock in the evening Mr Lister had arrived to find Dr Morris personally waiting to admit him.

It was one of the slickest pieces of bed manipulation that Goldblatt had ever come across, and he would have been proud of young Dr Morris if it hadn't been such a dumb thing to do. Why, he asked himself, couldn't Dr Morris use his awesome powers for good – getting rid of patients – instead of evil?

He would have stopped it, Goldblatt knew, if only the call from the other hospital had first come to him. He didn't know how, but he would have stopped it. Often, in later weeks, listening to Mr Lister pour out his endless complaints, Goldblatt knew that somehow, *somehow*, given half a chance, he would have blocked him.

Goldblatt examined him that morning. So did Dr Morris, for the second time, as well as Emma, and the HO. Ludo said she'd get around to it after she finished her Dermatology clinic. Mr Lister was thin. His ribs stood out when he took off his purple mock-satin pyjama top. Everyone asked him the same set of questions, and he finally exploded when Goldblatt asked him if he itched.

'Why does everyone ask me if I itch?' he demanded angrily. 'Do you think I've got lice or something? I don't itch. I never itch!'

Goldblatt couldn't believe that. 'You must itch sometimes.'

'Never!' declared Mr Lister.

'You mean you've *never* had an itch?' asked Goldblatt, genuinely intrigued. He wondered if he was looking at the makings of a case report for the *Lancet*. 'A Mattress-Maker with PUO Who Never Had an Itch.'

'No, Dr Goldblatt,' retorted Mr Lister irritably, scratching at his thigh. 'I've never had an itch.'

'Then how do you know what the word means?' enquired Goldblatt.

Mr Lister peered at Goldblatt. He glanced at the HO, who was standing beside him.

'Of course I know,' he said at last. 'Everyone knows.'

Goldblatt nodded. 'Look, Mr Lister, I know we're asking you a lot of questions, and I know you're worried about what's going on. Our job is to find out what that is. If we're going to do that, we have to know as much as we can. We're not asking you these things to upset you. There may be a detail you may not realize is important, but which we need to know about. For instance, the reason we ask you whether you itch is because there's a certain disease that sometimes makes people itch. It also gives them fevers and sweats, like you've been having.'

Mr Lister frowned. 'What disease is that?' he asked quietly.

'It's called Hodgkin's disease, and—'

'That's a cancer!' cried Mr Lister. 'My uncle had Hodgkin's disease. He *died* of it!'

'We just need to cover all the possibilities,' said Goldblatt. 'I'm sure you don't have Hodgkin's disease.'

'How do you know that? My uncle had it! How can you be sure?'

'Well, we're not absolutely sure yet. But I'm pretty certain. Besides, you don't itch, do you?'

Mr Lister thought about that. 'I don't think so.'

'What about after you have a hot shower?'

'I don't have hot showers.'

'All right, what about after cold showers?'

'I have baths.'

'Cold?'

'Hot.'

'Do you itch?'

'When?'

'After hot baths.'

'No.'

'There you are, then,' said Goldblatt. 'Most people with Hodgkin's disease do. Now let me look at your knee.'

Dr Morris thought he had been able to detect a slight swelling of Mr Lister's right knee, and wondered whether he had stumbled across the clue that would unlock the mystery of Mr Lister's illness. Goldblatt couldn't detect anything. He called Dr Morris, who admitted he hadn't been absolutely certain he could feel a swelling, but if there was even a possibility of excess fluid in the joint they would have to extract it for analysis. Goldblatt went back to put a needle into the knee and draw off the fluid that Dr Morris may – or may not – have felt.

The HO came with him. She had never seen a joint aspiration. Goldblatt asked Mr Lister to roll up his pyjama trousers, and he examined his bony knees for the second time that day. Then the HO followed suit, trying to copy Goldblatt's technique. She thought she could feel a swelling on the left.

'The left?' asked Goldblatt.

The HO nodded.

'Not the right?'

The HO glanced shiftily at Mr Lister's thin white knees. 'What did Dr Morris say?'

'Never mind what Dr Morris said,' said Goldblatt. 'Where did you feel the swelling?'

The HO gazed at Mr Lister's knees. 'The right,' she blurted out abruptly.

'Wimp.'

'Where did *you* feel it?' she asked.

'Me?' said Goldblatt, peeling the wrapping off a needle and attaching it to a syringe. 'I couldn't feel a swelling at all.'

Mr Lister was staring at the needle in Goldblatt's hand. 'What are you doing?'

'I'm going to take some fluid off your knee.' Goldblatt swabbed the inner aspect of Mr Lister's right knee with iodine. 'If you've got some fluid in there, we can check it out in the lab and it may tell us what's wrong with you.'

'From the fluid?'

Goldblatt nodded.

Mr Lister gazed down at the sterilizing yellow stain that had been spread across his skin.

'Will it hurt?' he asked.

'It won't take long,' replied Goldblatt, who preferred to avoid giving direct answers that were likely to make patients behave unexpectedly when he was holding an unsheathed needle. Of course it was going to hurt. Hadn't Mr Lister ever seen a needle before? Besides, as far as

Goldblatt could tell, there was no excess fluid in Mr Lister's knee. When there is, hitting the fluid is easy. Just slide your needle smoothly into the depression that marks the gap between the back surface of the kneecap and the femur behind, draw on the plunger, and watch the fluid flow. But a normal knee contains only a minute volume of thick, viscous liquid, which can be a lot more elusive to find. And there are a lot of sensitive structures in the vicinity that you're bound to hit before you strike oil. In another second the needle in Goldblatt's hand was going to be poking around inside Mr Lister's knee, nosing its way into bone, ligament, and cartilage.

The kindest thing Goldblatt could do for Mr Lister, he knew, was to do it quickly, efficiently, and without fuss.

'I'm just going to put the needle gently in,' he said to Mr Lister. 'I'll tell you before I do it. You'll feel a jab. Hopefully it will be over in a few seconds.'

Goldblatt pointed out the anatomy to the HO, showing her how to locate the point for the needle to enter. 'OK, here we go,' he said to Mr Lister, and slid the needle in. Mr Lister winced. Pulling back on the plunger to suck up any fluid on the way, Goldblatt advanced until he hit something, cartilage or ligament.

'Are you all right?' he said to Mr Lister, whose brow was starting to glisten with little beads of sweat.

Mr Lister nodded hurriedly.

'Almost there. I'm doing it as quickly as I can.'

Goldblatt withdrew the needle partway, changed direction a little and advanced the needle again, still drawing back on the plunger. Eventually a drop of viscous, yellow fluid appeared in the barrel of the needle, stained with a streak of blood. Goldblatt pulled the needle out of Mr Lister's knee, pulled down on the plunger to suck the droplet of fluid into the syringe, detached the needle, squirted the droplet into a sterile container, and handed it to the HO to label and send down for analysis.

'Looks normal,' Goldblatt said to Mr Lister, who was staring at him with horrified amazement.

'I never knew you could put a needle into a knee.'

'You'd be amazed where we can put needles.'

'Don't tell me, doc,' Mr Lister said earnestly.

Goldblatt laughed.

'Will you be doing other tests?' asked Mr Lister, as Goldblatt put a plaster over the puncture hole in Mr Lister's knee.

Goldblatt nodded. Dr Morris was planning a whole opera of investigations.

'A lot?' asked Mr Lister anxiously.

'As many as we have to do,' said Goldblatt. 'Not a single one more. I'll come back later and explain them to you so you'll know what to expect.'

'Are they going to hurt?'

'That's about as bad as it gets. There'll be X-rays, and things that don't hurt at all. Give me half an hour and I'll come back and explain.'

Mr Lister smoothed down his wispy hair. He didn't say anything else. He glanced nervously at Goldblatt and the HO, then looked back at his knee, where a plaster and a yellow stain were the only evidence that a needle had been sticking into it a couple of minutes before.

'We'll get to the bottom of things,' said Goldblatt. 'Don't worry.'

And they did. Or tried to. Mr Lister's blood would be assayed for antibodies, his bone marrow trephined for tuberculosis, his spinal fluid tapped for neurosyphilis, his skin biopsied for inflammation, his circulation injected with radioactive particles and his body exposed to X-rays and ultrasounds and CTs and MRIs with and without intravenous dyes and with and without guided needles to take biopsies of his tissues. And that was only part of it.

Was it a lymphoma hiding in the gutter between the spinal column and the aorta that was causing his PUO? Or a renal carcinoma tucked away under the cap of one of his adrenal glands? Or a VIPoma buried in the slippery, sliding wall of the gut? Or a tiny abscess loculated just under his diaphragm? Or inflammation of the microscopic leashes of blood vessels in his kidneys? Or another one of a thousand other possibilities?

They'd find out, eventually. The disease hadn't been invented that could elude Dr Morris for ever.

16

PROFESSOR SMALL DIDN'T APPEAR for her round on the Wednesday after the unit meeting, having important business in an undisclosed location – or at least in a location she hadn't disclosed to Emma, who could normally give an hour by hour account of the Prof's whereabouts. But when she arrived for her round the following Wednesday, she turned up with unusually benevolent demeanour. She was on time, for a start. And she didn't get upset when it turned out that no one had made the coffee. No one ever made the coffee, because, although it was understood that coffee should be made, it wasn't understood precisely whose job it was to make it. Every week the first ten minutes of the round were spent discovering, debating, and rectifying the fact that no one had made it in a festival of confusion that set the scene for the phantasmagoria that followed. But not this week. The Prof had a very collected, very serene look on her face. She suggested sweetly that the two medical students might wish to make the coffee, and the two medical students, realizing that they were being invited to perform an important task that was critical to their medical training, gratefully complied. The Prof chatted amiably with Dr Morris as she waited for them to come back.

Goldblatt glanced at her uneasily. Something wasn't right. Either the Prof was very happy about something – unnaturally, eerily happy – or someone had just shot her full of a major tranquillizer.

It wasn't the latter. A fortnight earlier, in one of her increasingly frequent visits to the Prof's office to complain about Goldblatt, Emma had told the Prof that Ludo, who was supposed to be filling in the Fuertler's files, wasn't filling them in at all. She, Emma, was forced to do it herself! The Prof had mentally filed away that piece of information in a special, dagger-filled cupboard in her brain, as she filed away all kinds of information, ready for the time when she might want to use it. And now, as far as the Prof was concerned, the time had come.

In reality, the time had gone. Only days after Emma had provided this information to the Prof, the improvisatory work of the Goldblatt Street Theatre had enabled Ludo to recover the files. Emma had tacitly conceded that her last and most cunning stratagem had failed – which meant that she hadn't been able to think of another one – and since then Ludo had been industriously – if such a word could be applied to Ludo – filling the files in. Emma hadn't dared to inform the Prof of this small but important development, because she couldn't work out how to do it without revealing why Ludo hadn't been able to fill the files in in the first place. But if Emma had known what the Prof was planning to do now with the information – or more accurately, the misinformation, as it had become – she might have summoned up the courage to bring the Prof up to date.

To put it plainly, the Prof was planning to slay Malcolm Goldblatt on her round and leave him lying flat in a pool of his own bubbling blood. From his very first day on the unit and his incomprehensible response when she had asked – very reasonably, she thought – to bring one of her patients in, the Prof had had a niggling feeling, playing constantly like a discordant tune in the background of her thoughts – or screeching at her like a siren in her head – that Malcolm Goldblatt didn't respect her. Inspired by the events surrounding Mr Siepl, Emma had raised the volume by telling the Prof bloodcurdling stories of Goldblatt questioning her decisions on ward rounds and countermanding her orders. And at the unit meeting the Prof had felt his eyes on her like a hot breath on her neck, watching, judging, laughing. The boy needed taking down a notch or three, and the Prof, after much deliberation in front of the Scale, had decided to do it. Just as she had been exposed at the unit meeting, so she was about to put him in his place in the best way possible – in front of everyone.

The instrument was to hand. She was ready to unleash the information provided by Emma from the knife-filled cupboard in her mind where she had stowed it. If the boy wanted to behave as he did – aggravating and alienating everyone around him, junior and senior alike – his own record had to be spotless. And it wasn't, was it? The SHO was supposed to be filling in the Fuertler's files. Today, on the round, when she opened them, the Prof would 'discover' that the SHO hadn't been doing her job, and that the SR had been compelled to fill them in for her. And if it's up to a consultant to discover that an SHO isn't doing her job, an SHO who is supposed to be supervised by the ward registrar, there's only one person to blame, isn't there?

The Prof already knew exactly what she was going to do. She had even rehearsed some of the speech. All of it, actually. And especially the really withering bits.

The Prof tittered at something Dr Morris said as she waited for the coffee. She looked around and asked the HO if she would be so kind as to pass her the Fuertler's files. Ludo almost wet herself with delight. Wasn't the Prof going to be pleased when she saw that every Fuertler's file was as full as a Fuertler's file could be!

The Prof fingered the files as she continued to talk with Dr Morris. Holding them on her lap, she rubbed her hand slowly over the one on the top of the pile, as one fondles something very precious, very comforting, very powerful.

The students came back. The coffee that was the object of their critical training mission was distributed. Everyone settled down, to the extent that they could, squashed thigh-to-thigh in the doctors' office.

The Prof invited the HO to start.

As the HO launched into the first patient, the Prof opened the top Fuertler's file and turned to the pages where the current assessment was supposed to be recorded. The entry was complete – but the writing was unfamiliar. It wasn't Emma's. The Prof peeked at the signature on the final page. Quite illegible, but again, not Emma's. The Prof glanced up at the SHO and saw that she was watching her excitedly. She took a peek at the second file. Same thing. She opened the third. The fourth. The fifth.

The Prof had stopped listening to the HO. She was opening one folder after another, dropping each one on the floor after she had finished with it. The last one went down.

The HO had stopped speaking.

The Prof looked up at her. 'Go on,' she said.

But the Prof's tone wasn't the gentle, mellifluous burble in which she had started the round.

Ludo couldn't say for certain, but she didn't think the Prof was as pleased with the Fuertler's files as she had expected.

The HO kept going. Emma stared at the Prof, trying to catch her eye. The Prof glanced at her and gave her the tiniest flicker of a smile. There was a lot of pain and effort in that smile. Emma started breathing again. The Prof wasn't blaming her! Emma didn't know what was wrong, but as long as the Prof knew it wasn't her fault, everything was all right.

But everything wasn't all right, that was the whole point, and the Prof had grasped it in an instant. The HO's voice droned on in a torrent of muddy, tedious information about her patients. Those Fuertler's files weren't meant to have been filled in. Not by the SHO, anyway. The Prof knew it, Emma knew it, Goldblatt knew it. There was only one possible conclusion. Goldblatt had deliberately had the files filled!

The filling of those Fuertler's files suddenly seemed to be the greatest single act of insubordination the Prof had ever faced. She would have to respond swiftly, vigorously, decisively, or lose whatever respect she still commanded altogether. To falter now, she felt, would be to invite a complete breakdown of her authority, which had been under threat ever since Goldblatt's unprecedented refusal to manipulate beds.

But how? The situation was almost impossibly tricky. After all, the Fuertler's files were *supposed* to be filled. The fact that it had been an unspoken understanding that they hadn't been filled merely made Goldblatt's treachery all the deeper. He knew perfectly well that she wouldn't be able to come out in the open and attack him for making sure that what needed to be done had been done. Well, there were other ways, and if Andrea Small couldn't devise one of them she might just as well hang up her stethoscope and give away her textbooks. All she needed was a pretext. A good, old-fashioned pretext, like the Fuertler's files themselves had been. But the Fuertler's files were no longer a pretext, they were a cause. It would be no exaggeration to say that they were a cause célèbre. And what the Prof needed now was a pretext that would give her the opportunity to celebrate. Quickly.

She found it lying in bed three when they went out on to the ward.

'Wait a moment, please,' said the Prof, with icy, whetted politeness. 'Did you just say Mrs Constantidis hasn't had her echocardiogram?'

The HO looked at the Prof in surprise. That was exactly what she had just said, but she had already mentioned it when she presented the case of Mrs Constantidis, the lady in bed three, in the doctors' office. The Prof, who had been looking through the Fuertler's files at the time, hadn't raised an eyebrow then. And Mrs Constantidis wouldn't be the first patient who would have had to come back as an outpatient for a test that was part of the Fuertler's work-up. Far from it. The various departments in the hospital were always cancelling and rescheduling, and patients would be in for weeks if you refused to let them go before every test was completed.

'*Did* I just hear you say that Mrs Constantidis has not had her echocardiogram?'

'Yes,' said the HO. 'The Cardiology department was supposed to do her yesterday, but one of their machines broke down and they couldn't—'

'I'm sorry,' said the Prof, who wasn't sorry at all and couldn't even make herself sound as if she was. '*Did* you say she hasn't had her echocardiogram?'

'Yes,' said the HO, rewinding to the start of the tape. 'The Cardiology department was supposed to do her yesterday, but one of their machines broke down and—'

The Prof, who had been staring fixedly out of the window while speaking to the HO, suddenly turned on her. The HO stopped. Her mouth stayed open, like a gulping fish.

'Every one of my patients gets an echocardiogram. It's part of the work-up. You have been told that. What have you been doing here for the past month?'

The HO stared.

'Do you expect me to check every test you order on every one of my patients? Well? What do you think you're *doing* here?'

The HO had frozen. The Prof's eyes, which hadn't left her face, turned her blood to ice.

Dr Morris was standing on the other side of the bed. Emma, following her loyalties, had taken a subconscious step towards the Prof. Ludo had taken four completely conscious steps in the opposite direction, trying to get behind Goldblatt. And no one helped the HO. The HO was out in the open like some nocturnal animal with short red hair caught in the spotlights of the Prof's icy rage, and everybody else was going to let her freeze. Freeze, HO, Freeze! No one helps an HO.

'Working her butt off.' Even as the words came out, Goldblatt wasn't sure whether he was actually saying them, or only thinking them.

No, he had said them. He caught a glimpse of the Prof's face. He had *definitely* said them.

Some kind of spasm streaked across the Prof's features. Outrage? Joy? Both. The one problem with the pretext lying in bed three was that the offence, strictly speaking, was the HO's offence, the kind of misdemeanour an HO commits every day, and there was no guarantee that she would succeed in shifting the blame to the registrar. But Goldblatt had just done her work for her. Insufferably impudent as he was, he had joined himself to the offence.

'And you, Dr Goldblatt. You *are* the registrar here, I understand.'

By this time there was complete silence in the room. No one else in there could pretend they weren't aware of the confrontation that had broken out amongst the doctors gathered around bed three. One of the cleaners, who had been mopping under the bed opposite, cautiously straightened up. The lady volunteer who pushed the trolley with the newspapers, and had been chatting to one of the patients about the latest royal scandal on the front page of the *Sun*, clutched the bar on her trolley and slowly turned her head. The other three patients in the room stared silently. And Mrs Eleni Constantidis herself, the cause and occasion of this awful confrontation, caught in the middle of the doctors, was staring at Professor Small, pale, open-mouthed, and rigid with fear.

'The echocardiogram is an elective investigation,' said Goldblatt evenly. 'Mrs Constantidis understands there was a problem with a machine. We've apologized to her, Professor Small. She's very kindly agreed to come back as an outpatient to get—'

'Mrs Constantidis,' said the Prof, whirling to face Mrs Constantidis, who bunched abruptly into a cowering, rabbit-like posture and pulled the sheet right up to her neck. 'Are you *very* upset that these doctors have failed to get your echocardiogram done?'

It took Mrs Constantidis a moment to realize that she was physically safe. After another moment she shrugged tentatively.

'I can see that you are,' said the Prof. 'I would be as well. It is intolerable. *Intolerable!* Is it true that they have asked you to come back?'

Mrs Constantidis smiled hesitantly.

The Prof sat on the edge of the bed. Mrs Constantidis shifted apprehensively, wondering what the Prof was going to do to her now that she knew she had agreed to come back to have the echo-thing done when it was intolerable. *Intolerable!* What was going to happen? She should never have agreed. If she had known it would make the Professor this upset, she would have told the little doctor that she couldn't do it. But the little doctor... she was just a young girl... who would have thought that such a sweet little doctor would ask her to do something intolerable? And now they were both in trouble. The Professor was going to punish the little doctor, and as for her, Eleni Constantidis, the Professor was going to send her away and never let her come back to the hospital again. Oh, what a lot of trouble she was in!

The Prof reached for Mrs Constantidis's hand. Mrs Constantidis gave it to her reluctantly, half turning her head away in an anticipatory flinch.

'Don't worry,' said the Prof, '*I'll* get your echocardiogram done, even if my registrar can't.'

The Prof gave Goldblatt a scornful glance. Then she looked back at her patient. Slowly, Mrs Constantidis realized that the Prof wasn't going to send her away after all. She gazed at the Prof gratefully, eyes wet with emotion and relief.

'Will you, Professor Small?' she asked in a tiny voice, scarcely believing in the miracle that had just taken place.

'Just see if I don't!' said the Prof.

The Prof got off the bed, paused only long enough to send a second withering glance in Goldblatt's direction, and marched off the ward with a vicious clattering of heels.

Goldblatt stared after her. Mrs Constantidis stared after her. Ludo, the HO, and Emma stared after her. Dr Morris stared after her. Sister Choy stared after her. The two medical students who had come on the round stared after her. The other three patients in the room, the lady who pushed the trolley with the newspapers, and the cleaner stared after her as well, even though none of them knew what they were staring at.

What they were staring at – or not staring at, since Professor Small had disappeared and they were actually staring at the empty space from which she had vanished – was a consultant walking off her own ward round. Simply walking off. Goldblatt had never seen it before. Neither had the lady who pushed the trolley with the newspapers. Neither had anyone else. And, apart from staring, no one knew what to do.

Goldblatt wondered whether they were meant to stay where they were until the Prof came back. He wondered if the Prof was ever going to come back. Who knew how long they might have stood there if the lady who pushed the trolley with the newspapers hadn't sighed, shaken her grey head, and started pushing her trolley again?

The cleaner dipped his mop in his pail and pressed hard on the pedal of the squeezer mechanism.

Dr Morris looked back at Mrs Constantidis. 'We'll try to get your echo-cardiogram done,' he said guardedly.

'Oh, it doesn't matter, doctor,' replied Mrs Constantidis. 'Really. I only live in Cricklewood. Like I told the little doctor, I don't mind coming back.'

Dr Morris smiled his mischievous smile. All at once there was a spring in his step. And he hadn't even moved.

'Right then,' he announced briskly to the others, 'let's keep going. Let's see how many of the patients we can get through before she gets back.'

They got through all the patients before she got back. Once the echoes of the Prof's footsteps faded away and they had recovered from their suspended animation, it turned into a quick, punchy, feisty round led with verve and gusto by Dr Morris at his clinical best. Once you let Dr Morris off his leash, his love of medicine took over, and there was no place for anything else in his sharp and inquisitive mind, not even the terrible prospect of the Prof's return. Instinctively, everyone joined in. They felt so carefree, so light. Even Ludo entered into the liberated spirit of the morning, trying her hand at a couple of wobbly answers when Dr Morris launched a Teaching Attack on peripheral neuropathies. Pretty soon it was hard to believe there had ever been a Prof. They were crazy, of course, unhinged by the sweet scent of freedom. The irrational elation of the doomed. As they were walking back towards the doctors' office, a certain familiar clattering of heels came towards them from around the corner.

The HO, who was pushing the notes trolley, stopped. Everyone stopped with her. Later Goldblatt wondered what would have happened if the HO had kept going. Would the Prof have turned and followed, running along-side the trolley as she berated them instead of dancing an ill-tempered little jig on the spot where she stopped to confront them? Like all the great questions in life – the size of the universe, the meaning of existence, the reason nerve fibres cross from one side to the other in the spinal cord – he would never know the answer. Because the HO, in fact, stopped.

'I don't know what you're all doing here,' the Prof shouted, without so much as a hello, 'if you can't even get a simple echocardiogram done on a patient!'

Goldblatt scrutinized the Prof carefully. Yes, she was mad. Absolutely insane. Whatever it was that had happened to her since she had marched proudly off the ward, it had driven her into a state of complete and certi-fiable lunacy.

'If I have to do everything myself, I don't know what's the point of having you all here!' she shrieked, stamping her feet in frustration.

'Are the cardiologists going to do the echocardiogram?' Emma asked brightly, thinking that she was throwing a Dorothy Dixer that would enable the great chief and leader to paint the glorious picture of her latest conquest.

Emma had just forfeited, with eight helpful words, all the credit she had built up by misinforming the Prof that all those filled-in Fuertler's files hadn't been filled in.

There had been no glorious conquest. There had been nothing but ignominious defeat. The Prof had just spent half an hour raving to an unimpressed cardiologist who, coolly glancing through the booking schedule, found an outpatient appointment next week for a non-urgent scan on a patient called Constantidis who lived four miles away in Crickle-wood with no known cardiac problems. He didn't see why he should turn his department upside down trying to slot this Constantidis in on his one remaining operational echocardiogram machine between the man with the failing heart transplant and the pregnant twenty-three-year-old with acute mitral regurgitation. And the Prof hadn't been able to make him see, no matter how many lies she told. He was wilfully blind. He had no guilt, either. Machines break down, he had said, shrugging with cardiological insolence. What can you do?

It had been a long journey back to the ward, and the Prof, who had almost decided not to make it, didn't need a Dorothy Dixer from some ersatz SR to remind her of the outcome of her joust in Cardiology.

The Prof impaled Emma with a venomous glance. 'They are going to try very hard,' she lied, and, before Emma could give her any more help, she grabbed Dr Morris by the arm and dragged him away.

Emma stood for a moment, glared at Goldblatt, and then went off to her office. Sister Choy slammed shut the nurses' communication book and stalked off, muttering something about consultants interfering with discharge plans. Only Goldblatt, Ludo, and the HO were left in the corridor.

The HO frowned. 'Shall I ring Cardiology and see what time they've booked her?'

Goldblatt shook his head.

'But she's going home today!'

'Correct,' said Goldblatt.

'Then what will I do?'

'If the cardiologists have a slot for her, they'll find her before she goes. If they don't have a slot, she'll come back next week as planned.'

The HO looked confused. 'But they might fit her in at the very end of the day! What if she's already gone?'

Suddenly Goldblatt felt very protective towards the HO. There was so much she still had to learn, so much to suffer. And then, having learned and suffered, she would be changed for ever.

'Clinical need,' said Goldblatt. 'Remember that? That's what matters. Forget what you saw here today. I mean, remember it, but only so you can forget it.'

The HO was watching Goldblatt intently, as if he were some kind of sage. It almost made him feel awkward. On the other hand, there was no doubt that the HO was extremely perspicacious for one so young, and probably knew a sage when she saw one. Who was he to doubt her judgement?

They walked back to the doctors' office.

'There was no clinical need to get that echo today,' he said. 'There was another need, but it wasn't clinical.' Goldblatt stopped and let the HO push the notes trolley into the office. He followed her in and drew up a decision tree on the whiteboard to illustrate the rationale. 'She goes home and comes back for the echo,' he concluded. 'Ignore the cosmetics and concentrate on the substance. Otherwise, you don't know what effects you're having. If she gets that echo today, she bumps someone else who needs it more.'

'The Broderip–Anderssen Principle?' said the HO.

Goldblatt looked at her in surprise. Obviously you had to be careful in front of the HO. Like many small people, she often remembered what you said.

'Exactly,' he replied.

Ludo laughed caustically. 'Don't you know where he got that principle—'

'Shut up, Ludo,' said Goldblatt.

Ludo looked hurt. Goldblatt thought that would please her.

He turned back to the HO. 'Send Mrs Constantidis home. If the cardiologists want to get her first, they can have her. Otherwise she comes back next week.'

Mrs Constantidis went home. The cardiologists didn't get her. They didn't try to get her. And the Prof did nothing else to make sure they would.

The Prof had no intention of doing anything else. The last thing she wanted was to prolong her involvement with Mrs Constantidis, who had probably never even needed a Fuertler's work-up in the first place. In fact, when the Prof came to think about it, she had only organized an admission for Mrs Constantidis because Mrs Constantidis had begged and begged in clinic, or at least agreed very readily when the Prof suggested that she should be admitted, and the whole affair had been very dubious from the start.

The whole affair had been even more dubious at the end. It hadn't turned out quite as the Prof had planned, or even remotely as she had planned, and the Prof had to admit that she herself was largely to blame for it. At the time, her spontaneous impulse to walk off the ward had seemed a stroke of inspiration that would put Goldblatt to shame, but it turned out to be a complete debacle, and the only way she could over-come its after-effects was to pretend that it wasn't, which just added to the humiliation because everyone knew that it was. As far as the Prof was concerned, the whole episode was distasteful and unpleasant and no one who was involved in it seemed to love her, except for Mrs Constantidis, and if the Prof was perfectly honest with herself – which she felt she probably had to be, given the circumstances – she had to admit that the only reason Mrs Constantidis loved her was because she had promised her something that she didn't deliver. By now it was very likely that Mrs Constantidis didn't love her at all. The sooner she forgot the whole unsavoury episode, the better.

Which is exactly what the Prof set out to do. When she got to her office, she shut the door in Dr Morris's face and locked him out. Then she turned and gazed at the Scale. It stood proud, upright, dependable. Immediately, the Prof felt calmer. Soon, she knew, the details of this nasty little event would be put out of her mind. The Prof had put many other nasty little events out of her mind in the past, and she didn't see why this one should be different. She closed her eyes, waiting for calmness to suffuse her.

But it didn't. Or wouldn't. Instead, she felt a slight wave of nausea. She opened her eyes. Now the Scale looked narrow, flimsy, and underfilled.

She had set out to teach Malcolm Goldblatt a lesson, but she felt that the opposite had occurred. He had taught her a lesson. Or at least she had taught one to herself, and somehow he had had a part in making her do it.

If anything, his insubordination was getting worse.

Not only that, she was starting to feel scared of him. Andrea Small had to admit, if she looked into her heart of hearts – which was always a difficult thing to do, whatever the circumstances – that Malcolm Goldblatt intimidated her.

What was she to do about the boy?

On the other side of the door that had been shut in his face, Dr Morris walked away in disbelief. The Prof had just staged the most divisive and destabilizing performance he had ever seen on a medical unit, and what had she done next? Locked herself away in her office and left him to pick up the pieces! Dr Morris had an awful premonition that this role was going to become more and more familiar, as were the tortuous conversations in which the Prof was now regularly embroiling him, leading him through the psychedelic pastiche of her professorial torments and intrigues.

He felt used and manipulated and resentful, but the pieces had to be picked up, and it was clear that the Prof had no intention of doing it.

He bleeped the team and had them meet in the cafeteria for a debrief over an early lunch. When they gathered he sent them off to buy sandwiches with strict orders to rendezvous at one of the unoccupied tables on the far side of the room. Once there, he sat at the head of the table as if he was the Father of the Unit, trying to patch things up after the silly tiff that everyone had just had with Mother and thus prove that they were one happy family once more. Unfortunately they had never been one happy family, or even an unhappy family, and Father Morris's plan was therefore doomed from the outset by the logical impossibility of imposing the restoration of a state of affairs that had never existed to begin with.

Not surprisingly, Father Morris was finding it difficult to start. It was one thing to get them all together as if he knew exactly what he was going to say. But he was just as shocked and demoralized at the Prof's performance as they were, and now that he was supposed to start talking he really didn't know if was going to be able to say anything that would sound as if he wasn't. He wished he was somewhere else, with some impossibly difficult patient, for instance, who suffered from ten obscure, life-threatening and undiagnosable diseases. Then, at least, he would have known what to do.

There was plenty of noise from the rest of the cafeteria, but at the table of the Small gang the only sounds were of concentrated chewing and swallowing. Between each bite of his sandwich, Dr Morris glanced around nervously, took a deep breath and cleared his throat, only to end up putting his sandwich back into his mouth. Unfortunately, as a prop, a sandwich has only a limited life, especially if you keep eating it. Everyone else's sandwiches were soon finished as well. Dr Morris's debrief was turning out to be very brief indeed, and was threatening to disappear into the same capacious void that had swallowed up the new echocardiogram appointment the Prof had promised to secure for Mrs Constantidis.

Dr Morris took another deep breath, cleared his throat, and made his mouth talk.

'Listen, I just want to say...' he began before frowning and stopping for a moment. Then he started again. 'Look, we're all in this together. Let's try to step back from what happened today and look at ourselves. We're a team, aren't we? Emma? Malcolm? That's how we work, like a team.' There was a wet and depressing doggedness in Dr Morris's voice, as if he knew – and he knew that they knew – that he was saying something that was completely at odds with reality, but there was nothing else he could think of to say. 'Come on!' he exhorted them beseechingly. 'We're a team!'

Faced with an almost pleading look on Dr Morris's face, Goldblatt nodded.

Dr Morris continued in his wet and dogged tone. Goldblatt glanced at Emma. She was staring at him. She looked away quickly. Her face began to flush.

Now Ludo was whining. 'But I filled them in! I had them all filled in and she didn't even care. All she cared about was that echo.'

'And that was the cardiologists' fault!' the HO added, with all the indignation she had bottled up when the Prof had turned on her. 'I went down there the day she arrived and booked it. They said they'd do it. Then they rang me up and said one of their machines was broken and they'd do it as an outpatient. It wasn't only Mrs Constantidis. They did it to Mr Galloway as well. And last week they did it to Mrs Patel. And to Mrs Golpher. And to—'

'All right!' said Dr Morris, who sensed that the big message was getting lost in a wealth of HO-ish detail. Besides, he knew that what had happened had very little, if anything, to do with Mrs Constantidis's cancelled echocardiogram. 'It's been a very unpleasant experience for everyone. Let's not dwell on the past. Let's see what we can do to make sure nothing like this happens again. If we can do that, we can make things a lot easier for ourselves. There are certain things the Prof wants done. She's the Prof and it's her unit. Whatever we might think of her and the way she does things and her abilities as a clinician—' He stopped himself. 'I mean, the point is, she's built this unit up, and we have to respect that. We have to respect the way she wants things done, and we have to make sure they get done in the way she wants. There's no way around that. Now, she wants the Fuertler's files to be filled in—'

'But they *were* filled in!' Ludo objected, injecting real passion into her whine.

'All right. She wants the work-up done on her patients—'

'But it *was* done!' snapped the HO. 'All except that echo, and it was all organized, and Mrs Constantidis was happy to go home and come back, and there wasn't—'

'All right! All right!' exclaimed Dr Morris in exasperation, covering his ears with his hands. He looked around for a moment. 'Listen, there's been a lot of stress for the Prof lately. And not just for the Prof. There have been a lot of changes recently on the unit, and they haven't been easy.'

'No, they haven't,' said Emma, her voice trembling.

Goldblatt looked at her. He hoped Emma wasn't going to start crying. He was going to be sick if she started crying.

'I know. It's been very difficult,' said Dr Morris with what seemed to be almost genuine sympathy.

Goldblatt thought he was going to be sick whatever happened.

'It's been... very hard,' said Emma.

'I know it has,' said Dr Morris.

Dr Morris did know. Emma had come crying to him a number of times – ostensibly about the way the unit was running, but mostly about Goldblatt – and he guessed these appearances were mere dress rehearsals compared with what she did in front of the Prof. The more he thought about it, the deeper seemed the divisions within the unit, and the more he wished that he could follow the Prof's example and lock himself in his room.

'It's been... awfully...' said Emma.

'I know,' said Dr Morris.

Goldblatt was going to pass out if this kept going.

'It's just...'

'I understand.'

'Yes,' said Goldblatt suddenly. 'It has been difficult.'

'Well,' said Dr Morris briskly, without any trace of the sympathy he had lavished on Emma, 'the point is, the Professor's been under a lot of strain recently. We have to recognize that. We have to recognize that this may have contributed to what happened today. So what I'm saying is that I want you all to understand it in that way and try to be sensitive to it.'

Dr Morris paused for a moment. No one said anything. Emma was gazing absently into the distance, lost in painful reflection on all the difficult changes that had taken place on the unit. Ludo and the HO were staring at the remains of their lunches on the table in front of them. They looked as if they were ashamed.

Goldblatt gazed at them. Of what? What had they done to be ashamed of? Not Ludo, but the HO, anyway.

'Let's just think beyond what each one of us is doing a little bit,' said Dr Morris. 'We're all working together, aren't we? No one's trying to make anyone look bad. No one's competing for anyone else's job. Malcolm's not competing for Emma's job. And Emma's not competing for Malcolm's job. Right?'

For a moment Goldblatt wondered about that. Was it even possible for someone to be competing for a job that was more junior than her own and from which she had just been promoted?

Dr Morris looked around the table earnestly. Suddenly he felt that he was really getting through to them. Maybe the idea of having this talk was going to pay off, after all. 'We just have to make sure we do the things the Prof expects,' he continued with a note of optimism creeping into his voice. 'All right? Let's do it, like a real team. We can do it, I know we can. Let's just do it and we won't have any repeats of today.'

'Excuse me.' Goldblatt pointed at the HO. 'Look at her.'

'What?' said the HO. She looked down in alarm to check the buttons on her blouse.

Dr Morris frowned. It had all been going so well, and it had been starting to sound so sensible, even to him.

'She's been a doctor for six weeks,' said Goldblatt. 'Six weeks, Dr Morris. And after six weeks, some professor subjects her to a personal attack in front of the patients she's supposed to be looking after. She didn't start with much self-esteem. Presuming it hasn't been totally destroyed, how's she going to go back to those patients with any credibility? And you're teaching her this is the way we treat each other? You're teaching her that when a consultant goes berserk, her job is to identify the trigger so she can find a way to prevent it happening again? What is she? The local slave?'

'Yes,' said the HO. 'What am I? I didn't start with much self-esteem. I've only been working for six weeks and—'

Goldblatt raised his hand. She stopped.

Dr Morris was staring at him. His mouth moved, groping towards articulation. But nothing came out of it.

'You're right, Dr Morris. The Prof's the Prof. And whatever we think of her, we have to respect that. It's her unit. She has the right to expect that certain things are done. And we have to do them. But she has to realize we can only work in the system we've got. This is the National Health Service, for Christ's sake. Shit happens. She knows that. And if she doesn't know it she ought to grow up and learn. She can't just take it out on the nearest person. In the end, what matters is the treatment her patients get. And *we* have the right to expect her to understand that.' Goldblatt smiled incredulously. 'She's under stress? We're all under stress. Look at Emma, for God's sake.'

Everyone looked.

'I have no intention of tiptoeing around because some professor can't control her urges,' Goldblatt muttered.

'That's putting it a bit strongly,' said Dr Morris.

'Look at her,' retorted Goldblatt, pointing at the HO again.

The HO gazed dolefully at Dr Morris with a hangdog look on her face. Her glasses slipped down her nose, and she let them teeter dangerously, too dejected to push them back up. The HO learned fast and was rapidly becoming a skilled and versatile accomplice. Her acting experience probably helped.

'I've only been a doctor for six weeks,' she said plaintively.

'All right,' said Dr Morris in exasperation. 'Just make sure everything gets done. Just get it done. And let's try not to let this happen again.'

'Everything'll get done, everything that can be' said Goldblatt grimly. He shook his head in contempt. 'That was abuse out there on the open ward. I've got a mind to put in a complaint against the Professor.'

Emma's mouth dropped in horror.

Goldblatt's bleep went off before he could say anything else. He got up and went to one of the phones on the cafeteria wall. Switchboard connected him with the husband of one of the Prof's patients who had rung to complain about his wife being cancelled.

Across the cafeteria, Emma was saying something to Dr Morris, shaking her head and frowning unhappily. Dr Morris nodded with an expression of forced sympathy. Or boredom.

Goldblatt watched them, still angry. After a moment he had to ask the husband on the phone to start his complaint again.

17

It was on the day after the Prof's performance with Mrs Constantidis that Dr Morris made good on his threat to play Goldblatt at squash. Goldblatt hadn't expected to hear anything more about the idea after Dr Morris's initial suggestion a few weeks earlier. When would he have the time? Dr Sutherland's unit was depositing clots and puddles of patients all over the hospital, and was already enjoying its third locum SR since the real SR had escaped to the US. Each locum seemed to be older, more weary, less knowledgeable, and to leave more quickly than the one before. And on any given day, just in case any spare time should craftily try to insert itself into Dr Morris's timetable, there were at least five fascinating patients waiting to be seen.

Thursday afternoons, as promised. Apparently there was a window of opportunity between the Immunology research meeting that ended at two o'clock on a Thursday and the Respiratory unit X-ray meeting that began at four. Strictly speaking, Dr Morris wasn't required to attend either meeting, but they were both too fascinating to miss. And it wasn't really a window between them. It was more of a wall, or perhaps a window that was bricked up with a million things Dr Morris had to do in those precious two hours, so many things that he had no chance of getting them finished anyway. He might just as well throw in a game of squash and get home an hour later than the hours-later that he normally got home. What difference would it make? He could still remember the gender and approximate ages of his two children, and he had never yet failed to identify them on sight. He had their pictures on his desk, and his wife supplied fresh ones every three months so he was always up to date. What could Goldblatt say? To refuse would be churlish.

One of the interesting aspects to all of this was that Dr Morris hardly knew how to play the game. And it wasn't just squash. He readily admitted that he had no formal training in badminton, tennis, racquetball, or any of the other racket sports that, he claimed, he also loved to play. He played every game with equal vigour, zest, and, he confided cheerfully to Goldblatt as they walked on to one of the two courts in the basement of the hospital, a complete lack of technical expertise.

'What I lack in technique I make up for in brute strength. That's what the North Wales badminton champion told me after he beat me in the Gwent regional heats,' he added in a very passable Welsh accent, closing the door of the squash court behind him.

'I don't suppose many people play badminton in Gwent?' mused Goldblatt.

'No,' said Dr Morris. 'Very few.'

Dr Morris also informed Goldblatt that he broke a lot of rackets. 'If I don't break a racket during a game of squash,' he remarked as he jumped from foot to foot in a strange ritual to limber up the ankle ligaments, 'I count myself lucky.'

'Must make it expensive,' observed Goldblatt.

'No. I don't play very much.' For some reason, Dr Morris was still talking in a Welsh accent. He had arrived dressed in blue shorts and a white T-shirt, and now, having prepared his ankles, he was doing bending exercises for his knees.

Goldblatt watched.

'It's the walls in squash, they're the tricky things,' Dr Morris remarked.

'Yes. Tennis is safer.'

'Oh, you'd be surprised.' As he methodically proceeded to loosen each of the major joints in his body, Dr Morris described to Goldblatt how he had once damaged his left kidney playing tennis. He had gone storming up the court to return a crucial, match-saving volley, which he reached at full stretch before spinning gloriously out of control and slamming his loin into the net post on the backhand side. The pain was severe, he was soon passing blood, and he knew that he had done himself some kind of urological injury. He got a nephrologist friend to meet him in the Ultrasound department at seven o'clock the next morning to do a scan before the department opened for business, and he had the result in his hand before he limped off for his morning ward round. Moderate haematoma at the upper pole of the left kidney. He took the scan home and waved it triumphantly in front of his wife, who was a general practitioner, six months pregnant, and who immediately forbade him to play any more dangerous sports. Dr Morris chuckled as he recounted the scene. Goldblatt understood. There's nothing more pleasing to a man than a moderate, fully reversible injury that shows up well on ultrasound and gives you the chance to display your stony fortitude in front of a fretting woman, even if it's only your wife. Dr Morris was soon plotting his next tennis match. Naturally, he also wrote his case up and sent it to a sports medicine journal, where it was published, together with an image of the ultrasound scan and a picture of the offending net post, under the title 'Urological trauma: an unusual tennis injury'.

'I'll get you a reprint if you like,' said Dr Morris.

'No thanks,' said Goldblatt. 'Did you win the point, at least?'

Dr Morris shook his head, grinning widely. 'Straight into the net.' He completed the last of his exercises, a painful-looking stretch of the shoulders. 'All right. Watch out, Malcolm!'

Dr Morris wasn't speaking metaphorically. On the second point, he chased a ball that Goldblatt had lobbed into the back corner. Pirouetting on his right foot, Dr Morris tried to return the ball by slamming it hard into the back wall. His racket slammed hard into the side wall, the ball ricocheted off the frame, hit the wall, and flew straight at his face. Dr Morris jerked his head away a split-second too late to avoid it and then, still pirouetting, went bouncing uncontrollably along the back wall until the opposite corner brought his escape to an abrupt halt.

Goldblatt walked over to the corner where Dr Morris had started his adventure, picked up the ball, and got ready to serve.

Not that Goldblatt himself was the world's greatest squash Meister, but he had played at university and could manage a decent game. After a while he tired of watching Dr Morris storm into the back corners of the court and hit himself in the chest, arms, abdomen, legs, and head as he failed to return the ball. He began to toy with him. He planted himself in the middle of the court and sent Dr Morris right and left, up and down the court around him, chasing balls that were placed so that, with a final lung-bursting lunge, Dr Morris might just get his racket to them. When he decided to end a rally because Dr Morris was about to keel over in respiratory distress, he lobbed one into the corner, ran for the front to avoid the helicopter-like rotation of Dr Morris's racket, and turned to watch the performance in the back court.

Goldblatt became aware of a sadistic pleasure and he surrendered to it unconditionally. He didn't know why. He hadn't the slightest ill feeling towards Dr Morris, not even after the grisly debrief in the cafeteria that Dr Morris had hosted the previous day. In fact, he liked him. He let Dr Morris win a few points so that he wouldn't lose heart altogether and stop running. Dr Morris staggered compliantly from side to side, gamely chasing the ball and growing more and more exhausted. By the third game he was tottering around the court in a semi-comatose state with a face the colour of a ripe tomato. His breathing was louder than anything Goldblatt had heard since the six months he had spent as an SHO on a ward full of patients with emphysema.

Suddenly, Goldblatt had a terrible premonition. Dr Morris was going to die. A major artery was going to rupture behind his eyes and he was going to die right there on the court, and tomorrow morning the Prof was going to be the only consultant left alive on the unit.

Goldblatt glanced over his shoulder as he was about to serve. Dr Morris's face was a stomach-churning patchwork of congestion. The areas around his eyes were as dark as liver, and his bulging eyeballs were fixed on the front wall with a frightening intensity. He was clutching his racket so hard that his arm was trembling. His thin white legs looked flimsy and unreliable.

'Are you all right?' Goldblatt asked.

No answer. The court echoed to the sound of Dr Morris's stertorous breathing.

'Are you all right?' he shouted.

Dr Morris still didn't look at him. But he must have sensed that Goldblatt was talking to him when the ball failed to appear against the front wall out of the edge of his field of vision.

'Can't think. Too tired. Just play.'

Dr Morris's voice had a sinister staccato quality that reminded

Goldblatt of people who have had cerebellar haemorrhages. Perhaps one of his arteries had already burst. Goldblatt couldn't help thinking that Dr Morris's death on the squash court would cut short a fine career and would be a great tragedy for Dr Morris, his wife, and his two young children, but it would be an even greater tragedy for himself, Ludo, and the HO, who would be left behind without any protection at all from the convulsive whims of Emma and the Prof.

'Come on. Serve,' came Dr Morris's robotic, staccato voice.

Goldblatt served. Don't die, Dr Morris, he thought as he hit the ball. Please don't die.

Goldblatt's sadistic pleasure had turned into masochistic dread. He ended the game in two minutes with a series of mercifully brutal shots that didn't give Dr Morris a chance. Dr Morris collapsed. Goldblatt sat down against one of the side walls, watching him warily and getting ready to spring into action if he stopped breathing. Dr Morris lay flat on his back, staring at the roof, and his chest went up and down like a bellows.

Eventually he turned over and started to crawl. He dragged himself towards Goldblatt and propped himself up beside him.

'All right?' said Goldblatt.

Dr Morris forced a smile on to the death mask that had replaced his face. 'Just need to get a bit fitter.'

'You looked like you were going to die out there. You would have left us all alone with the Professor.'

Dr Morris smiled wanly. 'Why do you think I was playing so hard?'

The lights in the court went out. They sat in the sunlight that filtered down from the windows in the gallery behind the court, like the half-light in a cathedral.

It was a strangely peaceful, contemplative atmosphere.

'You wouldn't really put in a complaint against Andrea,' said Dr Morris after a while, unceremoniously rending the tranquillity.

Goldblatt turned to look at him. 'Against who?'

'Professor Small. Remember? You said yesterday that you might.'

'Is it worth the bother?' asked Goldblatt.

'No,' said Dr Morris.

'You're not saying that just to stop me, are you?'

'No,' said Dr Morris. 'It isn't worth the bother. And it won't help you, you know. You're already in enough trouble with her.'

Goldblatt nodded. He thought about what he had said yesterday when the Prof was attacking the HO. The words had just come out of his mouth. That worried him. Actually, it scared him. He hadn't dared mention the episode to Lesley. He knew that sometimes he reached a point where he just didn't care any more, and then there was no knowing what he would do. It had happened in the past. He didn't want to reach that point on the Prof's unit. He couldn't afford to.

But he had the feeling that he had been in trouble with the Prof even before he had opened his mouth yesterday. He even had the feeling that her incomprehensible fandango on the round had been aimed in some obscure, indecipherable way at him.

'You just have to do what she wants,' said Dr Morris.

'I know that.'

'It's not that hard.'

'I thought that's what I was doing.'

The sounds of a game starting up came from the court next door. No one arrived to kick them off their court. They continued to sit in the half-light.

'I just can't stand the crap,' muttered Goldblatt reflectively. There was something about the half-light, the stillness, and the sound of the game next door – not to mention Dr Morris's near-death experience – that induced an almost confessional feeling.

Dr Morris looked up from his racket, which he had been examining for cracks.

Goldblatt glanced at him and shrugged. 'That's why I do things like that, I suppose. Like yesterday. I can't stand all the crap. I just want them to leave me alone so I can get on with the medicine.'

From next door came the *thwack* of the ball being hit.

'What are you doing here, Malcolm?' asked Dr Morris suddenly.

Goldblatt hesitated. He was always suspicious of questions with big existential overtones. 'Watching you recover from one hell of a beating?' he replied guardedly.

Dr Morris smiled. 'No. I mean on Andrea's unit. What are you doing in a locum job?'

'It was available. What happened to the old SR, anyway?'

'She left.'

'Why?'

Dr Morris hesitated. 'Differences with the Prof.'

'Such as?'

'Let's just say that certain expectations weren't fulfilled.'

'On whose side? On the Prof's or—'

'Look, Malcolm, that doesn't matter. Let's come back to you.'

Goldblatt didn't want to come back to him, but Dr Morris did.

'You're obviously a good doctor, you can certainly run a ward. There's no doubt you're SR level. That's the problem with Emma. Why can't you be a bit more patient with her?'

Goldblatt sighed.

'All right,' said Dr Morris. 'All right. But I still don't understand what you're doing in a locum job. You're too good for that.'

'Have you seen my CV?'

'I saw it when Andrea appointed you. Are you looking for an SR job?'

No. He wasn't looking for an SR job. He was hoping that, for the first time since the Big Bang sent matter flying into eternity across the starry spaces of the universe, time would stand still and he could be a locum registrar on Professor Small's Fuertler's unit for ever, or until he died, whichever was the later.

'Yes,' he said. 'I'm looking for an SR job.'

'Any around?'

'A couple.'

'Any good?'

'One is.'

'You're bound to get it,' said Dr Morris. 'You'd have a good chance at any job.'

Goldblatt wasn't sure if Dr Morris was putting on such an optimistic front for his benefit or if he really thought the world worked as simply as that.

'Where is this job?'

'The Nailwright,' said Goldblatt reluctantly. It was very tedious of Dr Morris to start talking about such depressing matters just when he was savouring the unsullied completeness of his victory on the squash court. Goldblatt was starting to wish that he had made him run just that little bit harder so that an artery of some kind really would have burst behind his eyes.

'I trained at the Nailwright,' said Dr Morris, as if that made any difference to Goldblatt or his prospects.

'I know.'

'Who's the job with?'

'Mike Coalport.'

'Mike Coalport? I was a registrar on Mike Coalport's unit!'

'I've heard,' said Goldblatt.

'Why didn't you tell me? It's a very good unit. You'll do very well there, Malcolm. Have they shortlisted?'

'Yes.'

'And?'

Goldblatt nodded.

'Excellent!' said Dr Morris. 'When's the interview?'

'Four weeks.'

'Have you been for the pre-interview?'

'Not yet.'

'Mike will want to get to know you. He always likes to see people before the interview.'

'I'm seeing him about a week before.'

'Good,' said Dr Morris enthusiastically. 'Well, this is excellent! I'll ring Mike and have a word with him.'

'That would be very kind,' said Goldblatt wearily. He couldn't be bothered explaining the futility of it to Dr Morris.

'I'm sure you'll get it.'

'No you aren't,' said Goldblatt.

Dr Morris looked surprised. 'Yes I am.'

'How can you be *sure*?'

'Well, I can't be absolutely sure.'

'I am,' said Goldblatt.

'What?'

'Sure.'

'That you'll get it?'

'No. That I won't.'

'Don't say that. I'm sure you will.'

Goldblatt looked at Dr Morris. Maybe he really did see the world in such simple terms. He was a dedicated, good-hearted man who mistakenly thought he had the time to play games of squash that were likely to kill him. He probably believed in the perfectibility of human nature.

'I won't get the job at the Nailwright,' said Goldblatt.

'Don't be so pessimistic. You'll never get the job if you go in there thinking you don't have a chance.'

'Look, I know I won't. I'm one of the Wise Men.'

'On the other hand, no one likes an arrogant candidate.'

Goldblatt shook his head. 'No. I'm one of the *Wise Men*. Don't you understand what that means?'

Dr Morris frowned.

Goldblatt sighed. Sometimes you had to explain everything. 'You know the story of the Three Wise Men?'

'Of course I know the story of the Three Wise Men.'

'And all those pictures with the Three Wise Men hovering in the back-ground, with the cats and the dogs...'

'The donkey and the ox.'

'And the gold and houndstooth and lambswool, or whatever it was they were bringing.'

'Gold, incense, and myrrh,' said Dr Morris, who had been to Sunday school.

'What are they there for?' asked Goldblatt.

Dr Morris looked at him suspiciously. 'What do you mean, what are they there for? They were there.'

'I'm sorry. I didn't realize you were a literal believer. I hope I haven't offended you.'

'I'm not a literal believer,' said Dr Morris, sounding as if he might really start getting offended if Goldblatt went around repeating slurs like that.

'What about your wife?'

'No.'

'Your kids?'

'What are you talking about, Malcolm?'

'All right, all right. So you're not a literal believer. I believe you, literally. So tell me, what are the Three Wise Men there for?'

Dr Morris frowned.

He obviously needed a push in the right direction. 'If we assume,' said Goldblatt, 'that they were never there historically, why are they there in legend?'

'Wait a minute!' said Dr Morris. 'You're saying they weren't really there?'

'Where?'

'In the stable.'

'You think there was a stable?'

Dr Morris stared. 'You're saying there wasn't a stable?' he whispered.

'I don't know. Maybe there was a stable. Maybe there wasn't. Children must have been born in stables occasionally. What I'm saying is, let's say it isn't all absolutely historical. The Three Wise Men part, for instance. Forget the stable, let's just look at that bit. Say it isn't historical. Say it's an embellishment. Say – odd as this might sound – that there weren't actually three kings who just happened to be wandering around the Judaean desert one December night – which, by the way, can get bloody cold in the middle of winter – looking for somewhere to offload their gifts. In which case, why would someone put them there? Why would they add them to the story?'

Dr Morris thought. He stared into the strings of his racket, as if the answer might be threaded subtly into the strands like the numbers worked into an Ishihara colour blindness chart.

'Well, they're there to... worship Jesus,' he said at last, looking up at Goldblatt.

'Right,' said Goldblatt. 'But why does Jesus need to be worshipped by Three Wise Men?'

Dr Morris hesitated for a long time, trying to guess what Goldblatt was thinking. 'Jesus doesn't need to be worshipped, does he?' he ventured.

'Very good,' said Goldblatt, who was genuinely pleased with the rapid progress Dr Morris was making. 'Jesus doesn't need to be worshipped.

He's Jesus. If he's divine, he'll be divine whether there are three kings or three beggars or nobody at all to worship him.'

Dr Morris nodded.

'But...'

'But we need to see him being worshipped!' exclaimed Dr Morris excitedly. A smile came over his face, and he shook his head in amazement.

Goldblatt watched him. It would never have occurred to Goldblatt that Dr Morris would get such a kick out of biblical exegesis.

'Why do you say you're one of the Three Wise Men?' asked Dr Morris.

'Why am I one of the Three Wise Men?' Goldblatt sighed. It was a long story.

'Why? I still don't get it.'

Goldblatt sighed again. Dr Morris was an intelligent man, but today he really needed everything spelled out for him. Maybe it was brain hypoxia. Lack of oxygen during the squash game had probably cost him a few choice neurons.

'All right,' said Goldblatt. 'Think of an interview. How many candidates do you have?'

Dr Morris shrugged. 'Three or four. Five, six. It depends.'

'Optimally, how many would you have?'

'Four,' replied Dr Morris.

'Exactly,' said Goldblatt. 'Why?'

'It gives you enough good candidates. If you interview more than four you're probably including people who aren't really up to the job anyway. You're just wasting your time.'

'And if you've already decided who's going to get the job?'

'Four makes it look all right. It makes it look as if you really tried to find the best—' Dr Morris stopped, eyes startled at what he had just heard himself say.

Goldblatt nodded. It was sad, he thought, that it had come out so easily. But Dr Morris wasn't to blame. There was never any point in shooting the messenger. It came out so easily because it was true.

'You need Three Wise Men in the background so the fourth can be seen to be the chosen one,' said Goldblatt.

'No, Malcolm.'

Goldblatt shrugged. 'You said it yourself. Look, I'm a very good Wise Man, Dr Morris. I've had lots of experience.'

Dr Morris shook his head. 'No. I'm sure you'll get the job at the Nailwright.'

'No. Wise Man. I can feel it. Wise Man again.'

Dr Morris gazed at him. He wouldn't know what it was like, thought Goldblatt. He would never in his whole life have been a Wise Man. He would always have been the chosen one, the one to be exalted.

'Have another look at my CV,' said Goldblatt.

'I'll talk to Mike Coalport,' said Dr Morris.

'That would be kind,' said Goldblatt tonelessly.

It was no idle boast. Goldblatt was a very good Wise Man. And he did have lots of experience. He had hovered in the background as a Wise Man at interviews at which some very fine physicians had got jobs. Some of those physicians had been so fine that it was almost an honour to have been selected to hover at their interviews. He had also hovered at interviews at which some not so fine physicians had got jobs. That was less of an honour. A less sophisticated mind might have perceived it as an injustice. But not Goldblatt. He was wise enough to realize that this was simply one of the things that happened to Wise Men. It wasn't all brandy and cigars. You were there to do a job, just like a bodyguard or publicist. Made no difference if you didn't like the star. You still had to do it. No point getting angry about it, and even less sense in trying to change it. It was an inherent drawback of the Wisdom profession, and as a Wise Man you simply had to come to terms with it.

But there was one thing that really did confuse him. How had he become a Wise Man in the first place?

That was something he definitely wanted to know, and he would have offered a substantial sum to anyone who could have given him a convincing account of the process. He couldn't remember having chosen to do it. Excluding the possibility that he had been drugged, kidnapped, driven to a deserted country house, and forced to volunteer for the job by cowled men under the flicker of tallow candles – which he was then unable to remember on awakening the following morning and finding himself back in his flat – there was only one possible explanation. Someone must have decided for him. But who?

Was it one person or was it many? Was there some body of Eminent Physicians who met secretly to nominate Wise Men? Was this body split into councils for the different specialities, like the Royal College of Physicians? Did they wear velvet robes and plumed berets when they deliberated? Goldblatt would have liked to meet these people. These were only some of the questions he would have asked them, and he would certainly have listened to the answers with attentiveness and tact, willingly signing any secrecy clause they put in front of him.

He wasn't the only Wise Man, that was one thing of which he was sure. He had seen others, hovering along with him in the background, but he had never spoken to them of their Wisdom. Maybe some of them weren't yet aware that they were Wise Men. Goldblatt himself had only become aware of it recently, but in retrospect he realized that he had been hovering in the background for over two years. He had become a Wise Man long before he understood that the transformation had taken place. Now that he understood this, statements and events that might once have seemed perfectly innocent took on a whole new meaning. The Wise Men and the Eminent Physicians were the two halves of an enormous, silent, and at least partially self-oblivious network that concatenated like the branching fibres of an unsuspected nervous system deep into every tissue and fibre of the body medical, determining the contraction of every one of its sinews and the movements of each of its joints, while the consciousness of the body itself, even as it moved in the direction secretly chosen for it, remained entirely ignorant of its operations. And he, Malcolm Goldblatt, at some undefined point in the past, had been inducted into it.

But if he had to be part of it, why did he have to be a Wise Man? Why couldn't they have waited a few years and inducted him as an Eminent Physician instead?

Recently, an even more horrible question had taken root in Goldblatt's mind. What would happen when his usefulness as a Wise Man was at an end? You could probably be an Eminent Physician until the day you died, but you couldn't remain a Wise Man for ever. You couldn't turn up at fifty and still be a convincing Wise Man while some lucky thirty-year-old got the job you had applied for. It just wouldn't look right. How did you get out of it? Assuming, unlikely as it might seem, that you wanted to resign your commission, to whom did you return it?

Obviously, he didn't mention any of this to Dr Morris when they were sitting on the squash court. Unless you had thought about it carefully and had weighed the overwhelming evidence, it would sound like a conspiracy theory, and Goldblatt, for one, detested conspiracy theories and found them entirely unconvincing. Besides, how did he know that Dr Morris wasn't part of the plot?

The manner and haste with which Dr Morris denied understanding what Goldblatt meant when he said he was a Wise Man was very suspicious. But even if he refused to acknowledge Goldblatt's role as a Wise Man, Dr Morris wouldn't be able to deny that Goldblatt had a problem. Fundamentally, it was a problem of imbalance, and one look at his CV was sufficient to reveal it. Goldblatt lacked some things that he needed, and he possessed other things that he ought not to have had at all.

Lesley laughed about it. Sometimes she cried about it.

'Only in medicine,' Lesley would say, with a depth of bitterness in her voice that Goldblatt found very moving. 'Only in medicine could they prefer those snotnoses to you.'

Goldblatt would have agreed, except it went against professional etiquette to refer to your colleagues as snotnoses, even if they had just beaten you at an interview, and it was a cardinal law of the profession that you never broke ranks in front of an outsider, even if you were having intercourse with her at the time.

'I can't believe they preferred that snotnose to you,' she would say after the latest Wise Man episode, 'just because he has a research degree.'

This was the thing that was most lacking in Goldblatt's CV. He had the right academic achievements, the right hospitals, the right experience. But he didn't have a research degree.

A research degree, either an MD or PhD, required you to interrupt your clinical training for two or three years, and people usually did it after they had passed their second part exam and done a year or two as a registrar and had acquired a patron who would help them get a place in a laboratory and then an SR job afterwards. It made perfect sense if you were one of the tiny minority who planned to combine a research career with clinical work, but for everyone else who had no intention of doing that, no one pretended that it made any difference to their ability to treat patients or to manage and develop junior staff, which were the two roles they would actually have to perform. Nonetheless, ninety-nine times out of a hundred, you had to have a research degree if you were going to get a job as a hospital consultant.

Goldblatt understood the situation. So it might have been supposed that he would have bowed to the inevitable, spent his two years in the lab, done his MD, and got it over with, like everybody else.

Malcolm Goldblatt? Bow to the inevitable? Like everybody else?

Nothing appealed to him less than the thought of incarcerating himself in a lab and burrowing blindly around some remote outpost of science to get results that might or might not make a difference to a tiny minority of the population in about thirty years' time. It wasn't what he had signed up for. He simply wasn't cut out for it.

But that was only half of Goldblatt's problem. It wasn't just what was missing that unbalanced his CV, it was what was there in its place.

'I can't believe they preferred that snotnose to you!' Lesley would say after the latest Wise Man episode. 'Don't they give a toss about everything else you've done?'

No, they didn't give a toss. In fact, it worked the other way around. The other things he had done were a stain on his character. And the biggest stain of all was the fact that he had left medicine to do a law degree.

This was one thing Lesley could never understand. Goldblatt didn't understand it either, but he had given up trying. It was just a fact. The profession regarded him with suspicion. He had been outside the fold. It was as if he had lapsed in some way, and even though he had returned, he couldn't be entirely trusted. Who knew what things he had seen when he had been on the outside? Who knew what contamination he had brought back with him? Who knew when he would lapse again?

He did the law degree after his second year as an SHO. He had just passed the second part exam and was poised, like his peers, to get a regis-trar job and go on with his specialist training. But unlike his peers, and against the strident advice of a number of consultants who warned him of the risks he ran if he ever tried to come back to medicine, he went off to do a law degree. Why? He had told himself many things at the time. He had told himself that he wanted a profession that would enable him to act more independently, a profession that would give him a greater intellectual challenge. He had told himself that he wanted to earn vast and unimaginable riches representing clients of dubious morals and unfathomable finances. He had told himself that his razor-sharp mind, his instinctive understanding of the human psyche, his victory in the school debating competition in the sixth form, and his collection of crime fiction all pointed clearly in one direction.

Which of these things were true, which delusion? Even now, he wasn't sure. Maybe he was just restless. Maybe it was just one of those phases in life.

He enjoyed doing it. He finished the degree and arranged a pupil-lage. Then he inexplicably deferred his pupillage and went to work on a six-month contract for Free from Bondage, a non-governmental organ-ization that campaigned against child slavery. Not that he necessarily believed that he had a self-destructive streak in his character, but if, for sake of argument, you wanted to build the case that he did have one – as Lesley had on occasion – this was as prime a piece of evidence as you could ask for. Free from Bondage, and its temporary, scantily funded job, took him about as far as you could get from the vast and unimaginable riches that supposedly were the reason he had done law in the first place. It was a tiny, newly established shoestring organization, and he was the legal department. He prepared their first ever submission to the UN Subcom-mittee on Slavery, and represented them at a conference in Manila. And then the six months were up and the grant that had funded him ran out. He would have stayed longer, but he couldn't. So he left. But something had happened inside his head. Maybe he doubted both the lies and the truths that he had told himself when he had started his legal odyssey. Or maybe he had just got over that phase in his life, if that's what it had been. Either way, he didn't take up his pupillage.

Lesley warned him. They had been together for only a year at that stage, but that didn't stop her. Not in so many words, but she warned him.

'Of course, if that's what you want, Malcolm,' she said, looking deep into his eyes. And then she shook her head.

It was the shake of her head that said it, more than any of the words she uttered. 'Don't do it, Malcolm,' said the shaking of her head. 'Don't do it to yourself.'

But Malcolm did it. He found himself a registrar job in a district hospital on the outskirts of London, which was mediocre enough to want him after he had been three years outside the fold – which gives some idea of how mediocre it must have been – and went back to medicine.

Over the next three years he worked himself back into the golden circle of London teaching hospitals, one reg job after another. But when he reached the point of progressing to SR, the jobs just slipped through his hands. He had been to a whole chain of interviews but was a Wise Man every time. One interview after the next. Always shortlisted, never appointed. The imbalance on his CV was killing him.

It made Lesley mad with frustration as she saw him become a Wise Man while the jobs went to snotnoses who had dutifully done their under-graduate training and their hospital jobs and their MDs and had never so much as taken a look at the world outside a hospital since they had arrived at medical school. Goldblatt was starting to feel guilty that he had ever dragged her into this horrible, impossible world of his. Perhaps she would have been happier if he had never asked her out for that first fateful drink. She was successful, she was sought after. As far as he could tell, her world was a cloud floating high above the realities of life, where the days – and many of the nights – passed in the prosecution of complex commercial cases involving the vast and unimaginable riches of which he had dreamed. Why did Lesley want to keep mixing herself up in the messy world of an unwanted hospital registrar?

'They're like Stalin,' she said.

'That may be taking it a bit far,' cautioned Goldblatt.

'It isn't. They're like Stalin. Once you've seen the outside world you can't be trusted.'

'Do you think they'll shoot me?' asked Goldblatt, who had read *Darkness at Noon*.

'Don't joke about this,' said Lesley. 'Joke about anything else, but not this.'

Goldblatt didn't see why he shouldn't. This was his joke. More than that, he was the joke. He couldn't see how you could reasonably be prevented from joking about it when, in fact, you were it.

'That bastard Oakley!' she said. 'He was the one. He killed you, Malcolm.'

Goldblatt didn't reply. Oakley hadn't necessarily been a bastard. Just weak, indecisive, cowardly, vengeful... all right, a bastard.

'And Rothman! He wasn't any better.'

Not much. But he told better jokes.

'How can you keep getting knocked back for these snotnoses?' she demanded in anguish. 'How can everything else you've done get constantly disregarded?'

'It's not having an MD,' he would say, almost feeling as if he was defending them.

'What about all the other experience you have?'

'True. That's another problem.'

'No!' she would cry. 'Only in medicine. Only in medicine would that be a problem! Anywhere else they'd value your experience. They'd say you're well rounded.'

'They say I'm not committed.'

'You came back. What more do they want? Do they want you to spill your guts?'

Possibly, thought Goldblatt.

'God damn them!' she'd say, and she'd mean it.

God damn them, Goldblatt thought. And he'd mean it as well. God damn them. God damn them to hell.

'Malcolm, how long are you going to keep doing this to yourself?'

When she got to that point, Goldblatt would shake his head helplessly. He didn't have a reply. He hardly knew why he had left medicine in the first place, all those years before, much less why he had come back to it.

He didn't know. He really didn't. Perhaps he had known once. He must have. He tried to remember the reasons. And that's when the old Jewish lady, who had come to him as a patient in one of his clinics, would spring to mind.

18

MR LISTER, THE MAN with a PUO whom Dr Morris had admitted with his tragically brilliant sleight of hand, had been on the ward for two weeks and still there was no end in sight to his stay. He was turning out to be one of those patients who transform themselves subtly but steadily into a fixture.

In principle, Goldblatt had nothing against fixtures, especially of the non-patient variety. All wards have them, mostly bolted to the wall. They don't say much. Or anything. But not Mr Lister. He spoke. A lot. He was sarcastic, dissatisfied, and unpleasant, and he brought to all of these qualities a complete absence of wit, which made him tedious as well. Every day he demanded to know when he was going home. An hour after every test he demanded to know the result. If he hadn't seen Dr Morris for twenty-four hours, he demanded to know when he was coming. In short, when he wasn't struck dumb with trepidation at the pain of a needle penetrating his epidermis for one of the thousands of tests that Dr Morris was running, he was a pain in the arse.

You didn't have to be Sigmund Freud to understand what was going on. Mr Lister was frightened. Underlying the anger and the demands, Goldblatt knew, behind the complaints every time a test was delayed, and the dissatisfaction each time a result was awaited, was fear of what all those tests might show. That was why he stayed, despite his almost daily threat to go home, as they put him through every test – biochemical, histopathological, haematological, microbiological, serological, radiological, and nuclearmedical – that Dr Morris could think of, and as Dr Morris began to procrastinate, asking for previous tests to be repeated and discovering new tests in journals which no one in the hospital laboratories even knew how to perform.

Goldblatt tried to make allowances for him. He told himself that the sheer horribleness of Mr Lister was merely the way his fear expressed itself, as in another patient it might express itself through obsessiveness, bravado, or denial. But as you approached his bed and got ready for the next barrage to hit you, you couldn't help wondering, if there were so many other ways for fear to manifest itself, why Mr Lister's fear had to adopt this one. Even though you knew it was his anxiety talking, and you knew that you couldn't let yourself be influenced by whether you liked someone or not, and you could attempt to make yourself feel sympathy for him, and sit by his bed and try to reassure him, and hold your tongue when you found yourself on the verge of saying what you really thought of him, he was still Mr Lister, he always had a complaint, and nobody found it easy to treat him.

Yet the HO could handle that. Mr Lister's irritability, sarcasm, and complaints didn't get under her skin. It was an altogether gentler, more pleasant patient who did, a Polish gentleman in his late seventies called Mr Sprczrensky. And he did it in a completely different way, out of the blue, on a Thursday morning.

Thursday mornings, when Goldblatt was in clinic, were Ludo's big chance to have her own round and play the starring supervisory role for which she had fought so hard and lied so shamelessly. In theory, Goldblatt would then come up in the afternoon after his clinic and run quickly through the names with the HO in the doctors' office to make sure everything was all right. But many perfectly sound theories break down in practice, and Ludo, for reasons of her own that she rarely saw fit to disclose, often missed her round. As she did on that particular Thursday morning.

The HO was therefore going happily around by herself, chatting with the patients, failing to recognize various warning signs and abnormalities, or recognizing normalities and thinking that they were warning signs, which is the way of HOs. Mr Lister's temperature had started its morning rise, and the HO stopped by just in time to see it top thirty-nine degrees and remind herself to add the day's attainment to the running charts she had started making of his fevers. On Dr Morris's suggestion, she was plotting the spikes of fever on a grid against the investigation results that were now regularly flooding back from the hospital's laboratories, in the straw-clutching hope that this cabbalistic exercise would reveal a hitherto hidden pattern and unpick the lock to Mr Lister's mystical illness. Then the HO moved on to the next bed, which housed Mr Sprczrensky.

No one on the ward could pronounce Mr Sprczrensky's name properly and they all called him Mr Sprensky. He didn't mind. Everyone called him Mr Sprensky, he said. He had white hair, pale blue eyes, a quiet, reserved manner, and he had fought at Monte Cassino. Apart from having a name unpronounceable by Anglo-Saxons – which can be either a handicap or an advantage, depending on your point of view – Mr Sprczrensky had only one problem, a case of moderate Fuertler's that manifested as skin lesions on his back and occasional pain in his hands and feet. He was an elective admission for the six-monthly work-up that was routine in every way, including the two cancellations that had preceded it and the fact that eleven months had passed since the last sixth-monthly admission. It went without saying that he was getting a Sorain infusion. Mr Sprczrensky had been very polite and considered when asked whether he thought Sorain had helped in the past. He couldn't say for sure that it had, but he couldn't say for sure that it hadn't. Except when he had seen the Prof on her round the previous day, when it had.

When the HO arrived to see him, Mr Sprczrensky was sitting in the chair beside his bed and a nurse had just connected the infusion pump to the cannula in his arm.

The fluid was stinging. The drip was in his right wrist. He held out his right arm, rolled back his sleeve, and rested his wrist on the edge of his bed so the HO could look at it. The skin at the puncture site around the top of the cannula was reddened.

'Does that hurt?' asked the HO, pressing the skin gingerly.

Mr Sprczrensky winced. 'A little.'

'Turn your hand over, Mr Sprensky,' requested the HO, peering at Mr Sprczrensky's wrist and trying to see how far the redness went.

Nothing happened.

The HO looked up. 'Would you mind turning your hand over, please?'

'I can't, doctor,' said Mr Sprczrensky.

'What do you mean?'

'It won't move, doctor.'

'But you moved it a second ago. I saw you.'

'I'm sorry, doctor. It won't move now.'

The HO stared at him. Mr Sprczrensky wasn't the type to play games. If this was a game, it was a silly one. 'Turn your hand over, Mr Sprensky.'

'I can't.'

The HO put two fingers into the palm of Mr Sprczrensky's right hand. 'Squeeze my fingers.'

Mr Sprczrensky's fingers didn't move.

'Squeeze please.'

'I'm trying, doctor.'

The HO whipped her fingers away from Mr Sprczrensky's hand as if it was red hot. 'Lift your arm up!' she shouted.

Mr Sprczrensky lifted his left arm up.

'Not that one. The other one!'

The muscles in Mr Sprczrensky's neck tugged. Nothing else moved.

The HO spun around to turn off the infusion pump. Panicking, she couldn't find the switch. She jerked on the cable and yanked the plug out of the wall.

An alarm beeped.

'Doctor?' said Mr Sprczrensky.

'What?'

'Doctor, what's happening? I don't feel so good.'

The HO froze, staring at Mr Sprczrensky, breathing heavily. 'I don't know,' she said, and ran away to find out.

When his bleep went off, Goldblatt was explaining the finer points of using a soft collar to an old lady in clinic. Soft collars are big pieces of wrap-around sponge with a notch for the wearer's chin. These complicated pieces of equipment can be worn in many ways – back to front, for instance, or upside down – and the old lady, who was using it for arthritis of the neck, had managed all of them. 'So when you go to put the collar on,' Goldblatt was saying to the old lady when he heard his bleep go off, 'remember, first of all place it on your neck with the Velcro strips at the *back*...'

He looked down at his pocket, recognized the number that had flashed up on his bleep as one of the ward phones, and ignored it. He had already

been up on the ward in the morning to sort out the admissions and cancellations with Debbie and draw lines through the names in the Book of Time.
There was only one way to teach nurses to collect their queries into one
big bunch, he thought irritably, instead of ringing him every time one of
them wanted to check something.

'At the back, doctor?' said the old lady.

'Yes, and then you do it up after that.'

'Tightly, doctor?'

'Not too tight. We want you to breathe.'

'Ooh, doctor. You are a one!'

Goldblatt smiled modestly. His bleep went off again. He checked the
number. This time it was the other ward phone. He sighed.

'Excuse me,' he said, and dialled the ward.

Someone picked up the phone before the first ring had finished. 'Hello!'

'Yes. This is Mal—'

'Malcolm! We've paralysed Mr Sprensky!'

'We've what?' said Goldblatt, recognizing the HO's voice.

'We've paralysed him! The Sorain's done it!'

Goldblatt frowned. The old lady was examining her collar intently.

'What are you talking about?' he asked.

'Mr Sprensky's paralysed.'

'When?'

'Now! He's paralysed now. Right in front of me. One minute he could
move, and now he can't.'

'Wait a minute. Hold on. Where's Ludo? Has she seen him?'

'Ludo?' retorted the HO sarcastically.

'She's supposed to be with you.'

'Ludo?' demanded the HO. 'When was the last time Ludo was around
when someone actually needed her? When was the last time Ludo—'

'All right. Tell me about Mr Sprensky. Quick. Is he conscious?'

'Yes.'

'Is he speaking?'

'Yes.'

'What part of him is paralysed?'

The old lady looked up sharply.

'His arm, Malcolm.'

'You mean his— Wait a minute. I'll call you back.'

'When?'

'Now.'

'Malcolm!'

'Put the phone down. I'll call you back.'

Goldblatt hung up. He told the old lady to practise with the soft collar and said he'd be back in a minute. Then he went into an empty clinic room down the corridor and rang the HO again.

'Malcolm!'

'What's going on?'

'Mr Sprensky's arm's paralysed, Malcolm. The nurses turned the Sorain on and five minutes later it was paralysed.'

'And you think the Sorain paralysed it?'

There was a silence on the phone. 'Didn't it?'

'What's his blood pressure?'

'Ah... I haven't checked it. Hold on! I'll go—'

'No. Just wait. Can he move the arm at all?'

'No! No! That's what I've been telling you!'

'What about his other arm?'

'Yes.'

'And his legs?'

'It's not his legs. It's his arm!'

'And his speech. Is it slurred?'

'No.'

'And his vision?'

'Ah... I haven't checked his vision. Hold on! I'll go and—'

'Wait. Just wait. Just calm down. Calm down, all right? If he's conscious, if he's breathing, you've got time. Stop. Let's think about this.'

'I turned the Sorain off.'

'OK,' said Goldblatt. 'That's all right. Look, it sounds like he's had a stroke.'

Silence.

'A stroke?' said the HO at last. Her voice was quiet, baffled, subdued. 'Why has he had a stroke?'

'I don't know,' said Goldblatt.

'I didn't know Sorain gave you strokes.'

'It doesn't.'

'Then why has he had a stroke?'

'I don't know.'

There was a silence again. 'Malcolm?'

'What?'

'It couldn't be a stroke.'

'Why not?'

'Because he was all right!' cried the HO, her voice rising again. 'One minute he was moving his arm and the next minute he wasn't!'

'That's what strokes do. That's why they're called strokes. Strokes. Like lightning.'

Silence.

'Listen,' said Goldblatt.

'What?' said the HO. Her voice sounded hollow once more. Detached. Lost.

'Go back and look at him. Check his pulse and blood pressure. Do a proper neurological examination. I'm coming up.'

'When?'

'Now. Don't worry. I'll be straight up.'

Goldblatt put the phone down. For a moment he continued to sit on the edge of the desk in the empty clinic room, thinking. Then he went back to the old lady with the arthritis in her neck.

She had managed to put her soft collar on the right way around all by herself.

Goldblatt sat down and started writing a return appointment slip for her. She watched him expectantly.

'Doctor?' she said. 'Is this right?'

'Yes. Very good,' said Goldblatt.

'Don't you want to check how tight it is?' she asked inanely, continuing the joke that had been cut short at a stroke.

No, thought Goldblatt. He got up and poked a finger between the old lady's chin and the collar. 'Feels right to me,' he said, sitting down again.

'I wouldn't want to get in trouble with my breathing,' said the old lady, who obviously came from the milk-it-till-it's-dry school of humour.

'You won't get in trouble with your breathing,' said Goldblatt, finishing off the appointment slip. He gave it to the old lady and managed a smile as he ushered her out of the room. He followed her out, told Rosa he'd be back in ten minutes, and left the clinic with Rosa calling after him that she hoped he knew he was already half an hour behind and his next four patients were waiting for him.

When Goldblatt got up to the ward it wasn't only Mr Sprczrensky's right arm that was paralysed. His right leg had gone as well. And the right side of his face drooped heavily.

He had been put back into bed. The HO was bending over him, listening to his heart.

'Mr Sprensky,' said Goldblatt. 'What's happened?'

The HO looked around. She put her stethoscope in her pocket and made way for him.

Mr Sprczrensky smiled crookedly with the half of his mouth that would still move. 'Dr Goldblatt,' he said, slurring the words.

'Let me just have a look at you.'

Goldblatt felt the pulse at Mr Sprczrensky's right wrist. He looked at Mr Sprczrensky's face and smiled reassuringly at him as he counted the beats.

'Can you lift your arm?' he said.

Mr Sprczrensky shook his head.

'Try,' said Goldblatt.

Mr Sprczrensky tried.

'All right,' said Goldblatt. 'Let me move it.'

He moved Mr Sprczrensky's arm, testing for the tone of the muscles. He tapped his reflexes, and tested Mr Sprczrensky's ability to feel touch on his skin. Then he went on to Mr Sprczrensky's other arm, and then his legs, and then he went up to his face, and tested his pupils, vision, feeling, and the movements of his facial muscles. Then he briefly examined the rest of him, his heart, the arteries in his neck, his chest and abdomen. The HO stood silently at the foot of the bed as Goldblatt did all this.

After he had finished, Goldblatt sat on the edge of the bed beside Mr Sprczrensky. 'Do you know what's happened?' he asked.

Mr Sprczrensky blinked. At least, his left eye blinked. His right eye rotated, but the lids didn't close properly. Fluid had dribbled out of the corner and left a snail track down his cheek.

'You've had a stroke, Mr Sprensky,' said Goldblatt.

Mr Sprczrensky nodded.

'Do you know what that means?'

'Yes,' said Mr Sprczrensky.

Goldblatt explained anyway. 'Have we rung your wife?'

'Not yet,' said the HO. 'I was waiting for you.'

Goldblatt nodded. 'We'll ring to let her know.'

'Thank you,' said Mr Sprczrensky.

'Mr Sprensky, we're going to do a couple of things. We're going to do a CT scan of your brain to make sure we know exactly what's happened. We're going to do some blood tests. And we may need to do a scan of your neck. Is that all right?'

Mr Sprczrensky nodded.

'Have you ever had a CT scan?'

Mr Sprczrensky shook his head.

'It's no problem,' said Goldblatt. 'You just lie there while it happens.'

Mr Sprczrensky gazed at him.

Goldblatt knew the look. He knew what was going to happen next. He knew Mr Sprczrensky didn't want it to happen, but he knew he wasn't going to last much longer.

The tears started rolling down Mr Sprczrensky's face.

Goldblatt was still sitting beside him on the edge of the bed.

'Dr Goldblatt?' said Mr Sprczrensky.

'Yes.'

'Dr Goldblatt. I'm frightened.'

Goldblatt nodded. He reached out for Mr Sprczrensky's hand.

'Frightened... Frightened.'

Goldblatt nodded again. He got a tissue and put it into Mr Sprczrensky's left hand.

Mr Sprczrensky cried.

'It's all right,' said Goldblatt. He continued to hold Mr Sprczrensky's other hand.

Mr Sprczrensky cried. Goldblatt sat with him and waited.

The HO stood watching at the end of the bed.

'Mr Sprensky,' said Goldblatt gently, 'you're at your worst now. You'll improve. It's early. It'll take some time. But you will improve. We're going to help you do that.'

Mr Sprczrensky nodded. He tried to smile and snuffled with the effort. The corners of his mouth went in opposite directions.

Goldblatt smiled back. He let go of his hand. Mr Sprczrensky wiped his eyes. He had stopped crying. Goldblatt looked around. At the end of the bed, the HO was just starting.

She turned and ran off.

She wasn't in the doctors' office when Goldblatt went in there to write his notes. He bleeped her number and didn't get an answer. He bleeped Ludo and dragged her out of the Dermatology clinic in the cafeteria and told her to get up to the ward and get an urgent CT scan organized for Mr Sprczrensky. Then he went back to the clinic and set to work on the backlog that had accumulated in his absence.

He headed up to the ward after he had finished in the clinic. The HO was there now. So was Emma, who had heard about Mr Sprczrensky's stroke. He found them near the nurses' station. Emma had the HO pinned with her back against the wall, giving her a dressing down in front of the passing cleaners for not having written her findings on Mr Sprczrensky in the notes.

'Emma, it's all right,' Goldblatt said. 'I've written in the notes.'

Emma ignored him. She wasn't talking to him, so why should she listen to him?

'It's not good enough!' she shouted at the HO. 'What would have happened if something else had happened to him? There was nothing in the notes. Don't you know about keeping notes?'

The HO stared at the floor.

Emma watched her in mock exasperation, her eyes narrowed, like a big, blonde cat toying with a mouse. Emma still hadn't forgotten the way the HO had run off to Goldblatt on her very first day when she had asked her to do an extra round. Well, if an HO chose to behave like that with her SR, she had to take what was coming when she did something wrong. And something was wrong. Very wrong. One of the Prof's patients had just had a major stroke, and the wrongest thing about it was that Emma couldn't be sure how the Prof was going to take it. The stroke would probably tie up a bed for weeks. Someone, somewhere, must be at fault.

'Well?' said Emma, still glaring at the HO.

'Fuck off, Emma,' said Goldblatt, and he dragged the HO away to see Mr Sprczrensky again, do a brisk round, and try to put some order back into the shambles of the day.

Each time they went back to see Mr Sprczrensky over the next few days, the HO stood by silently as Goldblatt examined him, watching with wide, grave eyes. Goldblatt was puzzled. Why was she so affected by this particular patient? Why did she stand there every day as if condemned to visit and revisit the scene of a crime, like some kind of Promethean punishment for a sin that she had never committed? She hadn't been this upset when the man with the VIPoma had died, and she had killed him almost single-handedly. And she had already publicly celebrated the death of one patient on his way in to hospital, or at least had celebrated it with Goldblatt, and who knew how many more deaths she had rejoiced in privately? All in all, she had been showing every sign of hardening up nicely, and could soon have been expected to have as tough, resilient, and scaly a clinical skin as anyone. Besides, she must have clerked in at least one stroke whenever she was on call. What was one more? Not enough to shed your skin over, surely.

'Do you want to talk about Mr Sprensky?' Goldblatt asked her in the doctors' office.

The HO shook her head.

'You know, these things happen,' he said, stating the obvious.

'I know,' said the HO.

'It wasn't your fault.'

'I know,' said the HO.

Goldblatt looked at her. But then the HO turned away and started doing something at the computer, hitting the keys very hard and very fast.

And he wondered, was she having nightmares of Mr Sprczrensky?

Or perhaps it wasn't really Mr Sprczrensky she saw. Perhaps, when the HO looked at Mr Sprczrensky, it was the ghost of the VIPoma she glimpsed there, hiding behind Mr Sprczrensky's gentle and half-paralysed Polish face. The VIPoma, whose barrel chest had crunched under the compressions of Steve's hands, and whose skin had burned under the paddles of the defibrillator that Goldblatt had applied, as the HO stood by and watched on that awful Sunday night five weeks before. Only five weeks before, yet a lifetime in the past.

Or perhaps it was the ghost of herself, of what she once had been, that she saw hiding behind the both of them.

19

IN THE DOCTORS' OFFICE the following Wednesday, the Prof listened to the HO present Mr Sprczrensky's case. The Prof already knew about him, of course, from Emma, who had informed her post-haste after Goldblatt suggested that Emma might care to leave the HO alone – or words to that effect – wanting to make sure that the news was delivered with the correct nuance and emphasis. Or to put it another way, wanting to make clear that she had had absolutely nothing to do with Mr Sprczrensky, either before, during, or after his stroke.

As far as Goldblatt was aware, in the six days that had elapsed since then, the Prof hadn't been up even once to the ward to see him.

'Well,' said the Prof pointedly, after the HO had presented the facts.

There was silence.

'Anything to suggest this isn't a straightforward stroke?' asked Dr Morris.

Goldblatt shook his head. 'Not unless there's an association between stroke and Fuertler's Syndrome.'

The Prof glanced at Dr Morris for a moment. 'I'm not aware of an association,' she said cautiously, 'but of course, Fuertler's Syndrome is such a rare and complex disease that it's perfectly possible that such an association does exist and we haven't identified it yet.'

Goldblatt had heard her say the same thing about Fuertler's Syndrome in one connection or another, or something like it, just about every week. It was wearing thin. Rarity and complexity: the Prof's mantra. Her excuse for any manner of ignorance and uncertainty.

The Prof looked at Emma. 'I wonder if it would be worth looking into the files about that?'

'Yes, Prof,' said Emma, and nodded her head very quickly, just as a small dog, thought Goldblatt, might nod at the prospect of being thrown a bone.

Thinking this might be a cue for her to achieve some recognition at last, Ludo grabbed the Fuertler's files on the ward's patients and held them out to the Prof.

'So, Dr Goldblatt,' said the Prof, ignoring her. 'What's happening with Mr Sprensky's discharge?'

'We're working on it.'

'Do you have a date?'

'Not yet.'

'Not yet...' repeated the Prof pointedly.

'We've referred him for rehab.'

'Maybe two weeks,' said Sister Choy, consulting her nurses' cardex.

'Two *weeks?*' said the Prof.

Goldblatt shrugged. 'He needs rehab, Professor Small.'

'I know he needs rehab,' retorted the Prof. 'I'm perfectly aware of that, Dr Goldblatt.'

Then what do you want? thought Goldblatt.

The Prof wanted Mr Sprczrensky gone. She wanted his bed for admissions for Fuertler's work-ups and Sorain infusions, and she didn't want those admissions to turn into cancellations because a patient was sitting in a bed as the result of a stroke that had absolutely nothing to do with Fuertler's Syndrome and therefore, it followed, had nothing to do with her. Cancellations, on the other hand, had a lot to do with her

Over the last few months, an ever increasing number of complaints had been coming in about cancellations on the unit. Letters arrived from patients, relatives, GPs, and consultants. What had started as a trickle was turning into a flood. They came in all kinds of styles. Some patients wrote simple notes full of spelling mistakes, while others wrote long, stiff letters full of tortured and apologetic politeness. The GPs sent reminders, and the consultants sent pointed demands for clarification. But all of them wanted to know the same thing: what had happened to the admission that the Prof herself had recommended for her patient three, five, eight, or even ten months earlier? It wasn't pleasant to get these letters. If anyone thought it was fun to face them as a regular feature of one's life – especially when one's secretary, who opened all of one's mail, carefully placed each letter face up on top of everything else, and then lay in wait to watch one's reaction as one spotted it – they could jolly well try it for themselves. It took all of one's strength to deal with them, and a lesser person might have buckled. But Andrea Small wasn't for buckling. She was made of sterner stuff. The Prof prided herself on always facing up to her responsibilities, and she had decided to face up to this problem in the most effective way she knew: by ignoring it. The Prof had great faith in this strategy, which was one of the skills she had learned in the early days in Liverpool, and had used it countless times in the past. She had committed herself resolutely to ignoring the letters, and she was sticking to that commitment with determination, no matter how difficult it proved to be.

But if she was completely honest with herself – which she was disinclined to be in this instance, for obvious reasons – the Prof was beginning to think that it would be impossible to ignore the rising flood of letters for much longer. A memo from the Director of Patient Services had washed in on the flood, and that had proven even more difficult – although not impossible – to ignore. The Prof was finding it harder and harder to avoid the sickening feeling that something, some time, would happen to make it impossible to ignore it all any further.

The prospect of having someone sitting in one of her beds for two whole weeks – and it could be more, because transfer to a unit like Stroke Rehabilitation was nothing if not a moveable feast – brought that sickening feeling bubbling to the surface. And with it, as she looked at Goldblatt, came another sickening feeling: the boy was enjoying it. She could tell. Look at the way he sat, look at the way he shrugged. Suddenly the Prof was certain he couldn't be happier that a stroke patient was blocking one of her beds, and that as a result there were going to be even more cancellations piled on top of the mountain of cancellations that at moments like these the Prof could feel weighing her down as if they were balanced precariously on top of her head. In fact, considering all the other things he had already done, she wouldn't have put it past him to have arranged this stroke deliberately. She didn't know quite how that would have been possible – but she wouldn't have put it past him.

'Who asked for this admission?' she demanded abruptly.

Goldblatt had no idea. Emma had booked it before he arrived.

Emma stared at the Prof.

'Give me the notes!'

Emma tore them out of the HO's hands. The Prof leafed through the pages feverishly, then came to a page and jabbed it with her finger. 'Just as I thought! It wasn't me, it was one of the clinical assistants!'

Goldblatt glanced at Dr Morris. He was sitting with his head resting against the X-ray box, his face composed in the Zen-like expression that he reserved for the most excruciating of the Prof's digressions.

'Well, he's here now, isn't he?' said the Prof, shooting a look at Goldblatt. She closed the notes and pushed them back at Emma.

There was silence.

'Go on,' said the Prof impatiently to the HO. 'Next patient. What are you waiting for?'

The Prof remained distracted and irritable throughout the HO's case presentations. When they went out on the ward, however, the outward signs of her anger magically evaporated. She drifted regally from bed to bed. When they came to Mr Sprczrensky she stopped, gazed at him sympathetically, placed a consoling hand on his forearm, and said: 'How are *you*, Mr Sprensky?' You might almost have been forgiven for thinking that she cared. She even left her hand there for a few seconds when Mr Sprczrensky cried and said he was frightened. Not that she made the slightest move to examine him, or ask any details of how the stroke had happened, or assess his recovery since then, or do any of the things that a doctor might have done. She stood back while Dr Morris, purely to satisfy his own insatiable interest, did it in front of her.

She threw an imperious glance at Goldblatt as she walked away from the bed, as if to say that whatever he chose to do, however many strokes he managed to put into her beds, *she* was still a professor, and *he* nothing but a jobbing locum registrar. Or at least that was what she hoped it showed, because inside, she almost felt as if the roles were reversed.

Goldblatt watched her walk on to the next bed with a faint feeling of disgust. He could just about have predicted everything the Prof had said and done on the round. So much about Professor Small was image, he thought, and so little was substance.

*

If Goldblatt had found the round demoralizing, Ludo had found it even more depressing. As far as she was concerned, its only redeeming feature was that it offered her something to whine about. Ever since the Constantidis Affair, the Prof had kept her distance from the Fuertler's files, and each Wednesday they sat neglected in a pile on one of the desks while the HO presented the patients, as if the Prof feared that merely opening one of them, Pandora-like, might unleash another whirlwind of chaos upon the round. This Wednesday, when Ludo had actually tried to force the files into the Prof's hands, had been no different, as she didn't hesitate to point out to Goldblatt when they were in the cafeteria that afternoon.

Once started, this particular whine on the devastating unfairness of the fate of the Fuertler's files – which was far from her first – promised to be one of Ludo's most accomplished. Goldblatt gazed absently at a nearby table of doctors as her voice droned on. The Fuertler's files had been her one chance to bring herself to the notice of the Prof, and that chance had been snatched away through no fault of her own. The Prof didn't care about them any more. But did that mean she could stop filling them in? No, she had to keep filling them in. It was Emma's fault. But did Emma care? No, Emma didn't care. Well, Emma could fill them in herself. But did you see Emma filling them in? No, Emma didn't fill them in. Emma came into the office at night to check them. But did Emma really want them to be—

Goldblatt looked back at Ludo sharply. 'How do you know Emma comes and checks them?'

'Of course she comes and checks them,' replied Ludo impatiently. She hadn't reached the end of her litany, and thought Goldblatt ought at least to have let her finish. 'She told me the Prof asked her to check every one and let her know if there's a single thing missing.'

'Well, don't worry then. The Prof knows you're still filling them in.'

'The Prof only knows what Emma tells her,' said Ludo bitterly. 'The Prof doesn't know I exist.'

Ludo may have been right. Obviously, there had been a period of at least a day when the Prof did know that Ludo existed, since she had invited her into her office to give her the chance to cry and lie her way out of being an HO, but who knew how good the Prof's memory was? Since then, there had been no sign from the Prof that could be unambiguously interpreted to mean that she was aware of the existence of a person called Ludo, much less that this person had some kind of a connection, however tenuous, with her unit.

'She never even talks to me,' whined Ludo, and she glanced impatiently at the coffee bar, wondering how much longer Goldblatt was going to keep her waiting before he bought her another coffee. 'The Prof's awful. She doesn't care.'

Goldblatt couldn't argue with that.

Ludo gave a disheartened sigh. She glanced longingly at the coffee bar again.

Goldblatt glanced at his watch.

'It's your fault, Malcolm. It's all your fault.'

Goldblatt stared at her.

'You know it is. Ever since that day with Mrs Constantidis. The Prof doesn't care about anything I do. Why did you do that to me?'

'I'm sorry, Ludo.' Goldblatt frowned, trying to understand. Really, he was trying. 'Just... *Do that to you?* What the fuck are you talking about?'

'And Emma as well. Ever since she stopped talking to you she won't say a word to me either.'

'Rubbish. You're always telling me what Emma told you. Emma told you this, Emma told you that...'

Ludo glared at Goldblatt resentfully. She shook out her hair as if it were weighing down her brain.

'Look, Ludo,' Goldblatt said wearily. 'You can always go and talk to the Prof.'

'And what am I going to say?'

'Tell her you're... enjoying working on her unit. Consultants love hearing things like that.'

Ludo looked at him mistrustfully.

'Tell her... you want to talk about the Fuertler's files. Tell her you'd like to use them to do a study.'

'I don't want to use them to do a study!' Ludo wrinkled her nose in disgust, as if something in what he had said reeked of putrefaction.

'Listen, Ludo,' said Goldblatt in exasperation, 'what do you need from the Prof?'

'What?'

'A reference.'

'Thank you. I'd never have realized that.'

'You've got to build a bridge.'

'A bridge, Malcolm?'

'A bridge, Ludo, is a thing over which a reference moves, so it doesn't get lost.'

'Where?'

Goldblatt thought for a moment. 'In the river.'

Ludo looked at him sceptically. Goldblatt himself was beginning to wonder where all this bridge and river stuff was taking him. Still, having come this far...

'Imagine a river. All right? You're on one side of the river and the Prof's on the other. A reference moves over the river, on the bridge, from her to you. You just have to build it.'

'The bridge?'

'That's right.'

Ludo stared at him as if she were looking at something very, very pitiful.

'Look,' said Goldblatt, 'if you want the Prof to give you a decent reference you have to find a way of putting positive thoughts into her brain.'

'Like you do, I suppose.'

Goldblatt ignored that. Or tried to.

'Or perhaps *you* don't need a reference.'

'Ludo...'

'When's your pre-interview for that job at the Nailwright again?'

'Next Tuesday. You're covering me, remember?'

Ludo nodded with a look of satisfaction, as if she had made an extraordinarily telling point. Goldblatt wondered what she thought it was.

'Ludo,' he said, 'if you didn't want me to help you, why did you ask?'

'Oh, Malcolm,' she teased, 'are we getting upset?'

Goldblatt restained himself.

'All right, Malcolm. I have to build a bridge? Is that what you said?'

'Yes,' replied Goldblatt cautiously.

'Over the river?'

He nodded.

'So the reference can cross?' said Ludo, and she grinned.

'Ludo, you've got to work at it! You can get her to like you. Tell her you want to do a study with the Fuertler's files. You heard her today. Strokes. Say you want to use the Fuertler's files to see if there's an association with strokes.'

'In case you didn't hear, Malcolm, that's what Emma's going to do.'

'Then think of something else. You know what? It wouldn't hurt you to do it. You might get a publication.'

'Why don't you do it?'

'We're not talking about me.'

'What about your bridges, Malcolm? Do you ever build them, or do you only burn them?'

Goldblatt stared. That was quite clever. The way Ludo was looking at him, she obviously thought so as well. He wondered for a moment whether it was possible to burn a bridge that had never even existed. To burn the possibility of a bridge, the prospect, the concept... His mind lingered on the idea.

'Anyway,' said Ludo, 'I'm not sure how strong the Prof's bridges are even if you do manage to build one.'

'What does that mean?'

Ludo smiled. 'Do you know what happened to the SR before you came?'

'Do you?'

Ludo continued smiling – the smile of a very skilled, very experienced interrogator who always got to the truth, no matter what it took.

'How did you find out?'

Ludo arched an eyebrow.

'Was it from Emma?'

The smile on Ludo's face, if possible, got smugger. Goldblatt shuddered to think what lies she had told – probably about him – to prise the information from Emma's lips.

'The SR went for a consultant job,' said Ludo, 'and asked the Prof for a reference.'

'As one does...' said Goldblatt.

'Yes, and the Prof said she'd give her a reference, *as one does*.' Ludo stopped to let Goldblatt connect the dots.

'The reference was... unhelpful?'

'Dr Goldblatt, I believe you've got it in one.'

'And she didn't get the job?'

'Right again.'

Goldblatt nodded. No wonder Emma hadn't been keen to divulge this particular example of her adored leader's behaviour. Within the profession, to promise a good reference and deliver a bad one was regarded as one of the most dishonourable things one doctor could do to another. The etiquette was to suggest to the putative referee that it might be wise not to request a reference at all.

'She walked out the same day,' said Ludo. 'Which left a gap. Which I believe is where you came in. So you see, I'm not sure about the Prof and her bridges.'

Fair enough, thought Goldblatt. But he didn't see how that helped her. Yet there Ludo sat, the smile lingering on her lips, as if the fact that she had just talked herself into not trying to get a reference from this job was some kind of victory.

Ludo glanced at the coffee bar. A group of house officers came into the cafeteria. Goldblatt thought about the HO. He was still worried about her. Whenever she went near Mr Sprczrensky she was quiet, solemn, withdrawn, and yet something constantly drew her back to him.

'Does someone over there interest you?' said Ludo. 'Do you like them young, Malcolm?'

'You're disgusting.'

Ludo shook out her hair.

'I'm just worried, that's all.'

'About what?'

Goldblatt rolled his eyes. 'Mr Sprensky's really knocked her.'

'You're so sweet,' said Ludo in the tone of voice you'd use with a maiden aunt of ninety who has long ago lost touch with reality. 'Malcolm, I didn't know you were such a sweetie.'

'I'm not a sweetie,' said Goldblatt, almost gagging on the word.

'She's fine. What are you worried about?'

'I told you.'

Ludo shrugged. 'It's only because Mr Sprensky had his stroke in front of her.'

'She didn't care this much about...'

'What?' said Ludo.

'Nothing.' Goldblatt had never told Ludo about the VIPoma. There was some ammunition that was just too powerful to put into her hands.

Ludo watched him with an expression that said not only that she knew he was hiding something, but that she'd find out. They could do it the easy way, or they could do it the hard way...

'You should have been there when Mr Sprensky had his stroke!' said Goldblatt suddenly. 'Why weren't you on the ward?'

'Oh, Malcolm,' whined Ludo, 'don't start that again.'

'What were you doing?'

'Something. What difference would it have made if I'd been there? It wouldn't have stopped Mr Sprensky's stroke, would it?'

Goldblatt grudgingly shook his head. Ludo rarely employed logic, but when she did, there was nothing more irritating. 'It's not Mr Sprensky I'm thinking about,' he growled eventually.

Ludo ignored that.

Goldblatt glanced at his watch.

'It's just because she's a house officer,' said Ludo. 'It's natural when you're a house officer.'

'Maybe.'

'Of course it is. Patients upset you. Things happen to them and you don't know how to deal with it. Can't you remember a patient who ever upset you like that?'

Goldblatt thought about it. He nodded. 'We had this patient who came in with lupus. I'll never forget her. She happened to look just like this girl I'd been going out with. We'd broken up a little while before. And then she went mad.'

'You were lucky you weren't still going out with her.'

'The patient, Ludo! She went completely mad. The lupus had involved her brain and she had the whole neuropsychiatric thing going on. One night I was on call, and they called me up to the ward, and she was climbing the walls. We had to sedate her. I had this syringe full of halo- peridol, and I was trying to get it into her bum and she was crawling away, scratching at me and the nurses and the porter and clawing at the sides of the bed and shouting all kinds of things. It felt like what I was doing was violent. I mean, I had to do it, she was a danger to herself and everyone else, but honestly, at that moment, I felt like the Gestapo.' Goldblatt paused, staring into his coffee cup, remembering that night. He smiled reflectively. 'It really had an effect on me. Must have been because she looked like this girl I'd been going out with. When I got back to my room, I cried. I actually sat down and cried.' Goldblatt looked up at Ludo. 'What about you?'

'Me?'

'Ever had a patient who affected you like that?'

'Don't be stupid, Malcolm.'

Ludo! He should have known that was coming.

Ludo laughed.

'You're sick.' said Goldblatt.

'Am I?'

'Yes.'

'How sick?'

'Very.'

'With what?'

'Don't you know?'

She shook her head. 'Diagnose me, Malcolm.'

Goldblatt laughed. He put a hand on her wrist, like a mock doctor feeling for a pulse.

But they weren't mock doctors. Neither of them.

Ludo looked down at Goldblatt's hand.

Her mouth opened a little. She looked up at Goldblatt, her eyelids hanging low over her blue irises.

'Some people would say that's sexual harassment, you know,' she murmured.

Goldblatt eased his hand away from her.

Ludo stood up. She put her white coat on with slow, deliberate movements, almost as if she were dressing in front of him. She shook out her hair over her collar.

'Thanks for the coffee, Malcolm.'

20

GOLDBLATT WENT TO THE Nailwright Hospital for his pre-interview the following week like a man voting in an election in Soviet Russia: knowing that the whole thing appeared to be about one thing whereas in reality it was about the direct opposite.

The first thing to grasp about a pre-interview was that it wasn't an option. To stand any chance of getting the job, you had to go and visit the unit in the weeks leading up to the interview. But on the face of it, there was something dreadfully wrong with this. In fact if you thought about it objectively, it might even have occurred to you that pre-interviews undid virtually everything that the selection process was designed to achieve. Medical jobs in the NHS are public service appointments and are supposed to be allocated on merit alone. In theory, therefore, the process for allocating them is constructed so as to ensure fairness, objectivity, transparency, reproducibility, and the elimination of favour. Yet pre-interviews, sitting down for a private chat with a consultant on the unit that is offering the job, are all about subjectivity, clandestinity, absence of scrutiny, irreproducibility, and the currying of favour. There was a solution to this apparent paradox, of course, and as a Wise Man Goldblatt had eventually worked it out. To understand it, you had to start from one stop further along in the process, the medical interview itself.

An interview for a medical job is a unique ritual with a choreography all of its own. The first thing you notice about it is its sheer size. A medical interview is attended by a whole horde of important people, each of whom represents one of the many groups who can claim an interest in the appointment of a doctor. Excepting patients, of course, who can claim an interest, but not representation.

At an interview for a specialist registrar position Goldblatt would be confronted by a minimum of six interviewers on the other side of the table. First, there would be a consultant from the unit that was offering the job. Second, a consultant from the academic department of medicine with which the unit was affiliated. Third, a consultant with regional responsibility for specialist training. Fourth, a consultant representing the relevant specialist college. Fifth, a consultant representing the hospital. Sixth, to leaven this consultative load, a layperson acting as a moderator. But sometimes, depending on availability, the layperson turns out to be another consultant. Alternatively, for the sake of variation, the consultant representing the hospital occasionally turns out to be a managerial layperson. And sometimes, just to add to the fun, a few additional consultants from the unit offering the job turn up to view the goods.

And the point of having a panel large enough to field its own side in a variety of team sports? Fairness and transparency, the qualities that the selection process is supposed to enshrine. It's fair to the candidate, fair to the hospital, fair to everyone who can claim a say. Every interest is represented, and how can anything underhand take place if six or eight people are watching?

On the other hand, how can anything useful take place? A panel of that size is just too cumbersome. So cumbersome, in fact, that firm measures are taken to prevent the whole procedure turning into a hopeless rout, and, more importantly, to ensure that no candidate's appearance exceeds twenty-five minutes, which seems to be the main concern of the panel. Each of the interviewers is restricted to two questions, with the possibility of a supplementary. Yet it's impossible to establish a sense of rapport, much less to develop a coherent understanding of someone's thought processes, in the space of two questions. And having six people ask two questions each isn't the same as having one person ask twelve. With all the chopping and changing, there's no opportunity to probe, to delve, to discover. The interviewers themselves generally don't do anything to make the best of the situation. They invariably converge five minutes before the panel is due to convene, and spend the next fifteen minutes exchanging hospital gossip until the moderator forces them to sit down. Tea is often provided, which makes it harder to get them started. Virtually impossible if there are biscuits. Few if any of them have had any formal training in interviewing techniques. There's no coordination of the questioning. At least one of them – and usually more – discharges their duty by lighting randomly on a previous post in the candidate's CV and asking him or her to describe the unit he or she worked on. The others all have a favourite stock question – The Social Issue, The State of the Health Service, The Research Programme – and their biggest worry is what they're going to do if someone else gets in with the same stock question first.

The medical interview, therefore, is perfect, with the congealed, nostalgic perfection of something very beautiful, very fragile, and utterly useless. With its exquisitely balanced panel, paralysed by its own size, and its fastidiously designed procedure, mummified by its own rigidities, the interview is like a flawless Fabergé egg. And, like the most flawless, glittering Fabergé egg, it's hollow. All is spectacle, and nothing is substance.

Yet medical interviews take place, and people are appointed, and jobs become vacant, and interviews are repeated. So how does the system function? Why doesn't it implode into the vacuum of its own unblemished futility? For a very simple reason. Inside the dark interior of the Fabergé egg, away from the light and the glitter, is a little secret: the consultant from the unit offering the job has the veto.

Of all the consultants sitting at an interview table, the one who is actually going to have the successful candidate hanging around on their ward for a year or two has the right of refusal. Not the right of appointment – but the right of refusal. Yet in an interview that is designed so that no one can determine anything useful about a candidate, it amounts to the same thing.

Naturally, this generates its own perverse logic, as dark little secrets do.

One can't possibly tell anything meaningful about the candidates for a job from the twenty-five flawless minutes of the medical interview, as everyone knows. But somehow, *someone* has to find out about them. And if the consultant from the unit offering the job has the veto, it ought to be them. So that consultant had better meet the candidates beforehand. They had better get to know them. They had better work out the reasons that they're going to reject them if they have already decided who they want to give the job to. Quietly, in private, without anyone to watch or listen to the questions they're asking. Without any of the golden horde that will troop in a week later and sit down around the table so that everything will apparently be fair and transparent and objective... after the one with the veto has already met the candidates and made up his or her subjective little mind without anyone to help or restrain the process.

That was the pre-interview. Something that was supposed to be about you getting to know the unit – but was actually about the unit getting to know you. You might get a perfunctory glance at the ward if you were lucky. Goldblatt had been to pre-interviews where the consultant simply sat you down in their office, pulled out your CV, and went through it. Not even the pretence of showing you the unit or introducing you to anyone else. After that you went home and came back a week later for the epilogue.

That was the pre-interview in its highest form, following the cruel logic of evolution to its ultimate stage. But it wasn't until the day Goldblatt sat down opposite Professor Mike Coalport at the Nailwright Hospital that he understood just how cruel evolution can be.

At the appointed time, Goldblatt knocked on the door of an office on the fourth floor of the Nailwright. He heard a grunt, and a moment later the door was opened by a short man in his late forties. His belly hung over his belt, and his jowls were heavy, floppy, and pugnacious. He had a thick, light brown moustache, and receding hair that was curly at the sides, giving him the look of a debauched cherub. There were papers everywhere in the office, on chairs and cupboards and on the desk and on the floor. Coalport shook hands with Goldblatt perfunctorily and waved him towards a chair that was wedged against a wall between two tall filing cabinets that were stacked even taller with papers. The chair had its own pile of papers, but Mike Coalport grudgingly picked them up and dropped them on the floor in Goldblatt's honour.

There was a larger, more comfortable chair in front of Coalport's desk, but this was stacked with papers as well, and these were obviously too important to be moved for a mere job candidate. Goldblatt therefore sat in the offered chair, cramped between the two leaning stacks of paper that rose four feet above his head on his right and his left, hoping they weren't going to fall on top of him, while Coalport himself sat down behind his crowded desk three yards away on the other side of the room.

Goldblatt didn't know much about Mike Coalport, but he had seen plenty of doctors and most of the varieties of arrogance that they practise. The first minute in Mike Coalport's office was enough to show him that he was in the presence of the meanest, hardest, most self-opinionated and injurious arrogance there is. Mike Coalport was the kind of doctor who prides himself on being known by his colleagues as a bruiser. He was at the height of his powers, more than capable of destroying the career of any trainee doctor who was foolish enough to cross his path. If Malcolm Goldblatt was a Wise Man, Professor Mike Coalport was an Eminent Physician. He wasn't just an Eminent Physician, he was an EMINENT PHYSICIAN, and no one thought he was more EMINENT than he did.

Coalport glanced appraisingly at Goldblatt for a moment, like a second-hand trader about to offer a quarter of the value of a cherished heirloom to an anguished and starving widow. Then he picked up a sheaf of pages, glanced at it scornfully, flipped a page, and eventually fanned his face with it, as if it was a crumpled, stale theatre programme. From a play that wasn't very good.

Mike Coalport said: 'So, Dr Goldblatt. Have you done a research degree?'

And Goldblatt knew. He knew it. He was a Wise Man again.

Coalport was going right for the jugular, and he wasn't even waiting for the interview. Goldblatt didn't think he'd even bother telling Lesley about this encounter when he went home that night. It would only get her angry. May as well hold that back for when the inevitable happened at the interview. No point getting angry twice, particularly when it was about the same thing each time, only in different settings.

'No,' said Goldblatt. 'I haven't done a research degree.'

Coalport looked up at him in mock surprise, unable to conceal his contempt. It wasn't even a contest. It was pitiful. Fancy coming along to get a job at the Nailwright Hospital – a certified Centre for Postgraduate Medical Studies – without even having done a research degree.

'So I take it you haven't done any research at all, then,' said Mike Coalport, chuckling silently to himself at the absurdity of such a person turning up to work at the Centre for Postgraduate Medical Studies.

'I haven't done a formal research degree.'

'So what have you done? Published a few papers, have you?'

'Some.'

Mike Coalport put on his most derisive face and flipped a page or two of the sheaf of pages that he was holding. Goldblatt watched him fatalistically, and wondered what it was that could turn a man into such a beetle-like creature. The Egyptians made gods out of a certain species of beetles and called them scarabs, but that didn't stop the beetles behaving as they had always behaved, slapping together balls of dung and rolling them home to eat in their tunnels.

'These publications?' he said, still staring at the sheaf of pages he was holding.

'Which publications?' asked Goldblatt.

Coalport looked up at him sharply. 'These.'

'Which?'

'These! These ones listed here. What's wrong with you?'

'I can't see what you're looking at.'

Mike Coalport eyed Goldblatt suspiciously. 'I'm looking at your CV. What do you think I'm looking at?'

'I have no idea. You haven't told me.'

Coalport sneered. 'Are these your publications or aren't they?'

'Are they listed on my CV?'

'Yes.'

'Then they must be.'

Mike Coalport shook his head and huffed. He glanced pointedly at his watch. '*Variation of Organ-Specific Autoimmunity with Disease Activity in Inflammatory Arthritis,*' he announced abruptly, citing the title of one of Goldblatt's papers.

'That's mine.'

'Wrote it with Sam Rothman?'

'Yes.'

'Tell me about it.'

Goldblatt told him. Mike Coalport had happened to choose the only one of Goldblatt's four papers that was any good, the only one in which he took some pride, and which he had written because he genuinely believed it would add to the sum of scientific knowledge rather than because a consultant had urged him to write it for the sake of his CV. He had written it during his last substantive job, drawing data from Professor Rothman's version of the Fuertler's files that covered his disease of interest. Somehow he had managed to fend off Professor Rothman's never-ending suggestions to cut corners or obscure confounders or overreach or over-interpret, or simply add undocumented figures that Professor Rothman swore he could remember, in order to make the paper 'more interesting'. It was amazing, Goldblatt had discovered, how benign corruption could be, and how difficult to resist.

Coalport interrupted incessantly as Goldblatt spoke, challenging every point so that he had to make it again. Goldblatt made every point again, knowing that everything he had done in the paper was defensible. Only when he had heard each point twice was Coalport satisfied that there wasn't some methodological or interpretational mine lying buried in there that he could explode in Goldblatt's face.

But at the end Coalport shook his head with dissatisfaction. It wasn't any good, it still wasn't any good. That was obvious. It couldn't be any good.

'You don't have any formal research training,' he reminded Goldblatt helpfully, in case he had forgotten. 'How do you know how to run a study or write a paper? You have to publish if you work at the Nailwright, Dr Goldblatt. But you haven't learned the scientific techniques.'

'Perhaps... it would help if I told you about one of my papers,' Goldblatt suggested.

Coalport tossed Goldblatt's CV on his desk.

'A mere undergraduate degree in medicine isn't enough if you want to make a contribution to the academic life of the Centre for Postgraduate Medical Studies. The specialist registrar is a clinical post, but you'd still be expected to make a contribution. It's a highly academic environment.'

'I'm not unfamiliar with academic environments,' said Goldblatt. 'I've also done a law degree.'

'Was that before or after you graduated in medicine?' Coalport countered swiftly.

'Does it matter?'

Mike Coalport's eyes narrowed. He gazed at Goldblatt for a long time, wanting to pick up his CV again, but feeling that it would be a sign of weakness if he retrieved the document that he had just tossed away. There was something unpleasant about this meeting, and Mike Coalport was beginning to suspect that it was beneath his dignity. Any meeting with someone who hadn't done a research degree was very likely to be beneath his dignity. His first instinct was to walk out, pugnaciously, taciturnly, and disgustedly, as he often did at conferences after having delivered a withering intervention that left the speaker floundering for his notes. By walking out he could deliver a *coup de grâce* to this despicable job applicant who clearly deserved it more than the many conference speakers to whom he had delivered such *coups* in the past.

But walking out now would be tricky. After all, this wasn't a conference hall. It was his office. He would have to wait around the corner and get his secretary to let him know when Goldblatt had left.

Finally he picked up Goldblatt's CV again and nonchalantly turned a page.

'This law degree of yours,' he said, 'was it a research degree?'

'No,' said Goldblatt patiently. 'It was a law degree.'

'Publish anything?'

'It was a degree,' said Goldblatt slowly. 'A *law* degree.'

'What sort of law degree?'

'Torts.'

Coalport raised an eyebrow.

'Negligence, litigation, criminal law—'

'But it wasn't a research degree!' Coalport said with obsessive perseveration. Goldblatt was starting to wonder whether Mike Coalport was suffering from some rare form of early-onset dementia characterized by grandiose ideation, aggression, and frontal baldness. Coalport's Syndrome. Why not? There was already an Alport's Syndrome, why not a Coalport's?

'And what about this Free from Bondage thing?' said Coalport, sneering sceptically at Goldblatt's CV and almost spitting the words out. 'What's that, anyway?'

'An NGO.'

'An NGO, eh?' Coalport snorted. 'Publish anything?'

'No,' replied Goldblatt wearily, 'I didn't publish anything.'

Coalport shook his head in sham disappointment. What could he do?

'I wrote a submission for the UN Subcommittee on Slavery.'

'Did you?' retorted Coalport jeeringly. Mike Coalport could tell a mile away when someone was trying to challenge him and was happy to meet them in combat anytime, anywhere. 'And what was this submission about?'

'Indentured child labour in Colombia. We called for a UN mission to go to Colombia to investigate the situation in the coal mines there.'

'And did they?'

'No.'

'Well, it couldn't have been much of a submission, then.'

'No,' said Goldblatt. 'You're right. The UN is usually incredibly responsive to demands made by small NGOs. It was a terrible submission.'

'And you didn't publish it?'

Goldblatt sighed. 'No, we didn't publish it.'

Mike Coalport smiled unpleasantly, watching Goldblatt with a bilious mixture of pity and contempt.

'So all your papers are medical,' he said. 'You've done all these other things, yet you haven't published anything. Not a single legal paper.'

'Would it be better,' Goldblatt asked, wondering if he had come for a job at the Coalport law offices by mistake, 'if they were all legal?'

Coalport tossed Goldblatt's CV aside. He shook his head. It wasn't any good. It just wasn't any good. It was even worse than before.

'As far as I'm concerned,' said Mike Coalport, 'if you don't publish, whatever you do is a personal indulgence.'

Well, thought Goldblatt, that was one way to give structure to your life.

'You haven't done a research degree.'

'No,' said Goldblatt. 'I haven't done a research degree.'

'Well, you see, this is what shows, Dr Goldblatt. I'm afraid it simply does. I'm sure we'd all be very happy for you if you continued as you are and were able to get exactly the sort of specialist registrar job you want, but I'm afraid that's very unlikely.' Mike Coalport paused for a moment and gazed at Goldblatt with superiority and derision written all over his debauched cherubic features. When he continued, it was with the air of a man who is too busy for any more diversion. 'I have fifty grant applications to review there,' he said, sweeping his hand flamboyantly towards the pile of papers on the chair in front of his desk. 'I assess grant applications for the BSM. Hardly one of those grant applications will be of sufficient scientific standard for me to even consider. Many of them come from people who have never done a research degree. I'll be wasting my time.'

Goldblatt peered at the pile of papers.

'What are you looking at?' Coalport asked irritably.

'Those grant applications,' said Goldblatt.

'Why?'

'Is mine there?'

'Have you lodged one?'

'No.'

'Then how can it be there?' Coalport demanded.

'It can't,' said Goldblatt.

That was the point. But Mike Coalport didn't get it.

He gazed at Goldblatt, his lip curled in disgust. Then he stood up behind his desk. 'I've heard enough.'

Goldblatt nodded. He guessed that Coalport hadn't really needed to hear anything. He stood up too, being careful not to disturb any of the papers whose seat he had taken.

'Something very odd happened to me today,' said Dr Morris, standing in the doorway of the doctors' office after Goldblatt had got back to the hospital.

Not as odd as what just happened to me, thought Goldblatt. Or maybe odd wasn't the word.

'I bleeped you to ask if you could see a patient for me, and Ludo answered.' Dr Morris looked at him in surprise and horror.

'What did you do?' asked Goldblatt with interest.

'I saw the patient myself.' Dr Morris came in and sat on the edge of a desk. 'I didn't think... you know... Where were you, anyway?'

'I went to the Nailwright for the pre-interview.'

'With Mike Coalport?'

Goldblatt nodded.

'How was it?'

Goldblatt thought for a moment. 'Unpromising.'

Dr Morris laughed. 'Mike Coalport's like that. It doesn't mean anything.'

'I think it did.'

'It doesn't,' said Dr Morris.

'I really do think it did.'

'I'm telling you it doesn't. When's the interview?'

'Next week.'

'Well, that's his style. The more you think he doesn't want you to get the job at the pre-interview, the more likely you are to get it.'

'Then I've got it for sure,' said Goldblatt.

Dr Morris had come up to the ward to examine Mr Lister, which he did a minimum of three times a week in the ever-renewed hope that something would eventually show up to explain his fevers. He also wanted to talk to Goldblatt about what they would do if the latest test revealed nothing. They were getting to the end of the investigational line, which was more of an investigational loop, because by now they were repeating tests that Dr Morris had already ordered, often for the third or fourth time. If nothing else showed up, they would have to make a diagnosis of exclusion: a diagnosis you make not from positive evidence, but from the absence of evidence, a diagnosis you make only because you've ruled everything else out. If the tests showed nothing at all to suggest a malignancy , a chronic infection or a specific inflammatory disease – which so far they hadn't – the only possible remaining condition that could cause his symptoms would be a generalized, low-grade inflammatory condition, or vasculitis, and they would start him on steroids as the treatment.

Dr Morris wanted to explain this to Mr Lister himself. This was something the Prof would never have done. The Prof did her weekly round on Wednesday, and apart from that never came near the ward. In the time-honoured tradition of people who deal with problems at second hand in order to retain the option of blaming the people who are forced to deal with them at first hand, she would have sent Emma. Dr Morris, by contrast, was always arriving on the ward at the least excuse.

Yet something held him back in the doctors' office. Maybe it was just the prospect of talking to Mr Lister, which seemed like merely another task when you were safe in your clinic room six floors down, but became strangely more dreadful the closer you got to his bed.

'I've got no one today!' he announced suddenly.

'What do you mean, you've got no one?' Goldblatt said. No one? What did that mean, no one?

'There's no one on the Sutherland unit. The house officer's sick. The registrar's away. And the locum SR walked out.'

'When?'

'Last night.' Dr Morris looked at Goldblatt in genuine bemusement. 'Why do they keep doing that? We've got so many fascinating patients.'

'Ah...' Goldblatt searched for a kind way to explain it to Dr Morris, and gave up. 'No idea.'

'Their loss. Anyway, I've got no one. I've just been seeing the patients.'

'By yourself?' asked Goldblatt incredulously.

'There isn't anybody else to do it.'

Goldblatt stared. It was unprecedented for a consultant to be alone on his unit. Or maybe it had happened once or twice before. During the Black Death, for instance, it may well have happened. But it was an unprecedented event within living memory for a consultant to be alone on his unit, even if it wasn't really his unit. Yet Dr Morris had only himself to blame. Like a walking nuclear reactor, the pseudo-Sutherland pulsated stupendous waves of electromagnetic energy that attracted patients and drove everyone else away.

'We've got thirty patients already,' said Dr Morris, 'and we're on call from five o'clock.'

Goldblatt looked around the office for somewhere to hide.

Dr Morris grinned. He had obviously gone completely mad. And if he hadn't gone completely mad, that just showed he was even madder.

'Well, if you want me to help out...' Goldblatt began lamely, having failed to discover any hidden trapdoors, ventilation shafts, or false cupboards into which he could disappear.

'No,' said Dr Morris cheerfully. 'They told me they'd find at least two locums by five.'

'What if they don't?'

Dr Morris shrugged.

'Well, I guess this is when you find out whether the thirteenth law works in reverse,' said Goldblatt.

'Which thirteenth law?'

'The Fat Man's thirteenth law.'

'What are you talking about?'

'In *The House of God*.'

Dr Morris still looked puzzled.

'You know, the book. *The House of God.*

Dr Morris nodded. There was recognition somewhere in that nod of the dark, iconic book about medicine that had been published twenty years previously, but it was slow.

'Remember the Fat Man?'

'The fat man?'

'The Fat Man,' said Goldblatt. 'In the book. The Fat Man's thirteenth law: "The delivery of medical care means doing the most nothing." Now you get to see if it works the other way round: "The more nothing you do, the more medical care you deliver."

Dr Morris shook his head. 'I never read that book.'

Goldblatt's mouth dropped open. It was like listening to a man of thirty-six admitting he was still a virgin. Despite the fact that he had two children.

'You never read *The House of God*?'

'Someone gave me a copy. I read the first thirty pages and I stopped. It was just too cynical.'

'*Too* cynical?'

'Medicine isn't like that.'

'No,' said Goldblatt.

'You see?'

'It's worse.'

Dr Morris frowned. 'Do you really think so?'

Did Goldblatt really think so? For God's sake, *The House of God* was American. It had been written about interns in a well-known, lightly disguised American hospital. It was full of all kinds of American things. Like hope. There is no hope. There is no basketball court where HOs can shoot baskets together to drive the demons away. There are no policemen who sit around the Emergency Department all night offering homespun psychotherapy to terrified HOs who have lost all sense of self-worth. Evil-doers aren't redeemed. The system doesn't slacken. People don't find their niches. None of these things, which all happened in *The House of God*, happen in real life in medicine. Or at least not in Britain. In medicine, in Britain, real life was... Goldblatt searched for something desperate and miserable enough to depict the reality. There was only one word that could capture it. Ludo.

'I love medicine, Malcolm,' said Dr Morris. 'I just love it. For me, there's my family, and medicine. That's all.'

'What about squash?'

'I could live without squash.'

Goldblatt laughed. But Dr Morris was serious. He was troubled. 'Do you really think medicine is like that? Is that how it seems to you? Like *The House of God*?'

'I told you, it's worse.'

'Really?' said Dr Morris sadly.

Goldblatt looked at Dr Morris, who was gazing at him with an almost unbearable, childlike expression of dismay. 'Say it ain't so,' his eyes seemed to be saying. 'Mister, say it ain't so.'

He wasn't a bad man, Goldblatt thought. He had just done a round on thirty patients by himself, and he had probably taken their bloods as well. What greater love? How could you even think of such a man as bad? No, he loved medicine, that's all, and medicine loved him back. How could he understand what it was to love medicine, but, for one reason or another, not to be loved in return?

But if that was a failing, it was of a type of which everyone is guilty, in some aspect of their life, at one time or another.

Besides, maybe Dr Morris was right, in a way. Maybe medicine wasn't like that. For him.

He was alone on his unit. He was making history. The ship was going down in the Sea of Sutherland, and Dr Morris, all by himself, was doing his duty to the last. And he hadn't even tried to force Goldblatt to come aboard. The least Goldblatt could do was to lie a little in return.

'No, kid,' Goldblatt said softly. 'It ain't so.'

'Pardon?'

Goldblatt coughed. 'No, I don't really think it's like that.'

'Really?' said Dr Morris.

Goldblatt hesitated. 'Really,' he said.

21

THE DAY BEFORE GOLDBLATT'S interview at the Nailwright, Mr Sprcz-rensky finally got a bed on a rehab unit. For three weeks the Prof had heard about his case each Wednesday morning in the doctors' office, and each time had only one question to ask. When was he going? Then she would see him on her procession around the beds, each week spending less time at his bedside. By the end she couldn't even be bothered waiting for Dr Morris to examine him for signs of progress.

Mr Sprczrensky was still unable to walk. He could stand only with someone to support him. The slurring of his speech had improved, and he could raise a cup to his lips with his right hand, but lacked the strength to hold it there when the cup was full. The HO wanted to know his prognosis and Goldblatt told her that by now it was clear Mr Sprczrensky would never recover fully. Eventually he might learn to walk again with the stiff hemiplegic shuffle of a stroke survivor. The HO said goodbye to him and watched the porters push him away in a wheelchair while Mr Sprczrensky held his bag on his lap with his good arm. Goldblatt wasn't sure whether the HO was happy to see him go or whether she would have preferred to keep him there for ever as a living means to assuage her nameless guilt.

What was happening to her?

Everyone knows it's a dangerous profession. Those who fail to warn kids about the risks before they sign up for medical school have a serious case to answer. Alcoholism, divorce, suicide. The HO wasn't married. But she did have a life, or at least she had once had a life, and one day she might have a life again, regardless of whether she did or didn't have one at present. Maybe something serious was going on in her head, and her self-immolation on the altar of Mr Sprczrensky was the only way she had of expressing it.

The trick was to know whether something serious was happening before it happened. It was no great achievement to discover that it had been happening after it had happened. Goldblatt had worked with one consultant who had self-immolated himself for real, with a shotgun. Everyone knew it had happened after it happened, but there was very little use in knowing it had happened by then. It just made you feel guilty, and the whole experience suggested to Goldblatt that if you didn't know it was happening until after it had happened, it was probably better not to know that it had happened at all. And when he wasn't inclined to make a joke out of things – which wasn't often, since that was the way he had coped with just about everything since he was ten – he tortured himself imagining what that consultant must have gone through in his last days, and tried to think of what he himself could have done, and wondered how he had utterly failed to see the signs.

Ludo continued to tell him that he was worrying over nothing with the HO – which only made him think that he wasn't. After Mr Sprczrensky was wheeled off the ward to be taken to the rehab unit, and the HO had disappeared to do one of the million tasks written down on the pieces of paper in her pockets, he went to the cafeteria with Ludo for what was supposed to be a fifteen-minute break before going back to the ward to do a pleural biopsy on Mr Lister, the latest in the series of ever more desperate tests to which Dr Morris was resorting. But never in recorded history had Ludo moved within fifteen minutes once she had settled in at the cafeteria.

'You don't look very happy,' she said to him, interrupting her latest whine, which Goldblatt wasn't even pretending to try to follow.

'I am happy,' muttered Goldblatt darkly.

'What is it? Not that job at the Nailwright? Malcolm, you're too down about this job. When's the interview?'

'Tomorrow afternoon. You're covering me, remember?'

'*Again?*'

'I told you last week.'

Ludo gave him a glance of profound disdain, as if even allowing the possibility that she might have forgotten – which of course she had – was beneath her.

'And this time, if Dr Morris rings you, make it at least *sound* like you know what you're doing.'

The look on Ludo's face, if possible, got even more disdainful.

'I'll be leaving at one.'

'There's no point me covering you if you're so negative about it. You'll never get the job if you're thinking like that. You have to be positive.'

Ludo... positive... The words didn't go together. Things must be bad, thought Goldblatt, if Ludo was giving the pep talk. Really bad.

Ludo picked up her cup and drained the last of her coffee.

Goldblatt thought about Mike Coalport. Honestly, after the pre-interview, what was the point in going back there tomorrow? It was so obvious, he thought miserably. He wasn't sure that he would even bother going. Just give them the satisfaction of having another Wise Man on the scene.

But what choice did he have? There was no other job on the horizon. And this would be the last one he could apply for without giving Professor Small as a reference. Once you'd worked on a unit for a few months, even as a locum, people would smell a rat if you didn't include the head of that unit as a referee. Goldblatt didn't think much of a reference was going to be forthcoming from the Prof. And maybe he should be more worried if one was, after what Ludo had told him about the previous SR. He didn't know how things had gone so sour so quickly. He had started off really, genuinely determined to be the most biddable, compliant, tolerant, helpful, and likeable registrar the world had ever seen, and he had really, genuinely believed he was going to be able to do it. And now, after two months, it seemed the Prof could hardly look at him without some kind of spasm in her head. As for him, he could barely look at the Prof without a feeling of disgust. Even if he had ever really been capable of being biddable, compliant, tolerant, helpful, and likeable – which, he had to admit, was open to question – he knew that he was losing the will to try. And once he lost the will, he knew, he would lose the way.

He glanced at his watch. 'Come on,' he said, 'are you going to help me with this pleural biopsy or not?'

'Oh, Malcolm,' whined Ludo.

Goldblatt got up. 'Come on. You said you'd never seen one.'

'I've got a Dermatology clinic.'

'It can wait.'

'Do I really have to help you?'

'Yes,' said Goldblatt. In the absence of the nursing staff, who had predictably announced, through Debbie, that they wouldn't have time to assist, and the HO, who had two new admissions to clerk as well as the prospect of Emma coming to drag her away to the Prof's private patients, he had asked Ludo to volunteer. All she'd have to do was stand by, pass him the instruments, and hold the jar in which the biopsy specimen would be deposited.

He was sure that even Ludo could manage that. Pretty sure, anyway.

Maybe Ludo was right about the HO. Goldblatt thought about her as he headed up to the ward with Ludo to do the biopsy on Mr Lister, searching his memory for the kind of signs he had missed in others in the past and which, because he had missed them then, he was concerned that he might be missing again.

In one sense, the HO had nothing to complain about. She was harassed, hounded, exhausted, and irritated out of her mind by the demands that came at her from every side. But this, after all, was the life of an HO. An HO clerks patients in, takes blood, books tests, sites drips, arranges discharge plans, gets hounded by nurses, finds out why tests haven't been done, rebooks tests, prescribes drugs, cancels drugs, finds out why tests still haven't been done, rebooks tests, gets hounded by nurses, rearranges discharge plans, rebooks tests, and sometimes goes home. The bit about going home is optional. A HO's lot is to do every menial, tedious, demeaning or labour-intensive task that anyone further up the hierarchy can find a way to dump on them. If they don't enjoy it, too bad. In a year's time, if they're still standing, they'll be a senior house officer and can start the lifelong practice of dumping on HOs themselves, and will be able to enjoy watching others floundering in the role. But you can't enjoy watching others floundering as HOs unless you've been an HO yourself and just shut up and got on with it. This is one of the unwritten, brutal 'I've done it therefore you'll do it' rules that pervade the medical profession, and every

HO has to abide by it or face the consequences from their seniors, who have all been HOs at one time or another, as they never fail to remind them.

But the HO faced more than her fair share of obstructions, pitfalls, and snares on the battlefield that, for her, was Professor Small's ward. She was caught in the crossfire. On one side, Goldblatt was supposedly running the ward according to the Book of Time, and on the other side, Emma was running a black market in beds, doing a roaring trade as the front man for the manipulation scam masterminded by the local Mr Big, alias Professor Small.

The fact that Emma still wasn't talking to Goldblatt didn't make things any easier for her. Two or three times a week Emma put her head into the doctors' office, checked that Goldblatt wasn't there, and then started whispering to the HO as if she had a swag of dodgy watches under her white coat. There was a special patient the Prof had asked her to bring in. It was always a special patient. Since Emma wasn't talking to Goldblatt, it was the HO who had to break the news to him. And each one of the Prof's special patients apparently needed special treatment, even though this special treatment invariably turned out to be the usual Fuertler's work-up that the HO could have organized in her sleep by now, and often did after a night on call. Emma was always cornering her when Goldblatt wasn't around and demanding an update on the work-up's state of progress. If any decisions had to be made, Emma usually contradicted anything Goldblatt said, on principle, and would then be back in an hour or two to ask the HO how Goldblatt had responded to make sure she hadn't made a mistake. Then, while the HO still had twenty tests to order and three discharge forms to write and two new patients to clerk, she would drag the HO off to the private patients' wing on the ninth floor, to spend an hour or two admitting the Prof's private customers and organizing their work-ups.

Formally, the HO had no responsibility at all for these patients, but informally she had plenty. Private patients in NHS hospitals typically occupied a semi-corrupt twilight zone in which consultants tried to force the work on to their trainee doctors, and their trainee doctors sought tactful means of evading this extra-contractual imposition while not blowing their chances of a reference. Some consultants offered pitiful sums of money to their trainees at the end of their time on the unit, like a feudal lord throwing a scrap of meat to a grovelling peasant, amounting to perhaps one hundredth of the sums that their trainees had earned for them, and apparently expected them to be grateful. Even though it was Emma who accompanied the Prof on her visits to the private patients, it was the HO, like some palace servant scuttling around the corridors behind the walls but never being seen, on whom she dumped the tasks.

Of course, sometimes the HO did get to leave the hospital on time. No system is perfect. And she wasn't on call every single night, or even every single weekend, so she ought to have had no problem coping with the mind-numbing exhaustion, the endless flood of trivial ward tasks, the requirement for her to deal with problems far above her level of experience, the unwillingness of her seniors to help her, the sense of aloneness when her bleep went off after midnight, and the general fear of failure that awaited her every night she was on call. In short, the HO was now deep inside the cycle of psychological trauma that is the traditional framework of existence for an HO.

She had begun asking herself the questions all house officers ask. Why not give it up? Why continue? Why do this to yourself? The house officers joked about these questions amongst themselves in the doctors' mess, as house officers do, glancing at each other surreptitiously, wondering if any of the others would really be brave enough or desperate enough to break cover. And what about the next job, after the house officer year was over? An SHO job? More sleepless nights, more eviscerating weekends? While you were trying to study for your first part. And after that? Another SHO job? While you were trying to study for your second part? More sleepless nights, more eviscerating weekends...

'What do you think about an SHO job in Accident and Emergency?' the HO asked Goldblatt, walking into the doctors' office and sitting down as he was writing up his notes on Mr Lister's pleural biopsy. Ludo had gone off to one of her fictional Dermatology clinics as soon as the cap on the jar containing the biopsy specimen was sealed, probably worried that Goldblatt was going to expect her to label it as well, which would make for just too much work.

'No,' said Goldblatt, without looking up. 'I don't think I should settle for anything lower than registrar. Not at my stage.'

271

'For me, Malcolm!'

Goldblatt smiled and continued writing.

The HO was holding a plastic specimen bag that was filled with ice cubes. Amongst the ice cubes was a syringe from which the needle had been removed, containing four millilitres of blood that the HO had just drawn from the artery at a patient's wrist. Once capped, it had to be kept on ice until she took it down to the lab where it would be analysed for its content of oxygen and carbon dioxide. Testing arterial blood gases was a standard part of the Fuertler's work-up, and the HO had to do it on every patient who came in.

'I'm serious, Malcolm. What do you think?'

'What do I think? I think it's a stupid idea.'

'Why?'

Goldblatt glanced at the HO. 'Because it's boring as hell. Fractures, stitches, and myocardial infarctions. You won't learn anything unless you want to be an orthopaedic surgeon or a tailor. Do you want to be an orthopod?'

'No.'

'A tailor?'

The HO paused to consider the idea.

'Anyway, it won't count for anything. It won't count towards your training unless you want to be a GP, and if you want to be a GP you'll just end up doing it again when you get on to a training programme. So it'll be wasted time. You'll waste six months of your life.'

The HO put the bag with the ice and the syringe on the desk next to the computer. 'Other people say it's a good idea.'

'Yeah. Well, there are a lot of idiots around,' murmured Goldblatt, writing in the folder. 'You want to be careful who you listen to.'

The HO crossed her arms. She tilted her head to one side and closed her eyes.

Goldblatt glanced at her. Her face was pale, there were dark shadows under her eyes. She had been on call the previous night and it looked as if she hadn't got any sleep. He watched her, waiting to hear what he knew was coming next.

'At least it's shift work.'

'So?'

The HO opened her eyes. She pushed her glasses back up her nose. 'So I'll get to fucking sleep!'

'Is that all you care about?' demanded old Professor Goldblatt. 'You young doctors! When I was a house officer we slept on wooden boards in the back of the mortuary and were on call for the whole year without a single night off. They had to provide prostitutes because we couldn't get out to see our girlfriends. By the end of it we hadn't seen the sun so long we had rickets. And let me tell you, we wore our bandy legs like a badge of honour.'

'Thanks, Malcolm.'

'It's no fun wearing bandy legs. Take it from someone who knows. They aren't easy to come by, for a start. And don't even talk about the weight of them!' Goldblatt crossed his arms forcefully. 'Shift work! What'll it do to your social life?'

'Social life!' the HO said bitterly.

Goldblatt gave her a penetrating glance. 'When was the last time you went out?'

The HO glanced away guiltily.

'Tell me. I'm your registrar. You have no rights.'

'Tuesday,' the HO mumbled.

'Liar!'

'All right, Saturday.'

'Saturday?'

'All right, the Saturday before that. I was too fucking tired last weekend. I stayed home.'

'By yourself?'

The HO nodded.

Goldblatt stared at her. That was bad. The HO had a boyfriend. Goldblatt wondered how much more of this he was going to tolerate.

The HO glanced around angrily. It was just possible to detect a hint of smoke coming out of her small nostrils.

She took off her glasses and rubbed them on her white coat.

'Don't do a Casualty job,' said Goldblatt quietly. 'It's a waste of six months. It's a racket. They buy you with golden visions and promises of sleep.'

The HO didn't say anything. She picked the bag of ice up off the desk and stopped, looking at it, frowning.

'What's wrong?' said Goldblatt.

The HO held the bag out for Goldblatt to look at. At the bottom of the bag was a thin line of vivid scarlet.

'You didn't put the cap on the syringe.'

'I left the cap off! Fuck!' Smoke was hissing out of the HO's nostrils now. She shook the bag and the blood inside it smeared all over the ice cubes. 'Fuck! Fuck! I left the cap off!'

'You left the cap off,' Goldblatt confirmed.

'*Fuck! Fuck!*' cried the HO. The words shot out on the geyser of rage that had built up inside her. She stormed out of the office to get rid of the bag and stormed back in to get another set of identification labels from the patient's notes before going to take another sample.

Goldblatt didn't think the HO was in a fit state to attack a plastic bag with an ice cube, much less a patient with a needle.

'Sit down,' he said.

'I can't sit down,' the HO snapped. 'I've got too much to do. I've got to take these gases again and then—'

'Sit down!' said Goldblatt

The HO looked at him resentfully. After a moment she sat down.

'Go home,' said Goldblatt.

The HO stood up.

'Not yet. Sit down.'

The HO sat down.

'You need to go home.'

'You told me to sit down.'

'First you need to listen to what I have to say. Then you need to go home.'

The HO sat on the chair. Like a volcano waiting to erupt.

Goldblatt gave her a long look. 'Can the gases wait until tomorrow? Ask yourself. Are they routine or urgent?'

The HO stared at him sullenly.

'Routine,' Goldblatt answered for her. 'They can wait until tomorrow. Right?' Goldblatt waited for the HO to answer. 'Right?'

The HO was silent.

Goldblatt got up and drew one of his decision trees on the whiteboard.

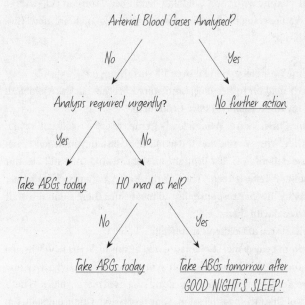

Arterial Blood Gases Analysed?

No / *Yes*

Analysis required urgently?   <u>*No further action*</u>

Yes / *No*

<u>*Take ABGs today*</u>   *HO mad as hell?*

No / *Yes*

<u>*Take ABGs today*</u>   <u>*Take ABGs tomorrow after GOOD NIGHT'S SLEEP!*</u>

The HO watched him angrily.

He sat down. 'That's dealt with. You'll do them tomorrow.'

The HO stood up.

'Where are you going?' asked Goldblatt.

'Isn't that what you had to say?'

'Sit down.'

'I can't. I've got three patients to clerk.'

'How can you have three patients to clerk? We only got two in today.'

'There's a private patient on the ninth floor.'

'Sit down,' said Goldblatt.

The HO sat down.

'It's four o'clock. You're paid to be here until five.'

'I never go home at five.'

'Today you're going home at five. Go home at five.'

'All right. Can I go now?'

'Where?'

'I've got three patients to clerk.'

'What's wrong with you?' Goldblatt demanded. 'You can't clerk three patients. You're going home at five. Fuck it, you're going home now! Give me your bleep.'

'No.'

'Give me your bleep. Hand it over. I'll sort things out.'

The HO held on to her bleep and stared fiercely back at Goldblatt. 'They're my responsibility! I have to do them.'

'Oh, for Christ's sake! What a load of crap. They've really got to you, haven't they? They've sold you the whole deal. Listen, you haven't even seen those patients yet. If I brought in eight, would they still be your responsibility? Ten? Fifteen? They're the Prof's patients. They're her responsibility. It's her responsibility to make sure there's enough staff around to deal with them.'

The HO stared at Goldblatt sceptically.

'You don't believe me?' Goldblatt gazed at this little HO who was just another one of the thousands each year duped by the hypocrisy and self-interest of their senior colleagues and supposed moral guides. 'That's the ethics of this fucking profession. Your profession. Our profession. I'm not making this one up. For once, this one isn't Malcolm Goldblatt's idea. Go and read the ethical guidelines of your own medical association. It's a consultant's responsibility – their *ethical* responsibility – to ensure that any doctor working on their unit is capable of carrying out the tasks they're given. It's an ethical responsibility, right? Not an option. Not a nice-to-have. A must-do. Now you tell me when any of the consultants you've worked for have ever bothered to come along and see for themselves that you're able to handle a given situation. Name one. Professor Small? One of the consultants you do Takes for? Did any of them ever speak to you about the man with the VIPoma? Did any one of them ever bother to find out why you didn't get his potassium level for three hours? Three whole hours when it was less than half the lower limit of normal? What have they done to make sure you can handle the things you come across at two in the morning? When have they ever even *asked* you if you've had a problem dealing with anything? When have they—'

He stopped. The HO was staring at him with wide, frightened eyes.

Goldblatt took a deep breath.

He smiled self-consciously. 'Sorry,' he said quietly. 'Look, this is how they get you. Don't you see? This is the lie they sell you, making you believe everything is your responsibility.'

The HO watched him. Did she understand? Goldblatt didn't know.

'Hand the patients over to Ludo and go home,' he said wearily. 'Ludo will clerk the admissions today.'

'Ludo?' said the HO, just as wearily. 'Come on, Malcolm. *She's* the one who goes home at five.'

'Not today.'

'She'll just hand them over to the on-call house officer.'

'Well, hand them over to the on-call house officer yourself.'

'I can't.'

'Why not? Don't they ever hand admissions on to you?'

'Sometimes.'

'So?'

'The on-call person will hate me. I hate them when they do it.'

'Let them hate you. Hate is what keeps the medical profession together. Listen, you have to learn to draw lines around yourself. Lines that no one can step over. People will hate you, but you have to do it. I do it. That's why people don't like me.'

'I like you, Malcolm.'

Goldblatt sighed. 'Apart from you. People don't like me, because I draw lines. That's how you survive.' Goldblatt peered intently at the HO, trying to see if she understood. Because it was important. Really important. She had barely begun to live as a doctor. It wasn't going to go away. It was going to get worse. 'The demands are endless. They never stop until you stop them. It's your right. Not only that, it's your duty. To yourself. You have to draw lines. Do the things that are important, the things that really matter to your patients. The rest of it is disposable. When you're more senior, you'll be able to draw the lines better. But that doesn't mean you can't draw any now. It doesn't mean you can't start. Understand?'

'Yes,' said the HO.

'Good,' said Goldblatt.

'Like Ludo?'

Goldblatt smiled. 'You don't necessarily need to draw as many lines as Ludo. Leave some space between them to actually do something.'

The HO laughed.

'Look, if there's anything you absolutely have to finish yourself, go and do it,' said Goldblatt. 'Not the admissions. And don't give them to the on-call person. Ludo will do one, I'll do the other one. Emma can deal with the one on the private patients' ward. Don't worry, I'll tell her. Leave me your bleep.' Goldblatt smiled. 'She'll answer that one.'

The HO grinned.

'Work out what you have to do, then give me your bleep and go home.'

The HO nodded. 'Can I go now?'

'Yes,' said Goldblatt complacently. 'What are you going to do?'

'Clerk the three new patients,' said the HO, and walked out.

Goldblatt stared after her. Then he shook his head and turned back to finish the note on Mr Lister.

But maybe the HO was right, he thought. Maybe there was no viable middle ground between blind, impotent, eye-scratching rage, and crawling, canine servility. One or the other, no place for the line-drawers in between.

Maybe it was the line-drawers who ended up as the Wise Men, and the canine crawlers as Eminent Physicians.

Then he had another thought: maybe you don't have to draw lines in order to survive.

It struck him with amazement. He felt stunned. Where had the thought come from? But maybe that was it. It would explain so much. Maybe he had been wrong all along, and everyone else was right. All the people who could have been his patrons, but hadn't been. Even Dr Oakley. If only he had realized it earlier, maybe he wouldn't be facing the Nailwright interview tomorrow with no patron, no support, nothing but his unbalanced CV to shield him.

For the very first time in his life, sitting in the doctors' office on Professor Small's unit and staring at Mr Lister's notes in front of him, Malcolm Goldblatt thought: maybe that was only the way *he* had survived.

22

Jobs in the medical profession are about patronage, and Goldblatt knew how patronage works. He also knew that he had no one to blame but himself for the fact that he had failed to take advantage of it.

The medical patron is a consultant, preferably a professor, with whom you develop your relationship as a registrar or SHO. They pulls the levers to get you your next job, find you a place to do your MD, and generally lean on people in your favour. In return, you perform the small acts of homage that a patron expects from their client. You treat them with the respect due to a great teacher, dance attendance whenever they arrive on the ward, put their name on every publication you produce even if they have zero input into it, and treat their private patients without a murmur.

That probably doesn't sound like much of an incentive for the patron, and you might wonder why they bother. But just as their peers will judge them by the number of papers they publish, the number of beds on their unit, the make and model of their car, so they judge them on the number and quality of their clients. A patron who has seeded his or her little neck of the medical woods with a succession of consultants who owe their training and positions to them is the equivalent of a big swinging dick on a bond trading floor.

It takes influence to be an effective patron, and there are only a limited number of consultants who are sufficiently powerful to play this role. On the other hand, there's a virtually unlimited number of young and aspiring doctors who want to be clients. The patron is therefore in the position of being able to choose which clients they will support, and which they will reject. Or to put it another way, it's a patron's market.

This was a very important point to bear in mind if, like Goldblatt, you were looking for one.

Goldblatt knew he had never been an attractive proposition as a client. Patronage isn't there to help people buck the system. It is the system. A consultant has little to gain by backing a registrar who doesn't want to do a research degree. It will take a cruel and unusual amount of influence to secure advancement for them, and the favours asked in return by other consultants are likely to be just as cruel and unusual. The legal interruption to Goldblatt's medical training had also severed many connections at a sensitive time in his career, and had put him back at square one in the competition for patronage. Yet despite this, Goldblatt had almost succeeded in acquiring a patron in the person of Sam Rothman during the year that he had worked as a registrar on his unit.

Professor Rothman was perhaps not the greatest heavyweight in his specialist area. He had a habit of answering with anecdotes when he was asked questions about concepts. One of his favourite stories was about the time he almost got a bean in his eye.

Goldblatt first heard it on one of his ward rounds. The house officer was looking particularly unwholesome, making everyone queasy with the unpleasant post-mortem pallor of his face, and explained that he had had no sleep at all while on call the night before. Professor Rothman laughed heartily, brought the round to a halt in the middle of the ward, leaned one elbow on the notes trolley, and nostalgically recounted the tale.

'I remember the day after my first night on call as a house officer,' he began. 'I hadn't got a wink of sleep, just like young...'

'Richard,' whispered Goldblatt.

'Like young Richard here. Not a wink. If I did, I was too tired to remember it!'

Professor Rothman laughed. He threw an amiable glance at the patient in the next bed, who was listening with interest as she waited for the doctors to reach her.

'Anyway, I had a girlfriend at the time,' Professor Rothman continued, as Richard closed his eyes and began to rock on his feet. 'She'd invited me to her place for supper. That very night! So I sat down, and she brought my plate of soup out and then she went back into the kitchen to get her own. I can remember seeing her go out, and that was the last thing I did remember. I don't know why she hadn't brought out the whole pot

– maybe she didn't think it would be polite. At that stage we still didn't know each other very well.' He paused and gave a small sigh. 'Anyway, out she went to get her plate, and when she came back she found me face down in the soup. She'd only been gone for a minute, but I was so tired I'd keeled over and gone to sleep!'

Professor Rothman laughed merrily at the anecdote. Dr Serenstern, the SR, smirked. Goldblatt stared at Professor Rothman incredulously.

'Did you drown?' he asked.

'No,' said Professor Rothman with avuncular bonhomie, 'but I almost got a bean in my eye!'

Still, Professor Rothman wasn't without clout. He was very nice and sometimes amusing, and these blameless attributes made him generally liked, and even bought him a moderate degree of influence. The sheer number of papers that carried his name, produced by the hordes of clients who attached themselves to him, also had an effect. Many of these papers, as everyone knew, were of doubtful quality, being derived from clinical records that were rarely complete, and they often appeared in second-tier journals that couldn't attract anything better. But there were a lot of them. Professor Rothman also ran a lab from which emerged papers of better quality that appeared in journals of higher regard. So he had been able to ensure that his current SR, Dr Serenstern, who had first arrived on his unit as a registrar, had received a grant to do an MD in his lab and had then gone on to his current post. It was also common knowledge that Dr Serenstern would get the consultant position that would become vacant in a couple of years when one of the other consultants on the unit, Dr Bracket, retired. Dr Serenstern, who had been told by Professor Rothman to keep it all under his hat, smugly pretended to be worried about his future.

After Goldblatt had been on the unit for a month or two, Professor Rothman started coming up with ideas for a few doubtful papers that would add to Goldblatt's publication record, and he gave Goldblatt access to his equivalent of the Fuertler's files so he could write them up. He began mentioning rumours that he had heard on the grapevine about SR positions that would be falling vacant, and began speculating about which ones might be best for him. For a while it looked as if Professor Rothman was prepared to throw around whatever weight he had in order to help Goldblatt get an SR job.

But wouldn't he need to do a research degree, at the very least an MD? No, Professor Rothman declared, not with *his* backing.

Unfortunately for Goldblatt, Professor Rothman's greatest strength was also his greatest weakness. The core of his niceness was an acute and overwhelming agreeableness, reflecting the fact that Professor Rothman's opinion on any matter strongly tended to echo the last opinion he had heard on the subject. His attitude underwent a change that coincided uncannily with the first SR interview that Goldblatt went for, and in particular with a phone call from one of the members of the interview panel that he received the day afterwards. The interviewer, who was a personal friend of Sam Rothman, had rung to let him know that the panel thought that Dr Goldblatt, while clearly an intelligent man and capable clinician, needed to do an MD before applying for any more SR posts. The panel, said the interviewer, thought Sam would want to know its opinion since he had been so strongly supportive of Dr Goldblatt's application. Sam did want to know its opinion, and was very grateful to his friend. Professor Rothman called Goldblatt into his office and, in a fatherly voice, said that the interview just proved what he had suspected all along: Goldblatt needed to do an MD.

'An MD?' Goldblatt looked at Professor Rothman suspiciously. Professor Rothman nodded. 'An MD?' But this was the very man who, one month earlier, had assured Goldblatt that it was certainly possible to get an SR job without having an MD – as long as he had *his* backing – and if he didn't get this job he would certainly get the next. This was the very office in which he had said it! 'An MD?' This time Professor Rothman looked at him blankly, as if he couldn't remember any of the things he had told Goldblatt earlier, and didn't particularly want to be reminded.

In fact, there was a deeper message. When the consultant from the interview rang, it wasn't simply to tell Professor Rothman that Dr Goldblatt needed to do an MD. There was a subtext, which was that Dr Goldblatt, *more than anyone*, needed to do an MD. That was the only way he could remove the doubt that hung over him now that he had been outside the fold. It was the only way he could prove that he had really come back for ever. He had to do it harder than everybody else, be purer than pure Otherwise, the stain on his record was going to stay there for good.

Goldblatt understood the message now, as clearly as if it were written in front of him. Had he really failed to see it back then? Or had he simply refused to acknowledge it?

But Professor Rothman wasn't cutting him adrift. Not at all. He mentioned the idea of applying for a research grant with Goldblatt. Perhaps Malcolm could do an MD in his lab, as Dr Serenstern had done. But Professor Rothman, an indiscriminate and therefore unreliable patron, had offered the identical gift of a place in his lab to other clients as well, and a lab has only so many places to go around. And Goldblatt, an unwilling and therefore unreliable client, didn't really want to do an MD anyway. So the idea drifted along for a while without anything happening, as different grant applications were written with different, more enthusiastic registrars, and might have drifted along for even longer had not an event taken place that was to kill Professor Rothman's patronage stone dead.

This event, as such events are, was the end result of a long chain of preceding events that culminated in a particular place at a particular time. Had it culminated earlier, or later, or somewhere else, it would have had no effect at all on Malcolm Goldblatt, and who could say how the course of his life might have been different? But it culminated when it did, and Goldblatt was standing slap bang in its way.

To summarize a long and bitter political struggle, the cardiologists, who had been agitating for years to withdraw their registrars from the medical Take rota, suddenly achieved their objective. This meant that the on-call commitments of the Cardiology registrars had to be redistributed amongst the remaining registrars on the staff. Someone in Medical Administration, whom Goldblatt had never met, sat down, drew up a new rota, and sent it out. And that person, whoever it was, probably expected to hear no more of the matter.

Goldblatt didn't want to do any more on-call work. It wasn't a huge amount more that he was expected to do – just an extra night every couple of weeks – but his contract specified exactly how much on-call work was required from him, and this wasn't included. So he went to talk to Dr Oakley, who was the consultant on the unit who ran the administrative side of things.

Dr Oakley was a generally compliant character who would have liked to see every side of an argument, but couldn't, now that his life had become a continuous series of skirmishes over the running of the unit. This role had been more or less forced on him by his two colleagues. Professor Rothman had academic interests to attend to, and Dr Bracket was too long in the tooth to bother with any of this new-fangled management hoo-hah, so if anyone was going to do it, it was going to be Oakley. When it all got too much for him, Dr Oakley would spread his papers out in piles on the floor in his office and go down on his knees, trying to sort out his correspondence. Often when Goldblatt walked past his office he would see him down there mumbling to himself in despair.

Goldblatt had a good relationship with Dr Oakley. He thought – he really did think – that Dr Oakley would recognize that the demand for him to do additional on-call work was a simple, straightforward breach of his contract, and that would be that.

Dr Oakley did recognize that it was a simple, straightforward breach of Goldblatt's contract and said he'd talk to the appropriate person in the hospital management. He talked to the appropriate person in the hospital management and came back and told Goldblatt that all the other registrars had readily agreed to the change, which Goldblatt found interesting, and quite sad, but hardly relevant. All right, said Dr Oakley, and he went back to the appropriate person, and the appropriate person sent him right back, and this time Dr Oakley asked Goldblatt if he wouldn't change his mind, 'just for me'. Sorry, said Goldblatt. All right, said Dr Oakley, and said he'd respect Goldblatt's decision – which he respected for about a day, until he went back to the appropriate person and she told him she couldn't possibly stand for that kind of insubordination and she didn't understand how Dr Oakley could either. At which point she declared that she was prepared to come and talk to this troublesome Dr Goldblatt if Dr Oakley thought it would help. Dr Oakley didn't know if it would help but he didn't think he was being given much choice in the matter.

When Dr Oakley told Goldblatt that the appropriate person wanted to talk to him – but there was still time to avoid this terrible meeting, if only he'd change his mind – Goldblatt sensed that he was being intimidated. A few seconds after that, he sensed that he was standing up for a principle. Once he realized he was standing up for a principle, there was no way he could back down. By now Dr Oakley couldn't back down either, but in his case it was less of a principle and more of an expediency.

So Goldblatt got to meet the appropriate person, who turned out to be a dumpy, pasty woman who introduced herself as Sue Bigelow, wearing a dark suit, with dyed blonde hair, and a lot of foundation on her face. And a small folder under her arm, which she opened officiously as she sat down in Dr Oakley's office with Oakley and Goldblatt, as if to declare that the meeting was open.

Dr Oakley, Goldblatt noted, had cleared away all the papers from his floor for the occasion.

Sue Bigelow seemed genuinely surprised at Goldblatt's refusal to work the extra shifts. 'Why don't you tell me why you don't want to?' she said, as if talking to a four-year-old.

'Because I don't,' replied Goldblatt, happy to play the part.

'We'll pay you.'

'I don't want the money.'

Sue Bigelow shrugged. All right, the hospital wouldn't pay him.

'No, you don't understand,' said Goldblatt, 'I'm not going to do it.'

Sue Bigelow looked dumbfounded. She glanced at Dr Oakley. Dr Oakley looked back at her helplessly.

'Why do you say you're not going to do it?' Sue Bigelow asked eventually, as if she was really interested.

'Because I'm not,' said Goldblatt.

'Why not?'

Goldblatt sighed. Why explain? He had given his explanation twice already to Dr Oakley, which was once more than he ought to have been asked to.

'Let's try to see how we can reach a solution that's acceptable to both of us,' said Sue Bigelow in a controlled, reasonable, but firm tone, just as they had taught her at management school.

'All right,' said Goldblatt. 'Let's start by saying I'm not going to do it.'

'Why not?'

'Why don't you read my contract?'

'I have read your contract, Dr Goldblatt.'

'Good. Then you don't need to keep asking that question.'

'This is a hospital. We have to think of our patients, Dr Goldblatt, not just our contracts. We can't let the patients suffer.'

'The patients won't suffer,' Goldblatt replied in what he thought was a controlled, reasonable, but firm tone, which he imagined Sue Bigelow would appreciate. 'You'll hire locums for the extra nights. There are plenty of registrars doing research who want the work. I can give you some names if you need them. And then you won't find yourself in the position of trying to breach my contract, which must be very unpleasant for you.'

Sue Bigelow frowned. She looked down at her file and made a note with her pen. Perhaps, thought Goldblatt, she was writing down his excellent suggestion. No, he thought, surely that one would have occurred to her already.

But it really was an excellent suggestion. The only drawback to it was that it would cost the hospital somewhat more to hire locums than if they could coerce Goldblatt – who was paid only half his usual rate of pay for on-call hours – to do the work. Given the small number of nights they were talking about, the total sum at stake for the hospital over the course of the rest of the year was probably all of a couple of thousand pounds. Thus it was preferable, it seemed, to try to breach his contract.

Sue Bigelow looked up at him. 'It's not very much more we're asking you to do,' she said, back in her cajole-the-four-year-old tone.

'For who?' asked Goldblatt.

She looked puzzled. 'For you.'

'Oh. For me? Who are you to make that judgement?'

Sue Bigelow folded her arms in exasperation. Now, she was getting angry. She shot a cold glance at Dr Oakley. What was wrong with him? Couldn't he control his junior staff? Dr Oakley caught her glance and looked away quickly. This was going to get back to the Chief Executive and it wasn't going to do him any good. He glared at Goldblatt resentfully.

Sue Bigelow turned back to him. 'Dr Goldblatt. I am always open to suggestions. But understand one thing. I refuse to discuss issues with staff who have already made up their minds and will not consider alternatives. I am prepared to consider alternatives, but I will not speak to people who will not consider alternatives themselves.'

'Does that mean I can go?' asked Goldblatt.

'No, you can't go.'

'But I've told you I'm not prepared to consider alternatives. Doesn't that mean you refuse to talk to me?'

'Malcolm...' said Dr Oakley.

'No, Andrew,' said Sue Bigelow. 'I think Dr Goldblatt needs to understand this very clearly.'

'I don't understand this very clearly,' said Goldblatt. 'I'm very confused. Why did you ask me to come to this meeting if you were going to refuse to talk to me?'

'Dr Goldblatt, listen to me. I will *not* discuss an issue with staff who will not consider alternatives.'

'So I *can* go.'

'Maybe he should go,' said Dr Oakley.

'No, Andrew,' said Sue Bigelow, who had come to show Dr Oakley how to deal with his staff, and was determined to do it. 'Dr Goldblatt, nothing I have heard today shows me that you care anything at all for this hospital or its patients.'

Goldblatt restrained himself. He glanced at Dr Oakley. Oakley looked away before he could meet his eyes.

Goldblatt turned back to the manager who was sitting with her folder still open on the desk in front of her. 'You should be careful before you say that sort of thing to a doctor,' he said quietly.

'And what is that supposed to mean?'

'You should think before you say things like that. That's all. And speaking of caring for patients, I think I've wasted enough of my time with this ludicrous conver—'

'*Do* you care for your patients, Dr Goldblatt? Perhaps you'd care to prove to me that you do.'

Goldblatt glanced at Dr Oakley again. Again, Oakley avoided his eyes. What was wrong with him? Was he going to sit by and let some over-rouged manager impugn his own registrar? Oakley had worked with him. He knew whether Goldblatt cared or not.

But Andrew Oakley just sat there, his ears going red and his eyes fixed firmly on the floor, as if he wished his papers were still down there.

'You don't understand what it is to do on-call work,' Goldblatt said eventually.

'I think I do,' said Sue Bigelow.

'Tell me when you've ever done it. Which hospital? What rotas? One in three? One in four?'

'I don't think that matters.'

'Then you think wrong.'

'Then explain it to me.'

'Why should I bother?' Goldblatt didn't care enough about this person who already knew all the answers to explain one of the answers that she obviously didn't know.

'Because I asked you.'

'So?'

'Malcolm...' said Dr Oakley.

'No one who hasn't done it can understand what it is,' said Goldblatt wearily. 'All right? Take it from me. How many times have you stayed in this hospital for thirty-six hours straight? For sixty hours straight? When you've done it ten, twenty times, thirty times, then let's sit down and have a talk. But right now, until you've done that, you may think you can understand, but you can't. That's a piece of advice. Use it as you will. You may find it helpful the next time you try to make someone do something you've never done yourself.'

Sue Bigelow didn't want Goldblatt's advice. She threw a knowing glance at Dr Oakley. He managed a sickly smile in return.

'I think I can understand it,' she said.

'Good for you,' said Goldblatt, who was a long way beyond giving a fuck about what she thought she could understand, but knew that he was going to hear anyway.

'I think most women can. Any mother who has ever had to nurse a newborn baby can understand it.'

Goldblatt stared at Sue Bigelow with genuine astonishment. Then he glanced at Dr Oakley to verify whether he really had heard what he thought he had heard. This time, Dr Oakley was too stunned to look away. He gave a slight, amazed shrug in response to Goldblatt's glance.

Well, whatever happened now, thought Goldblatt, this meeting wasn't going to have been a total waste of time. It had been worth sitting through all the condescension and threats for this one surreal moment.

Sue Bigelow was watching him with a smugly triumphant smile.

'Do you think,' Goldblatt said eventually, really wanting to find out if it were possible, 'do you *really* think you can compare my relationship with the six *hundred* patients who are in this hospital on any given night, most of whom I've never even *met*, to the relationship a mother has to the baby to whom she's given birth? Is that how you see it: they're my babies and I'm their mother? All six hundred of them? Is that really how you understand what goes on in this hospital every night after you leave your little office, after you lock your little door, after you go home to your little family?'

Sue Bigelow blinked.

Goldblatt grinned. 'If that's your idea of motherhood, are you sure you're fit to bring up your kids?'

And then he started to laugh. It was so ridiculous, he couldn't stop. Sue Bigelow stared at him with cold, rigid fury. Goldblatt was still laughing as he got up and left. Out of the corner of his eye, he saw Dr Oakley's shoulders shaking with silent giggles.

But Goldblatt never forgave Dr Oakley. Silent giggles didn't wipe out his guilt, his failure to speak up when it mattered, or what he did later.

Goldblatt had won. He didn't do the extra shifts. There were no legal grounds on which he could be coerced. The hospital gave the work to a couple of research registrars, who thanked him for the chance to earn some extra money.

But he lost as well. A lot more than he won. Dr Oakley had been humiliated, first by Goldblatt, then by the manager, then by Goldblatt again. The knowledge that he should have stood up for Goldblatt in the first place only added a prickle of self-loathing to the contempt he sensed from Sue

Bigelow and the inadequacy he felt in trying to cope with his administrative role. And whose fault was that? Goldblatt's, of course. Why couldn't he have just agreed to do the few extra shifts like every other registrar in the hospital?

And having misjudged what Dr Oakley would do the first time around, Goldblatt misjudged him again. As Lesley said, he never anticipated that people would actually act on their anger, that they wouldn't just laugh the experience off as yet one more absurdity the world threw at them. That very deliberately, purposefully, they would do something to injure him.

Naturally, Dr Oakley often spoke with Professor Rothman. When he spoke with Professor Rothman, he expressed his opinion about all sorts of things. He expressed it about Dr Goldblatt. Until now, Professor Rothman had had a generally favourable opinion of Dr Goldblatt. But Professor Rothman never had an opinion of his own that couldn't be reversed by a more forcefully presented opinion of somebody else.

Professor Rothman reversed his opinion.

There was no more talk of an MD in Professor Rothman's lab.

Goldblatt didn't know that he really blamed him. Sam Rothman wasn't much of a patron, but to be fair, Goldblatt had to admit that he hadn't been much of a client. He had been right on principle but wrong in practice. A good client would have acceded to Dr Oakley's demands in order to protect his relationship with Professor Rothman. Goldblatt didn't. Hence, in the context of a patronage system, he deserved what he got.

The day he left Professor Rothman's unit five months later, with Dr Oakley glancing out of his office from time to time to see if he was finally gone, he stepped patronless, MD-less, into the cold, cold world of locumdom.

Twenty months of it, including the time he had spent so far on Professor Small's unit. And unless some miracle was about to happen at the Nailwright Hospital the following afternoon, it was twenty months and counting.

23

GOLDBLATT WATCHED HIS FACE mirrored in the window against the blackness outside. The Underground train swept through the tunnel in the rush of its own compressed sound. The seats in the near-empty carriage were yellow and orange, old, worn, and grimy.

The train surfaced into the afternoon light. It ran past the backs of long rows of sandwiched houses. Goldblatt stared at them vacantly. The houses swept past. He caught glimpses of rooms. There were people in some of them. A man at a kitchen table. A woman with a baby. The reflection of his face in the carriage window was very faint now, like an out-of-focus foreground in a film shot. He felt as if he could have sat in the empty carriage for ever, if only the houses with the people in their rooms would keep rushing past.

He felt very detached and already empty. It was a familiar feeling that had arrived, peculiarly, a few hours early. It felt as if the interview was already over. It wasn't the right feeling to have going in. Not an optimistic feeling. Weary, hopeless, disgusted. He wasn't sure why he was even going. As an act of defiance? Just because he could? Because there's always a chance? After the pre-interview, only the most insane optimist would believe that. Mike Coalport didn't even want him there. Maybe he wouldn't be able to go through with it. Maybe, when the time came, he'd just turn around and walk away.

The train stopped. His stop.

He got off. Further along the platform another couple of people got off as well. He followed them out of the station.

It was a cold day in late March. The sky was blue. There was a piercing clarity in the air. Goldblatt turned left out of the station and followed the street, walking past parked cars and a couple of corner shops, overtaking an old lady with a blue woollen hat who was going home with a small bag of shopping. He felt as if he had done it all before, over and over again. He felt as if he were watching himself, Malcolm Goldblatt, walking along a street on a bright March afternoon. A man of thirty-three, average height, dressed in a dark overcoat over a blue suit, walking with his hands in his coat pockets for warmth. Dark hair, blue eyes, and a nose probably going red from the cold by now. A man walking along a street, not walking very fast.

Goldblatt glanced up. The main block of the Nailwright Hospital rose over the roofs of the houses ahead of him.

There were three others at the Nailwright that afternoon. There were meant to be four, but one of them had withdrawn, according to a candidate who was already there when Goldblatt arrived. The Mike Coalport treatment had obviously achieved the desired effect on at least one person. They waited in the lobby on the second floor of the medical school building. Chairs had been left out for them. Very dignified. People went up and down the stairs, glancing knowingly and smirking at the suited figures sitting in the lobby.

There's a dull, insensate, almost inevitable brutality to the way medical interviews are arranged. Another one of those things doctors would do only to each other. The candidates are all asked to arrive at the same time, and then they're meant to sit there for the next three hours, watching each other go in and come out, and then, as the last twist in the whole excruciating business, after the last candidate has emerged, after you've all been sitting around for three hours, everyone is meant to hang around for another thirty nail-biting, quick-chewing minutes while those with the power inside the interview room play with destinies and make up their minds. Then someone emerges and announces a name to the assembled candidates and invites the possessor of that name to come into the room and receive their reward. Just as if it doesn't really matter, as if it's only a game and the candidates are all good sports and don't mind being present to drink to the bitter dregs the experience of someone else stomping on their faces on their way up the ladder, and as if they really mean the forced congratulations they're ritually required to mutter as the victor leaves them behind to go into the interview room and be formally anointed.

The consultants had already gone into seminar room B, where the interviews were to be held, said the man who knew about the candidate who had withdrawn. He introduced himself as Anthony Thomas. He seemed to know a lot about the other candidates. He predicted the arrival of a woman who was finishing her PhD in Professor Murray's lab in Oxford, and three minutes later, behold, that woman did arrive. He also knew that the fourth candidate in the group had just disappeared to go to the toilet minutes before Goldblatt arrived. Presumably Anthony Thomas had predicted Goldblatt's arrival to the other man before he had left to relieve himself.

'And where are you working at present?' Goldblatt asked him.

'Oh, I'm just finishing my MD.'

'Really? And where would that be?'

'In Mike Coalport's lab,' said Anthony Thomas.

Of course you are, thought Goldblatt, and he heard the last piece of the puzzle clunk into place.

This job had probably been waiting for Anthony Thomas for two years. All they needed to do now was get enough Wise Men together to make sure it wasn't indisputably obvious.

The panel was assembled. The charade began. Soon enough the first candidate had been dealt with, and Goldblatt's turn came around.

Seminar room B contained a long table, a jug of water, and as fine a collection of Nailwright consultants as one could ask for. Goldblatt sat down, and they were soon under way.

The first interviewer on the panel took it upon himself to demonstrate comprehensively and without risk of ambiguity or omission, using Goldblatt's CV as prima facie evidence, that Goldblatt didn't have a research degree. This was an important public service, and Goldblatt understood why he spent so much time on it. Mike Coalport interrupted once or twice when there seemed to be a danger that he might not linger sufficiently on the point. Interrupting out of turn was usually considered to be a disruptive and unhelpful form of behaviour that threatened the precarious perfection of the medical interview, but everyone understood there were circumstances that justified it.

Well, thought Goldblatt, at least they've finished with the research degree.

'So it's true, Dr Goldblatt,' asked the second consultant, 'that you don't have a research degree?'

'It's true!' said Mike Coalport.

Goldblatt nodded briefly in Coalport's direction. Always acknowledge another's help, that was Goldblatt's maxim.

'May I ask why you chose to break off your career to do a law degree?' enquired the third interviewer when it was his turn, passing on to the next of Goldblatt's crimes.

Goldblatt had an answer. He had been asked the question so many times that he certainly had one. More than one.

But suddenly he felt just as he had felt in the train on his way to the hospital. It was exactly the same deep, hopeless feeling. It rose out of his bone marrow, seeped into his blood, and welled up into his brain.

Why did they always ask why he had left medicine? Why did they never ask why he came back?

Goldblatt gazed wearily at the consultant on the other side of the table who had asked the question. He had been introduced as a professor of something or other, the dean for postgraduate education in the region. He was a tall, well-built man with bronze skin, brown eyes, and thinning silver hair. Haemochromatosis, thought Goldblatt. That would be the diagnosis, if he had to hazard a guess. 'Bronzed diabetes', to give it the old-fashioned name. The body, genetically unable to process iron properly, lays it down all over the place – skin, liver, heart, pancreas, joints, pituitary gland, gonads. Iron in the balls. Why didn't he ask him about that? Ask about something relevant, for once, instead of asking why he did law. Why didn't this professor-whoever-he-was roll up his sleeve and ask Goldblatt to give him a diagnosis? Why didn't he then ask him to demonstrate how he would break the news to him if the diagnosis had just been made?

The bronzed professor with the iron balls was watching Goldblatt quiz-zically, waiting for an answer.

'Dr Goldblatt?'

Goldblatt had betrayed himself too many times answering that ques-tion for people like the ones on the other side of the table and still ending up a Wise Man. He couldn't bear the prospect of spilling his guts to yet another medical vivisectionist who was going to scoop them up and sniff them and throw them back in his face.

Yet finally he began, starting reluctantly on the well-trodden path of one of his standard explanations. Like a lamb, knowing exactly where the foul-smelling path leads, yet unable to stop himself following it.

'I wanted the challenge, I think. I thought I'd be able to combine both aspects of my training in a medicolegal career.'

'Defend your old colleagues, eh?' said Iron Balls sardonically, finding something amusing, apparently, in the thought.

Goldblatt gazed at him. All of a sudden, the empty, detached feeling was gone. It had welled up so far that it had blown the top off his skull, and now he was a wild, half-headed maniac with steam and anger belching out of his ears. What did they *want* from him? Why did they bother bringing him here if it was for this? Couldn't they think of anything better to do with their time, or at least something more original?

Goldblatt smiled. 'Defend my old colleagues? No, I'm more of a pros-ecutor by nature. I wanted to see every negligent, ignorant, arrogant doctor who had ever damaged a patient standing arraigned in the dock.'

Iron Balls didn't say anything for a moment. He stared at Goldblatt icily.

Goldblatt stared back. On closer examination, Iron Balls' bronzed diabetes looked as if it came out of a sunlamp. Goldblatt could easily picture him in the dock. An old-fashioned dock in an old-fashioned court. His tanned skin would go nicely with the wood panelling.

The room was quiet. It had been quiet to start with, a bland, cream-coloured quiet of boredom and predictability. Now it was a hideous, lurid, violet quiet of expectancy and strain.

He'd got their attention, anyway. No fidgeting. Everyone was looking.

'And now?' said Iron Balls eventually, taking up his supplementary question.

'Negligent, ignorant doctors?' said Goldblatt. 'I still want to see them in the dock. Don't you?'

Iron Balls gazed at him for a moment longer, his brown, appraising eyes disapproving. Then he looked at the pad in front of him and jotted something down, shaking his head.

It was disappointing. If the regional dean for postgraduate education didn't want to see negligent doctors in the dock, who would?

Now there was only one thing for Goldblatt to decide. Get up and walk out, or stay for the rest of the interview?

He realized that he had just thrown away all the chances he had never had of getting this job. That wasn't the problem. The problem was that now he had nothing to lose. And he still had just enough sanity left to recognize that that was when he posed the most danger. To himself. If he stayed, he didn't know what else he might end up saying to this bunch of Nailwright jackasses whose braying, he had discovered, was starting to irritate him. He sensed that in another moment even that last shred of sanity would be gone.

He needed to decide quickly. Now. Before he opened his mouth again.

He ought to leave. He knew it. The medical world is a small place. Word gets around. It would be unwise to stay. Too dangerous. It might be fun.

The next consultant to question him was Mike Coalport.

Fuck it, thought Goldblatt. He *couldn't* leave now.

Having seen the main issue of Goldblatt's interview dealt with twice over, and having just watched Goldblatt shoot himself in the foot – blow his foot right off, in fact – Mike Coalport squared his shoulders with relish and got ready to inflict more damage, hoping to see Goldblatt amputate his other leg. There was nothing he enjoyed more than seeing a candidate stagger out on two bloody stumps. He launched into one of his stock questions.

'I'd like to get your thoughts on a social issue,' he said.

Nine times out of ten, the social issue raised in a medical interview just happens, coincidentally, to be the same social issue that has been highlighted in one of the main medical journals the week before. Nine times out of ten the interviewer can't resist the temptation to provide his own thoughts on the subject as a preamble to the question, usually at far greater, meandering length than any answer he is prepared to tolerate from the candidate. Goldblatt had often been advised by consultants and successful candidates never to disagree outright with the interviewer's opinion. At most, if agreement was impossible, it was necessary to acknowledge the legitimacy of that view before briefly mentioning an alternative. But no consultant who had ever advised him could actually think of an opinion with which, for a period of five minutes and with a job hanging in the balance, they would find it impossible to agree.

'No, I don't agree,' said Goldblatt, when Mike Coalport had concluded his introductory oration, for which he had assumed the famous tone and posture with which he had delivered so many *coups de grâce* at conferences both in Britain and abroad.

Mike Coalport looked up at him in outrage. He had just given what he felt to be a scholarly, sweeping, and masterful exposition of his theme, which wasn't some plagiarized Social Issue culled from the previous week's *Lancet*, but was, in fact, his favourite Social Issue and of his own particular construction. The argument, in brief, was that doctors who focus their research on rare diseases are misguided, profligate and irresponsible. Instead, they should direct their efforts to more common illnesses, on the grounds that they would thus relieve more suffering. Coalport's technique was to deliver it in a tone that intimated that he was prepared to brook no opposition. When the candidate duly offered no opposition, he would then counter with an equally aggressive argument for the opposing point of view and demand to know what the candidate thought of that!

Goldblatt would have happily argued for the position that Coalport was advocating. On the other hand, he was happy to argue against it. After all, the gloves were off. The holds were unbarred. Even as he had listened to Coalport's punchy voice droning on, his mind was peering with alacrity down the many alleyways by which he could attack. It was like being a barrister again, or at least a trainee one, which was all Goldblatt had been. If Mike Coalport really wanted to debate a Social Issue, it was his lucky day.

'So you disagree?' asked Coalport, gazing at him in delighted contempt.

'Yes,' said Goldblatt.

Mike Coalport licked his lips, the pleasure of the entertainment in prospect making him look more like a debauched cherub than ever. He glanced from side to side, as if making a special and particular invitation to each of his colleagues to come to the Coliseum and enjoy the slaughter. Iron Balls, who was obviously an inveterate jotter, shook his head and jotted some more.

'Why?' asked Coalport eventually.

'How would you feel?' retorted Goldblatt quickly.

Coalport snorted. 'Is that how you would make a decision on a social issue?'

This was already Coalport's fourth question, and it was clear that he was going to run amok. Goldblatt appealed mutely to the lay moderator at the interview, who happened to be a professor of cardiology, giving her a final chance to stop proceedings. If she let it go from here, everyone knew, she would have to let it go to the end.

The professor of cardiology had no intention of missing the spectacle.

Goldblatt turned back to Mike Coalport. '*Is* this a social question?'

Coalport guffawed. He looked around again to see if anyone present had ever witnessed such a stupid man on the other side of an interview table.

'Or a question about you, Professor Coalport, as a moral agent?'

Coalport glanced back at Goldblatt abruptly. For a second he looked just like any fat, confused man. He blinked. Then he recovered his balance in the only way he knew.

'Do you think *you're* qualified to make that distinction?' he enquired sarcastically.

'That depends,' said Goldblatt. 'Are *you* qualified to think?'

Coalport was speechless with rage. Iron Balls dropped his pen and stared. Other mouths opened.

'I ask this in an ontological sense' Goldblatt continued, since no one appeared to be in a fit state to stop him. 'When you ask me "Are you qualified to make that distinction?" you're making the common mistake of confusing a moral with a technical judgement. The question you have asked is a moral one, not a technical one. Once we understand this, Professor Coalport, then we can see why your question entirely misses the point. This is a moral judgement, and by definition, we're all qualified to make moral judgements. That's why we're all subject to legal process. Those of us who aren't capable of making moral judgements – infants, or the insane – aren't subject to legal process. If I stood up right now and punched you in the face, for example, I would be subject to legal process, correct?'

Coalport stared at Goldblatt with hateful incredulity.

'Correct,' said Goldblatt, helping him out. 'Therefore I don't stand up and punch you in the face. Not that I'd want to, of course. But even if I did want to, I wouldn't, because I'm capable of making a moral judgement. Therefore it goes without saying that I'm capable of making this distinction.'

Goldblatt sat back in his chair and folded his arms. He glanced along the line of faces opposite, looking for a sign of life.

'But I haven't answered your question, have I?' he added.

'No, you haven't!' retorted Coalport, instinctively recovering his scorn even as he struggled to remember what his question was.

Wrong answer. Coalport should have taken the chance to bring the exchange to an end, not prolong it. No one pauses in an argument to remind you that he hasn't answered your question because a sense of fair play has suddenly forced him to own up to his evasiveness. He's asked you because he's got something else in store for you, and it isn't going to be pretty.

'And you haven't answered mine,' said Goldblatt.

'May I remind you that this is an interview, Dr Goldblatt,' interjected the moderator.

'Thank you, m'lud.' Goldblatt turned back to Mike Coalport. 'You haven't answered it.'

'What was it?' demanded Coalport combatively. He wasn't going to back down in front of some would-be SR who didn't even have a research degree.

'How would you feel?'

'How would I feel if what?'

'If you had some rare disease.'

'Oh, please. Do you really mean—'

'How would you feel if you had some common disease?'

Coalport frowned.

There was another one of those silences in the room, but it was different, all at once it was aimed at Mike Coalport. Maybe one or two of the consultants had realized where Goldblatt was taking him.

'Do you know how you would feel?'

Mike Coalport hesitated.

'Do you or don't you?' asked Goldblatt evenly. 'Do you *really* know?'

'Of course I don't!' retorted Mike Coalport with all the bluster he could muster.

'Well your analysis of this social issue, as you call it, presumes that you do.' Goldblatt shook his head and heaved a heavy, disappointed sigh. 'You know, Professor Coalport, your way of thinking is very old-fashioned. It used to be called utilitarianism. It requires a notion of a calculus of pleasure – or suffering, in this case. But I'm sure you require no instruction in the fact that the problem with utilitarianism is that it fails on the impossibility of intersubjective comparison. You can't tell me how much a person with a rare disease suffers, and you can't tell me how much a person with a common disease suffers. Only they can do that – which means that you can't quantitatively compare them. It's perfectly possible, for example, that a person with a rare disease but with *exactly* the same degree of objective physical disability as a person with a common disease experiences a much more intense degree of subjective psychological suffering precisely because of the very rarity of his or her disease. The fact that no one understands it, the lack of fellow sufferers with whom to share it, the sense of abandonment generated by people who go around saying that... well, making the intellectually contemptible argument that you just made. Or possibly they don't. The point is that this calculus of suffering that people like you would like to construct – it can't be built. Which means you can't say whether treatment of a few people with a rare disease relieves more suffering than treatment of many people with a common disease. Can you?'

Coalport wanted to say that he could. He *wanted* to say it. But he didn't.

'And that's why I disagree with your analysis, Professor Coalport.' Goldblatt smiled. 'Such as it is.'

Mike Coalport stared at him. Goldblatt couldn't remember ever having seen such malevolence and disbelief mixed together in a single pair of eyes. He could feel himself still smiling, ever so slightly. The icy smile of the ruthless but professional executioner, who can offer his victim only the comfort of his technical expertise, the sharpness and speed of the blade. He couldn't help it. For that one moment, and in front of all these people, he *was* Mike Coalport's executioner, even though he already knew that for the rest of his life Mike Coalport was going to be his.

Mike Coalport looked away, glancing down at the CV in front of him. After a second he shuffled it pointlessly.

There were muffled snickers. Iron Balls, who had picked up his pen again, smiled despite himself as he resumed jotting. The moderator allowed the pause to drag on a little longer before turning to the next interviewer. She didn't like Mike Coalport. Nor did anyone else. Naturally, she was thoroughly appalled at the insolent and subversive performance she had just witnessed from the candidate – but that was no reason to hurry on as if it had never happened.

Anyway, it turned out that the other interviewers didn't have many questions. And Goldblatt didn't wait around after his interview to witness the calling of Anthony Thomas and add to the glory of the anointed one's ascent by his own self-effacing presence.

He knew it was wrong to leave. For a Wise Man, it was an inexcusable dereliction of duty. It cast in doubt the entire point of his attendance at the interview in the first place.

Goldblatt thought about that as he retraced his steps to the Underground station. Maybe, he thought, he just didn't have the stomach to be a Wise Man any more.

24

HE FELT NUMB. HE had known he wasn't going to get the job and yet... and yet... until today, until the moment he had walked into that interview room, there had still been a possibility, however remote. A *possibility*. Only now, when the job was gone, as he sat on the train going over the macabre experience in his mind, did he realize that a tiny, treacherous flame of hope had been flickering within him all along. For all his bravado, it turned out, he had been holding on to that. And now that hope was extinguished. Where there had been light, no matter how faint, how tremulous, there was only a black, black pool of despair lapping at his feet.

He went back to the hospital. It was after five, but there were a few things he needed to do. Ludo had already gone, leaving his bleep in the doctors' office. He began looking through the results on a couple of patients that he wanted to check. The numbers passed in front of his eyes. He couldn't take them in.

Dr Morris bleeped him to find out if he was back and then came up to see him. He asked how the interview had gone. He needn't have. Goldblatt could see he already knew.

'I'm sorry, Malcolm.'

Goldblatt shrugged.

'How do you feel?'

'Not too bad,' he lied. 'I didn't expect to get it. It's not exactly the first time.'

'I heard it was a... difficult interview.' Dr Morris tried to hide a grin. He had spoken to someone who had spoken to someone who had been in the room. Word about the drubbing of Mike Coalport at the hands of a locum registrar was getting around.

But it wasn't a grinning matter. Malcolm Goldblatt was going to do himself serious damage if he went around talking like that to people like Mike Coalport. No one talked like that to Mike Coalport. But on the other hand... he *had* talked like that to Mike Coalport.

The grin widened on Dr Morris's face despite his best efforts to suppress it. 'I've always thought his thinking was rather old-fashioned myself, you know.'

Goldblatt buried his head in his hands.

'*You require no instruction...*'

'Don't. Please.'

'So it's true?'

Goldblatt groaned.

'Why did you do it?'

'Don't ask,' said Goldblatt miserably.

Dr Morris sat down.

Goldblatt looked at him. Dr Morris shook his head disbelievingly.

'How's the Sutherland unit?' asked Goldblatt.

'Between you and me, Malcolm, Dr Sutherland runs a terrible ship. If I ever practise medicine like that, take me out and shoot me.' Dr Morris stared thoughtfully at the floor. 'You know you can't do things like that,' he said eventually. 'You just... no one will give you a job.'

'I know. You don't have to tell me.'

'Then why did you do it?'

'I don't know. I just did. I was never going to get that job. I knew it before I even went in.' Goldblatt paused. 'You told me I'd get it for sure. After the pre-interview, remember? The worse it was, you told me, the more chance I had.'

'Well that was... not entirely based on experience.'

'You lied?'

Dr Morris shrugged sheepishly. 'I thought it would help with your confidence. You never get a job if you don't believe you've got a chance.'

'Did you know about Anthony Thomas?'

'Who?'

Of course he knew, thought Goldblatt. That 'who?' was too forced, too self-consciously nonchalant. He watched Dr Morris for a moment. Then he sighed. It didn't matter what Dr Morris knew. What had happened wasn't

Dr Morris's fault. 'I was a Wise Man again. I always knew I was going to be.'

Dr Morris pretended he didn't remember what Goldblatt was talking about. Then a look of recognition – obviously carefully crafted – came over his face.

'Well,' he said, 'it's always hard to beat a local candidate. It's not a reflection on you.'

Goldblatt nodded glumly. It was a reflection of something else entirely. Not that that was any comfort. Quite the opposite. If it had been a reflection of something about himself, at least there would have been a chance that he could change it.

'But you still can't do something like that, what you did to Mike Coalport.'

'I know.'

'Well, fortunately for you, it was Mike Coalport. He'll hate you for ever, but a lot of people will secretly admire you for it. Mike has a lot of enemies. He steps on everyone's toes.'

'You were his registrar.'

'Have I ever shown you my feet?'

Goldblatt laughed.

'Not that he's not a good physician,' added Dr Morris quickly. 'And an excellent scientist. I learned a lot from him.'

Dr Morris, thought Goldblatt, couldn't you just for once say something critical about a colleague and not—

'But he's a bastard,' said Dr Morris. 'An absolute *bastard*.'

That was better.

'People will think you did it because he's such a bastard.'

'Naturally,' said Goldblatt, instinctively clutching at the straw of a rationalization that Dr Morris had sent floating towards him.

'But you can't *do* things like that, Malcolm. People might secretly admire you, but that doesn't mean they'll give you a job.'

'I know.'

Dr Morris nodded. 'All right. Enough said. I know this is disappointing, but don't let it get you down. You never had a chance. You'll get a job, Malcolm. Any other applications in the pipeline?'

'I haven't seen any other good jobs around.'

'What about locum jobs?'

Goldblatt laughed. There were always locum jobs. You couldn't do them for ever.

'Malcolm,' said Dr Morris seriously, 'I've been meaning to say, I had another look at your CV. I want to ask you something. Have you ever thought of doing an MD?'

Goldblatt stared. Had he ever *thought*...

'You'd probably find it easier to get an SR job if you did.'

'Do you really think so?'

'Yes, I do.'

'Hmm,' said Goldblatt, putting his finger theatrically to his lips. 'I wonder why I've never thought of that...'

'All right, Malcolm. I get it. I'm sure you've got your reasons. Maybe we can talk about it another time. I'm just trying to be helpful.' Dr Morris smiled a smile that was so transparently intended to cheer him up that it made Goldblatt even more depressed. 'Come on. You'll get a proper job.'

'No. I just can't see how it's going to happen. You've seen my CV. Twenty months. That's how long I've been doing locum jobs. What's going to change? What's going to be different next time compared with today?'

'That's why I say you should consider an MD.'

'I have considered it!' Goldblatt stopped, conscious of his voice rising. 'Sorry. Look, I have considered it. Two years of my life? It's just not me. I'm not cut out for it. But you know what? Tell me it would make a difference – a single, meaningful difference – to my ability as a clinician, and I'd do it tomorrow. I'd spend two years with the mice in the lab. Just tell me – honestly, truthfully – that it would make a difference.'

Goldblatt waited. Dr Morris didn't reply.

'Exactly. Anyway, what's the point of even thinking about it? I don't have a patron.'

Dr Morris looked at him suspiciously. 'A patron? That's not another Wise Man thing, is it?'

For a moment Goldblatt thought of making something up – a story about three patrons, perhaps, presenting rosewater, honey and wax at an outhouse in ancient Mesopotamia – but he couldn't be bothered. Not even for Dr Morris, who probably would have enjoyed it, to judge from their last foray into bible studies. 'No,' he said.

'You'll get a proper job.' Dr Morris forced a note of encouragement into his voice. 'You've just got to keep trying. I'll do whatever I can to help. I'll give you a reference. You can count on me for that. But you could do a few things to help yourself with the Prof as well, you know.'

Goldblatt sighed. Dr Morris seemed to have taken a crash course in stating the obvious.

'You could try.'

'Believe it or not, I do. Look, Emma hates me. And she talks to the Prof. I'm sure she does.'

'She doesn't hate you.'

'She does.'

'She doesn't.'

Goldblatt gave Dr Morris a very searching look. 'She does.'

'Well,' said Dr Morris, 'only a little bit.'

'I don't know what to do.' Goldblatt shrugged helplessly. 'I really don't. I've tried to talk to her, but it doesn't work. I don't know what to do to make her stop thinking that I'm... I don't even know what she thinks.'

'Who? Emma or the Prof?'

'Both of them!'

Dr Morris laughed for a moment. 'You're in an impossible situation. You're caught in the middle. They're both as mad as hatters. You're the meat in the sandwich.'

'The meat in the hatters' sandwich,' said Goldblatt. 'That'll make a good epitaph.'

'Don't talk about epitaphs.'

'Seems like a good day for it. Does Emma talk to you as well?'

'About what?'

'About me.'

Dr Morris looked away guiltily.

'How often?' asked Goldblatt.

'Not often.'

'Once a week?'

'Sometimes...'

'Less?'

'More.'

'Does she cry?' asked Goldblatt.

'Not every time. Try to understand. It's hard for Emma. She hasn't got much confidence. This is her first job in a teaching hospital. Come on, Malcolm, imagine what it's like for her. We've always worked in this kind of environment, we take it for granted. We're used to it. Emma isn't. It's understandable that she finds it intimidating. And with someone like you...'

'I'm sorry,' said Goldblatt. He just wanted Dr Morris to stop.

'No, don't be sorry,' said Dr Morris.

'I'm not.'

'Why did you say you were?'

'Because I just said it. It's absurd. You've just told me you want me to understand why someone hates me because she lacks confidence. So I thought if that's a good enough reason for her to hate me, then I suppose it's a good enough reason for me to pretend I'm sorry. I mean, I'm sure she doesn't *like* hating me. So I should probably be sorry for making her feel bad about that as well.'

Dr Morris closed his eyes for a moment. 'All right, Malcolm. It's been a hard day for you. We'll talk about this properly another time. I just want to let you know that I'll do anything I can for you. I'll support you. But you have to keep trying, all right? Remember that. Don't give up.'

Goldblatt nodded. Dr Morris got up and left.

A few minutes later Emma came in, saw that Goldblatt was there, and hesitated.

'She's not here,' he said, guessing that Emma wanted the HO. 'Maybe she's already on the private ward.'

Emma looked at him for an instant longer and went away.

Goldblatt thought about Dr Morris. He really would do whatever he could for him, Goldblatt believed that. And one day, there would be a lot that Dr Morris would be able to do. But not now. Dr Morris was too young and too new. He didn't have the clout.

One day, Goldblatt was sure, Dr Morris would make a very good patron, and many registrars would benefit. But not in time for him.

*

Just as there are five phases of grieving, so there were five phases in Lesley's response on interview nights. Shock, denial, and dismissal took about two minutes, then there was sympathy – and then there was anger.

Lesley always started out with good and sympathetic intentions, and by the time she and Goldblatt were into the second bottle of wine she was always in a boiling rage. Her anger was diffuse, uncomprehending, and extreme. It went looking indiscriminately for targets amongst consultants, hospital managers, and the entire medical profession, but since there were no consultants or hospital managers on the sofa with them, it inevitably ended up aimed at the only representative of the medical profession who happened to be available.

'Why are you doing this?' she demanded. 'What's in it for you?'

'What?' said Goldblatt.

'This. This whole thing.'

'I don't know what you mean.'

'It's killing you Malcolm. Why are you doing this to yourself?' Lesley fixed him with her gaze. 'It's the old Jewish lady, isn't it?'

Goldblatt didn't reply.

'It is. I hate her.'

'Don't say that.'

'I hate her!'

'How can you hate her? She's an old lady.'

'I hate her!'

'You're an anti-Semite.'

'I'm an anti-Semite? No, I don't hate her because she's Jewish, Malcolm. I hate her because of what she's doing to you. I hate her, I hate her, I hate her!'

'She's dead, Lesley. Isn't that enough for you?'

'No. It isn't enough.'

'Wash your mouth out with soap.'

'She isn't dead. She's alive in your head.'

Goldblatt rolled his eyes.

Lesley slapped him on the head. Not playfully.

'In there,' said Lesley. 'She's alive. Isn't she?'

Goldblatt was silent.

'Isn't she?' She slapped him on the head again.

'Stop it,' said Goldblatt.

'Is she alive? Yes or no?'

'No. She's dead.'

Slap! 'She's alive. Admit it.'

'No.'

Slap! 'Admit it!'

'All right!' said Goldblatt, throwing his hands around his head. 'She's alive. I'm a doctor, remember? I'm allowed to bring people back to life.'

'No, gods do that, Malcolm. Not doctors.'

'What do you want from me, Lesley?' Inside him something suddenly flared. 'Tell me. What do you want? It wasn't the best day for me today. In case you haven't heard, I got dumped at another interview, and on the way I managed to humiliate one of the biggest fucking kahunas in the business.'

'Why did you *do* that?'

'I don't know why!'

'You're your own worst enemy.'

'At least I know what my enemy's doing.'

'Actually, I don't think you do. I don't think you've got any control over what you're doing at all any more. Don't you think this episode today tells you something? Have you ever heard of self-destruction?'

'Spare me the psychology, Lesley. I just did it. What difference does it make? I was never going to get the fucking job anyway!'

Lesley stared at him. Then she nodded. 'All right, Malcolm.'

Goldblatt shook his head. The realization that, deep down and almost unknown to himself, he had been holding on to the tenuous hope that he might actually get the Nailwright job had grown stronger as the hours since the interview had passed, and the prospect of what lay ahead correspondingly bleaker. Dr Morris's well-meaning attempt to encourage him had just made him feel even worse. If Dr Morris did give him a reference, people would still find it odd that Goldblatt didn't offer one from the Prof, the senior consultant on the unit. And a reference for what? Not even Dr Morris could make a substantive SR vacancy materialize out of nothing.

He was snookered. He was fucked.

'Malcolm?'

He looked at Lesley.

'Why don't you leave? Why don't you just leave this whole thing behind and do something else with your life?'

Goldblatt shook his head helplessly.

'I'll support you while you work out what you want to do. If you want to go to the bar, or train in something...' Her voice petered out. Lesley didn't say anything for a while. Then she took a deep breath. 'You know, I've been thinking...' she shrugged, her mouth trembling slightly. She took another deep breath. 'Maybe you'd be happier without me. Why should you have to explain yourself to me? You shouldn't have to keep doing that. You know, you could be like you always told me you used to be. No commitments. Sleep around with the nurses.'

'And doctors,' said Goldblatt. 'You're insulting me, Les. It wasn't just nurses.'

'Well, anyway...'

'You know, I did exaggerate a bit, when I used to tell you about that. It wasn't really like that, Les. I mean, not all the time. Or even much of the time, actually.'

She didn't reply.

'Les, what are you talking about? What are you trying to say?'

She frowned. Then she shook her head. 'Nothing. Look, it's all right. It's fine.'

Goldblatt stared at her.

'It's just... You're killing yourself, Malcolm. And when someone you love is killing themselves and there's nothing you can do except watch and...' She shook her head again. 'I can't bear to watch it.'

'If you can't bear to watch it, imagine what it feels like for me.'

It was meant to be a joke, but it fell flat before he had finished saying it. Even for him.

Lesley shook her head again. 'Malcolm Goldblatt, always joking. Always with the jokes.' She looked at him with a deep, searching stare. 'Malcolm, I just don't know how much more I can take.'

25

THEY MADE LOVE THAT night. It was long, slow, silent, intense. Hardly even physical. They gazed almost unbearably into each other's eyes. Goldblatt didn't understand what it meant. In the morning, he left early, before Lesley was up. He went to the hospital and got himself a coffee and sat in the doctors' office.

He pulled out Mr Lister's notes. Two days previously, Dr Morris had finally taken the plunge and started Mr Lister on steroids on the assumption that he had some kind of low-grade inflammatory illness that they couldn't detect, since they had excluded everything else. The previous day, Mr Lister had still run a fever. If the steroids were going to work, the fever would subside within the next couple of days. If it didn't, they were back to square one. Goldblatt flicked through Mr Lister's notes, looking over his test results, searching for clues, indicators, anything that he and Dr Morris might have missed as to the nature of what they were actually treating.

But staring, mostly. Staring blankly at the pages of results in front of him.

What Lesley said had scared him. What did she mean? What would she do? Was she just thinking about leaving him? Or had she already decided? Their lovemaking the previous night, had it been an affirmation or a farewell?

He flicked through a few more pages of Mr Lister's notes.

He almost laughed, it was all so awful. He was fucked. He was so fucked. He was never going to get a substantive job.

What right did he have to drag Lesley into this world of his? Each night he brought it home with him and she was forced into it, like it or not. She deserved better. It wasn't her world. It was sad, miserable, absurd. It was Ludo's world, not Lesley's.

He looked up and gazed slowly around the room. The HO had decided to stick the spiky charts of Mr Lister's fever up on the wall like some kind of frieze. The pages ran all the way across two walls and a good part of a third, giving the office an ancient Greek look, like something out of a neoclassical painting.

The door opened. The HO came in.

'How did it go yesterday?' she asked.

'No luck,' said Goldblatt.

'Oh.' The HO frowned. 'I'm sorry.'

'Thanks.' Goldblatt smiled ruefully. He paused. 'Listen, sit down. I'm worried about you.'

The HO looked at him uncomprehendingly.

'The day before yesterday. You were mental, remember? The blood gases?'

'Oh, that. I was just a bit... frazzled.'

'You weren't just frazzled. You were at the end of the diving board getting ready to jump head first into the deep end.'

'At least I knew where I was going.'

Goldblatt stared at her. It was like being confronted by an auditory mirror, if there could be such a thing. For an instant he wondered if he was creating a monster. Or a second him. 'You know, jokes like that aren't going to help you. Take it from someone who knows. Now listen to me. It's only a job. Right? It's not worth dying over. Tell me if it's too much.'

'It's too much.'

'I'm fucking serious!' he shouted. 'Do you understand? Tell me! Tell me if it's too much.'

The HO's eyes went wide. She pushed her glasses up on her nose. 'OK,' she said quietly. 'I'll tell you.'

'Promise?'

'Promise.'

Goldblatt took a deep breath. 'Good.'

Ludo arrived, wearing one of her inevitable woollen skirts. She sat down. The blue fabric stretched over her thighs.

'What happened yesterday?' she asked.

'He didn't get it,' said the HO.

Goldblatt nodded, waiting for whatever was coming next. The snide comment, the malicious jibe. Ludo's trademark.

Nothing. Ludo frowned slightly. Then she said: 'I'm sorry, Malcolm.'

Goldblatt gazed at her in surprise. Ludo looked back at him. Their eyes met.

'What's going on?' said the HO.

Goldblatt looked around. 'Nothing.'

He was dictating discharge summaries in the doctors' office that afternoon when his bleep went off. Goldblatt finished the summary he was working on, released the button on the Dictaphone, and dialled switchboard.

'Dr Goldblatt,' said the voice on the phone when switchboard had patched it through, 'this is Margaret Hayes.'

It was a loud contralto voice, the kind designed more for control than communication. Goldblatt had never met Margaret Hayes, but he had heard about her. He didn't say anything in reply. Although it was obviously an important voice, full of latent demands and the threat of unmitigated retribution, he didn't think having a name like Margaret Hayes was such an amazing announcement that it required any response.

'It's Margaret Hayes here,' said the voice again.

'I know,' said Goldblatt.

'How do you know?' asked Margaret Hayes quickly, unable to conceal her pleasure. Margaret Hayes was a person whose ears often burned in the knowledge that someone, somewhere, must be talking about her and the incredible feats she performed in the service of the Fuertler's Foundation.

'You told me,' said Goldblatt.

'When?'

'Just now.'

There was a disappointed silence on the line. 'Do you know who I am?'

'Margaret Hayes?'

'I am the secretary of the Fuertler's Foundation.'

'Really? That sounds like a very interesting job.'

'It is,' said Margaret Hayes with dignity. 'I count myself lucky to be in a position to serve.'

'Although I suppose there's a lot of typing involved.'

There was a puzzled silence for a moment. 'This *is* Dr Goldblatt?' said Margaret Hayes. 'Professor Small's Registrar?'

'Yes it is,' said Dr Goldblatt.

'Dr Goldblatt, I have rung about a patient. She is supposed to come in under Professor Small and she has been cancelled three times!'

Goldblatt didn't say anything. Margaret Hayes had been on the phone for all of a minute and already this was the second time she had made a perfectly commonplace announcement and expected him to react as if it were the most astonishing declaration. It was quite an irritating habit.

'Did you hear me, Dr Goldblatt?'

'Yes,' said Goldblatt.

'Well, what do you think about it, Dr Goldblatt?'

'It's not good, I'll say that much.'

'No, it's not good.'

'On the other hand, it's not bad. Yesterday I cancelled someone who had already been cancelled four times.'

'Who was that?' demanded Margaret Hayes.

'Someone,' said Goldblatt.

'Who?' demanded Margaret Hayes again. 'Was she one of mine?'

Goldblatt frowned. Was she one of mine? Now, just what was that supposed to mean? It was one of the quaint anomalies of the British justice system that there was no actual legislation specifically outlawing slavery in the United Kingdom, but for all practical purposes it had been banned indirectly by a variety of statutes for over two centuries, not to mention being prohibited under a number of more recent instruments of international law. His old colleagues at Free from Bondage, he suspected, might be interested in learning more about this Margaret Hayes and her claims to ownership of persons. She'd be an easier target than Colombian coal-barons, that was for sure.

'Dr Goldblatt?'

'What?'

'I have a patient here who has been cancelled three times. Her name is Mrs Watt. I want to know when she is now planned to be coming in.'

'Haven't we written to tell her?'

'Yes.'

'When did we say?' asked Goldblatt cagily.

'May the twelfth,' said Margaret Hayes.

'Then I'd say... May the twelfth?'

'Yes, that's what I said.'

'Exactly. That's when she's coming in.'

'Can you guarantee that?'

Can you *guarantee* that? Goldblatt wished there was some way he could have recorded the conversation. Honestly, it was priceless.

'No,' said Goldblatt. 'I can't guarantee that.'

'What is she coming in for?' asked Margaret Hayes.

'What did we say she was coming in for?' asked Goldblatt cagily.

'She doesn't know. Why do you think I'm ringing?'

'Why doesn't she know?'

'I don't know why she doesn't know.'

'Maybe you should find out and give me a call back.'

'Dr Goldblatt!'

'Didn't anyone tell her why she was coming in?'

'No.'

'What's wrong with her?' asked Goldblatt.

'She has Fuertler's Syndrome! Dr Goldblatt, I am the secretary of the Fuertler's Foundation.'

'No,' said Goldblatt. 'I mean, why can't she ring up herself? Is something wrong with her?'

'She has asked me to ring for her.'

'And you agreed?'

'Of course I agreed.'

That was unfortunate, thought Goldblatt. He couldn't just divulge treatment information to some secretary.

Goldblatt leaned back in his seat with a sense of anticipation. This was going to be a treat, and he could certainly use one after what he had been through at the Nailwright the previous day. There were few things he enjoyed more than making an intransigent and utterly immovable ethical stand on an inconsequential and completely trivial matter before intrusive relatives, friends, officials, and functionaries, and none of the things that he did enjoy more could be done in a doctors' office at four in the afternoon. Not by himself, anyway.

'I can't tell you that,' said Goldblatt.

'Why not?' demanded Margaret Hayes, with genuine interest as well as hostility in her voice. She was accustomed to getting any information she wanted out of Professor Small, usually without even having to ask for it.

'It wouldn't be ethical. That's confidential information. I'm sure Mrs Watt wouldn't want me to tell you.'

'She asked me to ring for her!'

'And you agreed?'

'Dr Goldblatt, I am ringing as Mrs Watt's advocate.'

Her advocate! Ooh, that was a frightening word. Margaret Hayes was obviously an accomplished bully. Goldblatt almost admired her.

'Is she paying you?'

'Dr Goldblatt! I have never—'

'Don't worry, I also happen to be a lawyer. I can assure you that if she isn't paying you, you're all right. She can't sue you.'

'*Sue me?* For what?'

'For not getting the information. I assume you told her you were going to get the information?'

Margaret Hayes hesitated for an instant. 'Yes.'

'And you aren't. But don't worry. As long as you didn't agree on a payment, she can't sue you. No consideration – no contract.'

'Dr Goldblatt,' said Margaret Hayes coaxingly, 'why don't you just tell me what Mrs Watt is coming in for?'

'Mrs Hayes,' replied Goldblatt accommodatingly, 'why don't you just ask Mrs Watt to ring me?'

'She can't ring you! The poor woman's a wreck. She's in tears. She's been in tears for a week.'

Goldblatt seriously doubted that anywhere near as much lacrimation as that had been going on. As if to confirm his suspicion, ten minutes after he put down the phone, Mrs Watt herself rang. Her week-long spell of weeping had miraculously ended, she had salvaged herself from the wrecker's yard, and sounded like a perfectly rational woman who just wanted to know what she was coming in for. Apparently the Prof hadn't quite got around to telling her in the clinic. In the eight months that had passed since then, Mrs Watt had come to the very reasonable conclusion that if she was going to get upset when she was cancelled every twelve weeks, she may as well know what she was getting upset about. Margaret Hayes had discovered this during the telephonic sweep of the infantry that she held every year, and had immediately ordered Mrs Watt to sit tight and wait until she found out for her.

She hadn't found out for her. Mrs Watt had found out for herself. But that wasn't the end of it. Two days later, the Prof received a letter.

At first glance, when she saw the letter on top of the pile of mail in her secretary's office, the Prof thought it was just another one of those irritating letters that had been arriving in rising numbers over the last few months and to which she had been tirelessly applying her strategy of ignoration. On second glance, when the Prof recognized the letterhead at the top and then quickly looked for the signature at the bottom, she realized it wasn't like the others letter at all. To ignore this letter wouldn't be strategic, it would be suicidal.

The letter, like its author, was blunt and bullying. It was not tolerable, wrote Margaret Hayes, for admissions for members of the Fuertler's Foundation to be cancelled so often. It seemed to be a phenomenon that was increasing in frequency and was now becoming routine. If the Prof wanted her to write to the hospital Chief Executive about the situation, she would be happy to do so.

The Prof lived in dread of offending Margaret Hayes. Since it was Margaret who had been instrumental in promoting the myth that Professor Small was the only doctor in Britain who was capable of treating Fuertler's Syndrome, and since this myth was the chief cause of her unit's dizzying rise – and since it was, after all, a myth – it followed that Margaret could ruin the Prof just as easily as she had made her. She never missed an opportunity of letting the Prof know it. If Andrea Small was king, Margaret Hayes was the kingmaker. But more to the point, as the Prof realized all too well, even if she wasn't king, Margaret Hayes would still be the kingmaker.

With one letter, the Prof realized, her entire strategy was in tatters.

But the last thing the Prof wanted was for Margaret Hayes to write to the hospital Chief Executive. The hospital already teemed with envious consultants from other units who were just waiting to stab her in the back, many of whom, she suspected, had spies in the Chief Executive's office and knew what came and went in his correspondence, and all she needed was for Margaret Hayes to slip a dagger into their hands. She was on the phone in ten minutes to make sure she didn't. Margaret was in a meeting and couldn't take her call.

A meeting, thought the Prof bitterly. What could it be about? Surely Margaret wasn't meeting Dr Jenkins from Leicester! Dr Jenkins, the Prof knew, had been putting himself about as a Fuertler's expert for years, and it was the Prof's worst nightmare that Margaret Hayes was conspiring to offer full recognition and establish diplomatic relations with him.

The Prof rang back. Margaret Hayes was still in a meeting. She was in a meeting for the next three hours according to the reply the Prof received to each of the fourteen phone calls she made before Margaret finally came to the phone.

'Margaret, I don't think that complaining to the Chief Executive would be helpful,' the Prof whimpered.

'It wouldn't be a complaint,' said Margaret Hayes. 'I'd never complain about you, Andrea. But I could enquire about the possibility of more resources being allocated to you. Considering all that the Fuertler's Foundation has contributed to your unit, the hospital should be prepared to invest a little more. Don't you think so, Andrea?'

'Of course I think so, Margaret. But we're at a very delicate stage just at the moment. I don't think it would be helpful at this point. Perhaps in a couple of months.'

'But something must be done *now*, Andrea. Our patients can't wait a couple of months. If you can't handle all of our patients yourself, maybe we should consider another option. As you know, we at the Fuertler's Foundation have always thought we should concentrate our efforts in building up your unit as the one centre of excellence for the treatment of Fuertler's Syndrome...'

'And you have!' cried the Prof. 'It is!'

'But maybe we were wrong. Maybe one centre isn't enough. Maybe we should consider a second centre. You know Dr Jenkins, don't you?'

No!' shrieked the Prof, swivelling her chair and turning instinctively to the Scale. Unable to suppress the horrible image, she visualized the column of red slithering down the wall. 'Margaret, leave it to me,' she pleaded. 'I'll handle it.'

In reality, Margaret Hayes would as soon have exchanged ambassadors with Dr Jenkins in Leicester as she would have handed over control of the Fuertler's Foundation itself. Dr Jenkins had been making Fuertler's passes at her for years, and had even gone so far as to hint that he had accumulated a list of forty-three patients who were not members of the Foundation that he would turn over in exchange for the Fuertler's Foundation recommendation as a centre of excellence. But Margaret Hayes wasn't going to be seduced by glittering baubles, even forty-three of them. Dr Jenkins was much too independent, and Margaret Hayes would have been blind if she couldn't have seen that she would never be able to exert the kind of control over him that made her relationship with Andrea Small so rewarding. The only use she had for Dr Jenkins was as a counterweight to keep Andrea Small in a state of continual suspicion and fear, and as far as Margaret Hayes was concerned the Cancellations Crisis was merely a new and pungent condiment to spice up the threat.

'All I want to know is how I can help, Andrea.'

'You do more than enough already, Margaret.'

'I can never do enough, Andrea.'

'You're so dedicated, Margaret. You should think of yourself a bit more.'

'Well, it is Fuertler's Syndrome, Andrea. If we don't do anything for our patients, who will?'

'No one, Margaret. That's the tragedy.'

But that was only a minor tragedy. The major tragedy would be if Margaret withdrew the funding she channelled into Andrea's research projects and started letting her patients go elsewhere. That would be more than just a tragedy. It would be a catastrophe.

After she put down the phone, the Prof sat in a state of catatonic stupor, staring at the Scale. The Scale was still stuck at 960. Was it never to rise any higher? What would happen if it began to fall? The Prof would have to buy some white paint and use it to blot out the red. She didn't think she'd be able to do it. She just didn't think she could.

And what was all the fuss about, for God's sake? A few patients who couldn't get in on time. What did everyone expect? It was a public system, for heaven's sake, and it was tottering towards collapse. Wasn't that what everyone always said? 'It's tottering, it's tottering.' One heard it all the time. Why blame her? Why not put the blame where it belonged for once? Why not put it... well, where it belonged? For once?

The Prof felt angry, bitter, and panicky. She called Emma.

Emma came straight away. The Prof told her that she had just had Margaret Hayes on the phone and Margaret wasn't happy because of all the cancellations that were happening and as a result she might not be able to provide all the funds she had been expecting to provide. Then the Prof stopped and watched Emma's face. The money for the MD that the Prof had hinted that Emma would be able to do in the lab with Bolkovsky was meant to be coming from the Fuertler's Foundation. It didn't take long for Emma to make the connection. Suddenly she was angry, bitter, and panicky. She stumbled out of the Prof's office almost overwhelmed by the injustice of it all, her eyes stinging with tears. She went looking for Goldblatt to tell him what a filthy coward and cheat he was for keeping all those patients out of the hospital and threatening her MD, and she would have told him, too, had she not remembered just in time that she wasn't talking to him.

The Prof felt much better. She rang the South Bank box office to book a pair of concert tickets to give to Emma as a reward.

But driving Emma to tears, while satisfying, was only a partial solution to the problem. The Prof knew that the time was past when she could simply ignore the crisis. Something else must be done. She didn't know what it was, but she knew that it must. And it was unlikely that Emma would know what it was, since it was Emma who, as registrar, had presided over the rising tide of cancellations in the first place.

With a horrible, sinking sensation, the Prof knew exactly who she would have to talk to.

26

GOLDBLATT PUT HIS NEWSPAPER down. It was Monday morning – Monday after a strange, detached weekend in which he and Lesley had said little to each other and yet the words she had spoken on the night of the Nailwright interview blared between them like a foghorn, leaving him troubled and confused. Now Goldblatt watched in amazement as the Prof appeared in the doorway, poked her head in, looked around, came in and closed the door behind her.

'Good morning, Dr Goldblatt,' she said.

'Good morning, Professor Small,' replied Goldblatt, silently cursing Ludo. It was her fault that the Prof had found him there. Ludo was late for their round – starting the week, naturally, as she hoped to continue it – and the HO had gone off to take bloods while they were waiting.

'I would like to talk to you about something, Dr Goldblatt.'

Goldblatt nodded. She probably wanted to talk about the Grand Round, the medical department's weekly meeting for all the doctors in the hospital. On Thursday of the following week it would be the turn of Professor Small's unit to present a case. He had been hoping that Emma would get saddled with the work of preparing the presentation.

The Prof sat down. 'I wanted to ask you, Dr Goldblatt, if it is really true that my patients are being cancelled?'

Goldblatt stared.

'Frequently, I mean,' said the Prof. 'Not just now and then.'

Goldblatt still stared. Was it possible she didn't know? The Prof was looking at him anxiously. Her face, with her hair brushed back from the forehead, was more cadaverous than ever. No, it wasn't possible. It just wasn't. Goldblatt wondered whether it was even possible for her to think that he didn't know that she knew. No, surely that wasn't possible either.

'Dr Goldblatt?'

'Yes,' said Goldblatt gravely, as if giving some very bad news to a nervous and debilitated patient. 'Your patients are being cancelled frequently.'

'How frequently?' asked the Prof, her eyes wide with trepidation as she waited for the answer that she already knew, but which, for contorted reasons of her own, she couldn't let Goldblatt know that she knew.

'Hardly ever!' cried Emma, rushing into the office.

Emma was breathing heavily and collapsed on a chair, pulling her white coat tightly around her heaving bosom. She had spotted the Prof getting into the lift on the ground floor and, with none of the other lifts available, had run up the stairs, all seven flights. The Prof never went near a patient without asking her to attend, and if she was heading up to the wards without inviting her, there was obviously something fishy going on. It was a blinding flash of inspiration that drew Emma straight to the doctors' office, where, she knew, Goldblatt was probably sitting. After Margaret Hayes's threat, these were crucial days, and Emma wasn't going to make the mistake of letting the Prof talk to Goldblatt alone.

The Prof gave her an appreciative smile. She felt much less uncomfortable now that Emma had arrived. If she looked into her heart of hearts – which would be inconvenient at this particular moment, obviously – the Prof knew that having Emma around during this conversation was the exact opposite of what she really needed in order to have any chance of elucidating the facts. She knew that she ought to ask her to leave. But she couldn't bring herself to do it. Like Potemkin, who supposedly ordered the construction of false, prosperous-looking villages for Catherine the Great when she insisted on leaving Moscow to see how her subjects lived, Emma could be relied upon to tell the Prof whatever she wanted to hear. And like Catherine the Great, who had allowed herself to go along with Potemkin's charade for fear of what she would see if she looked elsewhere, the Prof couldn't bring herself to send her away.

'I wouldn't say hardly ever,' said Goldblatt quietly.

The Prof jerked. The smile on her face froze, cracked, and disappeared. She looked back at Goldblatt reluctantly. Her head was starting to shake in the rapid, tremulous motion that always seemed to agitate it when something that was just too disturbing or unpleasant tried to get in.

'How often would you say?' asked the Prof hesitantly. Her voice was choked. The words came out in a weird, quivering rhythm that matched the wobbling of her head.

'Every day,' said Goldblatt.

'Only one!' cried Emma. 'Only one every day.'

The Prof, as if repelled yet mesmerized by the grotesque tale that Goldblatt was telling her, didn't even glance at her.

'I wouldn't say only one,' said Goldblatt, who couldn't stop now that he had begun to reveal all.

'How many *would* you say?' whispered the Prof.

'Two, sometimes three. Occasionally we've cancelled four.'

Four? The Prof mouthed the word. She couldn't actually bring herself to say it.

Emma glared at Goldblatt.

'Why?' said the Prof.

Goldblatt wanted to laugh. Why? What sort of a question was that from the world's greatest practitioner of the Broderip–Anderssen Principle? What did she think happened every time she rang Emma and asked her to manipulate a bed?

'It's a zero-sum game, Professor Small,' said Goldblatt.

The Prof stared at Goldblatt uncomprehendingly.

'It's that stupid principle of his,' said Emma.

Goldblatt ignored her. He didn't think it would be wise to revive the Broderip–Anderssen Principle with the Prof, even if she was its greatest practitioner. For a start, it was just possible that Emma had written the formula down in the hope of catching him out. And in the second place, there was always the possibility that Ludo would barge in at the wrong moment and reveal the origins of the principle in the servile hope of currying favour with the Prof and regaining some of the ground she had lost over the filled-in unfilled Fuertler's files.

Besides, the big problem wasn't the Broderip–Anderssen Principle. That was just a small problem that had grown like a minor malignancy on the backside of the big problem. The big problem was in the numbers. Maybe the Prof could understand those.

Goldblatt opened a drawer and pulled out the Book of Time. He opened it in the future and handed it to the Prof. 'Professor Small, look at this.'

The Prof glanced at Goldblatt and reached timorously for the admissions book. Goldblatt got up and went to the whiteboard. As the Prof looked at the book, hesitantly turning a few pages, Goldblatt wrote the numbers up on the board, the same numbers he had given to Emma a few weeks before.

The door opened. The HO took a step into the room and stopped. The Prof didn't take her eyes off the book. Goldblatt glanced at the HO and shook his head. The HO retreated.

A few seconds later, Ludo pushed the door open a few inches, peeked in, and closed it again.

The Prof was turning pages. Page after page after page.

'You see, Professor,' said Goldblatt, pointing to the numbers on the whiteboard, 'you just can't do it. With the Sorain infusion, you've got five-day admissions. You're booking four patients a day. With that level of bookings, you're *always* going to have cancellations. Even with sixteen beds you wouldn't be able to keep up, and since Dr Morris joined the unit, you've only got thirteen beds. That's why the cancellations have been getting worse. As it is, on average, forty per cent of the patients at a minimum are going to be cancelled, and more than that when you take emergencies into account. It's as simple as that. The numbers don't add up.'

But the Prof couldn't add up either. Or wouldn't. She glanced at Emma.

'What about weekends?' demanded Emma. 'He hasn't thought of those. Ask him about weekends.'

'What about weekends?' asked the Prof.

'Weekends are irrelevant,' said Goldblatt.

'He says weekends are irrelevant,' the Prof told Emma.

'I know,' said Emma.

'How do you know?'

'Because I've told her before,' said Goldblatt in exasperation. 'We've discussed this.'

The Prof gave Emma a suspicious glance. 'Have you?'

'No!' cried Emma. 'I'd never do that, Prof.'

'Why not?' asked the Prof.

Emma frowned, trying to work out why she wouldn't do what she had done only a few weeks earlier, when she had still been talking to Goldblatt, and which had seemed a perfectly normal thing to have done until two seconds ago when she had suddenly said she never would.

'You know, there's a way to solve this,' said Goldblatt.

The Prof looked at him expectantly, and blinked a couple of times.

'You can bring people in less frequently. Do the work-up once a year unless there's a particular indication of a problem, or do it as an outpatient, and if you still want them to have Sorain in the interim, you could ask their local hospitals to give it. There's no reason they can't. You could still review them in clinic, of course.'

The Prof stared at him blankly. She just stared. Goldblatt had absolutely no idea what was going on behind her eyes.

'Patients don't want to go to their local hospitals!' asserted Emma on her behalf. 'They want to have their Sorain here with the Prof.'

Goldblatt shrugged. Not every patient. In fact, it was a patient who had had to come up all the way from Somerset who had given him the idea a few days before. 'Dr Goldblatt,' she had said to him during his round, 'what's the reason I can't have this infusion in my local hospital in Taunton?' And the fact that there was no reason was so obvious – once someone had asked – that Goldblatt hadn't been able to think of an answer, not even an invented one.

The Prof continued to stare. Emma looked at her apprehensively, then shot a malevolent glance at Goldblatt, as if holding him responsible for putting the Prof into this scary catatonic trance.

Suddenly the Prof looked back at the admissions book. She started to turn the pages again, page after page with the impossible four bookings per day that Emma had entered. As if Goldblatt hadn't said a thing.

'Who wrote these in here?' she demanded.

There was silence.

The Prof continued doggedly turning the pages, page after page with Emma's writing, and with each turn of a page it was as if she tweaked another of Emma's nerves, just as if they were strings on a violin. The Prof was a virtuoso instrumentalist. Emma began to flush. The warm blood started rushing to her ears.

Goldblatt gave up on the numbers and sat down. Since they constituted irrefutable proof of what he was saying, they were going to be ignored. Naturally.

By now the Prof had gone far into the future, much further than Goldblatt ever looked unless he wanted to make himself especially depressed for the day.

The Prof had gone so far that she had reached the part where Goldblatt had started writing names in. But Emma's writing was on these pages as well.

Goldblatt had put names down in twos and threes and had left empty days on Fridays, to accommodate the rush of Broderips that always came from the Prof's clinic. This had worked for a while. Then Emma had started surreptitiously adding names after he had gone home, to top up the number on each page to four. For a while Goldblatt had crossed out the magical additions that appeared each night. But the names always reappeared, like poltergeists that couldn't be evicted, and eventually Goldblatt had stopped trying to drive them away.

Still the Prof turned the pages.

'What difference does it make who wrote them in?' asked Goldblatt eventually, despising himself for making even this puny effort in Emma's defence. He hated people who made themselves so vulnerable that he was unable to hate them.

'I want to know who wrote these names in!' the Prof repeated, like some kind of stupid, angry headmistress. Her head was shaking again. She looked just as she had looked the moment before she lied to Mrs Constantidis about getting her echocardiogram done.

Obviously, the Prof was one of those people who find that a good way to deal with a major issue is to identify some piffling misdemeanour that can be pinned on a specific individual, shout about it for ten minutes, and walk out in disgust. Goldblatt glanced at Emma. Emma was staring as hard as she could at her shoes. Something very interesting must have been going on with those shoes, because Emma couldn't take her eyes off them.

He turned back to the Prof, who had gone back to the start of the book and was now leafing through the crossed-out battlefields of the past.

'Is that really the issue?' he asked.

'Yes!' said the Prof vehemently. 'Someone wrote these names in and there are too many. You don't deny that there are too many names, do you, Dr Goldblatt?'

'No, I don't deny it.'

'Then whoever wrote these names in wrote too many names, didn't she?'

'Well, I think whoever wrote those names was under pressure to write that many names.'

'Under pressure? From who?'

Suddenly Goldblatt felt nothing but disgust. From who, Professor? he thought. Who do you think?

The Prof shut the book loudly and threw it down on the desk. She stood up theatrically.

'Well, it's done now! It's done, isn't it? Someone wrote all those names and there are going to be cancellations. That's what the numbers show, isn't it, Dr Goldblatt? You said so yourself. And now we've got Mrs Hayes upset.'

'Mrs Hayes?' said Goldblatt. 'What about Mrs Watt?'

'Who's Mrs Watt?' demanded the Prof.

'Mrs Watt is one of your patients who rang me up a few days ago because of all her cancellations. She was the one who got Mrs Hayes involved in the first place.'

'She was the one who— *Get her in!*' cried the Prof. 'Can't you manip— Emma, can't you find a bed for poor Mrs Watt?'

Emma looked up sullenly. 'Certainly, Prof,' she mumbled.

'Well!' said the Prof. 'That's something then. We've accomplished something, haven't we? That's a start.'

Suddenly the Prof seemed much more cheerful. She turned to go. Emma got up to go with her. Taking her cue from the Prof, she seemed to have developed a spring in her step as well.

'Don't worry, Prof,' Potemkin advised the czarina earnestly as they walked away. 'He's wrong. Honestly. He didn't take weekends into account.'

*

A couple of minutes after the Prof had gone, the door opened and Ludo and the HO peered in. They came into the room hesitantly, as if some kind of toxic miasma might remain from the Prof's presence.

'What was that about?' asked Ludo.

'Cancellations,' said Goldblatt.

'Not enough?' said Ludo.

'That's right. One can always strive for more.'

They went out on the ward to do their round. The patient in bed eight was going home to Norfolk after a course of Sorain. Goldblatt told her the customary lie that they'd get her back in six months for another infusion. Then he told her an uncustomary truth. 'But you know we probably won't.'

'I got cancelled twice this time, you know.'

Goldblatt nodded. Then on a whim, he said: 'They could give you the infusion in your local hospital.'

'Could they?' The patient looked at him in amazement. 'Really?'

'I don't see why not. Talk to your local doctor about it. I'll mention it in my discharge letter.'

Goldblatt said the same thing to another couple of patients before they were finished.

When they got back to the doctors' office, Ludo gave him one of her schadenfreudian smiles. 'Malcolm, I didn't realize you were so brave. The Prof will kill you if she finds out you've been telling her patients to get their Sorain locally.'

Goldblatt nodded. Very probably. She'd try to freeze him to death with her ice-crystal stare, at the very least.

'Well, it's your funeral.'

And Ludo would probably tell Emma what he had said in return for some trifling piece of gossip, thought Goldblatt – which would make her one of the undertakers.

Ludo sat down with the HO's copy of the *British Medical Journal* and began to leaf through the advertisements, looking for a course that would teach her everything she needed to know to pass the second part exam. Goldblatt had already told her they didn't make courses that big, but Ludo had more or less given up on the fantasy of studying for it in any other way.

The HO had started checking results at the computer screen. After

Ludo scanned the advertisements for courses, she turned to the job ads. It was only a six-month post that she had on the Prof's unit, and it was already time to start looking for her next position. It would be another SHO job unless she could convince an interview panel that a person who had failed the first part five times, and hadn't yet actually tried for the second part, should be a registrar. In fact, she had started wondering whether she even ought to try for the second part at the next exam session in June. What was the point? She had a feeling she wasn't going to be ready. When she had a feeling like that, as she had discovered from her multiple attempts at the first part, it was almost always right. Five times out of six, anyway. No, it was going to be another SHO job for sure. Ludo smiled bitterly to herself, running her eyes down the columns of ads.

Goldblatt watched her.

Ludo looked up. She raised an eyebrow. 'You can have it in a second, Malcolm.'

The HO glanced over her shoulder from the computer screen. 'Malcolm, Mrs Levy's U&Es have just come through. Her creatinine's gone up.'

'How much is it?' asked Goldblatt.

'130.'

'And it was 105 originally, wasn't it?'

'106,' said the HO.

'What do you think?' asked Goldblatt.

The HO narrowed her eyes in thought. 'I think we should get the renal people to see her.'

'You're right. Let's get someone else to sort it out.'

The HO nodded enthusiastically.

'Are you sure?' said Goldblatt. 'For a creatinine of 130?'

'But it's on the way up.'

'You're right! It could be 135 by now. Call the renal reg! Get her up here now!'

The HO grabbed the phone.

'Put it down,' said Goldblatt.

The HO put the phone down and looked at Goldblatt in confusion.

'She's got a mild degree of renal impairment. Let's think about it. What are the causes?'

'Polycystic kidneys!' yelled the HO, as if it were a reflex for her to shout the least common cause she knew for any condition.

'Ah... I think I've got a Dermatology clinic,' said Ludo, and she got up and left, taking the HO's *BMJ* with her.

'Polycystic kidneys?' said Goldblatt to the HO. 'In that case we'd better book her a transplant.'

'How do we do that?'

'Call the Renal reg.'

The HO lunged for the phone again.

'Put it down,' said Goldblatt. 'Did you examine this patient when she came in?'

'Of course I did,' said the HO.

'Did you feel polycystic kidneys?' asked Goldblatt. Polycystic kidneys are big, lumpy things that even medical students can palpate.

'No,' said the HO.

'Then does she have polycystic kidneys?'

'Maybe. Twenty per cent of patients with polycystic kidneys have kidneys that aren't palpable at the time renal failure is diagnosed.'

Goldblatt peered at the HO distrustfully. That sounded just like the kind of statistic he would have made up to bluff his way out of a tight spot.

But it sounded right. The percentage, as he recalled, was something like that.

'How do you know?' he asked cautiously.

'I just know,' said the HO. 'I know a lot about polycystic kidneys.'

It was possible. By definition, between gaps in a person's knowledge there must be islands of fact. Some things just stick better in some people's brains than they do in others. Maybe there was a place inside the HO's brain where polycystic kidneys just stuck. Maybe the HO had had polycystic kidneys in a previous life. As a merchant. In Guangzhou. With two pet parrots in a cage.

'What are the presenting features of polycystic renal disease?' said Goldblatt, just to check.

'Stones, haematuria, infection, progressive renal failure, and palpable kidneys,' the HO replied confidently.

Not bad, thought Goldblatt. 'What about clot colic?'

The HO rolled her eyes. 'That's included under haematuria.'

Fair enough. 'Let's go through them, then,' said Goldblatt. 'Does Mrs Levy have kidney stones?'

'There's no history of it.'

'Symptoms?'

'No.'

'Haematuria?'

The HO checked the notes for the results of Mrs Levy's admission urine test. 'No blood.'

'Infection?'

'No evidence of it.'

'Palpable kidneys?'

'No.'

'Renal failure?'

'Yes!' yelled the HO, just as if Mrs Levy was a patient who was meant to turn up at three in the morning but had died on the way in. Goldblatt almost expected her to punch the air.

'All right. Calm down,' said Goldblatt, regretfully preparing the HO for the demolition job that he was obliged to perform on her hypothesis. 'Mrs Levy developed renal impairment over four days. Does renal failure develop over four days in polycystic disease, or is it an insidious progression over months or years?'

'It can develop rapidly,' replied the HO, fighting her shrinking corner to the last. 'Superimposed infection or obstruction due to stones can precipitate renal failure.'

'True. Is there superadded infection?'

'No evidence of it.'

'Obstruction due to stones?'

'She doesn't have stones!' replied the HO impatiently.

'So would she have developed renal failure over the last four days if she had polycystic renal disease?' asked Goldblatt, who believed that he could finally see the light at the end of the tunnel and hoped the HO could see it as well.

'No,' said the HO.

'So does she have polycystic renal disease?' asked Goldblatt.

'No,' said the HO.

'Then what does she have?' asked Goldblatt.

'I don't know. That's why I wanted to call the renal reg, remember?'

'Pretend I'm the renal reg.'

'You're not the renal reg.'

'Pretend,' said Goldblatt. 'What would I say to you?'

'How should I know? You're the one pretending to be the renal reg!'

Goldblatt laughed. But the HO was serious.

'All right. I'd say, for a start, remember the three causal categories of renal failure: pre-renal, renal, and post-renal. I'd say, with that in mind, the first thing to do is examine your patient. Go and check her blood pressure, pulse rate, and jugulovenous pressure to ensure she isn't dehydrated. Listen to her chest and feel her abdomen. Auscultate for bruits. Ask about her urine output, and get the nurses to record a fluid balance chart. And get a urine specimen, dipstick it for blood and protein, and get it sent for biochemistry, culture, and microscopy.'

The HO had grabbed a spare lab request slip and started scribbling on the back.

'And?' said Goldblatt.

'What?' said the HO.

'The first thing you should always do.'

'I thought you said the first thing to do was examine the patient.'

Goldblatt smiled. Ah, the HO... Always listening to what you said.

'What's so funny?' she demanded.

'Nothing. Well? What's the other first thing you have to do?'

'Ring the renal reg?'

'No! Don't say that again. I'm serious. No matter what question I ask, do not say that again.' Goldblatt paused. 'Well?'

The HO stared. 'I'm not going to ring the renal reg,' she muttered.

'Check her drugs. That's the first thing you do. Always check the drugs.'

'Which drugs?'

'The drugs you prescribed that have given Mrs Levy renal failure.'

The HO screwed up her nose. 'I have *not* given Mrs Levy renal failure,' she retorted indignantly.

'Yes, you have,' said Goldblatt.

'Have I?'

'Yes. The frusemide you started last Friday has given her renal failure.'

'The frusemide? No, I didn't give her the frusemide. *You* gave her the frusemide, Malcolm. You're the one who told me to.'

Goldblatt sighed. It was so quaint, the instinct of self-preservation at the expense of others. 'Who wrote the frusemide up on the drug chart?'

'Me,' said the HO.

'Who signed the order?'

'Me,' said the HO.

'Then you gave it to her.'

'But I only wrote it because you told me to!'

'Prove it,' said Goldblatt.

'I never do anything unless you tell me to!'

'I'm glad to hear it. Now prove it.'

The HO's shoulders slumped. She buried her face in her hands. 'Fuck! I've given Mrs Levy renal failure. This is terrible.'

'It's not so terrible.'

The HO looked up hopefully.

'If you gave Mrs Levy renal failure, you can take it away.'

'Can I?' said the HO.

'Yes,' said Goldblatt. 'You are a doctor!'

'I am a doctor!' the HO repeated.

'You can't do much to alter the natural course of human life, but you can often reverse the treatments inflicted by your colleagues. Or yourself. Patients appreciate it. Remember that. Do it as often as you can. It's what we call A Good Thing.'

'A Good Thing?'

'Yes,' said Goldblatt. 'A Very Good Thing.'

The HO nodded, impressed.

'Go,' said Goldblatt. 'Examine Mrs Levy. And while you're there, halve her frusemide.'

The HO got up.

'Wait. What have you learned?'

'That frusemide can cause renal failure?' said the HO.

'And?'

'That you can treat renal failure caused by frusemide by reducing the frusemide?'

'And?'

'I don't know,' said the HO.

'Don't do anything you don't understand! That's what you've learned. Following orders is no explanation. It's not even an excuse. When you stand up in court, it's not going to be a defence to say that someone told you to do something. And by the way, no one's ever going to admit they did.'

The HO looked troubled. 'I don't understand anything. I'm always doing things because I'm told to. You tell me to do things. And the Prof does. And Dr Morris does. And Emma does.'

'And Ludo?' asked Goldblatt.

'I never do what Ludo tells me. What's going on between you two, anyway?'

'Nothing's going on between us.'

'No?'

'It's just... too much coffee.'

The HO stared at him sceptically. But it was true. There had been too much coffee. Much, much too much.

'Don't just listen,' said Goldblatt. 'Don't just do as you're told. Ask why. Make sure you understand. That's how you learn.'

'All right,' said the HO.

She left the office. A second later her small tousled head reappeared.

'Malcolm, why are we only halving Mrs Levy's frusemide? Why don't we stop it altogether?'

Goldblatt sighed. 'Because I said so.'

'All right,' said the HO, and her small tousled head went back to wherever it had come from.

Goldblatt smiled. The HO... Was he really worried about her? Most of the time she seemed determined, eager, and resilient, as she seemed right now, but still there were moments when he could imagine her exploding into hideous violence with a bag of bloodied ice cubes. Probably directed against herself. But maybe that was only his imagination. But maybe it wasn't.

He sat back in his chair and looked up at the spikes of Mr Lister's febrility frieze that the HO had put up around the wall. The frieze didn't really remind him of ancient Greece. It was more... Aztec. He'd miss it when Mr Lister went. If he ever did go. Perhaps they'd leave it up.

Goldblatt sighed. His gaze fell on the admissions book, which was still lying on the desk where the Prof had dropped it.

What had happened here this morning when the Prof came in? Goldblatt ran through it in his mind, as you run backwards and forwards through the scenes of an incomprehensibly surreal experience, vainly searching for a way to make sense of it.

27

As far as the Prof was concerned, the Cancellations Crisis, and the martyrdom of Mrs Watt, were over the minute she had walked out of the doctors' office with Emma and left Goldblatt behind.

She sent Emma away when they reached her office, and as soon as the door was closed she sat down and went over everything in her mind. It had been a short crisis but an intense one, and the Prof felt drained and exhausted. She also felt a sense of lingering uncertainty about the way she had succeeded in bringing it to an end so abruptly.

It had obviously been a master stroke to have a talk with Dr Goldblatt, but even in her wildest dreams the Prof wouldn't have imagined that it could bring such comprehensive success. How had she managed it? Wasn't there something more she should have done, some definitive act of administrative genius? The Prof could remember no such act. She could remember only a morbid haze of despondency that had become thicker every time Goldblatt had opened his mouth. And then he had mentioned a patient called Mrs Watt who had spoken to Margaret Hayes, and the Prof had ordered Emma to manipulate a bed for her. *That* was a definitive act. But it was a very particular type of definitive act. Very specific. Very personalized. It wasn't exactly a definitive act of administrative genius. Yet it had worked, hadn't it? That was what mattered. But could it really have been so easy to lift the terrible cloud of Margaret Hayes's disapproval, which had hung over her like a violent electrical storm waiting to break?

The Prof had a niggling feeling that there was some small but important matter she had forgotten to deal with, some light in the horrible mausoleum of the Cancellations Crisis that she had forgotten to switch off before locking the door and leaving it behind for ever. But what was the use of brooding about it? She wasn't going back in there to check, not unless

someone dragged her kicking and screaming. The Prof determinedly set
her mind not to brood. The niggling feeling soon went. A few minutes of
intense contemplation of the Scale was enough to drive it out, together
with any last doubts that may have been hiding behind it.

She gazed gratefully at the Scale. The morning, which had started
so unpromisingly with Dr Goldblatt in a quagmire of cancellations, had
turned into a day full of hope and anticipation. It was without question
one of those days when the Scale looked more full than empty.

The Prof experienced a wonderful, cathartic feeling. She was aware
of a wave of exuberance and elation building up in her, and she waited
expectantly for it to peak and carry her away. It was a shame she had told
Emma to leave. She was never more capable or incisive than when being
carried away on a wave of exuberance and elation, and she felt that Emma,
who displayed little exuberance and was rarely elated, should have the
opportunity to benefit from these waves when they came. There was much
that Emma had to learn if she were ever to make a successful Prof in her
own right. And the Prof had decided that Emma should one day become
a successful Prof in her own right, if only because the success of such a
protégé would be a vindication, perhaps the last and most outstanding,
of the Prof's own successful profdom.

The Prof allowed herself a moment of contented reflection. Now that
the crisis was safely behind her, she could indulge in a sensible modicum
of congratulation. As she thought about it, she realized that she had
achieved a number of important things.

For a start, she had humiliated Emma, who was obviously the person
who had foolishly written all those names in that awful book that Goldblatt
had insisted on showing her. The Prof had recognized her handwriting at
once. The fact that the girl couldn't bring herself to admit it merely proved
how great her humiliation had been. Humiliation was just as important
a part of Emma's education as exuberance and elation, and the Prof
jealously guarded her right to inflict it on her, preferably at least once a
fortnight, although not necessarily in front of Dr Goldblatt. Humiliation
in front of Dr Goldblatt was probably worth two normal humiliations. The
Prof opened the diary on her desk and glanced through it to see when
the next humiliation was due. She almost picked up her fountain pen to

make a note to cancel it. But she didn't. It would do no harm for Emma to be humiliated in front of Dr Goldblatt occasionally. The Prof closed her diary, driving the idea of such an extravagant concession from her mind.

In the second place, the Prof had organized the admission of a patient called Mrs Watt, who obviously needed urgent care, and whom Dr Goldblatt would probably have left to die in the street if she hadn't intervened. The Prof was fond of opera and found herself thinking of *La Bohème*, which she had seen at Covent Garden only a couple of weeks earlier, and the wonderfully romantic death of Mimi, the opera's heroine, in a garret. Perhaps, if she hadn't saved her, Mrs Watt would have died alone in a romantic garret as well. But she *had* saved her, that was the point. And a more important point was that her rescue of poor Mrs Watt would be a priceless point in her favour with Margaret Hayes.

The Prof opened her diary again. She wrote MRS WATT in big letters across the page to make sure she remembered the name of this important patient so she could nonchalantly remind Margaret Hayes about her the next time they spoke. Underneath MRS WATT she wrote Urgent Admission. The Prof gazed at the page contentedly. Seeing Mrs Watt's name there in black ink refreshed and strengthened the impression of all that she had achieved in overcoming the crisis. She could have gazed at Mrs Watt's name with perfect satisfaction for an hour.

And in the third place, she had stood up to Dr Goldblatt.

The Prof closed the diary sharply.

Standing up to Dr Goldblatt gave her immense satisfaction, more than she would have got from the salvation of a hundred dying Watts crawling up the hospital steps. But that was precisely the problem. There was something not quite right about a professor getting satisfaction from standing up to a registrar, and a locum registrar at that. And there was nothing at all right about the nerve-racking apprehension she felt at the thought of ever having to do it again.

From the day Goldblatt had refused to manipulate beds she had felt that there was something dangerous, reckless, and even unstable about the boy. And that was the first day he had joined the unit! None of her other registrars had ever refused. She had asked him nicely. The Prof still found the memory of his voice on the phone that day almost too difficult to deal with and she tried to think about it as infrequently as she could. Unfortunately, that wasn't infrequently enough. She should have nipped it in the bud then and there, on the very first day. Manipulate beds when you're told to, she should have said to him, or get off my unit!

That's what she should have said, like Dirty Harry or somebody.

The Prof had to admit to herself that she felt intimidated by the boy. In fact, if she was perfectly honest with herself – which she was certainly capable of being, of course, if the occasion called for it – she had to admit that he intimidated her down to the marrow. Especially after Emma reported back on that dreadful lunch they had all had following the unfortunate episode with that poor lady who didn't get her echocardiogram, when Goldblatt had apparently threatened to put in a complaint about her. The Prof had felt a spasm in her heart when Emma told her about that, and for a moment she had seriously wondered whether she was having a heart attack. That incident was even more intimidating than a refusal to manipulate beds, and the Prof therefore had to try even harder not to think about it. The very notion of someone saying such a thing out loud was too dreadful for words.

For a long time after that the Prof had wondered whether she should say something to Goldblatt, or pretend that she knew nothing about it. She could pretend she knew nothing about it because, officially, she did know nothing about it. Who would ever guess that Emma reported such things to her? Or all the other things Emma reported?

She decided to say nothing. The fact that she knew she had brought the whole thing on herself, in a way that she still found largely inexplicable, certainly helped with the decision. Who knew what else she might bring upon herself if she chose to reopen the terrifying Pandora's box out of which Goldblatt had leapt on that ward round? Or if she chose to open anything else with him, for that matter? By the time she decided this she had been thinking about it for so long that she didn't really have a choice anyway. It would have seemed odd to bring it up after a month. Another chance to nip it in the bud gone, she thought bitterly.

And here he was, this very morning, suggesting that patients could just as well get their Sorain infusions in any old hospital in any old corner of the country. She had almost choked in shock! Did he understand nothing,

nothing, of what it took to create and maintain a centre of excellence? Of course he did. He wasn't unintelligent. Far from it. He was rather too intelligent, it seemed, for his own good. No, it was nothing if not another naked attempt to humiliate and intimidate her.

Well, there was only one way to deal with someone like that, and that was to stand up to him – no matter how terrifying the prospect. The bud, which had become a full-blown carnivorous flower, had to be nipped. And hadn't she done it! Hadn't she just! She had shown him who was boss that morning. She had gone on demanding the name of the person who had booked all those admissions until he been forced to back down with some pathetic complaint about the pressure of the job. The pressure of the job! Ha! That was an admission of defeat if ever the Prof had heard one.

The Prof lingered over the memory and savoured the unwholesome satisfaction it gave her. She very much doubted, she told herself, that Dr Goldblatt would refuse to manipulate beds for her again. Not that she would ask him. He had had his chance and now he had lost it. She was almost inclined to be grateful that Margaret Hayes had precipitated this crisis so that, in solving it, she had had the opportunity to show the boy comprehensively who was in charge. It would be a long time before Dr Goldblatt would be able to intimidate Professor Small again!

The Prof felt she was very close to convincing herself that all of this was true and immediately decided to think about something else before she changed her mind.

She took out a draft of a paper that Bolkovsky, her Russian post-doc, was supposed to be writing, and began to read it. The spelling was atrocious. The Prof suspected that Bolkovsky refused to use the spell checker on his computer just to spite her. He was a horrible, foul-mouthed man with bad breath, and the Prof often wished that she didn't need to keep him.

Suddenly she felt deflated. She had always been surrounded by horrible men, ever since her first day as a medical student in Liverpool. Blunt, blustering, blundering men. When she looked at Tom de Witte, for instance, she wondered how someone like that could possibly exist. So big, hearty, and stupid, he was like a massive object made of rubber. With a penis. It would never have occurred to him that he wasn't supremely good at what he did, whether as a bronchoscopist, which was his speciality, or as a gastroscopist or uroscopist or proctoscopist. Or a milkman or a baker for that matter. Boys were like that. Or some boys were. So were some girls, or at least they pretended to be. Andrea herself pretended to be. But she wasn't. Yet Tom de Witte was. He never pretended to be anything. He was too big, hearty, and stupid for that.

Andrea Small had been through two husbands. The first was a very young mistake. The second was an older mistake. She had no desire to make it three. She didn't even know why she continued seeing Tom de Witte. In fact, officially, they both pretended they weren't seeing each other. Andrea didn't know why they did that either, and sometimes she wondered whether she should be outraged about it, on the assumption that they were doing it because in some way he was ashamed of her. But to become outraged over it would mean admitting that Tom could be ashamed of her, which would mean admitting that there was something which could, even theoretically, be regarded as shameful about her, which was even more outrageous than letting Tom de Witte simply get on with hiding the fact that they were seeing each other in the first place.

Anyway, Andrea Small wasn't altogether sure that she wanted to admit that she was seeing Tom de Witte. Maybe it was she who was ashamed of him! She would have liked to see the look on his big red face if she had told him that. It would never have occurred to him. It should have, since he had already been divorced once himself. But as far as Andrea was aware, Tom had never been guilty of the sin of introspection. Andrea, on the other hand, often felt as if she were drowning in introspection. At times like these, for example.

She threw a glance at Bolkovsky's horrible paper. She pushed it further away. She could hardly bear to read it.

The Prof looked up. The Scale was watching her. Sometimes it seemed as if the two 0s of the 1800 at the top were a pair of big, owl-like eyes that could see right through her. Right through the professorial façade and into the core of her being.

She gazed at the number, with its probing, owl-like eyes. It mocked her. 'I am unattainable,' it seemed to be hooting at her. 'Unattainable.' Not only was it unattainable, but deep in her heart Andrea Small expected that one day the tide would turn and the red column of Fuertler's patients would begin inexorably to slip down the wall.

She stared at the Scale, pondering it in despair. The Scale was stuck. It had been stuck at 960 for months. Perhaps the turning point had been reached...

Suddenly she shook her head. 'No, Andrea,' she said to herself, possibly aloud. 'Pull yourself out of it!'

She remembered how she had been feeling earlier, before she had picked up Bolkovsky's appallingly spelled paper. Elated. Exuberant.

'Come on, Andrea! Pull yourself together!'

She took a deep breath. And another, trying to recover that feeling.

'You showed him, didn't you? Well? Think of that!'

She thought of that. She had taught the boy a lesson. She had shown him who was boss. Was that worth nothing? After this, he'd respect her. He wouldn't be so quick to turn down the chance to manipulate a bed. If she ever gave him one, which she wouldn't. He wouldn't be so quick to talk about making a complaint.

The Prof looked up at the Scale again. Yes, Scale. Strong Scale. Good Scale. He'd respect her now.

And the Prof rushed out of the office, hoping that she would succeed in still believing it even when she came back.

On the seventh floor, Emma Burton was sitting in her bathroom-turned-office, on the phone to her sister, who was at her desk in the City. Emma had rung her as soon as the Prof shooed her away. She would be seeing her sister again that evening, when she got back to the flat they shared, but this couldn't wait.

It was weeks since Emma had stopped talking to Goldblatt. It hadn't been easy. It was hard not to talk to someone you were supposed to be working with. Not just working with, but supervising. Sometimes you felt foolish. You had to eat your lunch in your own tiny little office, where there were never any newspapers to read. If you didn't, you had to listen to him talk about where your blood went when you flushed and ask whether he could stroke you. And was it worth it? Had he done a single thing to persuade her to start talking to him again? No, he had gone on just as before, humiliating her, deriding her, undermining her with the Prof. Emma saw now how foolish she had been to expect anything else, how pointless it had been to give him so much time to make amends. Was a person like that even capable of caring whether other people talked to him or not?

Yes, it was all clear to her now.

Glancing secretly up from her shoes, she had seen the way Goldblatt had allowed the blame to drift directly towards her during the meeting with the Prof, letting the Prof's question hang for so long that the air had become almost too heavy to breathe. He hadn't let slip a single chance to emphasize her responsibility for the cancellations shambles on the unit. Emma shuddered to think what else he would have said had she not stumbled on the secret meeting, which only someone without a shred of decency would have arranged with the Prof behind her back. And anyway, what was the sum total of her responsibility? She had booked the patients in as the Prof demanded. Was that some kind of crime?

She laughed bitterly. On the other end of the line, her sister, who had heard it all a hundred times before – apart from the events of that morning, which so far she had heard only once – supportively murmured something in disbelief. She was a very loyal sister. Being an accountant, she also had a high boredom threshold, which helped.

Emma had tried to be welcoming. Hadn't she done everything she could to integrate Goldblatt into the team and not make him feel uncomfortable just because she was the SR and he was only the registrar and would have to take orders from her? But it was too late now. He had had his chances. She had given him more than his fair share.

'Much more,' said Emma's sister, whose loyalty often got the better of her judgement.

She had been waiting for Goldblatt to be dealt with in the appropriate way. After all, it wasn't her job to put him in his place.

'But you are the SR,' her sister pointed out. 'So you're senior to him.'

'But it's not my job!' retorted Emma, wondering if everyone was against her.

'Whose job is it?' asked her sister.

'The Prof's,' said Emma.

'Of course,' said her sister.

But the Prof hadn't done her job. Time after time, she had refused to act.

Emma couldn't understand it. The Prof knew what was going on, Emma made sure of that. Goldblatt had stopped turning up to her SR ward rounds, for instance. He had simply stopped coming! Emma had barely been able to believe that someone could even think of doing such a thing, and would have been too stunned to say anything to Goldblatt about it even if she had been talking to him at the time. Which she hadn't. But she told the Prof. The Prof was just as stunned. She shook her head in disbelief for at least a minute. But in the end what did she do?

'Nothing,' said Emma's sister, who knew the answer to that one.

'Exactly!' Nothing at all. The Prof didn't even talk to him about it. And what about his threat to make a complaint after the ward round with Mrs Constantidis? The Prof couldn't believe that one either, but again what did she do? In vain Emma waited for the Prof to drag Goldblatt across the carpet in the same way that she regularly dragged her across the carpet. What more did the Prof need? How much longer was she going to wait? Was there something about her carpet that meant Malcolm Goldblatt couldn't be dragged across it?

Well, maybe the Prof could afford to wait, but Emma couldn't. Today's meeting had shown her that. Emma couldn't afford to ignore him any longer, treating him to the silence that was more than he deserved. She couldn't afford to sit around as a target while he took shots at her. His aim was perfectly clear to her now. Turn the Prof against her, and he could have her job for himself. Where would she be then? Without the Prof's support, how would she ever find a place to do an MD? And without an MD, *she'd* be the one doing one locum job after the next.

'I need that MD, Kate,' she said to her sister.

'I know you do.'

'I'm sick of being nice to him.'

'He doesn't deserve it.'

Emma's eyes narrowed. 'It's him or me, Kate. It's not my fault. He started it. If he thinks he can stab me in the back, I'll do the same to him.'

'What are you going to do?'

Emma eyes narrowed further. She glanced calculatingly around the office, with its piles of illegally secreted notes and its collection of missing mugs. 'I'm going to tell the Prof the truth.'

'I thought you already had.'

'No, I mean the *truth*. What he really thinks of her.'

'Do you know what he really thinks of her?'

'Of course I do.'

Emma had learned a lot since she had joined the unit. She still failed to recognize that it was her defects that the Prof most valued about her, and consequently remained in a constant state of anxiety and readiness to panic, but there were other things she had begun to recognize about the Prof after all the time that she and Andrea Small had spent roaming the hospital wards together. At the start, Emma's sycophancy had been instinctive, but by now it had become far more knowing. She had begun to see that the Prof craved, needed, demanded to be loved. Well, Emma could do love, as much as was needed. She could do obsequiousness, adulation, abject gratitude, and servility as well. In fact, they came naturally to her.

But Emma had also begun to understand something else, something equally important: what the Prof feared. What she wilfully blinded herself to, what she couldn't bear to hear. Paradoxically, it was Goldblatt who had shown her that – or if not Goldblatt himself, the Prof's reaction to him. Her behaviour on the ward round with Mrs Constantidis had been an eye opener. After that, Emma had watched the Prof ever more closely, recognizing the signs of her fear in every truncated glance, in every tittered half joke.

With that realization had come a form of power. A power so terrible, so awesome, so potentially destructive – to herself – that Emma hadn't dared wield it. But if the stakes are high enough, the risks a person will take are commensurate.

She told her sister what she planned to say.

There was a sharp intake of breath on the other end of the line.

'It's true!' said Emma. 'I'm not saying anything that isn't.'

'I'm not saying you are.'

'So?'

'I just wonder...'

'What?'

'If it's wise.'

'Do you think I haven't thought about it!'snapped Emma

'When are you going to do it?'

'Tomorrow morning. The Prof's asked me to meet her. We've got the Grand Round next week and she wants to discuss it. I'll tell her then. I'll find a way to get it into the conversation.'

'Emma,' said her sister tentatively, 'I know you've thought about it, but... don't you think it's a bit risky?'

Emma laughed bitterly. 'What choice have I got?'

28

'WHO SHOULD WE PRESENT, Emma?' said the Prof.

Emma stared at her.

'Emma. It's a Grand Round. We need someone special. Think!'

Emma's mind was blank.

'Well?'

'Mrs Grahame?' whispered Emma.

'Ridiculous! Mrs Grahame? Why? What's special about her?'

Nothing but the fact that it was the first name that had come into Emma's head. She had seen Mrs Grahame with the Prof at the previous Thursday clinic and for some reason had just thought of her.

The Prof shook her head in disappointment.

Emma began to flush. She tried, in vain, to control it. The more she tried, the worse it got. In a minute she'd feel the warm blood pounding in her ears.

Once a year, when her turn came for the Grand Round that was held at eight o'clock on Thursday mornings, Andrea Small faced the same problem she faced before her unit meetings each month, finding someone interesting enough to present. But her unit meetings were small, trivial affairs, involving hardly anyone outside her own team, while the hospital Grand Round was a huge meeting involving half the doctors in the hospital, many of whom turned up, in accordance with ancient medical tradition, solely in order to attack the speaker as viciously as they could. So the problem was correspondingly bigger. There simply weren't that many angles to Fuertler's Syndrome, and it just wasn't that easy to come up with an interesting case every year, or even every couple of years, at least not for a non-Fuertlerological audience that wasn't going to shiver with delight at every tiny dot and squiggle in a Fuertler's skin biopsy.

The Prof wasn't the only one who faced this kind of difficulty. Dr Fulbright, the epilepsy specialist, hadn't presented an interesting case in years. He could spend hours ecstatically examining every spike and wave on an electroencephalogram, but who else cared? Few people attended the Grand Round when it was Dr Fulbright's turn. Those who did attend groaned when his SR began projecting the hieroglyphic tracings of the inevitable electroencephalograms, which no one could decipher except a great epilepsy specialist like Dr Fulbright, and wondered why they had bothered.

The only really interesting case for a general audience that the Prof had had for months was Mr Gust, the man with bruises on his back. But the man with bruises on his back hadn't had Fuertler's Syndrome at all. At a pinch, they could present him as 'A case of Porphyria Cutanea Tarda masquerading as Fuertler's Syndrome', but the Prof thought that would be unwise, especially with Dr Mowbray in the audience, considering that the case had masqueraded for all of about four seconds once Dr Mowbray had begun to look at it.

The Prof really did need to pick a patient. The Grand Round was next week, which left barely enough time if Emma was going to do all the work required to prepare the presentation.

She pressed Emma to suggest a few more names, just to see who she would come up with, and laughed at her after each one. When it was clear that Emma wasn't going to come up with anyone the Prof hadn't been able to think of herself, she said: 'What about Mrs Grahame?'

'I mentioned her already!' cried Emma.

'Did you?'

'Yes. And you said there was nothing special about her.'

There *was* nothing special about her. Mrs Grahame was a garden-variety Fuertler's who had had the disease for years, slowly progressing, until she had recently stabilized. But it's the way you present something, as much as what you present, that makes things interesting. Or so the Prof had often found, and she had learned a lot in this direction from watching the way politicians successfully presented the horrendous things – or 'spun' them, as she understood the correct terminology to be – that they were constantly doing to the health service.

'The fact that she responded to Sorain so dramatically is interesting,' remarked the Prof.

'But she didn't respond to Sorain,' said Emma.

'Yes, she did,' said the Prof.

'No, she didn't,' said Emma. 'It was months after she had her last dose of Sorain that her condition stabilized. I can remember you saying it was far too late for the Sorain to have worked.'

'You must have misheard me.'

'But I remem—'

'I said you must have misheard me.'

Emma bit her lip. She hadn't misheard her! She had been with the Prof in clinic and had heard every word distinctly. But there was only so far she would go in disagreeing with the Prof, especially today. There was too much at stake.

'How do you know it wasn't the Sorain?' asked the Prof.

Emma hesitated. 'You said so, Prof.'

'No, Emma. I would never have said it wasn't the Sorain. I said it may have been the Sorain and it may just have taken a very long time. You'll need to do a literature search looking for everything that's been written about Sorain's duration of action. Are there any other examples of a delayed effect? What are the characteristics of patients who respond in this way? You see, it really is an interesting case. You'll have to check the data in the Fuertler's files as well, of course.'

'But how will I know who's had Sorain?'

'Almost everyone's had Sorain.'

'But there are hundreds of them, Prof!'

'Yes,' said the Prof with satisfaction, 'there are.'

Emma stared at the Prof in despair. 'I can't look through hundreds of folders just for a Grand Round, Prof.'

'Can't you, Emma?'

Emma flushed with shame.

'All right. I have a list somewhere of the names of patients who got better some time after their Sorain,' lied the Prof, thinking that she must be able to remember a couple of others if she tried. For an instant, she wondered whether there wasn't some way of organizing the files so you could find out things like that without having to trawl through every single one. Or make up the results.

'Thank you, Prof.'

Maybe Sorain really did have a delayed effect in some cases, the Prof mused. She wondered how she could get Emma to look through all the Fuertler's files properly. Or maybe that SHO could do it, the one with the name that sounded like something out of a Christmas cracker. But she was such a strange, heavy girl, the SHO, and as far as the Prof was aware, had never shown the slightest enthusiasm for anything. Sadly, the Prof didn't see how she could avoid commenting on this lack of enthusiasm in any reference she would be obliged to write on the SHO's behalf.

Maybe she should tell Emma she was doing a study. Maybe she really should do a study. Was it possible Sorain actually did have a delayed effect that no one had recognized before? What a wonderful discovery that would be, not only for her patients, but for herself, whose chief claim to therapeutic expertise was the ability to handle this difficult and complex drug.

The Prof was starting to feel very hopeful, very hopeful indeed. This might well be the most interesting Grand Round she had ever given.

'This will be very good, Emma! I'm sure it will be. Don't you think so? As long as you speak clearly and don't mumble. You mumble when you get nervous. Did you know that?'

'Yes, Prof,' said Emma. 'You've told me.'

The Prof laughed. 'Sometimes you get so nervous one can't make out a thing you say. Nothing. Did you know that?'

'Yes, Prof.'

'We'll rehearse the presentation, of course.'

And not just once! Emma, as the SR, would present Mrs Grahame's case to the audience before the Prof stood up to take questions about the wonderful new delayed effect of Sorain that she had just discovered. There was no way the Prof was going to let Emma muddle her way through the case history. It had to be crystal clear. It had to have the right 'spin', as she understood the terminology to be.

'There won't be anything for you to be nervous about,' the Prof said reassuringly, just in case she had gone too far with the remarks about

Emma's nervousness. 'But there's still a lot more work for you to do,' she added, just in case she had gone too far with the reassurance.

Emma nodded.

The Prof smiled brightly.

Emma didn't. The time had come. It was now or never. Emma looked at the Prof glumly.

'What is it?' said the Prof.

Emma shrugged.

'Don't you want to do the Grand Round?' asked the Prof, for whom the alternative – getting Malcolm Goldblatt to do it – was almost unthinkable.

'Yes,' replied Emma miserably. The alternative was just as unthinkable for her.

'Then what is it?' demanded the Prof in exasperation. Emma was such a sensitive creature that the slightest turbulence could shatter her for days. Sometimes the Prof wondered where she got the strength to cope with her.

'Oh, nothing,' said Emma leadingly.

'It will be a very good presentation, Emma, really. I'm sure it will be.'

'I hope so,' Emma said listlessly.

'Well?'

'Oh, it's nothing.'

'Don't tell me you don't want to do the presentation. I know it isn't easy, standing up in front of everyone. The way they all want to attack you, pick you apart, jump on any mistake you make, ask impossible questions just to... Yes, well... But you must learn to do it. You must, Emma. You'll never get anywhere if you don't. And I didn't really mean it before, about the way you mumble when you get nervous. I mean, you do mumble when you get nervous, but I didn't really mean it. And you won't be nervous, will you? Because we'll rehearse it and you won't have anything to be nervous about.'

The Prof stopped and looked at her hopefully.

'It isn't the Grand Round,' said Emma, sighing.

'Then what is it?' asked the Prof gently, leaning a little closer across the desk that stood between them.

'You know what it is,' said Emma.

'Do I?' said the Prof.

'Yes,' said Emma.

The Prof did. She drew back across the desk

'I just can't work with him!' Emma felt tears spring to her eyes. She let them flow.

'I know,' said the Prof, who wouldn't have been averse to shedding a few tears herself, and might have started, had Emma not beaten her to it. Although the Prof didn't think it was a good idea to cry in front of staff, especially in front of Emma, before whom more than anyone else it was essential to maintain an air of impassive mastery. 'A lot of us find him difficult,' said the Prof, struggling to find her tone of masterful impassivity. 'But he's only here for a short time.'

'Not short enough,' Emma sniffled.

'Perhaps not,' said the Prof wistfully.

'No one can work with him. The patients don't like him.'

'I know,' said the Prof. 'You told me.'

'He's so arrogant!'

'I know,' said the Prof.

Emma reached for a tissue from the box on the Prof's desk.

'You should get rid of him,' she said abruptly, and glanced covertly at the Prof, with her nose in a tissue, to see how the Prof would react.

The Prof frowned. 'That would be difficult,' she murmured at last.

'No, it wouldn't. You're the Prof. It's your unit. You can do whatever you like.'

The Prof's frown deepened. It never felt as if she could do what she liked, even if she was a Prof and even if it was her unit. Sometimes it felt as if the more of a Prof she was, the less people would let her do.

'No,' said the Prof eventually, shaking her head. 'It would be difficult.'

'Why?' said Emma.

'Well, for a start, because... how would we find someone to replace him?' demanded the Prof, relieved to have discovered an explanation that circumvented all the unpleasant questions that the other explanations would have raised. 'It would take time. And who would do his work?'

'I would!' said Emma.

'And who would do your work?'

'I would!' said Emma.

'No, no, no, Emma.' The Prof chuckled indulgently, barely daring to imagine the catastrophe that Emma was volunteering to engineer.

Emma glanced at the Prof resentfully, pretending to blow her nose again.

She hesitated, nervously unsheathing the verbal dagger she had prepared for the occasion. The consequences of using it to stab the Prof were unpredictable. The Prof, she knew, would bleed. But the Prof was just as likely to pull out one of her own daggers – ten times bigger – and stab her back, perhaps fatally. If it went wrong, in other words, it would mean the end of the beautiful relationship she had established with the Prof. On the other hand, if it went right, it could mean the end of Goldblatt. But since Goldblatt had obviously dedicated himself to ending the beautiful relationship anyway, and since it looked as if he was going to succeed unless he was removed, Emma didn't really see that she had anything to lose.

She took a deep breath – and stabbed. 'He doesn't respect you!'

The Prof's face went very still. After a long pause she said: 'I don't know if that's true.' Her voice was very soft, as it usually was when she was lying to herself.

'It is true, Prof. Someone needs to tell you what he's saying. He laughs at you,' said Emma, stabbing again. 'You should hear him! You should hear the things he says. Calls you the great Fuertler's... fraud. He says you don't know any more about Fuertler's than he does. He says you couldn't tell Fuertler's from Porphyria Cutanea Tarda. He mocks you all the time. He doesn't care who hears him. Doctors, nurses, physios...'

'Patients?' whispered the Prof.

'Oh, the patients!' exclaimed Emma, stabbing with abandon. 'Prof, you should hear what he says to the patients! He tells them... he tells them... he tells them they should all go and get their Sorain somewhere else. With Dr—'

'Not Dr Jenkins?'

'Exactly. With Dr Jenkins. Or anybody else. Anybody would be better than you, he says. He doesn't take you seriously, Prof. He doesn't respect you, he doesn't respect anything about you. He doesn't respect the way you run the unit and he doesn't respect the way you treat the patients and he doesn't respect—'

'*Enough! Stop! Stop stop stop stop stop!*'

Emma stopped. She lowered her eyes, and then glanced secretly at the Prof to try to discern what effect her words had had.

The Prof leaned back in her chair, eyes closed.

Emma peered at her. 'He doesn't respect you, Prof,' she said quietly, twisting the blade and pushing it home. 'Someone has to tell you. It's not easy, but I had to say something.' She watched as the Prof continued to sit with her eyes closed. Emma felt an enormous sense of power. After all the times the Prof had reduced her to speechlessness, it was finally the Prof's turn to sit dumbly in front of her. An extravagant image came into her head of the Prof, not her, trembling once a fortnight. 'He says you're scared of him, Prof, and you'd never do anything to get rid of him. I've heard him say it, exactly those words. *She'd never do it.* But you would, wouldn't you? You can show him. You're the Prof. You can do what you want.'

With a huge effort of will, Emma stopped. There was so much more she wanted to say, but something told her that she had said enough. Less was more. That was what her sister, knowing what Emma could be like, had told her the previous night. A dozen times. Less was more.

Less was something, anyway. The Prof was silent. Emma stared at the Prof, suddenly fearful. Her blood lust had abruptly given way to terror. Had she gone too far? She was desperate to know what was going on behind the Prof's closed eyes.

Suddenly the eyes opened. 'Have you dictated your letters from last week's clinic yet?' demanded the Prof, her tone like ice.

Emma jumped. Then she flushed. 'Almost.'

'Go and finish them!'

'When?'

'Now!' said the Prof. 'And I want to see them when they're done!'

She held on until Emma had closed the door behind her. As soon as it was shut, the Prof leaned back in her chair and closed her eyes again. When she opened them, she had dropped her façade. She was naked and shivering in front of the Scale.

The shell of false confidence in which the Prof had encased herself for twenty-four hours, after the worryingly simple resolution of the Cancellations Crisis, had shattered completely. It had been fragile enough before Emma spoke to her, but at least the Prof had been able to ignore its fragility by the trusted expedient of not thinking about it. Avoiding Goldblatt like the plague had also helped. But thanks to Emma and her big indiscreet mouth, the Prof could no longer avoid facing up to it once more.

A horrible image came into her head. Everyone was laughing at her. Doctors, nurses, physiotherapists, occupational therapists, even that awful social worker who only came to her ward round for five minutes each week. She saw them in her mind's eye. Laughing. Pointing at her. Laughing.

No, it wasn't possible. Suddenly the Prof was filled with a crimson tide of hatred for Emma, that big lump of blonde obtuseness. She wished she had never appointed her. What had she been *thinking*? What did she expect from someone like that? Stupid girl. She wouldn't know whether someone like Malcolm Goldblatt respected her or not. How could she? She wouldn't recognize respect for a professor if it came along and knocked her on the head.

But Goldblatt didn't respect her. A depthless, sickening feeling threatened to suck the Prof down into its gaping void. The boy had never respected her, and never would. But she respected him. Not only did she respect him, she was scared witless of him and what he might say or do. The Prof knew that, despite everything she had told herself the previous day, in her heart of hearts – a place best avoided, for obvious reasons – she had never really believed otherwise.

With a sensation of clammy nausea, the Prof began to wonder how long it would be until Goldblatt undermined her irreversibly with everyone on the unit. Perhaps he already had. If he was putting seditious thoughts into Emma's head, which ought to have contained no thoughts but the ones she put there herself, no one was safe from his influence. She wondered what he had been saying to that impressionable young house officer who never got any tests done on time, or to the SHO with the ludicrous name. Maybe it was her duty to save them from his malign effect. The Prof took her educational duties very seriously, and made a strict point of never letting an HO leave her unit without first learning her name. Which reminded her, she must get her secretary to find out what it was...

Maybe she should get rid of him. What a relief that would be! Maybe she really should.

Then she remembered who had suggested it to her. Emma! That insolent, jumped-up SR, who, instead of showing even an inkling of gratitude for all the Prof had done for her, was running around telling people – or one person, at least – that Goldblatt didn't respect her.

But he didn't respect her. But that didn't mean Emma should be saying it, or even thinking it!

Not for the first time in her life, the Prof found herself overcome with animosity and resentment towards someone who had told her something that, if she had been brutally honest with herself – which one could hardly expect her to be, not now, not having had such a shock – she knew was perfectly true.

But Emma could wait. There was plenty of time to work out what to do with her. What to do with Malcolm Goldblatt was a much more urgent question.

It was a difficult one. The Prof wasn't even sure what the rules were, and whether, even if she wanted to sack him, she could do it without stepping into a legal minefield. On what grounds? Imagine announcing that she was going to sack him and then finding out that she couldn't! That would be worse than anything. Worse than having the boy on her unit for another three months. Her enemies would have a field day.

But talking to the HR people would be risky. It would get back to the HR director, and from there who knew where else it would get to? The HR director, she knew, was close to a certain endocrinology professor, and probably to various of her other enemies as well.

Yet she needed to talk to someone. And it had to be someone she could trust to keep quiet.

'I'm sorry. What did you say, Andrea?' said Dr Morris, shaking his head and blinking. The Prof had enticed him into her office and launched into a long conversation about the latest twist in her struggle to have an extra physiotherapy session allocated to her unit, which she had been waging for almost a year. It wasn't really a conversation. More a monologue. It had lulled him into such a state of stupor that he wasn't sure if, in the midst of all that, she had casually slipped in the question that he thought he had just heard.

'I said: "By the way, do you think I should get rid of our friend Dr Goldblatt?"'

'Is he a friend of yours?'

The Prof shook her head impatiently.

Dr Morris climbed upright in his chair, having slumped during the physiotherapy tirade. For a while now he had begun to feel that he was becoming the Prof's psychological crutch, and he wasn't enjoying the experience of being an orthopaedic support. How had she managed before he joined the unit? The way he had been left to clean up the mess after the business with Mrs Constantidis made him realize that the Prof was turning him into her consigliere, accomplice, and confessor. But most of all she was turning him into something at which she *talked*. Her 'little chats' usually turned into Hitlerian monologues that could last up to an hour. A searching and excruciating – if not overtly paranoid – analysis of the Prof's most recent conversation with Margaret Hayes was almost always on the menu, usually followed by a dose of vitriol poured over the character of Dr Jenkins in Leicester. Dr Morris had met Dr Jenkins a couple of times at conferences, and considered him a perfectly reasonable chap. And there was of course the omnipresent, Byzantine plot to force the head physiotherapist to allocate another three hours per week of outpatients' physiotherapy to the Prof's patients, bitterly opposed by the evil Dr Mowbray out of sheer bloody-mindedness, on which Dr Morris got a mind-numbing update at least twice weekly.

And now, if he heard correctly, she wanted to get rid of Malcolm Goldblatt?

'Why?' asked Dr Morris, totally bemused.

The Prof scrutinized him carefully. 'Don't you think he's difficult?'

'Do you?' replied Dr Morris, who was wide awake now and knew that at all costs he had to avoid committing himself to an opinion that would definitely be used against him later.

'I thought I could remember you saying that you did, Anthony,' said the Prof, resorting to an old trick.

'No, I don't believe I did, Andrea,' said Dr Morris, weighing each word before he spoke.

'Oh,' said the Prof.

Frankly, Dr Morris was shocked. Call him an old-fashioned traditionalist, but sacking another doctor wasn't a step you took every day, not unless the doctor in question had been up to something with a patient, or had forgotten to turn on the oxygen supply during an anaesthetic. It wasn't a step Dr Morris had taken on any day, or had ever been party to. He didn't want to be party to it now.

'Don't you think he's difficult?' asked the Prof, probing again.

'Difficult is one thing, Andrea, but getting rid of him is something else.'

'So you *do* think he's difficult!'

'I didn't say that,' replied Dr Morris quickly, realizing that he had only one opportunity to set the record straight. 'You know I didn't say it.'

The Prof glanced calmly and imperviously at the desk in front of her.

'I didn't say it, Andrea.'

'Oh, all right, Anthony, you didn't say it!'

'He's a perfectly good doctor.'

'I didn't say he wasn't a good doctor. Heavens, Anthony, what do you think I'm saying? That would be a libel. He's an excellent doctor. I have the greatest confidence in him. If my own mother were unwell and—'

'Andrea,' said Dr Morris, 'what is this all about?'

'I just wanted to know whether you thought we should get rid of him.'

'Can you get rid of him?' asked Dr Morris.

'Of course I can!' replied the Prof with as much false confidence as she could manage. Nine times out of ten, she knew, it didn't matter if you really had the power to do something, as long as people thought you did. If you were forceful enough no one would even check. That was one lesson she had learned from all the years she had been forced to spend amongst brusque, blustering men who constantly claimed the power to do all kinds of things they had no right to do, and usually got away with it. 'He's a locum, Anthony! I can sack him if I want.' She watched Dr Morris closely to see how he would respond. It was, she felt, an important test.

'I see,' said Dr Morris glumly.

The Prof felt tentatively buoyed. 'So you do think I should get rid of him?'

'No! Of course I don't! I can't believe you'd even consider it. Isn't that obvious?'

The Prof gazed at him. 'Well, I shall have to think about it,' she said at last. 'But I'm glad to have your opinion, Anthony.'

Dr Morris was glad to have given it. Maybe he genuinely believed the matter would end there, as if it really were his encouragement, and not merely his acquiescence, that the Prof had been seeking.

'You won't mention this to anyone, will you, Anthony?'

'Of course not.'

And thinking the matter was closed, he didn't, not even to Goldblatt.

29

Mr Lister was going home. The fever had gone. Not a chill, not a shake. Not a flush on the cheek, not a sweat in the bed. The mercury didn't break 37 degrees. They kept him in for another four days to make sure. Four times a day the nurses pulled the thermometer out from between Mr Lister's cracked lips and examined it in disbelief. The HO stuck the thermometer in his mouth every time she was in his room. His wife stuck the thermometer in his mouth every time she came to visit. Mr Lister stuck the thermometer in his own mouth when no one else was there to stick it in for him. No one believed they couldn't get a fever out of him if they tried hard enough. But they were wrong. Mr Lister was cured. Or at least his fever was gone.

On the morning of his departure he looked more doleful than ever. The nurses on the ward all stopped by to say goodbye. Didn't he want to go? Of course he wanted to go, he replied sombrely. He didn't look very happy, they said brightly, trying to cheer him up.

Why should he look happy? One of the nurses had conscientiously explained the potential side effects of steroid therapy to him long before Dr Morris had finally made the decision to use it, carefully emphasising the most extreme possibilities. Mr Lister could already feel the fluid that the drug was attracting into his tissues, the fat that it was depositing around his ribs, the cracking of the bones that it was thinning, the level of the sugar that it was elevating, the looseness of the skin that it was atrophying, the multiplication of the bacteria that it was nurturing, and the throbbing of the blood pressure that it was raising. He had come in with a fever and a daily sweat, and the drugs they were going to give him would turn him into an osteoporotic, hypertensive, diabetic buffalo with thin skin.

'They won't,' said Goldblatt during his round with Ludo and the HO on the morning Mr Lister was leaving.

'They will,' said Mr Lister.

Goldblatt shook his head. Even after they've had differences with you, most patients want to part amicably in the end. 'We're going to reduce the dosage as soon as we can, which keeps the side effects down. Hopefully you won't experience anything. If you do start to develop side effects, we'll deal with them as they come up.'

'Why don't you wait and see if you get them before you start complaining?' said Ludo.

Mr Lister glared at her. He didn't like Ludo. He felt that she had never taken his fever as seriously as she should.

'All right?' said Goldblatt. If it wasn't all right with Mr Lister after six weeks in hospital, four CT scans, five ultrasounds, three MRIs, an echocardiogram, a barium enema, a gastroscopy, a colonoscopy, a gallium scan, a white cell scan, a knee aspiration, two lumbar punctures, two bone marrow biopsies, a pleural biopsy, four skin biopsies, three hundred X-rays, and fourteen million blood tests, many of which no one but Dr Morris understood, something really was wrong with him and he should be admitted at once for further investigation. Preferably to a hospital north of the Scottish border with good psychiatric facilities.

Mr Lister didn't say anything.

'We'll see you in clinic in two weeks,' said Goldblatt. 'Don't forget.'

Mr Lister nodded disconsolately.

'And you should ring us earlier if the fever comes back, like Dr Morris explained. All right? Check your temperature four times a day.'

Mr Lister nodded.

'You know how to take your temperature, don't you?'

'No, doctor. No idea.'

Oh, how he was going to miss Mr Lister, thought Goldblatt. 'Has someone actually watched you do it?'

'Watched me?' demanded Mr Lister incredulously.

Goldblatt turned to the HO. 'Come back and make sure. And make sure he has a thermometer to take home.' It was amazing how often patients were expected to know how to do things properly just because they had seen them done a hundred times, and how often it turned out that they didn't. Or couldn't, because someone had forgotten to give them whatever they needed in order to do it.

Mr Lister looked at him sourly. For a moment, it was just possible to catch a glimpse of the fear in his eyes. That was what lay behind his irritability and sarcasm, of course, as it had done ever since the dreadful night when Dr Morris had used his pseudo-Sutherland sleight of hand to have Mr Lister admitted. Then he had been afraid of what the diagnosis might be. Now he was scared that they hadn't got the diagnosis right. Scared, after six weeks in hospital, to be going home.

'Listen,' said Goldblatt, 'it's going to be all right. Just take the Prednisolone, take your temperature four times a day like we've told you, and let us know if your temperature is over thirty-eight or if you're feeling unwell.' He paused, wishing he didn't have to say what he had to say next. 'You've got the hospital's number. Ring, ask them to bleep me. Any time. I'm here.'

Mr Lister stared at him.

'Any time. If you have any concerns, call.'

Mr Lister nodded grudgingly.

'I'll come back and make sure you've got everything before you go,' said the HO as they moved away.

But the HO wasn't happy. She looked almost as miserable as Mr Lister. Anyone would have thought she was being sent home as well.

'What if he does have an infection somewhere?' she asked when they got back to the doctors' office. 'What if we just didn't find it?'

It was a good question. After weeks of tests that revealed nothing but the unimpeachable normality of Mr Lister's organs and tissues, with the exception of a couple of equivocal, non-specific biopsy findings and a few suspect blood tests, Dr Morris had made the diagnosis of exclusion and concluded that Mr Lister must have vasculitis – but no matter how many tests had been done, it was still a diagnosis of exclusion, and no one likes settling for that. What if you've missed the real diagnosis because you haven't looked hard enough or in the right place? What if the real disease is then masked by the medication you give for the one you've wrongly diagnosed, and silently progresses until declaring itself again, too late for treatment? What if the treatment for the non-existent disease actually makes the real disease worse?

Prednisolone, the steroid used as the treatment for vasculitis, also impairs the body's immune defences, enabling an infection to spread.

'If he had an infection,' said Goldblatt, 'we would have found it. There was nowhere left for it to hide.'

'But what if he does?'

'He doesn't have one,' said Ludo.

'Well, we just put him on Prednisolone,' retorted the HO. 'If he does have one, it'll kill him.'

'*You* put him on Prednisolone,' Goldblatt corrected her.

'Oh, no I didn't!' she objected vigorously. 'I specifically wrote in the notes that Dr Morris told me to.'

'Good idea,' said Goldblatt. 'And who signed that entry in the notes?'

'I did,' said the HO.

'That's going to look very good, then. You'll be able to prove that someone else told you to start Prednisolone because you wrote that someone else told you to start Prednisolone. Does that sound a little bit circular to you?'

'But Emma told me to always write things down in the notes. And you did as well.'

'True,' said Goldblatt.

'And I did!' yelled the HO. 'I fucking did.'

'Good,' said Goldblatt.

The HO collapsed into a chair. 'What do you want from me?'

'I told you something else.'

'What?'

'Lists are good,' said Ludo.

'Shut up, Ludo,' said the HO.

'Yes, Ludo, shut up,' said Goldblatt. 'I told you something else.'

'What? Draw lines around myself! It's those fucking lines, isn't it?'

'No,' said Goldblatt. 'It's not the lines. It's much simpler than that. Don't do anything you don't understand.'

The HO let her head fall back and closed her eyes. 'Don't do anything you don't understand,' she repeated numbly. 'Of course! That one.'

'Malcolm Goldblatt!' cried Ludo in outrage. This was the first she had heard of Goldblatt's latest piece of revolutionary propaganda. 'Did you tell her that? She's a house officer. She doesn't understand anything. What do you think will happen if she follows that rule? Nothing will get done.' She turned to the HO. 'Don't you listen to him!'

The HO listened.

'If you think it's dangerous to put Mr Lister on Prednisolone you shouldn't have put him on it,' said Goldblatt.

'Malcolm! Stop it!' cried Ludo, putting her hands over the HO's ears.

The HO pushed her hands away.

'It doesn't matter who tells you to do it,' Goldblatt continued. 'If Dr Morris tells you to do it then ask Dr Morris why. He'll explain. If he can't explain it to you, then he can't explain it to himself and he shouldn't be doing it. If he can explain it to you and he can't be bothered, then he can write the drug up himself.'

'If Dr Morris tells you to do something, you *do* it!' said Ludo vehemently. 'You don't need to ask anything.'

'Ask,' said Goldblatt. 'Dr Morris will be glad you did.'

'Try asking the Prof,' sneered Ludo. 'See if she's glad.'

The HO was still watching him with an anxious frown. 'It's OK,' said Goldblatt. 'We've excluded everything else. Mr Lister's responded to the Prednisolone. He's OK to go.' He grinned. 'I was beginning to wonder whether he was going to outlast me.'

'He didn't miss by much,' muttered Ludo.

Goldblatt looked at her. 'What does that mean?'

'Nothing.'

'Then why did you say it?'

Ludo arched an eyebrow. 'No reason,' she said, and she got up and marched out, already slightly late, to one of her fictional Dermatology clinics.

'Malcolm,' said the HO.

Goldblatt looked around.

'Malcolm, is it really OK? Should I have put him on Prednisolone?'

'Yes. He doesn't have an infection. He has a vasculitis.'

'How can we be sure?' asked the HO.

Goldblatt sighed. 'We can't. We can only think it's *very, very, very, very, very* likely and take all the precautions we can in case we're wrong.'

'Then shouldn't we keep him in a bit longer just to see?'

'No. We'll see him again in two weeks.'

'But what happens if his infection gets worse and kills him before that?'

'Then he dies,' said Goldblatt. 'What kind of a question is that?'

'I mean, what happens if his infection gets worse?'

'Which infection? The one he doesn't have?'

The HO nodded.

'We'll see him in two weeks. We've told him to check his temperature. You're going to make sure he knows how. We've told him to ring us if he thinks the fevers are coming back or if he's unwell.'

'What if he doesn't check his temperature? What if he doesn't ring?'

'And the infection that he doesn't have is bad enough to kill him before he comes back to clinic?'

'Yes.'

Goldblatt shrugged. People had to take responsibility for themselves at some point.

The HO still looked troubled.

'You'd like certainty,' said Goldblatt. 'Sometimes you don't have it. In medicine, all you get is probabilities, and that's what you have to work with. If you can't cope with that, you'd better be a surgeon.'

The HO stared at Goldblatt for a moment longer. She wrinkled her nose and pushed her glasses up, considering what he had said. Then without another word she climbed on the desk and started taking down the frieze of Mr Lister's temperature.

'You should be happy when a patient goes home, especially when they've been in this long,' said Goldblatt, looking up at the HO.

'I am happy,' the HO muttered darkly, ripping down a part of the frieze.

Goldblatt watched her, as he had been watching her ever since her reaction to Mr Sprczrensky's stroke.

He thought of asking her if she was all right, but stopped himself. He had told her to tell him if it was too much. He believed that she knew he really wanted to know. You couldn't keep saying it. You could end up smothering someone.

'There'll be other PUOs,' Goldblatt said. 'Of course, it's hard. He was your first.'

The HO snorted and kept going until she had taken all the pages off the wall.

It was hard. Not very hard, just a tiny bit hard. There was a certain sense of emptiness on the round the next morning, Goldblatt had to admit, when they arrived at Mr Lister's old bed, subconsciously steeling themselves for a blast of irascibility and venom, and found an ordinary Fuertler's patient in front of them, a kind, amiable and softly spoken old gentleman who was waiting for the work-up and the juice of the Sorain tree, as if Mr Lister had never even existed.

But emptiness never lasts long in medicine. Late that afternoon Goldblatt got a call from one of the doctors in Casualty. One of the Prof's Fuertler's patients had been brought in as an emergency.

A Fuertler's patient? Brought in as an emergency? As he took the lift down to Casualty, Goldblatt wondered if someone was playing a prank.

30

He pushed open the swinging plastic doors of the Casualty department. Immediately, Goldblatt glimpsed an incredibly ill-looking woman lying in the fourth cubicle from the entrance. He looked away. But by then it was too late, because of the infallible Law of the Glimpse, which states that any patient you glimpse out of the corner of your eye and wish you hadn't glimpsed is inevitably... your patient.

Nonetheless, being by nature doomed to rebel against the immutable laws that governed his existence, Goldblatt didn't go straight over to her. He stopped a passing nurse and told her who he was and asked where he could find the patient he had been called about. The nurse glanced at a whiteboard covered in the secret symbols of nursing code, looked back at him, and said: 'Over there. Her name's Sandra Hill.' And she pointed, just in case there was any remaining doubt, straight at cubicle four.

There's a look people have when they're really, really ill – not merely off colour, or in pain, but marrow-sappingly, heart-stoppingly, breath-strugglingly, just-let-me-die-in-peacely ill. Even from the other side of the department, Sandra Hill had that look. She was easily the sickest human being in a Casualty department that was otherwise populated by old ladies with broken wrists and people wheezing with acute asthma and big men grimacing with acute gallbladder pain.

She lay with her eyes closed and her lips pursed under an oxygen mask, and her whole frail, emaciated face focused on the effort of sucking in air.

Through some miracle of efficiency that must have been a mistake, her medical notes had already turned up. Goldblatt glanced through them. Sandra Hill was one of the rare cases in which Fuertler's turns into severe fibrosis of the lungs, laying down dense, tough tissue over the delicate membrane that lets molecules of gas waft in and out of the bloodstream, and obliterating tier upon tier of those tiny cavities where the wafting is meant to take place. According to the notes, she had had all the treatments Tom de Witte could throw at her.

Goldblatt closed the notes and went over to her.

Her eyes were still shut as she drew breaths under the oxygen mask. She was a thin black woman of about forty with the blotchy skin of Fuertler's Syndrome. Some of her skin was thickened and puckered, and some was thinned and de-pigmented, like fallen white leaves stuck on her wrists and neck.

Goldblatt glanced at the gauge on the wall to check the concentration of oxygen flowing into the mask. Sixty per cent. Even at that concentration she was breathing in and out continuously, the muscles in her neck straining to contribute to the leverage on her ribcage. In physiology lectures at medical school, Goldblatt had been taught that the total surface area of a pair of average human lungs, if you could unravel and smooth out the microscopically thin and bulb-like membranes within them, is the size of a tennis court. That's the absorptive surface the human organism needs in its chest to trade its carbon dioxide for oxygen at an adequate rate to breathe easily, with some to spare. Sandra Hill didn't have a tennis court of absorptive membrane left inside her chest. She didn't have a badminton court. Or even a squash court. He guessed that maybe she had a table tennis table.

Goldblatt closed the curtain behind him and stood beside her at the head of the trolley.

'Hello,' he said.

She opened her eyes.

'I'm Dr Goldblatt, Professor Small's registrar.'

She nodded.

'Is your breathing always this bad?'

'Worse... recently,' she whispered.

'Over how long has it been getting worse? Days? Weeks?'

'Days.' She paused, sucking in a couple of breaths, then shrugged slightly. 'Weeks.'

'You didn't think it might have been a good idea to come in earlier?'

She gave another slight shrug, almost lost in the effort of her breathing. 'Don't like... hospitals,' she whispered, and then she laughed, more with her eyes than her mouth.

Goldblatt liked her at once. It took spirit to laugh in her situation. He didn't know if he would have been able to do it.

He proceeded to take a history from her. She gave short answers. He kept to the bare minimum and tried to ask Yes/No questions. Not exactly the open-ended interviews the textbooks recommend, but life isn't always like a textbook. He examined her. She managed to sit up for a minute or two for him to listen to her chest.

When he had finished, Goldblatt put his stethoscope back around his neck. 'Don't worry, Sandra,' he said, 'we'll sort you out.'

From behind her mask, Sandra looked at him with an expression he found difficult to decipher, perhaps accusing him of lying, or thanking him for lying, or ignoring the fact that he was lying in the face of what she knew was finally happening to her after all these years with Fuertler's fibrosis of the lungs. Goldblatt didn't know which. But he could see that she knew the truth. She smiled, as if to show that she knew it, and was far beyond caring.

She smiled again later, when Goldblatt punctured her lung.

Sandra was dehydrated, and her chest X-ray showed pneumonia on top of her underlying lung devastation. She needed intravenous fluids and antibiotics. By five o'clock she had arrived on the ward, and the HO came along to put in a drip, bringing with her a third-year medical student who had taken it into his head to attach himself to her for the afternoon. The HO poked four needles into various places in Sandra's Fuertlerized skin, more in hope than in any real expectation of hitting a vein, and gave up. She called Goldblatt. Goldblatt examined Sandra's arms, swapping the tourniquet from right to left and back again, and couldn't see, feel or even imagine there was a vein he could hit.

'They always have... trouble,' Sandra said.

Goldblatt looked at her feet and tightened the tourniquet around her shin like a garter. There was a vein there, on the back of her foot, no thicker than a matchstick, and, once you stuck a cannula into it, it was likely to blow in a matter of hours.

Goldblatt unsnapped the tourniquet. 'Let's put in a central line,' he said to the HO. He looked at Sandra. 'Have you had a central line in before?'

Sandra nodded ruefully.

'Neck or chest?'

'Both,' she whispered.

Goldblatt smiled. 'So you know what it'll be like?'

Sandra nodded.

A central line is a cannula that goes directly into one of the large veins of the chest or neck, and the technique for putting one in is straightforward, so straightforward that the HO clamoured to do it, and Goldblatt almost let her until she admitted, while they were loading the equipment on a trolley, that she had never done one and had seen it only twice, both times from the back of a pack of students in Emergency. Goldblatt told her to get a little closer this time and watch carefully. The medical student, who looked as if he wasn't used to being around sick people, stared at Goldblatt with wide eyes. 'You should come and watch as well,' Goldblatt said to him before they went back to wheel Sandra's bed into the treatment room.

There wasn't a nurse free to help, apart from the one who strolled in about halfway through the procedure because she wanted to watch, so at the start it was Goldblatt and the HO and the medical student, who was apparently called Tim. Goldblatt opened a sterilized pack containing the equipment he needed and laid it out on a trolley, then washed his hands and put on a pair of gloves, instructing the HO and Tim to take Sandra's pillows away and tilt the bed head-down in the position required for the procedure. Then the HO arranged Sandra's nightie, baring the right side of her neck and upper chest.

Goldblatt swabbed Sandra's skin with cotton wool soaked in iodine. The light above the bed was hot and yellow, and the iodine ran down the side of her neck, staining the sheet, and collected in a murky brown pool in the V of her throat. Goldblatt wiped it away.

The HO snapped open two ampoules of local anaesthetic, and Goldblatt drew the local up and then injected it under Sandra's collarbone, ending with a fat bleb beneath the skin. Then right through the middle of the bleb he slid in a large-bore needle connected to an empty syringe, letting the needle ride under the lower surface of the collarbone, and drawing back on the plunger as he went so he'd know when he'd hit the subclavian vein. He talked to Sandra as he did it.

Sandra winced as he changed the angle of the needle and searched for the vein. He elevated the butt of the needle slightly to increase the angle of penetration, explaining the anatomical landmarks to Tim and the HO. The HO was standing on the other side of the bed, with her hand on Sandra's wrist.

Sandra closed her eyes.

Suddenly a rush of dark blood flooded into the syringe.

'The needle's in, Sandra. That's the worst bit.'

He detached the blood-filled syringe, using his gloved thumb to stopper the hub of the needle that was still embedded in Sandra's chest, and handed it to the HO, who turned away to squirt the blood into a series of tubes for lab tests. With his free hand Goldblatt picked up a flexible metal guide wire that was about two feet long, taking care not to desterilize it as it waved drunkenly in his hand. He removed his thumb from the hub of the needle, inserted the end of the guide wire through the blood that began to drip as soon as he unstoppered it, and began to feed the wire down the hollow needle. Once it was two thirds of the way in he would pull out the needle, leaving the guide wire in place. Then he would slide the plastic cannula over the guide wire into the vein. Finally he would extract the wire out of the end of the cannula, leaving only the soft plastic tube in position, with its tip sited inside the superior vena cava. That was the objective of the whole procedure.

The guide wire stopped about halfway in.

Goldblatt pushed cautiously. There was resistance. That usually meant the guide wire had started going up towards the neck. Not uncommon. When the guide wire reaches the point where the jugular vein meets the subclavian, it can either go up towards the neck, or down to the chest, which is the desired direction.

Sandra writhed a little, twisting her neck.

'Is it hurting you, Sandra?' asked Goldblatt, pulling back on the guide wire. He rotated it between the blood-stained rubber of the glove ensheathing his fingers to see if that would make it go down towards her chest when he pushed it further in again.

Sandra didn't say anything. She took deep breaths on the oxygen that was streaming over her face.

'Tell us if it hurts,' said the HO.

Goldblatt gently pushed the wire further in. It went another couple of centimetres and got stuck once more. Goldblatt was starting to feel hot under the light. He was starting to sweat. He pulled back on the wire and twirled it again, then pushed it in, feeling for the resistance to give way.

Sandra moaned. She let go of her oxygen mask and her fingers searched for the HO's hand.

Goldblatt drew back a little on the wire and held it still. He looked over at Sandra's face.

'What is it, Sandra?'

Sandra shook her head from side to side.

'Sandra, keep your head still.'

'Sick,' she murmured, shaking her head.

Goldblatt watched her.

Sandra was lying with her head tilted down for the procedure. Not a good position if you're going to vomit. Things coming up from people's stomachs have a tendency of running down into their lungs when they're head-down on their backs.

Sandra gasped. Runny yellow fluid came out of her mouth and nostrils and bubbled in the stream of oxygen inside her mask.

'Get her up!' cried Goldblatt, and with one gloved hand pressing down over the needle and wire, he threw his other arm behind Sandra's back and in a single movement dragged her up before the HO had even got a hand behind her from the other side. Sandra was coughing and gasping and the vomit poured out of her mouth and coated the inside of her mask. Goldblatt pulled her mask off and the thin acid fluid ran down her chin and on to her nightie, staining it yellow-green.

Goldblatt noticed something on the bed beside Sandra. The needle had come out. He looked under his hand and found that only the last couple of centimetres of the wire remained in Sandra's skin. The rest of it now was non-sterile and couldn't be reinserted. He had no choice but to pull it out, then press hard with his thumb on the puncture site under Sandra's collarbone. He grabbed a piece of gauze off the trolley and then pressed with that. The centre of the gauze turned red.

Sandra had stopped vomiting. She was sucking in air as fast and as deep as she could. Goldblatt asked the nurse to get another mask, and when she brought it they connected it to the oxygen. In the meantime he and the HO had raised the head of the bed and packed the pillows up behind Sandra's back. They cleaned the blood and vomit off her chest, and Goldblatt stuck down a fresh piece of gauze over the puncture wound under her collarbone. After a few minutes Sandra was breathing a little more easily. The HO looked at Goldblatt.

'Go and organize a chest film,' he said.

The HO left. Goldblatt picked up his stethoscope and listened. Wherever he placed the stethoscope, he heard the dry, papery crackles of lung fibrosis, which he had heard when he examined her earlier. He didn't hear anything new, no sloshing of fluid as Sandra breathed in and out. But that was a coarse sign, and its absence didn't mean that she hadn't aspirated any of her vomit in the few seconds that she had been head-down on the bed.

'It's OK,' said Goldblatt.

Sandra nodded.

Goldblatt turned around. The medical student was still there. Goldblatt had forgotten about him. He hadn't said a word.

'Ever seen a case of pulmonary fibrosis?' Goldblatt asked.

Tim shook his head silently.

Goldblatt looked questioningly at Sandra. She nodded.

'Come on,' said Goldblatt. He held the diaphragm of his stethoscope against Sandra's skin and offered the earpieces to Tim. 'Listen. You'll hear crackles. Very dry, like paper rustling.' He waited as Tim listened through his stethoscope. 'Hear it? Those dry crackles? A bit like tissue paper? That's pulmonary fibrosis. Remember it. You'll never hear a better example.'

They wheeled Sandra out of the treatment room and back on to the ward. Goldblatt listened to her lungs again. He made sure she was comfortable.

Then he went out to the nurses' station to wait for the radiologist. Tim sat down as well.

There was a copy of some kind of women's magazine on the desk of the nurses' station, and Goldblatt picked it up and leafed through it as he waited. Ads for women's underwear. Who let nurses bring this kind of pornography into hospitals? And what was wrong with women, anyway? Why were their ads for underwear so sexy? Surely they didn't enjoy looking at this stuff. This was stuff for men. Men enjoyed looking at this stuff. Goldblatt could vouch for that.

He could sense Tim glancing surreptitiously at him. He looked around. 'What?'

'Dr Goldblatt,' said Tim, in the hushed tone that third-year medical students use when addressing a personage as exalted as a registrar, 'was that... all right?'

'Was what all right?'

'That.'

'That?' asked Goldblatt.

Tim nodded.

'What do you think?'

Tim glanced away nervously. Then he looked back at Goldblatt, trying to guess what he was thinking. 'Yes?' he said.

'You really think that was all right?' asked Goldblatt. 'She was vomiting in her mask, for Christ's sake.'

'So it wasn't all right?' asked Tim.

'It depends,' said Goldblatt. 'It was all right if I was trying to make her vomit. It was all right if I wanted to add an aspiration pneumonia to the bacterial pneumonia she already has.'

The whirring noise of the portable X-ray machine was coming up the corridor. A moment later it appeared around the corner, pushed by the radiographer, a red-haired woman with an ample figure in a white uniform. Goldblatt pointed towards Sandra's bed.

'Dr Goldblatt?'

Goldblatt looked around. Tim was still there.

'You weren't trying to make her vomit, were you?'

'No,' said Goldblatt. 'I wasn't trying to make her vomit.'

'Because you could have been,' said Tim, trying to show that he wasn't just another dumb medical student. 'If she had come in with an overdose or something.'

'True,' said Goldblatt. 'But it wouldn't be a very good way of making her vomit. There are better ways. Try Ipecac. That's good. Or a stomach washout. That's good, but messy. Just remember one thing. If you want to make someone vomit, don't lie them head-down.'

'All right,' said Tim seriously. 'I won't lie them head-down.'

'And another thing. You didn't really think that was all right, did you?'

Tim looked at him guiltily.

'You only said that because I'm a registrar.'

The guilty look got guiltier.

'Here's a rule. Never ever let anyone's ranking in the hierarchy...' Goldblatt stopped. He was sick of making up rules. To judge by the way his career was going, they were all wrong. This one more than any of the others.

'Never let anyone's ranking in the hierarchy what, Dr Goldblatt?'

'Nothing. Figure it out. Think of it as a test: complete the sentence. Give me the answer next time you see me.'

Tim nodded, a look of determination in his eye. He pulled a notepad out of the pocket of his white coat and wrote down the words.

The radiographer left the ward with her machine and they waited for her to come back with the X-ray.

'Interesting,' she said when she returned, handing the film to Goldblatt.

'Interesting?' said Goldblatt, his heart sinking. 'Is that "interesting" as in "I'm really bored tonight and even a normal chest X-ray is interesting?" Or is it "interesting" as in "I hope you live in interesting times"?'

'"Interesting" as in "It's interesting that this patient has a pneumo-thorax."'

'A pneumothorax?' repeated Goldblatt mechanically.

'I've got two films to take in ITU,' she said by way of reply. 'Give me a call when you want me to come back.'

Goldblatt watched her go. Patients with poor pulmonary function don't thank you for giving them a pneumothorax. Some of them die just to show what they think of you.

He flicked the switch on the viewing box behind him and its white light blinked into life. He put the film up and got the one that had been taken earlier in Emergency and put it up beside the new one for comparison. He stared at them grimly. They both had the wispy, reticular pattern of lung fibrosis. There was nothing new to be seen in the lower lobe of the right lung, which is where aspirated vomit usually ends up. But something else was different. A perfectly clear rim had appeared around the edge of Sandra's right lung on the later film. It was no wider than a centimetre on the film, except where it expanded to a small cap on the top. Not a single lung marking crossed this space. It was a pneumothorax, a pocket of air trapped between the two pleural membranes that separate the lung from the chest wall, and there was only one place that air could have come from. A hole that Goldblatt had put in Sandra's lung. He must have nicked the top of it as he was searching for her vein with the needle.

'What's this?' asked the HO, who had just come back.

'A pneumothorax,' said Tim. As if he knew.

The HO reached up and ran a finger down the clear crescent at the edge of the lung. 'Is this it?'

Goldblatt nodded.

'Wow! I've never seen one of those before.'

The HO had never seen anything before. Goldblatt didn't see why she had to make such a big thing out of one little pneumothorax.

'Neither have I,' said Tim.

'What?' said a nurse, who had stopped behind them to see what was going on.

'Pneumothorax,' said the HO, pointing to the film. 'See the edge of the lung?'

'Wow!' said the nurse.

Ludo walked past. Ludo? After five o'clock? The evening was going from difficult to surreal.

'Malcolm just gave Sandra Hill a pneumothorax,' said the HO.

'Oh, Malcolm,' said Ludo reprovingly, and clicked her tongue. 'Who's Sandra Hill, one of the Prof's specials?'

'No, she isn't one of the Prof's *specials*,' Goldblatt retorted through clenched teeth. 'And what difference would it make if she was?'

Ludo looked at Goldblatt haughtily. 'Don't take it out on me, Malcolm. I'm not the one who gave her a pneumothorax.'

'She's a Fuertler's patient who's come in with end-stage pulmonary fibrosis,' Goldblatt said gruffly. 'All right? I just gave her a pneumothorax trying to put in a central line.'

'Where's the cannula?' asked Ludo, looking for the thin curve of the plastic tube, which is always made out of radio-opaque material so as to be visible on X-ray.

'I didn't get it in,' said Goldblatt.

'You didn't get it in and you *still* gave her a pneumothorax?'

Goldblatt nodded. 'Thanks.'

'What are you going to do?'

Goldblatt gazed at the film and frowned. 'I'm not sure.'

'We could hand it over to the on-call team,' suggested the HO, glancing at her watch.

Goldblatt stared at the HO. That wasn't funny, even as a joke. If the HO was going to start drawing lines, she had better learn where she was allowed to draw them.

'We stay till it's sorted,' he growled. 'It's our responsibility. Mine, anyway. I gave her the pneumothorax so I stay to deal with it. You can go.'

The HO stayed.

Goldblatt looked back at the X-ray. 'Ludo,' he said, half-heartedly launching a Teaching Attack, 'give me the causes of pneumothorax.'

There was no answer. He turned around. Ludo was gone. For a moment he wondered whether she had ever been there, or if it had been some horrible, mocking apparition emanating from the culpability in his own mind.

The HO and Tim were still watching him.

He went back to Sandra Hill's bed. Her breathing didn't look any more laboured than when he had first seen her. Maybe it couldn't get more laboured. Goldblatt asked her if he could listen to her chest again, and then stuck the ends of his stethoscope in his ears.

Pneumothoraces are things you hear by not hearing them, by the abnormally low volume of the breath sounds. The layer of air between the chest wall and the lung muffles the noise. He hadn't picked it up before.

It must have been small, as it appeared on the film. Even knowing it was there, he still couldn't definitely discern it when he listened.

Sandra looked at him knowingly, waiting to hear whatever it was that he was obviously going to tell her.

'Sandra, there's a problem.'

Sandra shook her head expectantly, looking at him.

'You've got a pneumothorax.'

Sandra frowned.

'I punctured your lung.'

Her eyebrows rose.

'I'm sorry, Sandra. It does happen sometimes when you put in a central line. It's one of the risks. Looks like it happened just now.'

She nodded.

'There's some air around your lung now. It's not a disaster, but it won't help your breathing. How do you feel? Is your breathing any worse?'

'The same,' said Sandra. 'Don't tell me... can it... get worse?'

'We'll have to get the air out.'

She shrugged with resignation.

'I'm sorry, Sandra. You're really getting your money's worth tonight.'

Sandra smiled.

'Get some arterial blood gases,' Goldblatt said to the HO. He turned back to Sandra. 'I'll be back soon.'

Goldblatt went out and stood in front of the X-ray again. He shook his head. He had never managed to give anyone a pneumothorax while putting in a central line, even though it was a recognized risk of the procedure. And of course he just had to go and do it now to someone with zero lung reserve. Less than zero.

He estimated that the area of empty space on the film occupied well under twenty per cent of the right lung field. The teaching was that you could treat a pneumothorax of that size by simply inserting a needle and aspirating the air, leaving any remaining gas to be absorbed. But not in a person with significant underlying lung disease. A person with underlying lung disease needs the works, a big chest tube introduced between the ribs and connected to a water seal for two or three days to empty out every last bit of air and keep it out. And if there was one thing that Sandra Hill had, it was underlying lung disease, as the X-ray in front of him showed.

Goldblatt sat down at the nurses' station. The HO came out from behind the screens, waved a tube of blood packed in ice at him, and rushed away.

He didn't want to put a chest tube in. It's a horrible, traumatic thing to do to a person, involving an introducer as long as a skewer and as thick as your little finger that you force through the layers of muscle between the ribs. He had a bad feeling about putting one into Sandra Hill. It felt like the trigger for a sequence that could only end in tears. As mighty oaks from small acorns grow, so medical catastrophes from small complications begin. The patient who comes in for the elective hernia operation gets a local wound infection, which sets off his subclinical diabetes, which dehydrates him, which throws his kidneys into acute renal failure, which puts him into the intensive care unit, which is where he gets the antibiotic-resistant pneumonia, which is the last straw for his atherosclerotic heart, which has the cardiac arrest that kills him. Something would happen when he put the tube into Sandra's chest. He'd hit an intercostal artery. Or the tube would block. Or it would get infected. Something. It was just a bad, bad feeling that he had about this chest tube. Irrational, he knew that. He probably just didn't want to put Sandra through the muscle-splitting pain of the procedure. He wanted to slip a nice thin needle over a rib, suck out the air, pull the needle out, and leave her alone.

On the other hand, if she really needed the chest tube, it would be settling for the nice quick needle that would trigger the sequence of catastrophe.

'Dr Goldblatt?'

Goldblatt looked up. Tim was sitting next to him again.

'Giving her a pneumothorax... that wasn't all right, was it?'

Fast learner! 'No,' said Goldblatt. 'It wasn't.'

'Does that happen very often when you put in a central line?'

'Pneumothorax? That's my first.'

Tim looked at him doubtfully.

'You don't believe me.'

'No, Dr Goldblatt. I do!'

'Don't. Never believe people who say things like that.'

Tim looked puzzled for a minute. 'It is your first, isn't it?'

379

'Yes,' said Goldblatt.

Tim smiled. For some reason, that seemed to make him very happy. He opened the magazine and began to look at the lingerie ads that Goldblatt had been looking at earlier.

Suddenly Goldblatt made a decision. Arbitrary, spontaneous, definitive. The best sort. When the HO came back with the arterial blood gas results, if Sandra's arterial oxygen came in over nine, he'd aspirate the pneumothorax with a needle. If it came in under nine, he'd go for the tube.

And if it was nine exactly?

Fuck it, he thought, I'll go for the needle.

The HO came back.

'Well?' said Goldblatt.

She handed him the printout. Nine point three.

Goldblatt got up. 'Have you ever seen anyone aspirate a pneumothorax?'

The HO saw him do it. So did Tim. Goldblatt put a sweet little 16-guage needle in over the top of Sandra's third rib, sucked out about a hundred millilitres of air, and pulled the needle out. It took less than a minute, Sandra hardly felt it, and then it was over. Then he sent the HO off to organize another X-ray. Half an hour later the X-ray came back. The pneumothorax looked a lot smaller. When he compared it with the previous film, he didn't even have to talk himself into believing that it was.

In the meantime he had sited a drip in the one remaining vein in Sandra's foot, hoping that it would last overnight. The HO wrote up fluids and antibiotics, while he wrote an extended account of his numerous puncturings of Sandra Hill in the notes. The HO sat beside him and watched with a gratified look while he finished. It was after seven, but this was one night she didn't mind staying back. One of the few things that makes life as an HO worth living: watching your registrar sweat.

The HO left. The vein in Sandra's foot still worried Goldblatt. She'd be lucky if it lasted until morning. Tomorrow, he'd get one of the anaesthetics SRs to put a central line in. But it still bugged him. He could just imagine what would happen if that vein packed up overnight. First the on-call HO, then the SHO, then the reg would come along one after the other to try to resite it. She could easily have ten or fifteen needles shoved into her arms and feet, probing for veins that weren't there. He wasn't going to let that happen. He called the on-call anaesthetics reg and told him about Sandra and asked him to put in a central line if the vein packed up. Then he went and found Debbie and asked her to hand over to the nurses on the night shift that they were to call the anaesthetics reg directly if that happened. Then he went back to the doctors' office to write the instruction explicitly in the notes.

And when he looked up, Ludo was in the doorway.

This time, he wasn't going to be fooled.

'You're not real,' he said, and he went back to writing his notes.

The Ludo-vision came into the doctors' office and sat down.

Goldblatt looked at her again. 'I know you're not real.'

'What are you talking about, Malcolm?'

'What are you doing here? You're not on call, are you?'

'Dr Morris offered to take a few of us who are studying for the second part through some patients.'

'How did it go?'

Ludo sighed. She threw back her head with a toss of her hair.

'That good?' said Goldblatt.

'How did you go with that pneumothorax?'

'I aspirated it.'

'How is she?'

'She's got pulmonary fibrosis.'

'Is she sick?'

'End-stage.' Goldblatt shook his head. 'End-stage, end-stage.'

He turned back to the folder and finished the last instructions in his notes. He put the folder in the notes trolley.

He thought about what he had said. End-stage end-stage. Where do you go after that?

He looked back at Ludo. She hadn't moved.

He frowned. Ludo was watching him.

And the words just came out. 'Do you... I don't suppose you want to go for a drink?'

31

THE PUB WASN'T FAR from the hospital. Ludo had suggested it. It had
a seedy, dilapidated air, with stained carpets and small, chipped tables.
Ludo sipped her gin and tonic. She was whining about her flatmate. Or
maybe it was about the washing machine that the flatmate had broken.
Or the smelly man who had come to fix the washing machine. Occasionally Goldblatt made some kind of a noise when it seemed that Ludo was
expecting a response, which wasn't often. She whined about something
else. It wasn't the washing machine, Goldblatt was pretty sure about that.
He wasn't listening. Ludo probably knew it.

He watched her. In his head, he had turned off the sound, like watching
television with the volume off. Her mouth moved. Presumably words were
coming out of it.

What was he doing here, he asked himself suddenly. What was he
doing with Ludo in a pub?

There had been a kind of unspoken truce at home for the last week.
Whatever it was that Lesley had started to say to him on the night of the
Nailwright interview, she had put it away. But it wasn't gone. Sensing that
it wasn't, Goldblatt had been just as careful to keep away from it. There
had been no sex since the silent, immensely concentrated episode that
night, which had been almost scary in its intensity. Everything they said
to each other was safe and inconsequential. And every safe and inconsequential thing they said to each other was a reminder of the very unsafe,
consequential matter that was waiting for them.

Goldblatt got a second round of drinks. Ludo whined some more.

He watched her.

He didn't even like her. She was selfish, cruel, unreliable, dishonest,
egotistical, lazy, unhelpful, and had entertained a war criminal. Worst of

all, she was depressing. She was apparently convinced that the nosedive into which her career was heading, with no one but herself to blame at the controls, was a tragedy of truly global proportions that should concern somebody other than herself. And the only thing she seemed able or willing to do about it was to whine.

But still there was something sexy about her. He would, he knew. All things being equal, he'd sleep with her. He knew what he had been like before he met Lesley. Nurses or doctors, he didn't even have to like them. The job did it. Why? It was probably the same for them. Expunging some mutual, nameless thing that had to be driven out, that couldn't be expunged any other way than in an aching carnal frenzy, and which couldn't be expunged except with someone who had the same nameless thing bottled up inside them.

He'd sleep with her, and then he'd want to get away as quickly as he could, and then a couple of days later he'd be back to sleep with her again.

And she wanted him to. Maybe not get away as quickly as he could, but the rest of it. He knew it as much as he had ever known what a woman wanted from him.

She flirted with him. All the time. True, Ludo flirted with most males within reach, including ward clerks, porters, and the men who came to change broken light bulbs in the patients' rooms. He had even seen her send a suggestive remark in the direction of the spotty youth whose job was to find the misplaced medical records that were hidden in Emma's office, which had gone right over his spotty head. But she didn't flirt with them the way she flirted with him. She didn't look at them as she looked at him, a kind of tentative, hesitant, searching look, ready to transform in an instant into a flash of defensive, Balkan haughtiness.

More importantly, sometimes she didn't flirt with him. Sometimes you only know when something's there when something else goes missing.

What kind of a woman was she? The kind who went out looking for wild sex with a new assortment of multiple partners every night? Or the kind who stayed at home trembling with timidity? Goldblatt watched her as she drank her second gin and tonic, and wondered. For some reason, it seemed to him that she had to be one or the other. But which?

Ludo, he thought. Ludo, Ludo, Ludo. What was it all about? The listlessness of her entire life, her inability to sit in front of a textbook for more than eight minutes at a stretch, the general grey hopelessness with which she infected anyone who was prepared to have a coffee with her... And those coffees, those endless coffees she wheedled out of people – mostly him – what were they but an oral gratification of an altogether different need?

Not that sex was everything. No, not even Goldblatt believed that. But it was something.

Suddenly Goldblatt had a very alarming thought. She couldn't be a virgin, could she?

He gazed at her closely. So closely that she stopped in mid-whine, and said: 'What?'

'Nothing,' said Goldblatt.

She looked at him suspiciously for a moment before continuing.

No, she couldn't be. Could she?

How old would she be? Twenty-seven? Twenty-eight? She could be. Technically, that is. It was possible. A virgin at twenty-eight? Such things happened.

Didn't they?

'What?'

'Nothing,' said Goldblatt. He looked at his watch.

'Do you have to go?'

Suddenly he said: 'Do you want another drink?'

'Another drink?' said Ludo insinuatingly, as if she were in some kind of B-grade movie. 'Are you trying to get me drunk? What would your girlfriend say, Malcolm?'

Goldblatt frowned. He'd never told Ludo he had a girlfriend. Had he?

He tried to remember. Which was difficult, because at the same time he was trying to work out just exactly what he was doing asking Ludo if she wanted another drink. To invite Ludo to have one drink was a misfortune, to invite her for a second was careless. Goldblatt didn't think that even Oscar Wilde would have been able to say what prolonging the agony to a third drink was. He *had* just done that, hadn't he?

'All right,' said Ludo.

Apparently he had.

'But I don't have any money. You'll have to keep buying.'

Goldblatt shrugged. There was a surprise!

'No, Malcolm, I *really* don't have any money.'

'It's all right,' Goldblatt said impatiently.

'Well, I'll have another G&T,' said Ludo cheerfully. 'And get us some crisps, Malcolm.' She grinned. 'Since you're buying.'

Goldblatt went to the bar. He came back with the drinks and three bags of crisps in assorted flavours. Ludo grabbed one and tore it open.

'Look out there,' she said.

'Where?'

'Across the road. See that flat on the corner? The first floor. The one with the light on.'

Across the road were redbrick mansion blocks with shops at street level. Goldblatt found the flat Ludo was talking about. It was above a bank. A light was on behind a gauze curtain.

'Do you know who lives in that flat?' said Ludo. 'Guess.'

'Who?'

'Emma.'

Goldblatt looked back at her. She was grinning triumphantly.

'How do you know?'

'She showed me once.'

'You've been there?'

'No. I haven't been there. She showed me where it was one time when I was on my way catch the Tube. We might see her if we're lucky.'

Goldblatt didn't think it would be that lucky. 'Is that why you wanted another drink? So you could sit there watching Emma's window just in case you caught a glimpse of her?'

Ludo laughed derisively. 'Oh, Malcolm. I wanted another drink so I could be here with you.'

Goldblatt shook his head, smiling despite himself.

'Do you know what Emma told me?' said Ludo in a strangely lewd tone. She gazed at Goldblatt, crunching on a prawn cocktail crisp.

'What?' said Goldblatt.

'She said the Prof's going to get rid of you.' Ludo looked at him with greedy, lascivious expectation. Goldblatt could all but see the blood dripping off her fangs.

'Is that what you were talking about yesterday?' Goldblatt had assumed Ludo had been lashing out at him randomly in the doctors' office after Mr Lister went home. 'Do you spend *all* your time talking to Emma?'

'I hardly ever speak to her.'

'Except when she invites you to her flat.'

'I'd never go to her flat, Malcolm.'

'I bet you'd go with her to one of those concerts the Prof keeps giving her tickets for.'

'I would not!' Ludo laughed. 'I'm not that sad!'

Goldblatt took a sip of his drink. 'So did Emma tell you this in confidence or did she ask you to tell me?'

'What?'

'That the Prof's going to get rid of me.'

'Hmm,' said Ludo. 'Emma said she'd been working at the Prof to get her to do it for weeks and finally she came out and told her she should do it and it was going to be the best day of her life when it happened. The things she said to the Prof about you, Malcolm! Honestly, even I found them somewhat exaggerated. What do you think? Did she tell me in confidence?'

Goldblatt raised an eyebrow.

'Oh, what a naughty girl I am,' said Ludo, and put a finger to her pouting lips. 'Spank me!'

'I just might.'

'Really? Do you like that kind of thing, Malcolm?'

Goldblatt laughed. You couldn't script it. Someone would shoot you.

'Oh, Malcolm, the Prof's not going to do anything to you. That's just Emma.' Ludo laughed maliciously. 'Now she's terrified of what the Prof's going to do to her because of the way she spoke to her. Emma's an idiot. She's dreaming. The Prof's not going to get rid of you.'

'Who knows? It might be better if she did.'

'What do you mean by that?'

'Nothing,' said Goldblatt. 'Forget it.'

Ludo stared at him. 'Malcolm, you're not thinking of leaving?'

'Why? Would it make a difference?'

Ludo didn't reply. Suddenly she shook her hair out as if there were flies in it, and retreated into her chair, arms folded across her chest.

'Why?' he said.

Ludo glared at him. 'Because who'll buy me coffee?' she retorted angrily, and she gave him a long, resentful glance, and then looked away.

She was silent.

Strange, thought Goldblatt.

He opened a pack of salt and vinegar crisps and took a handful.

'Why do you think Emma hates me?' he said eventually, trying to bring Ludo back to life.

Ludo shrugged.

'Well?'

'You're very intimidating, Malcolm.'

'Really? Do you think that's it?'

'You don't realize it. You don't know how intimidating you can be.'

He crunched on a crisp. 'Are you intimidated by me?'

Ludo blushed a little. She shook out her hair and fixed him with one of her droopy-eyed stares. 'Do you think I should tell you?'

'Yes.'

'Why?'

'Because otherwise I'll have to guess. And you said yourself I don't know how intimidating I can be. So I can't guess, can I?'

Ludo didn't reply. She reached for more crisps. Goldblatt noticed her hand stop. She was looking down.

He looked down as well. Her hand was resting on the table beside the prawn cocktail crisps. His own hand was just a couple of inches away, beside the salt and vinegar.

And he knew. All he had to do was slide his hand across those two inches of wooden table.

And touch her.

In an hour's time, maybe less, they'd be in bed.

He could feel a surge of blood. His pulse beating faster.

He looked up at her. Saw her face, her eyes still staring at their hands.

She glanced up. Her mouth parted a little.

Goldblatt moved his hand closer. Her fingers twitched, as if by an involuntary, startled reflex. He saw her gazing down again, her breathing shallow. His hand stretched out.

He felt her, in his fingertips.

They looked at each other, their hands touching. Slowly, she rubbed hers along the side of his palm.

'Malcolm...' It came out quietly, long, like the way she might say it when she was under him.

In an hour. Less.

He drew his hand away. 'Let's get out of here.'

They walked towards the Underground station.

The chill of the night air hit him. Darkness, Reality. He glanced to the side, saw Ludo walking next to him. What was he doing? Lesley was at home. He was on a street with Ludo.

They stopped at the entrance to the station. A lift came up behind the ticket barrier and a crowd of people surged out, and for a minute or so was all around them. Then they were alone again.

His mind seemed to freeze. What was he about to do?

Ludo waited, her eyes questioning him.

He could feel the seconds passing.

'Well...' she said eventually, 'I suppose... thanks for the drink.'

Goldblatt nodded.

Suddenly she kissed him. Brushed his lips. She stood back and stared at him. There!

Goldblatt gazed at her. She smiled slightly. Uncertainly.

No. He stepped back. 'See you tomorrow.'

'Is it because we work together?' she said, reaching for him. 'Because I don't care, Malcolm.'

He felt her hand on his arm as he took another step back. He shook his head. He turned to go to his car.

'Malcolm.'

He looked back at her. Ludo was standing with her arms folded tightly against the cold.

'Um...' She tried to sound nonchalant. 'I'll pay for the drinks next week, if you like.'

She waited a moment longer, then turned and walked into the station.

32

'DR GOLDBLATT,' THE PROF said, taking a deep breath, 'let's start again.'

Andrea Small gathered her thoughts. She hadn't expected this to be an easy conversation, but she thought she was prepared for it. Yet it was turning out to be worse than she had imagined. Far worse. In fact, it was beginning to feel like a cruel joke that she had played on herself. The boy seemed unable to understand what she was talking about. Or unwilling, more likely. He refused to take a hint. Almost as if he were going to force her – *force* her – to come out and say exactly what she meant.

On the other side of the desk, Goldblatt smiled at her patiently, trying to work out what on earth she had been endeavouring to say for the previous five minutes. They were in her office. The Prof had bleeped him and asked him to come down, but to be honest, after she started talking, his mind had wandered, and not for the first time that morning. What had happened with Ludo last night? And what had almost happened? He told Lesley he had been kept late at the hospital. It was the first lie of that sort – or half-lie, because he *had* been kept late there, but not that late – that he had ever told her. What was the next lie going to be? Where was it leading?

'This is very difficult,' said the Prof, smiling with pain.

Goldblatt nodded. As a doctor, he knew how important a simple expression of empathy can be in alleviating another person's discomfort, even if you have no idea what is causing it.

The Prof closed her eyes for a moment.

'I just don't know what to do,' she said at last, shaking her head a number of times as if she were trying to dislodge something from her ear. 'On the one hand, it would be easier in many ways if the situation was resolved. But on the other hand, that means I'll have to find someone else. That can be very troublesome. Very disruptive for everyone.'

The Prof paused, looking at Goldblatt hopefully.

Goldblatt nodded again. It was a terrible dilemma that the Prof had just outlined to him. He could well understand her perplexity. On the other hand, he would have liked to know what on earth she was trying to say.

Like Dr Morris, Goldblatt was nothing but a fusty old traditionalist who associated the notion of one doctor kicking another out only with the most severe breaches of medical ethics or the most abject acts of incompetence. He was guilty of neither, as far as he knew. He had shrugged off Ludo's warning in the pub as a combination of Emma's penchant for malice and Ludo's penchant for exaggeration. That, together with his own preoccupation and the Prof's excruciating circumlocutions, and he really hadn't latched on to what was going on in her head.

The Prof, for her part, having failed to be fully reassured by her conversation with Dr Morris about getting rid of Goldblatt, had spent a lot of time trying to think of someone else whom she might safely ask for the opinion she needed. But she couldn't think of anyone – until it occurred to her to ask the boy himself. She could certainly ask him. And somehow, when she thought about it... well, somehow it had seemed to make sense. It wouldn't really be asking an opinion of him, it would be more in the nature of a warning. But in the guise of asking an opinion. It had made perfect sense. Then. But now, when she actually had the boy in front of her, it made no sense at all. Sense? It had never made any sense. What on earth had she been thinking?

'People say that you're... difficult,' said the Prof.

'Which people?' asked Goldblatt, thinking it might help them both if the Prof could be more specific.

The Prof sighed. 'People.'

'A lot of people?'

'Some people.'

'More than ten?' Goldblatt enquired, giving the Prof a lead. He waited. 'More than eight?'

The Prof frowned, calculating.

'Was it the lady in clinic, is that who you're talking about? The Armenian lady?'

The Prof looked puzzled. 'Which Armenian lady?'

'The one in clinic,' said Goldblatt. A couple of weeks earlier an Armenian lady he was seeing in clinic for knee pain had threatened to put in a complaint when he declined to check her blood pressure. According to her notes, the Armenian lady went to five different clinics for eight different conditions. One of these was high blood pressure, for which she had been on the same dose of the same medication for eleven years, and she was accustomed to having a cuff put on her by every doctor she saw, not even excepting dermatologists. Goldblatt thought it was unhealthy, all this taking of blood pressures, and had thought it important to tell her so. All that could come of it was obsessionalism and anxiety, and everyone knows what that does to your blood pressure.

'I don't know about any Armenian lady in clinic,' said the Prof.

'I'd tell you her name, but I can't.'

'Why not?'

'Unnecessary disclosure,' replied Goldblatt. 'I can't disclose patient details unless there's a valid medical reason.'

'Dr Goldblatt, I'm only asking for her name.'

Goldblatt shook his head.

'Dr Goldblatt, I am the head of this unit!' said the Prof, blinking rapidly.

'I know that.'

'And you won't give me her name?'

'Well, since you are the head of the unit, I suppose I could give you her name.'

'Then give me her name.'

'But do you need to know her name?'

'Of course I don't need to know her name.'

'Then why do you want it?'

'I don't!' shrieked the Prof. She was blinking and shaking her head like a mechanical doll that somebody had overwound. She took a deep breath. She was getting bogged down. How did the boy always manage to discompose her? Where had the Armenian lady come from? Who had mentioned an Armenian lady? The Prof didn't care about any Armenian lady. She just wanted to know whether she should fire him, and unless the Armenian lady could give her the answer, she didn't want to hear any more about her.

'Dr Goldblatt,' she said in barely a whisper, 'let's forget about the Armenian lady, shall we?'

'Fine by me,' said Goldblatt. He was almost sorry he had mentioned her.

The Prof took another deep breath. She looked down at the front cover of the diary on her desk and ran her fingers carefully along the sides of it. She examined the front cover for a long time.

'Malcolm,' she said suddenly.

Goldblatt's head shot up at the Prof's surprise move to his first name. This was a startling tactic but one that he seemed to recall she had used before, in one of her first conversations with him. In any case, she had certainly succeeded in putting him on the back foot for a second.

'Malcolm, let's start again,' said the Prof.

Goldblatt shrugged. They could start again if the Prof wanted, but that would mean wasting all the ground they had already covered. And it would be the second time they were starting again, which would make three starts in total. That was a lot of starts for one meeting. Personally, if it were him, and he needed so many starts, he'd probably want to reconsider whether it had really been a good idea to start at all.

'Do you like medicine?' asked the Prof.

Goldblatt stared at her.

The Prof smiled nervously. She blinked. 'It's just that... I wonder sometimes if you wouldn't be happier doing something else.'

Goldblatt wondered sometimes as well. Theoretically, one could always be happier doing something else. Existentially, the Prof's question was virtually meaningless, and he didn't see why he should bother answering it. Anyway, who was she? His mother?

'I just wonder,' said the Prof again.

'We always wonder about things, Professor Small,' said Goldblatt. 'I see it as part of the human condition. Ontologically, we're wonderers.'

The Prof gazed at Goldblatt in a state of apparent paralysis. She wasn't shaking her head now, not even a bit. Or blinking. Her facial muscles must have stopped working. Myasthenia gravis, thought Goldblatt, always keen to hone his diagnostic skills: the disease of muscle fatigueability. The Prof had blinked so much that now her periorbital muscles were too weak to blink any more. Goldblatt scrutinized the Prof's eyes surreptitiously to see whether she was developing a divergence in their direction of gaze, a common finding in patients with myasthenia gravis that usually occurs towards the end of the day when muscle fatigue is most pronounced.

The Prof kept staring.

No, no hint of divergence, Goldblatt concluded reluctantly. Both her eyes were gazing in exactly the same direction. A little manic in intensity, but straight, definitely. One couldn't ask for a better example of coaxial coordination. But it was only ten in the morning. Goldblatt made a mental note to look for divergence the next time he saw the Prof late in the day.

The Prof stared for so long that Goldblatt began to feel uncomfortable. He had been a lot more comfortable when the Prof wasn't in suspended animation and was attempting to ambush him by using his first name.

'It's an ontological proposition,' he said, to see whether that would reanimate her. 'But you can dispute it if you like.'

The Prof blinked.

Goldblatt drew a discreet sigh of relief.

'No, I don't want to dispute it,' she said.

Suit yourself, thought Goldblatt.

'You are difficult,' she said, as if she had finally made up her mind.

'Am I?' said Goldblatt.

The Prof nodded.

'I don't mean to be.'

'I know you don't,' the Prof lied. 'Can't you be nicer to Emma?'

'How much nicer do you want me to be?' enquired Goldblatt suspiciously.

'It's very hard for Emma.'

'I know,' said Goldblatt. 'It is very hard for Emma.'

'I mean it, Malcolm. We have to be understanding. She's not the most confident girl.'

Goldblatt nodded.

'And she's a woman.'

'I know,' said Goldblatt.

'It can be hard for women,' said the Prof, looking straight at Goldblatt, as if she were someone who should know.

Goldblatt nodded. The Prof seemed to expect him to nod, and he would nod to anything if only she would get to the end of this nauseating sexist blackmail.

'Sometimes women don't say things as openly as they should, especially to men. It can be hard for women to deal with that. It's easier for men.'

Goldblatt stared past the Prof at the wall behind her, desperately trying to distract himself from her voice. His gaze fixed on the Scale. He wondered what kind of a mind could have conceived of it and what kind of a hand could have wrought it. What would Blake have made of it? Probably would have written some stirring masterpiece on human insanity. How would it start?

> Scyle! Scyle! red and bright
> In the Fuertler of the night,
> What demented brain or eye
> Could frame you on the wall so high?
> What mad doctor? what crazed witch?
> What sad sour sulking—

'Couldn't you go to her ward rounds, at least?'

'Sorry,' said Goldblatt. 'What was that?'

'Couldn't you go to Emma's ward rounds, Malcolm? Couldn't you do that? For me?'

'Yes,' said Goldblatt, 'I could go to her ward rounds. I should, shouldn't I?'

'Yes, you should. That would be very good,' said the Prof brightly. 'I'm sure that would help.'

'Who?'

'Emma,' said the Prof. 'I'm sure that would help with her confidence.'

'Well, that's all right then,' said Goldblatt.

The Prof smiled.

'And I'll think about that other thing, shall I? Let's see how we go.'

Goldblatt frowned. 'What other thing?'

'Whether I should ask you to leave.'

'Whether you should ask me to leave?' said Goldblatt quietly.

Suddenly he realized what all that muddy verbiage at the start had been about. She really did feel she had a dilemma. And the dilemma was whether getting rid of him was more trouble for her than it was worth.

She was serious.

Goldblatt could feel a certain tightening of his chest. He tried to quell his anger.

The Prof was still staring at him pleasantly.

'Yes,' said Goldblatt eventually.

The Prof smiled.

'I'll think about it too.'

'I'm sorry?' said the Prof.

'I said I'll think about it too. Whether I'm prepared to stay.'

The Prof smiled an inane grimace of confusion.

'Well, what did you think I was going to do, Professor Small? You're seriously telling me you're thinking about firing me. Isn't that what you just did? How badly do you think I need this job?' Badly. Very badly. But he couldn't stop himself. 'How long do you thing I'm going to go on working in this atmosphere? How long do you think I'm going to put up with it? Surely you thought about that before you decided to speak to me.'

'I... What atmosphere?' asked the Prof timidly. She thought the atmosphere had become very pleasant in the last few minutes, and when Goldblatt said he would go to Emma's ward rounds – *for her* – she had almost convinced herself that deep down Goldblatt really did respect her, proving that Emma knew nothing – absolutely *nothing* – about what people thought of her.

'People telling me I'm difficult. The SR going behind my back and crying to the professor. The professor patting the SR on the back instead of telling her to grow up. It's difficult for me too.' Goldblatt felt a wave of foamy, artificial passion sweeping him away and decided that he may as well see where it took him. 'It can be difficult for men, you know. We don't open up enough. We're not in touch with our feelings. Many of us find it difficult to say what we think, especially to women. I just wish people would remember that sometimes!'

The Prof stared at him uneasily.

Goldblatt got up. 'I'll think about it. I'll let you know. Right now, that's all I can say.'

The Prof nodded speechlessly. Suddenly it seemed that she hadn't achieved anything at all in this interview. She hadn't got an answer from the boy about whether she should fire him. She hadn't even warned him. He had just warned her! He had managed to turn the tables. Now, it seemed, she was waiting for *him* to tell *her* whether he was going to leave. Somehow he was threatening her with the very action with which, she thought, she had been threatening him.

Goldblatt opened the door. 'Goodbye, Professor Small.'

He turned, and pulled the door shut firmly behind him.

'Goodbye, Dr Goldblatt,' whispered the Prof, after it had closed.

Dr Morris bumped into him as he was coming out of the men's toilets. He grabbed Goldblatt by the shoulders, glanced around shiftily for a second, and then pushed him back inside.

Goldblatt didn't know what Dr Morris had in mind, but he hoped it wasn't some kind of male bonding. At best, Goldblatt was ambivalent about male bonding, and he was downright suspicious of it when it took place in a public convenience.

Dr Morris pushed him towards the wall lined with washbasins. At least he wasn't taking him towards a cubicle.

'Well?' he said.

Goldblatt looked at Dr Morris uncomprehendingly.

'The Prof talked to you, didn't she?'

Goldblatt nodded.

'I saw you going in. What did she say?'

'She told me she was thinking about whether she should fire me.'

Dr Morris looked at him incredulously. 'What?'

Goldblatt shrugged.

'She's...' Dr Morris shook his head. 'You're in an impossible situation, Malcolm.'

'I know. You've told me.'

'It's crazy.'

'Emma's convinced her I'm a nightmare.'

'You haven't exactly helped yourself in that department. You know it's hard for Emma.'

'Everyone keeps saying that. Do you really think it is?'

'Yes,' said Dr Morris. He looked around for a moment, then went over to one of the urinals.

'I don't,' said Goldblatt.

'Why not?' asked Dr Morris over his shoulder.

'I just don't.'

Dr Morris began to pee. 'Do you really mean that?'

'No,' said Goldblatt to Dr Morris's back. 'I don't care. I don't care enough to give a fuck about her one way or the other.'

Dr Morris laughed. 'You don't mean that.'

'Of course I do.'

'What happened to your compassion for a fellow professional?'

'This fellow professional is making a profession out of getting compassion from her fellows.'

Dr Morris turned around and stared at Goldblatt. Fortunately, he'd zipped first.

'Don't ask me to repeat it,' Goldblatt said. 'I don't think I could.'

'Did you prepare that before?'

'Yes, it's one of my toilet jokes. I use it every time I have a discussion with my consultant in the toilet about an SR who's a pain in the arse.'

'It's very good,' said Dr Morris.

'Thank you. I practise frequently.'

Dr Morris washed his hands. 'What are you going to do?' he asked as he pulled a couple of paper towels out of the dispenser. 'Even if you do finish out your contract here...'

'So you don't think she's going to extend it?'

'I doubt it.'

'She might, though. Looking on the bright side.'

'You'd have to be looking on the bright side.'

'Do they still make sides that bright?'

'I once saw a patient who'd burned the retinas of both her eyes skiing,' said Dr Morris. 'It was the sunlight off the snow. She'd forgotten her sunglasses, but she skied the whole day anyway. You've never seen such oedematous retinas.'

'Interesting?' asked Goldblatt.

'Fascinating.'

Goldblatt was sure it had been – the thing he wasn't sure about was what it had to do with him. 'Anyway, she hasn't fired me yet. I told her I'd think about whether I wanted to stay.'

Dr Morris stared at him. 'You said that to her?'

Goldblatt nodded. 'I don't think I should ask her for a reference, though.'

'No,' said Dr Morris. 'You have to be careful asking her for a reference even when she wants to give you one.'

'So I've heard.'

'I'll give you a reference.'

'Thanks,' said Goldblatt.

'As long as you don't insult anyone else at interviews,' he added, only half-jokingly.

'I try not to,' said Goldblatt, 'but they keep asking these dumb questions.'

'Really, Malcolm. It makes it harder for those of us who want to help you.'

'Who's that?'

'Well, I want to help you, of course.'

Goldblatt looked very frankly, almost demandingly, into Dr Morris's eyes. It was a long time since he had bothered to look so expectantly at a consultant. Not since... well, not since he had looked at Dr Oakley in that way, almost two years before.

Silently, Goldblatt asked the questions. Are you going to do something about this impossible situation I'm in, or are you just going to keep telling me I'm in it? Are you going to stop me getting fired, which will take away whatever last slim chance I have of getting a real job, or are you just going to watch as it happens and then offer to give me a reference?

'I'll give you a reference,' said Dr Morris again. 'I'll be glad to Malcolm. Just let me know when you need it.'

'Thank you,' said Goldblatt.

'I mean it. I'll support you, Malcolm. I'll do whatever I can to help. Not just for locum jobs, but for substantive jobs as well.'

'I know you mean it,' said Goldblatt. 'Thank you.'

'Don't keep saying thank you,' said Dr Morris.

'Shall I say something else?'

'If you like.'

'Thank you very much.'

Dr Morris took a couple of steps towards the door. He turned back to Goldblatt.

'You're upset. I understand. Remember what I said. I'm behind you, Malcolm. I really am. I'll support you in whatever way I can.'

'I'll remember,' said Goldblatt. 'Thank you.'

Dr Morris left.

Goldblatt stayed there for a moment longer and almost went over to one of the urinals before he remembered that he had actually been leaving the toilets when Dr Morris pushed him in there.

Later that day, the Prof called Dr Morris into her office and told him that she had put Goldblatt on probation for a week. She had sat staring at the Scale after Goldblatt had gone, with no idea what to do next, until the notion of a week's 'probation' slipped into her mind as a fancy name for doing nothing and waiting for the whole thing to go away.

The Prof hoped that Goldblatt would turn up to Emma's ward round, and that Emma would stop crying about him, and that the whole sorry crew would somehow limp along so that by the end of the week's probation she could conclude that everything had improved – and that the same sorry crew could then keep limping along until Goldblatt's contract came to an end – and she could quietly shelve the threat of asking him to leave, which she now was almost too scared to use because she no longer knew whether it was aimed against Goldblatt or herself. But equally deep down, she doubted this would happen. She didn't really believe she had the makings of a good probation officer.

Incidentally, the Prof had omitted to inform Goldblatt of his week's probation, since she had decided to put him on it only after he had left, and the last thing she wanted to do was to call him back. As luck would have it, she also omitted to tell Dr Morris – who naturally assumed that she had told Goldblatt – that she had omitted to tell him.

In consequence of all of this, Malcolm Goldblatt ended up in the unusual – and some would say unenviable – situation of being on a week's probation without even knowing it.

33

GOLDBLATT REALLY DID MEAN it when he thanked Dr Morris. He wasn't just saying it. Well, after the first couple of times he was just saying it, but at the start he really meant it.

He appreciated Dr Morris's concern. Dr Morris really was being kind. He was also being useless. But he couldn't help that. That was just him, the way he had been educated, the conventions he had been taught to respect. Within those limits, giving Goldblatt a reference was the very best he could offer. And he didn't have to offer even that. Goldblatt had no right to expect it of him. So he deserved to be thanked.

But being kind didn't mean being effective. It didn't mean he was going to make a big speech to the Prof.

'Andrea,' it didn't mean he was going to say, 'I'm not going to stand by and let you fire Malcolm Goldblatt, even if you are the head of the unit. If you try to fire him, I'm going to take it up with the Medical Director. You don't fire a doctor just because you don't like him, or because one of your other doctors has trouble adapting. There's a proper way to deal with this. There's a degree of responsibility here. There's a question of fairness, even if he is just a locum. You don't do this to people's careers.'

Obviously, the full speech as it developed in Goldblatt's mind was longer, but those half-dozen sentences contained the core of it. They would have been enough by themselves, although each time Goldblatt went over the speech it grew, developing complex and stunning arguments and becoming embellished with exuberant rhetorical flourishes and irresistible appeals to natural justice. In the end the speech was quite a fine piece of oratory, and it was a terrible shame that Dr Morris would never utter it. Goldblatt knew he never would. He would never even utter the core of it, let alone the rhetorical flourishes.

Goldblatt didn't blame him for that. Dr Morris was what he was. In a way, Goldblatt envied him. Having come so far and so smoothly through the tubing of the profession's machine, having been stripped down, pulverized, moulded, and re-formed by its pressures, and then squirted out the other end as a perfect professor-in-waiting, Dr Morris was simply not capable of recognizing that perhaps it was time for him to stand up and demand that the machine be switched off for a second while someone shone a light to see what was going on in one of its many thousands of tubes and moulding chambers. The machine, to those who were its products, was a black box. It had to be taken as a whole. It couldn't be taken apart.

No, Goldblatt knew that Dr Morris would never make that speech. So Goldblatt made it for him.

To Lesley.

He couldn't help himself. Forgetting that everything was supposed to be safe and inconsequential, and not stopping to ask himself what might happen once the unspoken truce was broken. He had tried to hold it in, and had succeeded until the very last thing at night, when they were in bed. But once he started, like a trickle turning into a stream turning into a wild, surging torrent, it gushed uncontrollably out of him. He couldn't stop it.

It went on for twenty minutes. Lesley listened without interrupting. At the end she said: 'Yes, Malcolm, that's what he should say.'

'He should, shouldn't he?' demanded Goldblatt.

'Yes, Malcolm. He should.'

There was silence. Goldblatt waited. Lesley said nothing.

Goldblatt tried to put out of his mind what had happened with Ludo the previous night. There had been a few awkward glances between then during the day. For the first time since... for the first time he could remember, he hadn't bought her a coffee. He had caught the HO watching them a couple of times, obviously wondering what was going on. Goldblatt wished he knew. He wished he knew what he was going to do next. Lying here now with Lesley, the previous evening with Ludo was like something from a different universe. Not real.

Eventually he said: 'Can you believe what Professor Small said to me? Aren't you angry about it?'

'No,' said Lesley.

'Not even a bit?'

'No,' said Lesley.

That was scary.

'Don't you think I should fight it?' asked Goldblatt.

'You could.'

'The contract they made me sign was rubbish. Forcing me, as a locum, to waive my rights to appeal. That can't be legal.'

'Probably not.'

'There's got to be some kind of employment law on that.'

'Probably.'

'We could fight it, Les. You'd slay them in court.'

'Probably,' said Lesley.

Goldblatt reached for her hand. She withdrew it.

'Les?'

'What?'

'What's going on?'

'Nothing's going on, Malcolm. I'm tired, that's all.'

'Do you want to sleep?'

'No, I'm *tired*.' She turned to him. 'I'm tired, don't you understand? What was it your ex used to say?'

'She wished she'd never left me?'

'If there's a hard way to do something, you'll find it. I used to think it was funny, but it's not. She was right, it's exhausting. I'm tired, Malcolm. I'm tired of all of it. I can't stand it any more. What are you doing to yourself? What are you doing to us?'

Goldblatt flinched.

'I can't bear it any more. All right? That's all. No big deal. I've tried to tell you, but you never listen. So I'll say it as clearly as I can. I can't *bear* it any more.'

Lesley turned away from him.

'What can't you bear?'

She turned straight back.

'What can't I bear? My God, Malcolm. Do you have any idea what you're like? What it is to be with you? I just don't know why I'm with you any more. I try to think back to what it was like at the start to understand how I even ended up with you in the first place. Stand back and look at yourself, Malcolm. Just for once, please, just once, see yourself as you really are. You don't know what you've become. You don't see it, do you? Your anger, your frustration. You're eating yourself alive and you can't even see it.'

'What are you talking about? I've always been like this.'

'No, Malcolm! You haven't always been like this. You weren't like this when I met you. You were happy.'

'I've never been *happy*,' muttered Goldblatt, pronouncing the word with disgust.

'No, you've never been happy. You were dissatisfied, restless, and miserable.'

'Thank you!'

'But there's a certain kind of misery that makes you happy, Malcolm. And when I met you, you had that kind of misery. You were happy. When you were studying, you were happy. At Free from Bondage, you were happy. Even on Rothman's unit you were happy.'

'I was *not* happy on Rothman's unit!' declared Goldblatt. 'That's bullshit!'

'Well, you weren't like this. You're killing yourself, do you understand me? You are *killing* yourself!' Lesley grimaced in frustration, her hands clenched, shaking. 'Malcolm, I don't know what to say to you any more. I don't know what words to use. There are so many other things you could be doing with your life. You're so smart. You're so talented.'

'So handsome?'

'It's always a joke, isn't it? Listen to me! There are so many other things you could do, Malcolm. And you're killing yourself. For what? For *nothing*. For absolutely nothing.'

'It's not nothing,' he said quietly.

'No, it's not. You're right. It's not nothing.' Lesley was silent for a moment. She drew a deep breath. 'They're not going to let you do it. Can't you see that? You want to do it your way, that's the only way you're prepared to do it. Well, it's not going to happen. Accept it. They're never going to give you a substantive job. All right? I've said it. One of us has to. They are never... going... to give you... a substantive... job. *Finis*. They win, Malcolm. You lose.'

Goldblatt listened to the words.

'Face it. It's over. They've won.'

Goldblatt looked at her. Then he threw himself back on his pillow.

'I can't bear it any more. I love you, Malcolm, but I can't bear it any more.'

'What does that mean?' asked Goldblatt, staring at the ceiling.

'I don't know.'

'It sounds like a threat.'

'It's not a threat.'

'It sounds like it's medicine or you. It sounds like an ultimatum.'

'It's not. God, it's not.' Lesley gazed at him, eyes beseeching. 'I don't want it to be like that. It's the last thing I'd ever say to you. I'm just telling you how I feel. If you think this last week has been fun... If you think... I can't... I can't work, I can't concentrate. I'm supposed to be drafting an opinion and... All I can think about is this. Every single minute of the day.'

'I love you too, Les.' He looked at her. 'I don't think I've told you that enough, have I?'

Lesley laughed.

'Has it been so bad for you?'

'No, Malcolm. It hasn't been bad. I'm not saying it has.'

'Apart from the unbearable anger and frustration?'

Lesley smiled sadly. 'Yes, apart from that.'

Suddenly Goldblatt felt a foretaste of what it would be like, talking as if it were in the past, as if Lesley had left him. It was a terrible feeling. Lonely, empty, cold.

'Lesley, what should I do?'

'I don't know. I can't tell you any more.'

'You used to be able to tell me. You used to never be able to stop telling me.'

'Did I? You never listened.'

'I'll listen this time.'

Silence.

'I love you, Les. You know I do.'

'I've told you before, Malcolm. Lots of times. I've told you what I think.'

'Tell me again.'

She sighed. 'All right. I'll tell you again.' She got up on her elbow and stared down at his face. 'Come down from the cross, Malcolm.'

Goldblatt frowned.

'It's time. No one cares that you're up there. No one but you – and me.' Lesley gazed into his eyes. Then she shook her head. 'Look, there's no point me saying it. You have to want to do it. You have to do it for yourself. Don't do it for me. That would be worse than anything. You'd end up hating me.'

'No, I wouldn't.'

'Yes, you would. I'd rather we part now as friends than have that happen. I couldn't bear it.'

Goldblatt reached up to touch her cheek.

'Don't,' said Lesley, and she wiped at the tears herself. 'Just... don't.'

'I need you, Lesley. I don't know...'

'What? You don't know what you'd do without me?' Lesley laughed ironically through the tears. 'I thought you always told me hospitals are a hotbed of sex. No one hanging around? No little nurse? A little doctor somewhere?'

Goldblatt flinched.

There was silence again.

'I don't know what to do,' said Goldblatt eventually. 'It's easy to say. Leave it. Walk away. Words are easy, Les. How do I do it? Tell me. How do I *do* it?'

'You have to face her, Malcolm.'

'Who? The Prof?'

'No, you idiot. You know who I'm talking about. *Her.* You have to face her.'

Lesley gazed at him for a moment, then switched off the light and turned away.

'Lesley?'

No reply. He wanted to touch her. She was only a few inches away from him. But he knew he couldn't. He watched her. The back of her head in the darkness, her shoulders. What had he put her through? He didn't have the right to do it.

It was all out in the open now. How long before she left him? Making a joke of it wouldn't work any more.

'Lesley?'

No reply.

He stared at her hair, a darker darkness, falling over her shoulders.

She was right. Goldblatt knew who Lesley was talking about. Once and for all, he had to face her.

Maybe the old Jewish lady had never existed. Maybe she was just a myth in his mind. She had looked as if she existed when Goldblatt saw her in his clinic three years earlier. But only just. She was five feet tall, with papery skin, and fine grey hair, and tiny veins in her rosy cheeks. Her blue eyes had that milky band around the irises that old people get, and she wore glasses that magnified her eyes and gave her stare an intense, manic quality. She was as thin as a stick, and when she raised her arm it looked like a twig that was about to snap off at the elbow. Her fist was about as impressive as a sultana. Raising her twig-like arm with her clenched sultana-fist was a favourite gesture of the old Jewish lady, and Goldblatt was introduced to it within two minutes of meeting her. He was introduced to it again halfway through the consultation, and just in case he had missed the earlier introductions, he was introduced to it again towards the end of the old Jewish lady's visit, when she reminded him that she was a fighter.

'I'm a fighter,' she said, in a European accent Goldblatt couldn't place exactly.

Goldblatt smiled. 'Where are you from originally?'

'Where am I from? What a question. Where do you think I'm from?'

'Mexico,' said Goldblatt.

The old Jewish lady laughed. 'You know a town called Helmstedt, *mein Herr* Dr Goldblatt?'

Goldblatt shook his head.

'That's where I'm from. Helmstedt. In Germany.'

'In Germany?'

'In Germany,' said the old Jewish lady.

Goldblatt glanced at the date of birth on the old Jewish lady's notes, determining exactly when in Germany's history, in a town called Helmstedt, the old Jewish lady would have been born. He put down his pen and sat back in his chair.

The old Jewish lady waved her hand. She sighed. 'Well,' she said. It was only a single syllable, but she managed to inject it with a complex mixture of resignation, pain, bitterness, and unbearable longing.

Goldblatt nodded.

'But I'm a fighter!' said the old Jewish lady, raising her twig-like arm and clenching her fist like a sultana, with that intense, almost maniacal glint in the magnified pale blue eyes behind her glasses. 'You think I would have survived if I wasn't a fighter?'

No, she wouldn't have survived. Goldblatt believed her. She was a fighter. That was what she kept saying, and it was certainly true. What Goldblatt wasn't sure about was what she was fighting against now. But being a fighter was simply part of the old Jewish lady's mental constitution, and it didn't necessarily imply that at any given time she had an opponent.

Goldblatt met the old Jewish lady only twice. There wasn't too much that was wrong with her. She had a bit of blood pressure, a touch of rheumatism, her eyesight wasn't too good, she had maybe gallstones which gave her pain now and then but she didn't want to have an operation God forbid something should happen to her when they put her to sleep and she should end up depending on her lovely family who all had worries of their own.

'Wouldn't they look after you?' Goldblatt asked.

'Wouldn't they look after me? Sure they'd look after me. You think they wouldn't look after me? Put me in a home somewhere!'

'And you don't want to go to a home?'

The old Jewish lady gripped Goldblatt's wrist with her papery, dry fingers. 'Dr Goldblatt, you would want to go to a home?'

'I'm not eighty-four.'

'Please God you will be one day,' said the old Jewish lady, letting go of him.

'It's a very safe operation. They do it through a small hole in the skin. They don't make those big cuts they used to make.'

The old Jewish lady shrugged. Big cuts, small holes – she didn't want to know.

'All right,' said Goldblatt.

'Good,' said the old Jewish lady, nodding with satisfaction. No more nonsense from the doctor, at least.

The old Jewish lady was terrified of being dependent on her family and ending up in a home. That was the dominant motivating force in her life, and everything was subordinated to this one overwhelming objective. She lived by herself in a flat up a flight of stairs that Goldblatt didn't even want to imagine her climbing. She tottered around unsteadily on legs like beanstalks, refusing to use a walking stick or even consider a Zimmer frame, which would be the first step on the slippery path to immobility, dependence, and transfer to a home. Her blood pressure tablets made her dizzy, and she had fallen a couple of times when she got up in the mornings. It took all of Goldblatt's interrogation skills to make her admit it. At first she gave him the old line about slipping over her slippers.

'Slippers. I left them beside the bed. Like every night. I get up in the morning. I forget they're there. Down I go! Like a pack of cards. Slippers. Think. Think about it, doctor. What do you expect? Slippers. So I slip.'

Did she think he'd been born yesterday? Goldblatt had heard that one a million times before.

'Dizzy?' the old Jewish lady lied. 'I wouldn't say dizzy. A bit light-headed maybe.'

'All right. When are you light-headed?'

'Light-headed?' said the old Jewish lady. 'That's maybe a bit too strong. Let's say whizzy.'

Actually, with her German accent, she said 'vhizzy'.

'Vhizzy?' repeated Goldblatt.

'Vhizzy you don't understand?' asked the old Jewish lady.

Goldblatt shook his head.

The old Jewish lady shrugged.

Goldblatt decided on the direct approach. He knew the drugs the old Jewish lady was taking, and at her age if they didn't drop her blood pressure when she stood up there really had to be something wrong with her.

'In the mornings, when you get out of bed,' asked Goldblatt, 'do you feel dizzy when you stand up?'

The old Jewish lady peered at him suspiciously. Goldblatt could tell guilt when he saw it.

'And do you feel dizzy at other times when you stand up, for instance if you've been sitting down for a long time?'

'And what if I do?' asked the old Jewish lady defiantly. 'You're going to put me in a home?'

'I might change your tablets.'

'Why?'

'To stop you feeling dizzy.'

'Vhizzy,' the old Jewish lady corrected him.

'Vhizzy,' said Goldblatt.

'Which tablets? The blue ones or the orange ones?'

'Wait a minute.' Goldblatt hated it when patients expected him to recognize tablets by colour, size, or shape. No one ever stopped to think that he just wrote the prescriptions and never saw the drugs himself.

He looked up the old Jewish lady's drugs in the formulary, which gave a physical description of the tablets.

'The orange ones,' he said.

'The prazosin?' said the old Jewish lady. 'Why didn't you say so?'

Goldblatt nodded at the old Jewish lady, smiling. That's one to you, he thought. Her milk-rimmed eyes twinkled mischievously.

'Yes, the prazosin.'

'And what about my blood pressure?' asked the old Jewish lady, sounding like a grandmother who was teaching him to suck eggs.

'We'll find a different tablet for your blood pressure, one that's less likely to make you dizzy when you stand up.'

'Vhizzy,' said the old Jewish lady.

'Vhizzy,' said Goldblatt.

'All right, Dr Goldblatt,' said the old Jewish lady. 'That sounds fair.'

Goldblatt stopped the old Jewish lady's prazosin and substituted a drug that was less likely to cause postural hypotension. He saw her in clinic again a few weeks later, when she confided that her vhizziness was much better than before. And at her next clinic appointment after that she failed to appear. Something made Goldblatt suspect this wasn't the normal failure to appear that regularly wasted clinic slots in every hospital every day. He rang up the old Jewish lady's general practitioner. She was dead. How? She just died, the GP said. Her daughter had to get the police to break into her flat. They found her in bed. What had he written on the death certificate? Cardiac arrhythmia. The GP said he always wrote cardiac arrhythmia when an old person died in her sleep and there was no specific reason for it. He was an old-fashioned GP and he would have preferred to write old age as the cause of death, except the coroner wouldn't accept old age as a cause of death, and consequently no one was allowed to die of it any more.

The old Jewish lady had reminded Goldblatt of his grandmother, who had also been an old Jewish lady, and used to bake a special hard sweet biscuit for him when he was a little boy. He used to nibble and suck on it until it turned to delicious mush in his mouth. His grandmother had gone on making it for him long after he had grown up, right up to the time that her gnarled hands became too crippled for baking.

But it wasn't the fact that the old Jewish lady reminded Goldblatt of his grandmother that made her important. It was the fact that he had told Lesley about her, apparently many times over. He often told Lesley about patients when some awful malpractice had happened as his colleagues tried to treat them. But there was no malpractice attached to the old Jewish lady, as far as he was aware, and if there was, then he was probably the one guilty of it. No, the fact that he had told Leslie about her could mean only one thing: something was going on in his mind. Something deep, murky, foetid, and Freudian. He knew what he had to do.

That night, after Lesley had finally fallen asleep – or was breathing deeply and regularly to make him think she was – he got up, went into the kitchen, poured himself a drink, took a deep breath, held his nose and plunged into his id to find out what was going on.

Goldblatt's id was a horrible place, and he only went there when he absolutely had to. His superego was a cleaner and much more pleasant environment, although it did have its drawbacks. There always seemed to be some long, boring, and incredibly guilt-inducing Calvinist sermon in progress. But at least there was nothing frightening in there. Goldblatt had seen some truly bloodcurdling things in his id that made his hair stand on end. When he had to go down there he moved as fast as he could, went directly to his objective, and never looked around. When he got in there this time, therefore, he marched straight across to a place where he could see the lenses of a thick pair of spectacles glinting in the evil, reddish light. Sure enough, those were the lenses of her glasses, and behind them was a pair of milky blue eyes, together with the rest of the old Jewish lady, arm raised and fist clenched like a sultana, staring down at him with her manic, magnified gaze.

She had become a symbol – but a symbol of what?

Goldblatt knew at once. She was a symbol of everything that was most dangerous for him about medicine, its siren song, its treacherous allure, the cunning and carefully calculated control that it exerted over him. Lesley had realized it as well, even before he did, which was why she hated the old Jewish lady so much.

Wasn't that why he had gone back to medicine? Wasn't that the answer to the question? The old Jewish lady. And the others.

They didn't have to be old Jewish ladies. They could be anything, and had been. They could be men or women, young or old or middle-aged, they could be Chinese or Polynesian, black or white, and they didn't have to remind him of his grandmother. They could be a tailor from Budapest who had lived in Soho for forty years and came to Goldblatt's clinic on Professor Rothman's unit with an osteoarthritic right thumb after five decades of stitching clothes. Fifty years of stitching. Who had he made clothes for?

'The most famous person I made clothes for?' the tailor asked.

Goldblatt nodded.

'I would say... the Shah of Iran.'

Goldblatt stared at him. He put his pen down and sat back in his chair. 'You're joking.'

'No. A very elegant man.'

'The Shah of Iran?'

'That's nothing. My father made clothes for Admiral Horthy. You know who Horthy was?'

'Miklós Horthy?' said Goldblatt.

The tailor nodded, impressed. 'You've heard of him. No one remembers him today.'

'Should we?'

'No, the bastard. May he rot in hell. My father was his tailor. Uniforms, mostly. There was a lot of business in uniforms in those days.' The tailor chuckled. 'All the time he was going up there to his residence. I was a partisan, and he was making uniforms for Horthy!'

The tailor chuckled again, unconsciously rubbing his painful thumb.

'That's a big change, from being a partisan to being a tailor.'

The tailor shrugged. 'No, why? I was young. Best time of my life.'

'Really?'

'It was terrible. Really horrible, the things that were happening. But you look back now, and you see yourself like you were, and somehow... it's like you're looking at someone different. Fearless. Give us a gun, and nothing could stop us.'

'And you miss that?'

'Doctor, I don't miss it. Heaven forbid, it's not something you can miss. But...' he shrugged. 'No one understands. My own grandchildren don't want to hear. My daughter rolls her eyes if I start to talk.'

'So tell me.'

'What?'

'Why you miss it.'

These were the moments that nailed Goldblatt to medicine. These moments, as if a veil suddenly billowed back and revealed an open window behind it. You never knew when it was going to happen. Usually it didn't. But then it did. And this was what the old Jewish lady symbolized.

There was the fifty-three-year-old Irish woman with five children who had waited until the last of them was old enough to look after himself, and then run away from the husband who had beaten and raped her for thirty-two years. Goldblatt would never forget the way she told him. He had looked up from the folder where he had been jotting down his notes and had just stared at her from across the desk in amazement. Not at the beating and raping, but at the way she said 'run away', without the slightest hint of self-consciousness, just as if she were a child or a slave, and had escaped illicitly from her place of bondage.

'Run away?' he asked.

'I'd never been far from home, doctor. You don't understand. I was born on a farm and I married a man from another farm seven miles away. So I'd hardly ever been away from there, like, before I run away.'

'Where did you run to?' asked Goldblatt, putting his pen down and sitting back in his chair.

'Here, doctor. London. Well, I went to Liverpool, like, just on the way through. I've got a sister here and I stayed with her at the start. It's not easy, starting a new life when you're fifty.'

Goldblatt could hardly imagine. 'What did you do?'

'Oh, anything I could, doctor. Cleaning, mostly. There's always a call for cleaners, if you'll work. And, you know, being on a farm all me life, and bringing up five kids, it's not like I'd never had to raise a finger before.'

'Would you go back?' Goldblatt asked.

The Irish lady laughed. 'To what, doctor?'

Goldblatt shook his head. He didn't know what she would go back to, finding it difficult to understand what she had come from.

The Irish lady was watching him.

'You don't talk about this much,' said Goldblatt.

'Who wants to hear, doctor?'

Goldblatt didn't reply. He waited. She talked.

Those were the moments that nailed him, when he put down his pen and sat back in his chair, ignoring all the pressures of the clinic and the other patients waiting outside. The act of sitting back itself was important. He had come to understand that throwing the pen down and sitting back for a moment was an act of professional divestment, like a deep-sea diver taking off his diving suit and stepping out of it for a moment, even if he was going to put the suit back on and dive in again in another minute or two.

It was the opportunity – and the responsibility – for an instant of time that abruptly billowed open in front of your eyes, not to be a doctor, but to play a part in someone else's life. By asking, by listening, by nodding. Not as anyone else could play a part, not as a friend or relative, but nor as a complete stranger. To be both objective and involved, detached and connected, a part that was utterly unique and enormously important for that person at that moment. Each one of us is that person at some time

413

in our lives. At those moments, this was the greatest good he could do, to ask the questions no one else in their lives dared or cared to ask, but which they longed to answer, to listen as they went to wherever those answers took them, to nod without hint of judgement or critique. And this must have a value, because people don't speak, they don't let you in and ask you to play that part in their lives, unless they need you to. Unless there's something in it for them. Self-esteem, self-assertion, catharsis, acknowledgement. Something. That was the proof. The fact that they did ask him in – not always, not often, but sometimes – that they did let the veil over their deepest lives billow open for a moment.

Goldblatt had tried to explain this once to an interview panel. It was one of his earlier panels, before he understood that he had become a Wise Man. In those days his accumulating failures at interviews had seemed unrelated, and he hadn't yet understood the logic that connected them. Foolishly he believed that a display of passionate commitment might sway the junta in front of him.

'It's that unique satisfaction you get,' he said in response to an interviewer who had launched with the usual withering sneer into questioning his decision to come back to medicine after his law degree. 'It's that moment when you throw down your pen and you sit back in your chair and you're just with the patient in front of you, sharing some part of their life that they have a need to share.' Goldblatt paused, feeling a dangerous build-up of sincerity threatening to overwhelm him. 'That's why I love medicine. After all, isn't that what it's all about?'

There was a chilly silence. Goldblatt found himself looking at a wall of the blank, staring faces of a group of people who had never heard anything so grisly and nauseating in their entire lives and were certainly not going to stand for much more of this disingenuous drivel. In retrospect he was lucky the Eminent Physicians hadn't struck him off their list of Wise Men at their very next convocation. Somewhere, he knew, there must be a black mark against his Wisdom because of it.

But it was true. That was the cruel irony of it. Amongst all the extravagant and deceitful exaggerations he had ever spouted at interviews, and which had been swallowed whole, this small, modest truth had been rejected like bile.

It wasn't the other things that kept him in the profession. Not the prestige, the authority, the opportunity to ruin the lives of younger colleagues who were under your control. Handing out drugs that made people better – yes, that gave him a sense of satisfaction, often very powerful, and it wasn't something trivial, it was meaningful and important, but it was the same drugs for the same conditions, over and over, and the truth was anyone could do it if they learned enough lists. And it wasn't the adulation of patients that frequently resulted. He hated hearing patients like the Broderip talking about their consultants as if they were gods incarnate, and he despised consultants, like Andrea Small, who encouraged and cultivated the Broderips as their high priests.

On the other hand, running heroically down hospital corridors when you were called for a cardiac arrest, getting admiring looks from sexy young women visiting their grandmothers, did have its allure. But how often did you get to do that? It's a statistical fact that most cardiac arrests happen outside visiting hours.

No, it was the act of throwing his pen down on the desk and sitting back in his chair. As simple as that. It didn't happen much. But it happened.

That was the bait that really hooked him.

He came back quietly into the bedroom. Lesley was asleep or still doing a good impression of it. He sat down on the chair in the corner, which was piled with clothes she hadn't bothered to put away, and gazed at her in the dimness.

He was tired, with a tiredness that wasn't only physical, but there was more for him to do. In his mind, he attempted to see himself as an observer, from a distance, as Lesley had asked him to. He owed it to her at least to try.

She was right. He had insisted on doing it his way. He always had.

It wasn't just the fact that he didn't want to do a research degree. That was just the visible part, the tip of the iceberg, more the symptom than the disease. If he was honest with himself, it was that – and everything else. He hadn't become part of the machine. He still stood outside it. Watching, pointing, jeering.

He was the problem. Wasn't it time, finally, to admit it? Him. Not the profession. The profession was much, much more than that. It was a gigantic cluster of problems, a gulag of problems, a galaxy of problems cocooned like the millions of larvae of a parasite deep within the body of medicine. But you couldn't change something so big, so hallowed, so infiltrated into the tissues of its host. You had to bow in awe of it. Accept it or leave. Adapt to it or die.

His friends from medical school had adapted. He had seen them, over the years, one after the other, transforming themselves into the mirror images of the people they hoped, one day, to replace. A horrible Lamarckian evolution had got hold of them. All their greyest and most stereotyped attributes were burgeoning, while the individualistic and idiosyncratic parts of them shrivelled. These were people who had once laughed at authority and mocked pretentiousness. They used to mimic their consultants in pubs. Now they were senior SRs. A couple were already consultants themselves. They were serious people with concerns about waiting lists, hospital committees, and government targets. They took matters up with their 'senior colleagues' and thought things would really improve if everyone just 'worked together and made an effort'. Weren't you meant to get more cynical as you got older? What had *happened* to them?

Would he ever be like that? Could he make himself like that, even for the sake of the billowing moments? He doubted it. He'd fight against himself until the part of him that was doing it lay bludgeoned, beaten to a pulp by the rest of him.

The stupid, brutish, Pavlovian 'I did it therefore you'll do it' that came from the upper reaches of the profession disgusted him. Was there anything more inimical to rationality and reform? And yet, already, his friends were beginning to talk like that. Already their outrage was being extinguished as time made their memories rosy. Shoot me, Goldblatt thought, shoot me if I ever say such a thing.

And the Oakleys, sitting there, silently, staring at the ground, staring at the wall, staring anywhere to avoid his eyes. Shoot me, he thought, shoot me if I ever fall silent. If I ever stare like that.

Lesley was right. He would never change. He couldn't. And even if he could, he didn't want to.

And now the machine had discovered it and was vomiting him out.

For years it had queasily tolerated him. For the last twenty months it had struggled with him, like a beast with an indigestible piece of gristle bouncing around in its guts. Now it was expelling him.

To stay there, to hang on, to refuse to leave, somehow to resist the impetus of expulsion and try to force his way back into the machine, would kill him, as Lesley said. It already was killing him. It was to torture himself without end, to torment himself in a constant cycle of delusion and despair.

Maybe that's all he deserved. Maybe that's what he was born to do.

But Lesley wasn't. He couldn't expect her to stay with him as he did it.

He thought about Ludo. Why had he asked her for a drink the previous night? It was the old thing, wasn't it? After what had happened with Sandra Hill, after trying to save someone who was nudging on death's door and instead almost pushing her through it, the need to be with someone who understood, who could laugh in the way you could laugh at it, and which no one who had never been there could ever really do. To relieve the tension, subvert it, erase it from your mind until the next morning, the next week, when you would feel it again.

Ludo. It seemed almost impossible to believe that both she and Lesley lived in the same world, as if the existence of one negated the possibility of the other. What he had with Lesley – or what he had had with her – he would never have with someone like Ludo. It was ridiculous even to try to imagine it. When Lesley and he had first got together, he had felt like the luckiest man alive. He still felt like that when he bothered to think about it, when he wasn't too busy taking Lesley for granted. And now it was slipping away. He felt ill at the thought. He wanted to grasp on to it and keep it safe.

But even if he wanted to do what Lesley said, how to do it? The old Jewish lady was still in his head. Everything that she symbolized was still real. It was still precious to him.

Old Mother Medicine was an unrelenting mistress. Why else had he come back to her? Once she had you in her grasp she never let you go. She changed you. She raised you up and kicked you down, and you weren't the same. You were different. Better? Worse? Different. She cut a piece out of your heart and kept it. If you wanted it, you had to stay. You could have it while you were there but you could never take it with you. Leave, and you'd be for ever incomplete.

Maybe, deep down, that's what he had felt when he left medicine in the first place. He had lost something of what he had become, and practising law could never fill that gap. Maybe that's why, when the moment of ultimate truth arrived, the moment at which the break would become irreversible, he had turned tail and reverted. To have it back.

Well he couldn't have it back. It belonged to old Mother Medicine now, and if you had it, it was only on her terms.

He thought of what Lesley had said. Come down from the cross. Wasn't that it?

He was still nailed up there. If he tore himself away, the ripped shreds of his flesh would remain up there for ever, the scars on his hands would never disappear.

Did he really want to do it? Was he really prepared to? And if he was, how? How to tear himself off and come down?

34

THERE WAS NO ROUND the next Wednesday morning. The Prof, together with eighty other professors, was sitting in a lecture hall at a morning meeting on postgraduate training at the Royal College of Physicians. She had rescheduled her round for two o'clock in the afternoon.

At ten past two the Prof was rushing from the consultants' car park towards the hospital entrance. Lunch had been provided after the meeting at the Royal College, it had dragged on, and of course it was impossible to leave before it was finished. People did leave before it was finished, but it was impossible. The Prof knew she wasn't just eating lunch – although it was a very nice lunch that she was eating, the College always catered well – she was networking. It was an important thing to do, and it also put her petty troubles at the hospital into perspective. Even without the networking, an invitation to the meeting at the Royal College of Physicians always did that. There was so much tradition in the place, so much knowledge, goodness, and virtue that the Prof almost shuddered to think of it. Being invited to a meeting there helped her remember how important she really was, and she had managed to mention it three times during her last conversation with Margaret Hayes, to help her remember as well.

She entered the hospital lobby. The sound of her own heels clattering on the floor as she rushed towards the lifts was like an adrenaline-fuelled drumbeat in recognition of her return from such an important event. The Prof was almost in high spirits. She would certainly have been in high spirits, and not merely almost in them, if not for the fact that Malcolm Goldblatt would be at the round to which the drumbeat of her feet was carrying her. Without the boy's presence, her entire day would have been a spotless pleasure. Morning at the Royal College, lunch with the network, afternoon presiding over her round. Who could design a more spotlessly professorial day? Yet there was a spot, and the day, she knew, wouldn't be entirely pleasant.

On the other hand, the Prof had to admit, it was also partly because of Malcolm Goldblatt that she was almost in high spirits. Paradoxically, he was a cause both of her high spirits and of her failure to fully attain them. But that was so typical of the boy, she thought, almost allowing her almost-high spirits to be overwhelmed by irritation. Everything about him was a paradox.

It was nearly a week since the Prof had asked Goldblatt whether she should get rid of him and he had threatened to think it over. In many ways it had been quite a good week.

Preparations for the Grand Round, which was being held the next morning, had come along nicely. Emma had worked until midnight every night in order to go through the entire set of Fuertler's files, and had identified two other patients who had benefited from a delayed effect of Sorain – or could be interpreted as such. She had also found a paper that reported a similar effect in a patient in Brazil, which was one more paper than the Prof had expected her to find. Maybe there really was such an effect. And in their rehearsals, Emma had mumbled very little. It was obvious to the Prof that a lot of additional rehearsing had been going on.

Another good thing about the week was that Goldblatt, the Prof understood, had turned up to Emma's SR ward round, as he said he would. That was very good. On the other hand, Emma, once she heard that Goldblatt was coming, hadn't turned up, which was probably bad. It was always a bad idea not to turn up to your own round, or even to walk away in the middle of it, as the Prof herself had recently confirmed. But Emma seemed to regard missing her own round as a means of snubbing Goldblatt, which was probably good. Or maybe bad. The Prof wasn't sure. It was probably good. Although the Prof didn't want Emma thinking too highly of herself. That would definitely be bad.

As for what the Prof was going to do with Emma as a result of the incident in her office the previous week, she still hadn't spoken to her about that. It was perfectly plain to the Prof that Emma was going almost insane with worry, and would do anything for a sign that she had been forgiven for her outrageous assertion about Goldblatt's lack of respect. Naturally, that made the Prof disinclined to hurry. Emma could wait a little longer before the Prof relieved her anxiety. In fact, for a couple of days the Prof genuinely hadn't decided whether she would forgive her, but soon came to her senses. Surely the girl's outburst had been a Goldblatt-induced aberration of the sort that the Prof herself had experienced. What possible reason was there to think that there was anything more behind it? Emmas don't come around every day, and to cast Emma adrift, the Prof had to admit, would be cutting off her nose to spite her face, in particular since – if she was totally honest with herself, which was a risk she felt she had to take on this occasion – some of what Emma had said might have been true, or at least it was understandable that Emma might have thought it was.

Some, but not all. As the week passed, the 'some' became smaller and the rest larger in the Prof's mind. True, there may have been moments in the past, brief flashes of foolishness and misjudgement, when Goldblatt hadn't respected her. After all, young men are rebellious by nature, the Prof understood that. It's their hormones. They're like bulls, stallions. Even older men could be like stallions. Take Tom de Witte. The Prof was sure Goldblatt didn't have a girlfriend. That was certainly the problem with the boy. No one to soothe his passions, calm his storms, drain the hormones out of him.

But the events over this past week since she and Goldblatt had had their talk – or the lack of events, more to the point – strongly indicated that his disrespect – if indeed it had even existed – was in the past. What evidence was there to the contrary? None. Had he been impertinent to her? No. Had he contradicted her? No. True, she hadn't given him the opportunity. She had avoided him like the plague, sailing past him in corridors with a frozen smile plastered on her lips and her eyes fixed on some fascinating and invisible apparition far in the distance. She didn't dare to bleep him, relying on Emma for information, which was inconvenient because Emma had given up going to the ward for fear of bumping into him as well, and was relying for information on the house officer. But what did lack of opportunity prove? Nothing. The Prof, who prided herself on her truly legendary sensitivity to the needs, moods, and whims of others, could sense disrespect a mile off, with or without opportunity.

That was the reason that Goldblatt, despite being Goldblatt, almost made her spirits high. Whatever had happened in the past, it was clear now that he didn't disrespect her. Rushing back from her meeting at the Royal College, where she had sat together with eighty other fine and knowledgeable professors, the Prof could barely believe that she had ever thought otherwise.

Perhaps, thought the Prof as she stood in the lift and waited for it to deliver her to the seventh floor, I'll keep Dr Goldblatt. Perhaps I won't get rid of him. I expect I won't even feel intimidated when I see him at the round!

Now, Andrea, said a calmer, more reasonable voice inside her head, let's take one step at a time.

She opened the door to the doctors' office.

'I'm so sorry,' she said benevolently. 'I was at the Royal College. Couldn't get away.'

'We were just deciding whether to start,' said Dr Morris, who had been forced to reschedule a pseudo-Sutherland round to fit in with the Prof's rescheduling.

'Oh, you should have started, Anthony,' the Prof lied. 'Of course you should.' She sat down and looked around the room. Everyone was there except Jane, the South African social worker, who only dropped in to the rounds for five minutes anyway. It would take more than the absence of some useless Antipodean to upset her on such a day. And there was coffee on the desk! How thoughtful. If only it could be ever thus. The Prof glanced at Goldblatt, and blinked in a show of conciliation and good fellowship. Then she turned back to Dr Morris.

'I see the man with the PUO has actually gone, Anthony,' she said. 'I was beginning to think we might never get rid of our dear Mr Lister.'

Dr Morris grinned. Emma laughed with hearty loyalty at the Prof's excellent joke and looked desperately for an indication, a clue, a hint – no matter how small or fleeting – that the Prof accepted her abasement.

'It was amazing the way his fever came down!' said the HO eagerly. She started looking for his file on one of the shelves amongst a pile of notes waiting for discharge summaries to be dictated. 'Would you like to see his charts, Professor Small? They're here somewhere.'

'No,' said the Prof tolerantly, 'I don't think that will be necessary.'

'It won't take a second.'

The Prof ignored her. 'Vasculitis, Anthony?'

'Yes. We thought so in the end.'

'Yes,' said the Prof. 'I'm sure you're right. You started him on Prednisolone, I seem to remember. What dose, again?'

'Sixty milligrams,' said Dr Morris.

'Sixty milligrams,' mused the Prof with the air of a connoisseur. 'Mmm, I would probably have started with forty.'

'I thought forty,' said Emma quickly. 'Didn't I, Dr Morris?'

'We considered forty,' said Dr Morris.

'I *knew* it should be forty,' said Emma.

Dr Morris nodded wearily.

'Yes,' said the Prof, glancing at Goldblatt to ensure he was gaining the benefit of this erudite discussion. The starting dose of Prednisolone in any given patient is a fine judgement, depending on the patient's age, weight, clinical condition, and the balance of a complex set of other factors. Any young doctor could benefit from the experience of his elders, especially when one of those elders was a professor.

Goldblatt was staring at the ceiling, balancing a cup of coffee on his knee. The last few days had been dull, bleak, and depressing. He struggled to understand what was happening to his career and what he should do about it. He struggled to understand what was happening with Lesley. He didn't know what she was going to do, but eventually she was going to do something. Did he have a day, a week, a month before she had finally had enough? Was he going to go home one night and find that she had left? Tonight? Tomorrow? And it didn't help that at the hospital he had been on the receiving end of a lot of injured Balkan stares from Ludo, often accompanied by hair-flicking. Buying her a coffee didn't seem to help. The silences that followed were awkward, if not downright scary. She didn't even whine any more.

The Prof turned back to Dr Morris. 'I'm sure sixty milligrams will be all right.'

The Prof poured herself a cup of coffee. She glanced at Goldblatt again as she lifted the cup on to a saucer.

Sister Choy opened her ward diary and rested it in the crook of her arm.

'Shall we start?' said the Prof.

Goldblatt nodded to himself. Let's start, he thought. Let's fucking start.

The HO started. The first patient was a standard Fuertler's whom the Prof pretended to remember until it was obvious she didn't have the faintest idea who the patient was, and Emma helped her out. The next few were standard Fuertler's patients as well, and the Prof repeated the same piece of drama each time.

It would be interesting, Goldblatt thought, to know if she really thought she did remember them, or if she was consciously putting on an act each time. He sipped the last cold dregs of his coffee and wondered if the Prof even knew herself.

The Prof wanted to review all the test results for each patient, all the examination findings, demonstrating her complete mastery of the disease. She even picked up the Fuertler's files, for the first time since the Constantidis Affair, and checked each one, looking up at Ludo in satisfaction. Ludo watched in dazed rapture.

Goldblatt was getting bored. The Prof appeared to be cool, confident, and totally in control, which made him nauseated as well. He had come to the round, intending to be detached, controlled, and pleasant. Honestly. But he could feel it going. He could feel it slipping away.

And why did she keep glancing at him like that, and blinking, as if there was some little joke she wanted to share with him? Every time she glanced at him, he could feel something twist tighter inside him. He felt as if it was going to snap. Stop it, he wanted to shout. Stop with the blinking!

They had already spent half an hour, and not a single clinical decision had been made. It was nothing but checking to make sure the HO had run every sacred test and Ludo had filled every holy folder. Where was the medicine? It was as if the audit commission had come to town.

Was he really going to sit through this stuff for another three months? Or until the Prof, in her wisdom, decided it would be more convenient for her if he left?

Goldblatt turned his head and stared at her.

The Prof became conscious of his gaze. Her questioning of the HO became brisker.

The HO moved on to one of Dr Morris's patients and dealt with her in two minutes. The HO opened the next file.

'Sandra Hill,' she announced.

'Oh, yes,' said the Prof with immediate recognition, 'she's the lady with pulmonary fibrosis, isn't she?' She glanced at Goldblatt, as if to say that she could remember her patients if she wanted to.

If you couldn't remember a patient as sick as Sandra Hill, thought Goldblatt, you ought to hand back your stethoscope and recuse yourself from the profession.

'What's she in for again?'

'Pneumonia,' said Emma quickly. 'I told you, Prof. And Dr Goldblatt gave her a pneumothorax.'

'Of course,' said the Prof amiably. She looked at Goldblatt again. 'Well, it happens to all of us.'

To all of us, thought Goldblatt. When was the last time you put in a central line? Ever?

The Prof watched Goldblatt for a moment, wanting to be sure he had noticed her gracious commiseration. Then she looked back at the HO. 'Tell us about Sandra Hill.'

'Shall I go over everything?' asked the HO.

'Yes, please.'

The HO went over everything. When she got to the part about the pneumothorax, the Prof glanced at Goldblatt again, blinking in an expression of friendly sympathy that she desperately wanted him to see. But he didn't see it. He was leaning his head against the wall and staring at the ceiling again.

The Prof frowned. She let the HO keep speaking for a moment. Then she looked back at Goldblatt.

'Dr Goldblatt,' she said suddenly.

The HO stopped talking.

Goldblatt slowly turned his head and looked at the Prof.

It was twisting tighter, whatever it was inside him. The thing that was going to snap. Twisting. Twisting...

'What's up there, Dr Goldblatt?'

'Where?' said Goldblatt.

'On the ceiling,' said the Prof.

'Which ceiling?'

'That ceiling! That ceiling you keep looking at as if there's something terribly interesting up there. What's up there? I'm sure we'd all like to know.'

'Up there?' said Goldblatt.

'Yes, Dr Goldblatt.'

Goldblatt shrugged. 'A couple of lights.'

'Aren't you interested in this patient, Dr Goldblatt?'

Goldblatt gazed at the Prof in disbelief for a good ten seconds before he replied. The silence in the room grew heavy. Sister Choy lowered the communications book and laid it flat on her knees, as if she knew she wouldn't be needing it for a few minutes.

'I gave this patient a pneumothorax, Professor Small,' he said at last. 'What do you think? Wouldn't you be interested?'

'Yes. I would. I'd be very interested. I wouldn't be looking at the ceiling.'

'Where would you be looking?'

The Prof stared at him, trying to think of an answer. For a second she felt as if she couldn't breathe. What was happening? Everything had been going so well, and now everything was going so badly and it had all just happened in a second and she didn't know how or why or whose fault it was. She wanted to rewind. Rewind! To the part before the ceiling, please. No. She couldn't rewind. She could only go forward.

'I'd be looking at the patient,' said Goldblatt to help her out. 'I wouldn't be sitting here talking about her for two hours.'

The Prof twitched and continued to stare. Her myasthenia was playing up again. Goldblatt recollected that he never had managed to see if she developed gaze divergence late in the afternoon.

'We're just discussing the case, Malcolm,' said Dr Morris, in a despairing, half-hearted tone, as if he knew that anything he said now would be too little, too late, but he had to say it anyway.

'And I was just looking at the ceiling, Dr Morris. We all have our foibles.'

A frosty silence filled the office.

Ludo prodded the HO. The HO looked at her angrily.

'Go on,' Ludo hissed.

The HO went on. She brought the Prof up to date on Sandra Hill's admission.

'So Mrs Hill is better?' asked the Prof. She didn't really ask it. She stated it.

'A little bit better,' replied the HO guardedly.

'Well, she had a pneumonia and you've treated that. Dr Goldblatt gave her a pneumothorax but that's resolved. She's got pulmonary fibrosis and Dr de Witte is looking after that side of things. Why can't she go home?' demanded the Prof with perfect, icy logic.

Goldblatt clenched his jaw. Because she's dying, he replied silently. And if you'd bothered to come up and see her just once since she came in, you'd know it. Because she can't even get out of bed without oxygen. Because if she's going to go home she needs an oxygen supply and someone to look after her or she needs to go to a hospice, and the social worker, who might be able to organize some of this, but who's stopped coming to your round, Professor Small, because it's such a fucking waste of time, hasn't even been up to see her yet.

'Well, why can't she go home?' the Prof demanded again. 'Is there a reason? Or has no one bothered to arrange it?'

The HO sat there silently, looking at Goldblatt.

Goldblatt let his head fall back. It hit the wall with an audible clunk. Tighter it twisted... tighter... He stared at the ceiling, boring imaginary holes with his eyes through the ceiling tiles and electric wiring and air ducts and deep into the concrete of the floor above, still clenching his teeth to prevent himself speaking. Not trusting himself.

'Well?'

'She's still a bit too ill,' said Ludo hesitantly. 'I don't think we can send her home.'

'Then what are we doing for her?' demanded the Prof, glaring angrily at Goldblatt, who remained unresponsive to her stare. 'What are we *doing* for her?'

'There's nothing much we can do,' Ludo said.

Goldblatt frowned slightly. Ludo, the great evader, out in the open, taking the flak. For him. Not that she had much choice. Emma was sitting by and watching as his management of the case came under fire, smirking like a big blonde cat, and the only other person who could answer was the HO. Of course there was Sister Choy, and the physiotherapist, but it was unlikely they were going to say anything. And there was Dr Morris, but it wasn't his patient.

But at least she was doing it, thought Goldblatt.

'What do you mean there's nothing very much we can do for her?' demanded the Prof. 'Is she on steroids?'

'No,' said Ludo.

'Is she on cyclophosphamide?'

'No.'

'Has she had a Sorain infusion?'

'No.'

'No, no, no!' the Prof repeated in growing rage. 'Then who says there's nothing more we can do for her?'

'Dr de Witte,' murmured Goldblatt, without taking his eyes off the ceiling, barely moving his lips.

'Dr de Witte?' demanded the Prof, staring at Ludo.

'He took her off cyclophosphamide and steroids a couple of months ago,' said Ludo. 'He said her disease was so advanced there wasn't any—'

'*Give me those notes!*' cried the Prof.

Potemkin jumped up, tore the notes out of the HO's hands and presented them to the czarina. She stood protectively beside the Prof as the Prof started to flick feverishly through the folder. Dr Morris got up and looked over the Prof's other shoulder. Finally the Prof stopped at the most recent letter from Dr de Witte's clinic and lapped it up greedily. She looked up in triumphant scorn.

'Dr de Witte did *not* say that,' she announced, staring at Ludo with hostility. 'It was his SR, Dr Ramsay. Dr de Witte was away the last time she went to clinic. Dr Ramsay saw her instead. I don't trust Dr Ramsay. I wouldn't trust anything that doesn't come from Dr de Witte himself!'

Nothing like a personality cult, thought Goldblatt.

'Andrea,' said Dr Morris, who had read the letter over her shoulder. 'This assessment seems very reasonable.' He reached down and turned to the previous letter. 'And Dr de Witte says more or less the same thing himself at the previous visit.'

'I don't trust Dr Ramsay!' the Prof repeated, as if it were the one last thing in the world of which she was certain, shaking her head jerkily and clutching the notes to her breast.

'All right,' said Dr Morris, sounding like the exhausted parent of a spoiled three-year-old. He sat down. 'Why don't we arrange for Mrs Hill to go to Dr de Witte's clinic next week? We'll keep her in until we get his opinion. In the meantime, we'll see if we can set things up to discharge her after that, if it's appropriate. What day is his clinic?'

'Tuesday,' said Potemkin, seeing that the czarina was too preoccupied to answer.

Dr Morris turned to the HO. 'Will you organize that?' he said, thinking that the Prof could probably organize it a lot more quickly with Dr de Witte herself, if half the rumours about them were true. 'Find out if Dr de Witte will be there next week, and tell his SR that Professor Small has specifically asked for him to see Mrs Hill personally. All right? We want Dr de Witte to see her himself. If there's a problem, let me know and I'll give the SR a call.'

The HO nodded and scribbled a note on one of her bits of paper. Then she looked at the Prof, waiting for her to give the notes back. The Prof was staring vacantly at the floor, the notes still clutched to her breast. The HO didn't think it would be wise to prise them loose.

'Go on,' said Dr Morris quietly. 'Who's next?'

'Mrs Whittecombe,' said the HO.

'All right,' said Dr Morris, 'tell us about Mrs Whittecombe.'

'And in the meantime put her on cyclophosphamide and Prednisolone,' the Prof burst out, suddenly coming to life. 'We have to do something. How old is she?'

'Mrs Whittecombe?'

'No! Sandra Hill!'

'Forty-two,' said the HO.

'Forty-two! Forty-two!' shouted the Prof, as if this were the most harrowing age in God's catalogue. 'I can't just sit here doing nothing while a forty-two-year-old woman is dying.'

Goldblatt thought the Prof was underestimating herself. She had done a pretty good job of it over the last week.

'But we've... made her Not For Resuscitation,' stammered the HO.

'*Who* made her Not For Resuscitation?' demanded the Prof apoplectically.

Goldblatt closed his eyes.

'Dr Goldblatt,' whispered the HO.

'Dr Goldblatt! Dr Goldblatt had no right to do that. No right at all! Dr Goldblatt's going to have to answer to me about that. You make her For Resuscitation. Make her For Resuscitation right this minute.'

Right this minute? Another twist. Tighter... tighter...

'And start her on cyclophosphamide and Prednisolone.'

'But Andrea,' said Dr Morris, 'we were going to ask Dr de Witte to see her next week. If her condition's as advanced as Dr Ramsay suggested, then a few days more or less of treatment isn't going to make any difference.'

'I don't trust Dr Ramsay! She may be dead by next week, and Dr Ramsay will have killed her. I can't just stand by and do nothing while she dies.'

Yes, you can, thought Goldblatt. It was all any of them could do for her.

He had seen Sandra Hill every day for the past week. More than once every day. He had become accustomed to her tired smile and wry resignation. There was nothing he would have wanted more than to make her well. If he could have given her a new pair of lungs, he would have. He'd have given her his own. But he couldn't. He knew what she wanted. He had talked with her. He had sat on the edge of her bed and listened to her, even when she wasn't saying anything. He knew that she understood. She had come to the end. She had had every treatment she could have. She no longer felt angry. She no longer wondered why it was so unfair. She had been through so much. She was tired. When would peace come to her?

He didn't want to stand by and watch her die. But it was all he could do, the best he could do for her. Give her comfort as she died. Ease her suffering. Help her when the time came, if he could.

'All right,' said Dr Morris reluctantly, feeling more like a psychological crutch than ever and despising himself even as he allowed the Prof to lean on him. He turned to the HO. 'Put her on cyclophosphamide, twenty-five milligrams—'

'Fifty milligrams, Anthony.'

'Fifty milligrams. And Prednisolone – forty?'

'Sixty.'

'Sixty milligrams a day. All right?'

The HO stared at Dr Morris. Then she glanced at Goldblatt.

Ludo watched with horror. She knew what was going through the HO's mind. Goldblatt's latest principle, the most dangerous of all. Understand what you do. Understand what you do or don't do it at all.

Goldblatt met the HO's questioning eyes.

SNAP!

'No,' he said.

'Malcolm...' said Dr Morris plaintively.

'No,' said Goldblatt.

Dr Morris buried his face in his hands.

The Prof was staring at Goldblatt, speechless with rage, disbelief, and the old, bitter sense of inferiority that nothing she had achieved in her life had ever been quite able to bury.

'Professor Small,' Goldblatt said quietly, 'we treat patients... in order to treat patients. Not to treat ourselves. It's as hard for me to see a forty-two-year-old woman die as it is for you. But Sandra's still going to die. The drugs you want to give her, are they going to make her last days easier? Is that what you'd want? Someone to give you a drug as toxic as cyclophosphamide just so they could give themselves the illusion they were doing something?'

'I'm not—'

'I'm sorry. No.'

Goldblatt's tone was hard. What was wrong with her? He stood up. Something had taken control of him. He recognized the feeling, the same one that had swept over him in the interview at the Nailwright when Iron Balls had asked why he had done a law degree, and a minute later he had blown the top off his scalp and had told old Iron Balls exactly why he had done it. It was getting harder and harder to hold on to his head nowadays.

He found himself standing beside the whiteboard where he had drawn so many decision trees for the HO. But this one wasn't going to be for her.

'It's very simple, Professor Small.'

He drew. Calmly. Ferociously. He could hear nothing at all from anyone behind him in the time that it took him to complete it. The marker squeaked very faintly as he drew it over the surface. The time was endless and yet it was over before it began. It was outside time.

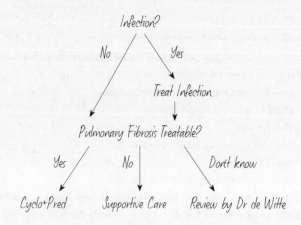

He turned around and stared straight at the Prof, sending a searingly cold gaze into her cloudy, veiled eyes.

'Where are we? We've treated Sandra's pneumonia, so we're here,' he said, turning back to the board and pointing at 'Supportive Care'. 'But because we all hate Dr Ramsay, we've moved to here,' he continued, drawing his finger across to 'Review by Dr de Witte'. 'But we're not... here!' he concluded, stabbing 'Cyclo+Pred' and pushing his finger hard into the words until they were broken and smeared and dead. 'We're not here.'

Goldblatt turned back to the Prof. She was looking away. Catatonic. A slight tremor rocked her body.

Goldblatt took his finger off the board. He dropped the marker and sat down.

There was an awful silence. It was as if a cloud of gas was choking everybody. Emma stared at the Prof in foreboding, desperately trying to work out whether this was going to make things better or worse for her.

'Go on,' said Dr Morris eventually to the HO in a hushed voice.

The HO looked at him.

'Mrs Whittecombe,' Dr Morris prompted her.

The HO nodded. 'Mrs Whittecombe,' she said hesitantly.

It took the HO about six minutes to get through the remaining patients. The only interruptions came from Dr Morris, who clarified a point here and there. The Prof was silent. She stared vacantly at a point on the floor beside one of the desk legs.

They went out on to the ward. Like any piece of show business, the round had started, so it had to be finished. Dr Morris conducted it, and the Prof stumbled along behind. She was silent. Her face was grey and her head trembled. She smiled automatically when the Fuertler's patients greeted her, as if even the acclaim of her adoring public could barely penetrate the haze of her injured self-absorption. Sister Choy hovered nearby, waiting to catch her if she fell.

When they came to Sandra Hill, the Prof just stood there as Dr Morris examined her. Sandra took off her oxygen mask and whispered Hello, and the Prof produced a fragile smile and kept it there, frozen in place, until they went on to the next bed.

As soon as they left the last patient, the Prof disappeared. Dr Morris, despising himself again, followed her. Goldblatt, Emma, Ludo, and the HO were left standing in the ward corridor with the notes trolley. There was a big sense of anticlimax in the air. Or it may have been preclimax. Goldblatt wasn't sure. But there was a climax lurking somewhere nearby, that much he knew, and this wasn't it.

'Coffee?' said Ludo.

Everything was wrong. They had trooped down to the cafeteria together. Emma hadn't run away from him as soon as she could. And then she actually spoke to him. She said, 'What do you want, Malcolm?' and he said, 'Coffee,' and she went over to the counter and bought it. That was bad. That was very bad. Goldblatt knew he was in trouble.

They sat there reflectively, the four of them, sitting around a table just like a real medical team in which everyone actually talked to each other.

Finally Ludo said to Goldblatt: 'You should have seen the Prof's face when you drew that decision tree.'

The HO nodded.

Ludo laughed cruelly. 'I thought she was going to cry.'

Emma couldn't suppress a guilty smile. Then her bleep went off. She got up to answer it at one of the phones on the wall.

That would be Dr Morris organizing a debrief, thought Goldblatt.

It wasn't.

Emma rushed out of the cafeteria, leaving her tea to get cold.

Ludo laughed again, watching her go.

'You didn't think it was so funny at the time,' said the HO.

'No one thought it was funny at the time,' said Ludo. 'Things like that are only funny later.'

True, thought Goldblatt. But not everyone gets the joke.

After ten minutes Emma came back.

'Guess who that was!' she said breathlessly, her face flushed.

No one guessed.

'It was the Prof! Guess what?'

No one guessed.

'She just gave me three concert tickets she happened to have spare for tonight! Isn't that great?'

'Three?' said Goldblatt. 'What a curious number.'

'Anyone want to go?' asked Emma, ignoring him.

'I'm on call,' said the HO.

'Come on, Ludo,' begged Emma, 'I don't have anyone to go with. The Prof will ask me what it was like tomorrow. She'll ask me who I went with, too.'

And what had happened to Emma, Goldblatt wondered. Suddenly she couldn't lie any more?

'What is it?' asked Ludo.

'Dvořák.'

'What's that?'

'Music,' said Emma. 'Come on. It'll be good.'

Ludo shrugged. 'All right.' She glanced pointedly at Goldblatt. 'I've got nothing else to do.'

'Great!' cried Emma.

Goldblatt watched in bemusement. What was she so excited about? Emma was almost jumping from foot to foot, clutching her white coat around her and flushing with pleasure.

'Isn't this great? It's fantastic! The Prof's not...' She stopped, suddenly realising that if she said any more everyone would know how desperate she had been for a sign that Prof wasn't going to crush her like a beetle.

'I'll bleep you at six,' she said to Ludo. 'We have to be there half an hour before it starts to pick the tickets up.'

'There's still one more ticket,' Goldblatt called after her as she left, but Emma didn't turn back.

Goldblatt looked at Ludo. She watched him for a moment from under her drooping lids. Then she threw back her hair. She grabbed her white coat and got up, saying something about a Dermatology admission.

'Malcolm?'

Goldblatt turned to the HO.

'What do we do about Sandra Hill?'

Goldblatt nodded. It was a good question.

Dr Morris had already answered it. When Goldblatt and the HO went back up to the ward they found Sandra's drug chart lying on the desk in the doctors' office. Dr Morris had been back and written up the Prednisolone and cyclophosphamide that the Prof had demanded.

Goldblatt shook his head in resignation. Sandra was dying anyway, but the unit had to live on. He held out the chart to the HO. 'Make sure she gets plenty of fluids. Write her up for three litres a day IV and keep an eye on her urine output. The cyclophosphamide will burn her bladder raw if she runs dry.'

The HO nodded and took the chart. 'Malcolm,' she said, 'I wouldn't have gone to that concert.'

'Thanks,' said Goldblatt.

'Did you hear what it was? Dvořák!'

Goldblatt smiled.

The HO grinned.

Not for the first time, Goldblatt felt like tousling her short red hair. 'Don't be too picky,' he said. 'It isn't every day you get a present from your Prof.'

Goldblatt was wrong. It seemed that the Prof was in an unusually generous mood, and Goldblatt himself wasn't going to be left out. His gift would be there the next morning, waiting in a sealed envelope on the desk in the doctors' office.

But in the meantime, there was one more night to get through.

35

HE GRABBED THE PHONE before the first ring had even finished.

He always woke like that, in a flash, no matter how deeply he had been sleeping. It was all the years of being woken. Then he always broke out in a sweat.

He answered automatically, feeling the familiar, clammy, cold disorientation sweep over him.

It was the HO's voice. She was on call in the hospital. It was one of the nights when Goldblatt was on call at home for the Prof's unit and Dermatology.

'Sorry to wake you, Malcolm,' she said.

'It's all right. What is it?'

'It's Sandra Hill. She arrested.'

Goldblatt closed his eyes for a second and shook his head.

'Malcolm?'

'Yes. Sandra arrested. What time is it?'

'Half past four. I resuscitated her, Malcolm.'

'You *resuscitated* her?' Goldblatt sat up. Beside him, Lesley stirred. They were still sleeping in the same bed although most of the time now it felt as if they were strangers in it. 'Wait a second.' He got up and took the phone out of the bedroom into the corridor.

'Malcolm?'

'Yes. OK. Go on.'

'What do I do next?'

'Where is she?'

'In her bed.'

'What does the medical registrar say?'

'He hasn't seen her.'

'What do you mean he hasn't seen her? I thought you said you called a an arrest.'

'No. I didn't call an arrest. I was on the ward and I found her and I resuscitated her before anyone called an arrest.'

'By yourself?' asked Goldblatt. Maybe he wasn't quite awake yet. 'You resuscitated her by yourself? What did you do?'

'I looked at her.'

'You *looked* at her?'

'Well, that wasn't all I did. I put her oxygen mask back on her as well. And she started breathing again.'

It was cold in the corridor. Goldblatt shivered. 'You have a gift. Do you know that? Have you ever thought about becoming a doctor?'

'Very funny.'

'What were you doing on the ward, anyway? What time did you say it is?'

'Half past four. I had to put a drip in someone.'

'And you say she's in her bed?'

'Yes.'

'And the med reg hasn't seen her?'

'No.'

'Is her blood pressure all right?'

'A hundred on sixty.'

'Is she conscious?'

'Yes,' said the HO. 'But she's in pain.'

'Chest pain?'

'Abdominal pain.'

'Have you felt her abdomen?'

'Yes.'

'And?'

'It feels sort of tight.'

'Bowel sounds?'

'I didn't listen for bowel sounds. Should I have listened for bowel sounds? Hold on and I'll go and—'

'No, just wait.' Goldblatt paused. 'Let me get the picture. Has she been vomiting?'

437

'I don't think so.'

'Does she need any analgesia?'

'I've given her diamorphine already.'

'For?'

'For the abdominal pain. She was in terrible pain, Malcolm. I had to give her something.'

'How much did you give her?'

'Five milligrams.'

'Intramuscularly?'

'Intravenously.'

'That's a big dose. Is she comfortable now?'

'I think so.'

'That blood pressure you mentioned, was that before you gave her the diamorph or after it?'

'Before.'

'Have you checked the BP since you gave her the diamorph?'

'No,' said the HO. 'Should I have checked her BP again? Hold on and I'll go and—'

'No, just wait.'

'Wait a second, Malcolm. One of the nurses is here. I'll get him to check it.'

Goldblatt heard the HO talking to one of the nurses. He tried to think. Decision trees are harder to draw in your brain at four in the morning than on a whiteboard at four in the afternoon.

'All right, Malcolm,' said the HO. 'The nurse is going to check it.'

'Get an ECG, a chest film, and an abdo X-ray. Make sure you tell the radiographer we're looking for a bowel perforation, so we're looking for free gas under the diaphragm, right? Tell the radiographer so they sit her up properly.'

'I don't think she can sit up, Malcolm.'

'Just tell them, all right? They'll prop her up. Get some blood gases as well. Make her nil orally.'

'I don't think she's going to be eating.'

'Just make her nil orally,' said Goldblatt impatiently. 'Make sure it's done so no one goes pouring anything down her throat. Are you writing this down?'

'Yes. ECG, chest film, and abdo film. Look for gas under the diaphragm. Blood gases. Nil orally. Anything else?'

'Get the surgical registrar to see her.'

There was silence.

'Did you hear me?'

'I can't ring the surgical registrar.'

'Why can't you?'

'I can't, Malcolm. You know what they'll say. She has to be seen by my registrar first.'

'No, she doesn't. Just ring the surg reg.'

'I can't, Malcolm. Can't it wait until you see her?'

'No, it can't wait until I see her. Listen, just do what—'

He stopped, imagining what it would be like to be an HO at four in the morning with that voice talking to you on the other end of the line.

'OK, that's fine. I'll ring him from here.'

'Thanks, Malcolm.'

'OK. And one other thing. Make her Not For Resuscitation.'

There was another silence on the phone.

'Did you hear what I said?'

'But we made her For Resuscitation today.'

'Well, you've saved her life now and it's time to make her Not For Resus again.'

'Malcolm,' said the HO, 'you know what happened today.'

'Listen. At this point, it's my decision. I'll take the consequences. I know what Sandra would want. She's Not For Resus. Right?'

'Can't it wait until you see her?'

'No. This can't wait. If she arrests before I see her I don't want anyone jumping up and down on her chest. Understand? She's Not For Resus. She doesn't get intubated. You don't shock her. She doesn't go to ITU. She gets fluids. She gets antibiotics. She gets pain relief. That's it. Nothing else. She's Not For Resus.'

The HO was quiet. 'I can't do it.'

'Why not?'

'You know the rules. A registrar has to do it.'

'Do it. Do it. Just write that I told you to do it.'

'That's circular, isn't it?'

Goldblatt realized he had created a monster.

'Do it! I'll fix it up as soon as I come in.'

'Are you coming in?'

'Of course I'm coming in.'

The tapping of his footsteps was loud as he crossed the dimly lit lobby of the seventh floor. Goldblatt went through the doors and on to the ward. A murmur came from somewhere. Somewhere else, a door closed. A piece of equipment beeped. His own footsteps. The sounds of a darkened ward at night. How many times had he heard them? How many times had he moved through this muffled night-time world?

He dropped his jacket off in the doctors' office. He went around the corner and saw the surgical registrar standing in front of the X-ray box on the wall behind the nurses' station. The fluorescent lights set into the front panel of the desk formed an island of light. Behind it, the X-ray box sent a white glow into the high-dependency area, where a nurse was checking a drip.

The surgical registrar looked around as Goldblatt came towards him. He was a big, cuddly-looking Asian guy, like a teddy bear, and the crumpled greens in which he had been sleeping bulged over the roll of fat around his middle.

'Malcolm Goldblatt,' said Goldblatt when he reached him, 'I'm the registrar looking after Sandra Hill. I'm the one who called you.'

'Ravi Menon,' said the surgical registrar.

'Thanks for coming up. I appreciate it. Have you seen her yet?'

'Just finished.'

'What do you think?'

Ravi Menon looked back at Sandra's X-ray. Goldblatt scrutinized it over his shoulder. It was a messy film. They hadn't managed to prop her up very far and she had slumped to one side and there were ribs everywhere. Even so, they could see that Sandra's abdomen was full of fat sausages of dilated, thin-walled, gas-filled bowel. If one of those sausages hadn't already burst its skin, it probably soon would.

Ravi Menon shrugged. 'Probably paralytic.'

'No bowel sounds?'

'Not that I could hear.'

'Perforation?'

Ravi Menon blew a puff of air out between his lips, shaking his head. 'Look at that film. How can you tell?'

The nurse came out of the high-dependency area and passed them silently, heading for a storage room.

'If she's perforated, would you operate on her?' asked Goldblatt.

Ravi Menon puffed again. 'She's sick. I met your house officer. She's got something wrong with her lungs, hasn't she? Your house officer was getting gases.'

'Pulmonary fibrosis. She's on forty per cent oxygen all the time.'

'Could she survive an operation? You tell me. You're the physician.'

'Unlikely,' said Goldblatt.

'Well...'

Ravi Menon turned away from the viewing box and sat down at the desk of the nurses' station with Sandra's notes in front of him.

'Why's she got pulmonary fibrosis?' he asked as he opened the notes.

'Fuertler's Syndrome.'

'Never heard of it. They get a lot of this?'

'Not a lot.'

'I'll see her again later today. Let us know if she gets fit enough for an operation. I'll write something in the notes.'

'Thanks,' said Goldblatt.

The HO came around the corner.

'Malcolm,' she said.

'Hi.'

'I'm sorry to have to get you in here.'

'You made the house officer's mistake.'

'What? Waking the registrar?'

'No. Resuscitating the patient.'

The HO managed a laugh. She was pale and drained, with dark smudges under her eyes. She looked as if she was going to keel over and fall flat on her face, squashing her already squashed nose even more.

All she needed was a bowl of bean soup in front of her.

'Have you got other stuff to do?' asked Goldblatt.

'There's a drip up here again. And I have to write up some drugs on someone the SHO's just admitted from Casualty. And they just rang me from some other ward about a patient who's having chest pain.' The HO pulled a piece of paper out of her pocket. She frowned, turning the paper upside down and then back to front. The writing on it consisted of names and numbers, and went in all directions.

'Have you been to bed?'

The HO narrowed her eyes and looked around furtively. 'Bed? What's that?'

'What happened with Sandra?'

'A nurse found her on the ground next to her bed. She must have tried to get up.'

'And?'

'I was in the next room and they called me in to look at her. I put the oxygen back on her face and she started breathing again.'

'Did she have a pulse when you found her?' asked Goldblatt.

The HO frowned.

'You know, a pulse?'

'I know what you mean.'

'Did you feel one? Did you check?'

'The nurse said she couldn't feel one.'

'But did *you* feel one?'

'She started breathing again, Malcolm!'

'I hate to say this, but I don't *think* she had an arrest.'

'You mean I didn't resuscitate her?'

'You normally have to do more than put an oxygen mask on a patient for it to count as a resuscitation.'

Ravi Menon glanced up from the notes and grinned.

'I really thought I resuscitated her,' said the HO. 'I've never resuscitated anyone.'

'You'll get your chance,' said Goldblatt.

The HO shook her head bitterly, as if she had been going to cut a notch in her stethoscope. She tried one last time. 'I'm sure I resuscitated her,

Malcolm, really. Are you *sure* I didn't?'

Goldblatt turned to look at Sandra's X-ray again.

'Do you need me?' said the HO. 'Only I've got this drip to do and there's still that patient with the chest pain and the patient from Casualty.'

'No, go on.'

The HO headed for the supply room to get a cannula for the drip. Goldblatt went to see Sandra.

The glow of a light filtered out from behind the screens that were drawn around Sandra's bed. Goldblatt saw a pair of frightened eyes watching from one of the other beds in the gloom. He smiled reassuringly as he went past. The patients in the other two beds were pretending to sleep. But who could sleep while doctors, nurses, radiographers, and X-ray machines as big as elephants spent the whole night going to and from the bed in the corner? Who could sleep while someone there was dying?

He went behind the screen. Sandra's eyes were closed. A nurse was checking her blood pressure. You never really got to know the nurses who worked nights as their regular shift. Goldblatt had seen her a couple of times when he had been on call before. He waited until she finished. The nurse let out the pressure from the cuff, took the stethoscope out of her ears, and turned around.

'Malcolm Goldblatt,' he said. 'I'm the registrar looking after Sandra.'

'Hi.'

'Is she comfortable?'

The nurse looked at Sandra. 'I think so.'

'What's the BP?'

'Eighty on fifty'

Goldblatt nodded. Not too bad, considering the dose of diamorphine the HO had walloped her with. He picked up the charts and examined them while the nurse stood by. He saw the HO's five milligrams of diamorphine timed, dated, and signed off. He flicked through the charts for a moment longer.

'Has she got a catheter in?' he asked.

'No.'

'Would you mind organizing that after I finish?'

'Certainly,' said the nurse.

'Thanks.' He handed the charts back to the nurse, who took out her pen to record the blood pressure.

He went to the head of the bed. Sandra was breathing evenly behind her mask, knocked out by the diamorphine. The oxygen made a bubbling noise in the background. The light above her shone straight down on Sandra's face and Goldblatt reached up and angled it away.

'Sandra,' he said.

Sandra breathed. Goldblatt shook her shoulder gently. Her head lolled a little.

'Sandra.'

Her eyelids fluttered.

Goldblatt smiled down at her. 'How are you feeling, Sandra?'

She mumbled something.

'All right?'

Sandra nodded. Her head moved slightly. 'All right,' she mumbled.

'Have you got any pain anywhere?'

Sandra shook her head.

'Is your breathing all right?'

Sandra didn't answer.

'I'm just going to have a look at you.'

He pulled aside the sheet that covered her and examined her briefly. Her belly was tight and distended, and when he pressed on it gently she winced.

'Does that hurt?'

Sandra nodded. Her eyes were closed and she was drifting in and out of sleep.

Goldblatt laid his stethoscope on the skin of Sandra's belly, just beside her umbilicus. He looked at his watch and listened for a full minute. Nothing. Not a single one of the bowel sounds you normally hear plentifully gurgling and rumbling away when you put your stethoscope to a healthy abdomen. Silence in the belly. Silence of the grave, as one of his surgery lecturers used to put it.

He pulled the sheet over her again.

'Sandra,' said Goldblatt. He shook her shoulder gently. 'Sandra.'

Sandra's eyes opened reluctantly.

'Sandra, you haven't got any pain?'

Sandra shook her head. Her eyes closed again.

Goldblatt hesitated, wanting to explain. But she wouldn't understand, the diamorphine had muffled everything, her perception of pain, her ability to think, consciousness. He looked at her. Under her oxygen mask, the skin of her nose was thickened and pocked with Fuertler's. Her face was scarred and puckered.

And he didn't know, even after all these years, after all the patients he had seen pass by before him. How important was it to know that you were about to die? That the time had come. How important was it to know why it was going to happen?

But Sandra knew already. She had known for days. For weeks, probably.

'Sandra,' Goldblatt murmured. He stroked her forehead, brushing back her hair.

Sandra breathed steadily. He was talking to himself.

'We'll keep you comfortable, Sandra.'

He adjusted her oxygen mask. He reached over to the dimming switch and dimmed the light right down. Then he stroked her forehead again, gazing down at her. He took a deep breath and turned to go.

The nurse was still there, watching him.

He stopped for a second, then smiled self-consciously. 'We'll keep her comfortable,' he said stupidly, and the nurse nodded.

Goldblatt went back to the desk at the nurses' station. Ravi Menon had gone. The HO had gone. He could hear the sound of a bedpan being flushed in the sluice room. He looked at his watch. Almost six o'clock. He looked out of the window on the other side of the ward. Still dark outside.

He pulled Sandra's notes across the desk and opened them. He looked over the ECG that the HO had done, and checked the arterial blood gas results that she had recorded. He read over the HO's note. It started with 'Patient arrested' and ended with 'NOT FOR RESUSCITATION ACCORDING TO DR GOLDBLATT'. She had underlined 'ACCORDING TO DR GOLDBLATT' three times. Goldblatt made a mental note to tell the HO that underlining didn't reduce circularity. He read Ravi Menon's note. Towards the end it said 'Unfit for surgery according to Med Reg'. It was true. All of it was indisputably true. He had said these things. It was funny how people took you seriously when you told them something. You say words and they become reality. Goldblatt took out his pen to add some more reality to the record.

When he was finished he turned to the front registration page of Sandra's notes. He found the number of the person listed as her next of kin, Mrs Jones, one of her sisters. He had met her briefly a couple of times on the ward.

He dialled the number. He heard it ring, imagining the darkened rooms of a house where its unwanted, ominous tones were cruelly slicing through the early-morning silence.

Goldblatt found the HO in the doctors' mess, slumped forward with her face in yesterday's newspaper, when he left the ward. The on-call night had only a couple more hours to run.

'Coffee?' said Goldblatt.

The HO jumped. 'Where?'

'It's Platonic,' said Goldblatt. 'The coffee hasn't been made yet. But it exists in our minds, as the form of coffee...'

The HO slumped forward again.

'We can make it real, if we want. Do we want?'

'Yes,' came the HO's muffled reply.

'I thought so,' said Goldblatt.

The HO keeled over sideways on the sofa.

'What happened with the man with chest pain you were going to see?' asked Goldblatt as he waited for the water to boil.

'It got better,' said the HO, dragging herself up to a sitting position.

'What was it?'

'No idea.'

'How did you treat it?'

'I didn't treat it. It went away by itself.'

'It's a gift,' said Goldblatt. 'I keep telling you.'

The HO shook her head wearily.

'Milk?' said Goldblatt.

'Yes, please.'

Goldblatt sniffed the milk. 'No, I don't think so.'

'How's Sandra?' asked the HO.

'The same. Five milligrams of diamorph intravenously is a big slug. For someone that size you should start with two point five.'

'I always give five milligrams,' said the HO.

'What do you mean, you *always* give five milligrams?' Goldblatt looked at her incredulously. The HO was too new to the business to 'always' do anything.

'Dr Warren always gives five milligrams.'

'Who's Dr Warren, the local euthanasathist?'

'No,' replied the HO stoutly, 'he's one of the medical registrars. He says you always need five milligrams to get rid of real pain.'

'And real blood pressure. And real breathing. You don't need five milligrams intravenously. Not in someone that size. Intramuscularly, maybe. But intravenously, hardly ever. Maybe with a severe MI.'

'But she was in pain, Malcolm! You should have seen her.'

'You can always give more. Start with two point five next time if you're giving it intravenously, all right? See how that goes, and check her BP and respiratory rate before you give any more.'

The HO looked discontented.

'Say: "I always start with two point five milligrams when I give diamorphine intravenously,"' said Goldblatt.

'No.'

'Say it.'

'Why should I?'

'Because the water just boiled and you won't get any coffee otherwise.'

'I always start with two point five milligrams when I give diamorphine intravenously.'

'Good.'

'Sometimes,' said the HO.

Goldblatt brought the coffees over and sat down beside her.

'I did an ECG on the man with chest pain.' The HO pulled a spooled ribbon of paper out of the pocket of her white coat. 'I wasn't sure if it showed anything.'

'Did you check it with the med reg?'

The HO shook her head. 'The pain went.'

Goldblatt held out his hand and the HO passed him the ECG. He unwound the long strip of paper and examined the saw-toothed trace.

'Inferior myocardial infarction,' he pronounced after a few seconds. He rewound the ECG strip and held it for the HO to take.

She stared at him in horror. 'But the pain went!'

'Pain does sometimes.'

'So you mean he had a heart attack? You mean he's had an infarct and I just left him there?'

'He's had an infarct at some point in the past.' Goldblatt paused. 'They're old changes on the ECG. Years old, probably.'

The HO closed her eyes in relief. 'Not last night?'

'Not last night.' Goldblatt held out the strip. 'You must have seen it on his old ECGs.'

'I didn't look at his old ECGs.'

'That'll explain why you didn't see it.'

'Should I go and check it against his old ECGs?'

'Yes,' said Goldblatt. 'You should always check an ECG against old ECGs. In fact, you should always check any test against old tests.'

'I should, shouldn't I?' said the HO, as if realizing a truth that had long eluded her.

'Yes, you should. And if you find any changes you can't understand, you should call your med reg.'

'Even if the pain goes?'

'Especially if the pain goes.'

The HO nodded. She got up.

'Not now. It's an old infarct. Trust me. The old ECGs aren't going to change if you drink your coffee before you check them.'

The HO sat down. She sipped her coffee. Goldblatt watched her. She looked ill with exhaustion.

'Got anything on tonight?' he said.

The HO nodded.

'What?'

She shrugged.

'Are you going?'

'Don't know. Too fucking tired to think about it.'

'We need to get you home on time,' said Goldblatt.

The HO laughed bitterly.

Goldblatt didn't blame her for laughing. How many times had he said that to her over the past couple of months? And how many times had she actually been able to do it?

'How old are you?' he asked suddenly.

'Twenty-three,' she said.

'I was right.'

'What were you right about?'

'Lots of things.'

The HO shook her head. 'Is Sandra going to die?'

'Yes. Her bowel will perforate. It's perforated already, I think. Nothing we can do. She wouldn't survive an operation. And even if she did ...' Goldblatt shrugged helplessly. 'What for?'

The HO nodded. 'Why did her bowel dilate like that?'

'It's paralytic. It stopped contracting.'

'Why?'

Goldblatt shrugged. 'The Fuertler's? Hypoxia? Who knows? It's pre-terminal. Dying people have to die of something.'

Goldblatt listened to what he had just said. It sounded like a law. He was too tired to think of a name for it.

They finished their coffees.

'Come on,' said Goldblatt. 'Let's go up and see what's happening with her, then you can go and check that patient's ECGs.'

The screens around Sandra's bed bulged, outlining the shapes of the people sitting on the other side of them. There were five members of the family around Sandra's bed. The nurses had been trying to organize a side room for Sandra to die in, but she was still in the four-bed room where everyone had been awake since the HO found her on the floor at four in the morning.

The family looked around as Goldblatt and the HO put their heads in through the gap in the screen. Mrs Jones got up. 'Hello,' she said. She introduced the other members of the family, starting with Sandra's mum. Goldblatt shook her hand.

'Should we have a talk?' said Goldblatt.

'I think Mum would appreciate that,' said Mrs Jones.

Goldblatt took Mrs Jones and her mum to the doctors' office. The others stayed by Sandra's bedside. Sandra's mum was a squat woman in her sixties who looked as if she had put on her best clothes. She was wearing a hat and clutching a small white Bible. Goldblatt invited the two women to sit down, but neither did, so Goldblatt didn't either. Mrs Jones held her mum's elbow all the time he was speaking to them.

Goldblatt had ended up being very frank with Mrs Jones on the phone when he had rung her earlier. She had demanded it. She had said to him bluntly: 'Sandra's dying, isn't she?' Mrs Jones was the kind of person who wants to know the facts, undiluted, unconcealed. Goldblatt gave them to her. It was people's right to demand as much or as little as they wanted. It wasn't his place to decide how much that was for them.

Sandra's mum wasn't like Mrs Jones, you could see that at a glance. Sandra's sister wanted a crisp and certain answer. Sandra's mum didn't believe in crisp and certain answers, and therefore didn't ask for one.

But she knew. She didn't need Goldblatt to tell her.

'Well, it be in the Lord's hands,' she said in a strong Caribbean accent, after Goldblatt had assured her that they would keep Sandra comfortable as they watched to see what happened. 'If the Lord want Sandra, he take her.'

Goldblatt nodded.

'It been a terrible hard life for Sandra, doctor. She been *so* sick. *So* many years. Sandra is my daughter. I love her, doctor. But she *so* sick. It be best for her now. The Lord take her.'

Goldblatt nodded again. Sandra's mum wasn't crying. She was looking straight into Goldblatt's eyes, and Goldblatt was looking straight back into hers. Soft brown eyes, bedded in densely wrinkled skin.

'Come on, Mum,' said Mrs Jones, and she led her by the elbow back to Sandra's bedside.

The HO was still there, speaking softly to the other family members. Sandra had slipped into a pattern of terminal respiration, taking a stuttering series of two or three deep, snoring breaths every minute or so, without breathing at all in between.

The oxygen was bubbling. It was pointless, but Goldblatt left it on. To turn it off in front of the family now, when Sandra was still breathing, would be too cruel.

Sandra snored in deeply. She had slipped down the pillows, and her head was slumped to one side. Goldblatt leaned over to straighten her up. He put his left arm under her back. Her head lolled against his shoulder. He felt her warm, listless weight in his arms, and braced to pull her up.

Sandra snored again. The breath cut itself short.

Goldblatt was still holding her. He frowned. Surreptitiously, he slid his hand on to Sandra's neck and felt gently for her carotid pulse. He probed deeper, trying to detect it. Then he glanced at the HO, who met his eyes questioningly.

Goldblatt straightened Sandra up. He arranged the pillows behind her head. Then he stepped back and smiled briefly at Sandra's mum. The family continued to sit around the bed as the oxygen bubbled, waiting for Sandra's next breath. Goldblatt left them behind the screens. The HO followed him out. In the corridor, they met one of the nurses coming towards them.

'Sandra Hill has just died,' Goldblatt said quietly to the nurse. 'The family doesn't know yet. Could you go in there and have a look at her, and then say you're going to get the doctor? I'll give them a few minutes, and then come back to declare her dead.'

In the doctors' office, the HO perched on one of the desks.

'You all right?' asked Goldblatt.

She nodded.

'Really?' He wondered if the ghosts of Mr Sprczrensky and the VIPoma were on their way back, if this was going to be the moment the HO broke.

'I'm OK. It was time for her, Malcolm. I'm glad she was Not For Resus.'

Goldblatt smiled.

The HO looked at him quizzically. 'She died in your arms.'

Goldblatt thought about it. So she had. The only one of his patients who had ever done it.

'She would have liked that,' said the HO.

'Right. Like she liked me giving her a pneumothorax.'

'No, Malcolm. She would have. You were her protector.'

Goldblatt glanced at her. The HO's tone was certain. As if she knew. But the HO never knew anything.

But maybe sometimes she did.

Goldblatt nodded. 'Thanks,' he said quietly. He frowned. For a moment he didn't trust himself to speak. You don't cry when your patients die.

The HO was silent. Then she noticed something on the desk. 'You've got a letter.' She picked up a small yellow envelope and handed it to Goldblatt.

Where had that come from? He had been here only ten minutes earlier with Sandra's mother and sister.

'I'm going,' said the HO. 'I've got to check those ECGs. I'll see you at the Grand Round.'

'Maybe.'

'Aren't you coming?'

'I'll see.'

'Come on, Malcolm, you've got to come. Emma's presenting. Can you imagine what will happen if she makes a mistake? It's worth going just to see that.'

Goldblatt smiled.

The HO looked at him seriously. 'I'll have to write a death certificate for Sandra, won't I?'

'Have you ever written one?'

The HO shook her head.

Of course not, thought Goldblatt. No one dies on a Fuertler's unit. Until today, anyway.

'We'll talk about it later. Go on, I'll go back and declare her. Check that ECG and then get some breakfast. I'll see you at the Grand Round.'

The HO left. Goldblatt picked up the envelope and stared at it. His name was handwritten on the front. Nothing else. He turned it over. Blank on the back. Sealed.

Goldblatt opened the envelope. It contained a piece of yellow notepaper. He unfolded it. He recognized the curly, strangely girlish writing.

Dr Goldblatt

On reflection over the past week and after yesterday's ward round I am now convinced that the unit's best interests are served by you leaving. May I suggest today as a suitable date. I will inform Mr Titherington in Human Resources to make the appropriate arrangements in lieu of your notice.

Andrea Small

Goldblatt let the note fall on the table in front of him.

He went out to shine a torch in Sandra Hill's eyes and lay his stethoscope on her ravaged, now-silent chest, and declare that she was dead.

36

THE GRAND ROUND HAD started by the time Goldblatt reached the lecture theatre on the ground floor of the medical school building. He had got caught up on the ward, checking the Book of Time and then cancelling all four of the admissions for the day. There were no beds. Even Sandra Hill's death didn't free one up. Her bed had been borrowed, taking the total over the unit quota, and Sister Choy was taking it back.

Goldblatt slipped into the lecture theatre via the back door. It was a large hall with an aisle running down the middle of steeply tiered seats. He went about halfway down the steps to an empty seat on the aisle. Ludo and the HO were sitting together further down. He could see the back of the Prof's head in the front row. A tall man was sitting next to her. No one else was near them. Only speakers sit in front rows.

The lights in the lecture theatre were low. Emma was speaking, standing behind a small lectern with a microphone on the platform at the front of the hall. A slide was projected on the wall above her head.

She was halfway into the fascinating case of Mrs Grahame. Emma ran through a sequence of slides. She spent most of the time half turned from the audience, looking at the wall behind her and reading them. A familiar technique that Goldblatt had seen practised by hundreds of medical lecturers in the past.

At one point Emma interrupted her presentation, and the man who was sitting next to the Prof, a histopathologist, got up and took the control from her hand. A big slide in pink and blue, with thousands of tiny nuclear dots, appeared on the wall. He ran through a couple of slides showing the microscopy of skin biopsies from Mrs Grahame, commenting on the changes typical of Fuertler's Syndrome.

Emma took over again. She went through the record of Mrs Grahame's remarkable recovery under the miraculous delayed influence of Sorain. Goldblatt recognized the format of the pages from the Fuertler's files projected in the slides, showing the changes in Mrs Grahame's skin test scores.

Goldblatt looked around. The lecture hall was about a third full. Consultants in suits, junior doctors in white coats. To his left were a couple of rows of medical students taking notes to add to the stacks of paper they must already have at home.

Goldblatt watched the audience. He often did that when he got bored at lectures or performances. It was the alonest kind of aloneness, being a spectator of spectators. It was like seeing the event reflected in a changing, human mirror. But people don't like it. If they noticed him they'd give him a confused or angry glance, and then they kept looking back at him, unable to forget that he was there. By the time that happened there was no point watching them any more. Goldblatt understood. It was as if he had violated some unwritten law, excluded himself from the collective, unspoken agreement that everyone was going to watch what was happening on the stage and not have to worry about keeping their guard up against other people watching them. No one likes that. No one likes people who set themselves apart. Never have. If you're not careful they end up burning you at the stake.

The audience gazed at Emma's slides. Some people sipped coffees they had brought with them. The medical students wrote. Goldblatt stopped watching. Medical audiences were never very interesting.

Emma's part had ended. She had presented Mrs Grahame's case and had also described the lone case report from Brazil that she had found in her literature search. She left the platform. The Prof got up and took her place. She switched the projector off and turned the main lights up. The Prof was wearing a grey-brown suit, and the silk scarf around her neck was yellow and orange. Her colours. Never blue, for some reason. Or red.

Question time. The first was a dumb question about whether these kind of skin changes were typical for Fuertler's Syndrome. Maybe the Prof had planted that one. She got to laugh indulgently and say 'Nothing is typical in Fuertler's Syndrome,' which would have made a good sound bite. If anyone had wanted one.

There were other questions. Not all were so benign.

'Your patient had Sorain,' someone was saying from the audience, 'and she improved, although she improved a long time after the Sorain was given. You yourself have just said that Fuertler's Syndrome runs an unpredictable course, Professor Small. What evidence is there that the Sorain actually contributed to this patient's improvement?'

'I think Dr Burton has reviewed the evidence very thoroughly,' replied the Prof.

'Dr Burton presented a single case report, Professor Small, and mentioned two other cases among your own patients, about which she told us virtually nothing. Is that all there is? What studies have been done looking at the effect of Sorain over this time frame?'

'I don't believe there are any studies looking at the delayed effects of Sorain.' The Prof looked away, hoping to spot a hand in the air somewhere else.

'I'm sorry, Professor Small. Can I follow this up?'

The Prof smiled icily, wishing someone would find a pillow and smother this awful man. She didn't recognize him. He looked about the right age to be an SR. Maybe he had heard about the Grand Round and come from a different hospital to see it, as people sometimes did when some of her other colleagues were presenting. The Prof would have regarded it as a profound compliment if his attitude weren't so obviously a profound insult.

'You have two cases among your own patients, but you've failed to tell us how many patients in total you have, so how are we to judge whether that's a significant number? Two out of how many, Professor Small?'

'It's three, actually,' said the Prof through gritted teeth. 'There's the main case as well as two others.'

'Out of how many?'

'I don't claim to have done an exhaustive review,' said the Prof, even though that was exactly what Emma had done. 'These are simply case reports.'

'But Professor Small...' persisted the awful man.

The Prof looked reluctantly at him again. Her ex-SR, she suddenly thought, had probably sent him along to make trouble.

'If these are simply case reports, and you have no idea how frequently this effect is seen, what exactly are we to conclude? Presumably, you'll be using more and more Sorain, hoping for this kind of delayed improvement. And I'm just asking what scientifically plausible evidence you have for it. No one can explain why the drug works even in the short term. Correct me if I'm wrong. People talk about inhibition of cytokine receptors, but as I understand it the evidence for that is very thin. So can you tell us what evidence you have of this delayed effect from solid, double-blinded, placebo-controlled trials in Fuertler's patients? Have you done any such studies? And if not, are you planning to do any?'

The Prof glanced nervously at the second row, where Professor Gold, the Director of the Department of Medicine, was sitting.

'Well, this is precisely the difficulty with Fuertler's Syndrome,' she said. Her head began to wobble. 'This is precisely the difficulty. It's so rare and complex a disease. As a result, we have a lack of therapies. Indeed, there are subgroups of patients with different manifestations of the disease. Subgroups of subgroups, indeed. We should be developing appropriate treatments for each of these different groups. But it's almost impossible to get a sufficiently large number of patients together even to look at the disease as a whole, not to mention the subgroups. The complexity of getting such a study to run is prohibitive. I've been trying to run any number of studies on all kinds of aspects of the illness and I can't even...'

Goldblatt gazed at the Prof. She looked frail, cadaverous, and anxious, and even now she might have aroused his pity. But he just felt bored. In ten years, she'd be giving the same answer, moaning about the rarity and complexity of Fuertler's Syndrome, and the difficulty of arranging proper studies, singing the praises of anecdotalism because she didn't know the techniques or have the inventiveness to do anything else.

Answer it scientifically or don't even bother, Goldblatt thought in disgust. Learn how to cook or get out of the kitchen. But stop *whining*.

'... and if people aren't prepared to put the resources behind this kind of work because they don't think something as rare and as complex as Fuert—'

Goldblatt stood up. Andrea Small stopped in mid-word. She hadn't even realized he was in the hall.

Heads turned towards him. There was a perplexed, bemused silence.

Goldblatt began to walk up the stairs to the back of the lecture theatre, plodding deliberately up one step after the other. The silence persisted, broken only by his footsteps, which echoed like the sound of slow hand-claps. He could feel everyone watching him, wondering who he was. The spectator of the spectators had turned into the spectacle.

He reached the exit and closed the door behind him.

He went to the outpatients' clinic and sat down in his consultation room and waited for the first patient to appear. Something was happening. The world was changing colour. It was going all rosy and tawny, as if Titian had been in overnight to do a paint job. And the old Jewish lady was there! Who had invited her? But there she was, sitting in a corner of the clinic room, raising her fist like a sultana, and saying she was a fighter.

'I'm a fighter,' she was saying to him. 'Are you a fighter, Dr Goldblatt?'

Goldblatt was too dumbfounded to reply. What was this, symbols asking questions? Symbols talking back? Something had obviously gone horribly wrong in his id, and at some point, he knew, he would have to go down there and sort it out. He would have to put the old Jewish lady back up on the wall where she belonged. But he couldn't face it right now. He was too tired. He had been up since four-thirty and he hadn't managed to get much sleep before that. He hadn't had much sleep for days, not since that last horrible conversation with Lesley that had left him wondering what she was going to do. Now he had that familiar day-after-the-night-on-call feeling, the light-headedness and the dull weight dragging him down.

'No,' he said to the old Jewish lady eventually, 'I'm not a fighter.'

The old Jewish lady looked at him with disappointment. 'Not a fighter?' she said.

'So?' replied Goldblatt.

The old Jewish lady turned up her nose as if she had just smelled a piece of carp that was going off. But she didn't go away. Even when the patients started to come in she stayed on her chair in the corner, her nose turned up in the air, behaving very properly, not saying a word, not interfering, yet still there. Goldblatt preferred her when her twig-like arm was raised and her sultana-fist clenched. He tried to ignore her, and made an effort to concentrate on the patients in front of him. But he couldn't resist slipping her a glance now and then, while he was filling in a request for a blood test or dictating a letter between patients, and the old Jewish lady knew how to exploit her opportunities. Goldblatt should have known she would be a grandmaster of the game of guilt. He didn't stand a chance. Her nose went higher in the air each time Goldblatt threw a glance at her, as if the smell was getting riper.

And then he came to the last patient on his list. A twenty-six-year-old woman with newly diagnosed rheumatoid arthritis. Goldblatt had the notes in front of him. He stared at them. For a moment he thought he just wasn't going to be able to get up and call her in. Suddenly it was too big. How could he do it?

Because it was the end, wasn't it? The last one he would ever see. And Sandra Hill was the last of his patients who would ever die. And that night had been the last time he would ever walk on to a muffled, darkened ward. Suddenly, he *knew* it.

Maybe if he just stared at the notes, maybe if he didn't do anything but just kept staring at them, he could stop everything, and he could sit here in this clinic, and be a doctor, for ever.

Then he heaved himself up, went to the door, and called her name.

She came in just as if she was a regular patient. It was funny, thought Goldblatt, how rarely you know the role you're playing in someone else's drama. Or never know it, perhaps. The consultation went quickly. Her arthritis wasn't well controlled, and Goldblatt changed her drugs.

'We'll see you again in four weeks,' he said after explaining what to expect with the new drug. He handed her a prescription, a pile of blood test forms, and an appointment slip. 'You'll be feeling a lot better. I'm sure of it.'

'I hope so, doctor.' She took the forms and opened her bag with swollen, painful fingers.

'You will. You'll notice a huge change.'

'Will you be here, doctor?'

'I'm afraid not.'

The patient looked up. 'Why?'

Goldblatt hesitated. It wasn't the first time he had told a patient in a clinic that he wouldn't be there the next time she came back to see him. He had done it hundreds of times. Doctors in training are always moving from job to job, and long-term patients get used to seeing new faces and having to go through their entire stories from start to finish, and hearing contradictory prognoses every second or third time they come in.

That wasn't the reason. Not this time. But she didn't need to know the grisly details.

Goldblatt smiled apologetically. 'We have to move around through jobs. It's part of our training.'

'Really?'

He nodded.

'Well, good luck, doctor,' said the patient, standing up.

'Thanks.' Goldblatt got up and opened the door for her. 'The new drug will do wonders. We'll see you in four weeks.'

She left.

Goldblatt closed the door. He stood behind it for a second and listened to it close.

He sat down and pulled out his Dictaphone. He dictated a note to her GP. The door opened a fraction. Dr Morris peered in.

'Finished? No more patients?'

'No,' said Goldblatt, throwing a glance at the old Jewish lady. The old Jewish lady sniffed, pretending to be insulted. Goldblatt ignored her. He knew the tricks of the game as well as she did. The old Jewish lady was dead. She understood perfectly well that she wasn't a patient any more.

Dr Morris came in and sat down on the other side of the desk.

'Look,' said Goldblatt, 'if it's about the Broderip–Anderssen Principle...'

Dr Morris grinned. But only for a second. He looked seriously at Goldblatt, as if there were something difficult he wanted to say but he didn't know how. Goldblatt was starting to feel worried. Maybe some horrible skin lesion had developed on his face since the last time he had seen himself in the mirror, and Dr Morris didn't know how to tell him it was there. He had to restrain himself from jumping up and running out to the men's toilets to check his face in the mirror. But even if he did run into the men's toilets, to judge by past experience, Dr Morris would probably just follow him in.

'Has the Prof said anything to you?' Dr Morris asked eventually.

Goldblatt was amused. That was a pretty limp way to get into it.

'She fired me,' he said flatly.

'I know. She told me she was going to.'

'When?'

'Last night. After the round.' Dr Morris paused. 'Well, that was one to remember, anyway.' He laughed, relieved it was out in the open. 'That decision tree – what was that? It was like something out of Monty Python. "This is where we are, but because we all hate Dr Ramsay we've moved to here." Fucking unbelievable, Malcolm.'

Goldblatt laughed. 'The Dead Decision Tree sketch.'

'The Dead Professor sketch.'

'The Dead Career sketch.'

They stopped laughing at that.

'She died, by the way,' said Goldblatt. 'Sandra Hill.'

Dr Morris nodded. 'I heard.'

'She didn't suffer. Someone gave her a five milligram slug of diamorph intravenously.'

Dr Morris raised an eyebrow. 'That must have helped things along.'

'Well...' Goldblatt drew a breath. Then he looked at Dr Morris speculatively. 'How long until the Prof retires?'

'About ten years, I suppose.'

'That's not too bad. You can survive ten years.'

'I don't know.'

'Of course you can. Ten years isn't long. Blink of an eye.'

Dr Morris smiled ruefully. 'What are you going to do, Malcolm? Have you thought about it? Have you started looking for another job?'

'I'm leaving medicine.'

Dr Morris stared at him. Goldblatt, if such a thing were possible, stared at himself. Stunned, but somehow unsurprised at the same time.

He had said it. And now it was true.

Dr Morris shook his head. 'It's not because you're a bad doctor. She told me herself she thinks you're a good doctor.'

'Who?'

'Professor Small.'

Goldblatt laughed. 'Do you think I give a fuck what kind of a doctor she thinks I am? She's not a good enough doctor to judge.'

Dr Morris frowned uncomfortably. He was, after all, part of the machine. One of its best products, but still a part of it. It had carried him to where he was, and it would carry him a long way further. Even with the best will in the world, and even after having stood by and seen a senior colleague do something that he couldn't condone or even explain very well, it was difficult for him to hear that colleague's abilities described for what they really were.

'You're upset,' he said, 'that's understandable.'

'No,' said Goldblatt. 'I'm not upset. She's rubbish! Come on. Andrea Small's a terrible doctor. If I was ill, I would drag myself out of bed and crawl to another hospital – *crawl* to another hospital – if that was the only way of getting away from her.'

Dr Morris smiled guiltily.

'No wonder they gave her a disease like Fuertler's to treat. Even then she fucks it up half the time. I wouldn't let her near me if I had a worse case of Fuertler's than old Jacob Fuertler himself.'

'Did Jacob Fuertler have Fuertler's?' asked Dr Morris with interest. 'I didn't know that.'

'No, he didn't have Fuertler's.'

'But didn't you just say he did?'

'I made it up. For effect. I do that.' Goldblatt paused. 'And by the way, all those journal articles I told you about,' he added, since apparently he was coming clean, 'I made those up as well. Most of them, anyway.'

'No wonder I could never find them.' Dr Morris gazed at Goldblatt thoughtfully. 'You have a very active imagination,' he said at last.

'That's the least of my troubles.'

'Yes,' said Dr Morris pensively. 'Listen, Malcolm. You can work for me. On the Sutherland unit. The SR I've got now's not going to last another week.'

'What do you *do* to those people?'

'What?' said Dr Morris.

Goldblatt laughed.

'I'm serious, Malcolm. You can work for me. It'll just be a locum job, but you can do it while you find a substantive post.'

Goldblatt looked at Dr Morris. It was kind of him. Really kind. The kind of kindness that can kill you.

But Goldblatt had said it now, and it was true. He was leaving. With every second that passed, the reality of it set harder. Already he sensed a kind of liberation. Almost a kind of elation.

He shook his head. 'I appreciate it. I really do. But let's face it, I'm never going to get a substantive job.'

'You will, Malcolm. You're too good not to.'

'Doesn't matter how good I am. That's the point, Dr Morris. That's exactly the point.' Goldblatt thought about it. It *was* the point. 'My career as a Wise Man is over. Finished. You can tell your friends.'

'Which friends?'

Goldblatt gazed knowingly at Dr Morris. You would have thought that now, when it no longer mattered, he could have stopped pretending.

'You're not a Wise Man, Malcolm.'

'Thanks a lot.'

'You know what I mean.'

'Look,' said Goldblatt, 'this is my analysis. I'm never going to get a substantive job as an SR in a decent hospital. The best I can hope for realistically – the very best I can hope for – is a job in some godforsaken, run-down, second-rate place out in the provinces where no one else will go. And that's if such a job exists, which I'm not even sure of. And if it comes up at the right time. *And* if Andrea Small doesn't go around saying things about me that are so bad that even places like that won't take me. And assuming I am lucky enough to get a job like that – and that by itself is a pretty heroic assumption, and I'll probably kill myself in the process of testing it – where does it lead? To the next thirty years as a consultant in some godforsaken, run-down, second-rate place out in the provinces where no one else will go. And that's not me. It just isn't. It'll kill me.'

'You can make it first-rate,' said Dr Morris with a half-hearted note of encouragement in his voice.

Goldblatt ignored that. Dr Morris would thank him for it later, he knew.

'Am I right?' said Goldblatt.

Dr Morris thought. 'Maybe.'

Goldblatt nodded. The analysis was indisputable. Goldblatt knew, because no one wanted to dispute it more than he did. 'Please, Dr Morris.

Don't make this any harder for me. Don't offer me a job as your locum SR. I might just take it.'

Dr Morris was silent for a moment. 'So what are you going to do?'

'I have a law degree. I have specialist physician training. And I have one hell of a grudge against medicine. Don't you think that's an interesting combination? I'm sure I can put it to some kind of use.'

'Do you really have a grudge against medicine?' asked Dr Morris sadly.

'No,' said Goldblatt. 'I love it.'

Dr Morris looked at him. His eyes were full of some soppy warm material that made Goldblatt cringe with guilt.

'And I hate it, as well. Everything that surrounds it. Everything that's been built up around it. Everything that you—' Goldblatt stopped.

'What, Malcolm?'

'Look, I'm just not like you. I think you're a great doctor. If I had to crawl away from Professor Small, I'd be crawling to you. Honestly. I think you're great.'

'I think you're a pretty great doctor as well,' said Dr Morris.

Goldblatt shook his head. 'I'm not like you. I just can't... I can't do it. I can't make the compromises. For you, they're not even compromises, they're natural, but for me... I can't fit in. It's killing me. It's like a woman you have to walk away from. You love her, but it's killing you. So you just have to walk away from her. And that kills you as well.'

Dr Morris looked at him with that same sad, soppy look.

'All right, that stuff about the woman, I just made that up. I've never actually walked away from a woman. They all run away before I have the chance.' Goldblatt paused. 'It just sounded good.'

Dr Morris smiled. 'I'll miss having you around.'

'So will I.'

'You're sure, then?' Dr Morris looked at him searchingly. 'This is what you really want to do?'

Goldblatt hesitated. It felt like a moment of truth, and he wished that it had never come. But he couldn't deceive them. Dr Morris, the man who really loved medicine, was waiting for an answer. And the old Jewish lady in the corner, who had come all the way up from his id for the occasion, had lowered her nose and was looking at him as well.

Goldblatt shook his head and shrugged helplessly. 'I suppose it is.'

Dr Morris nodded.

There was silence.

'Well, go easy if you've ever got me on the stand,' Dr Morris said. 'I'd hate to have you cross-examining me. Don't make me admit things I've never done.'

'I'll think about it.'

Dr Morris hesitated again. 'Let me know if I can do anything for you, Malcolm. I mean that. Look, I know you told me not to, but... if you change your mind, let me know. The SR job'll be there.'

'Thank you. I mean that as well.'

Dr Morris nodded.

Goldblatt nodded too. He felt that he should get up and bow or shake Dr Morris's hand or make some other manly and symbolic gesture to mark the moment. Dr Morris looked as if he felt the same way.

Then Dr Morris glanced at his watch. 'Must go,' he said, with the familiar thrill of anticipation creeping back into his voice.

'Got a patient to see?' asked Goldblatt.

'Chap who came in two days ago with a pericardial effusion. Now he's developed a rash!'

'A rash?'

'Fascinating!' Dr Morris stood up. 'Want to come? He's on Marsden ward.'

Goldblatt looked at his watch. 'I've got some things to do. I could meet you at one-thirty.'

'Sorry. Got to see him now. I'm going to be flat out again all afternoon with the Sutherland unit.'

'House officer away?'

'Not yet, but she's feeling ill!'

Dr Morris left. The door closed behind him.

A pericardial effusion, thought Goldblatt. Fluid between the membranes around the heart. He'd never go to see one again, with or without a rash. Never, never, never, never, never, never again.

He felt no sense of liberation now. No elation. Nothing seemed sadder. He felt a tearing. A slicing, twisting, ripping of his flesh.

He bleeped Emma. She hesitated when she heard his voice on the phone. Strictly speaking, even after yesterday's lapse, she wasn't speaking to him, which made the telephone an especially inconvenient medium of communication. For a moment all Goldblatt could hear was the sound of her breathing.

'Do you want to come on the round with us this afternoon?' he asked for the second time after he had listened to her breathing for a while. 'We'll do a handover.'

Goldblatt knew she was there. The breathing went on.

'Or do you want to do the round yourself? I'll tell the others. I don't care.'

'No,' Emma said eventually.

'No what?' asked Goldblatt.

'I don't want to come on the round. You do it.'

'You don't want a handover?' asked Goldblatt.

'No. The Prof's round isn't until next Wednesday. I don't need to know the patients until then.'

'Goodbye,' said Goldblatt, and he put the phone down.

He shook his head. Emma! If Ludo was right, Emma had put him to the knife. But who was more the victim? Him or her? Suddenly he laughed. The feeling of liberation swept over him again. Stronger than before. Lifted him up and made him feel marvellously light.

The old Jewish lady in the corner had disappeared. Goldblatt looked down at his hands. Punctured. Torn. Ripped. Chunks of flesh were missing. The holes left in them by the nails were ragged and bloody. But they were free.

37

THAT AFTERNOON, GOLDBLATT DID his last round with Ludo and the HO. Ludo turned up on time, which made Goldblatt think his sacking genuinely must have been an important event. To her, at least.

'Are you really leaving?' asked the HO as she pushed the notes trolley out of the office.

'Yes,' said Goldblatt.

'You'll have to do things you don't understand now,' Ludo said to her.

'She does that anyway,' said Goldblatt.

'Only when I have to,' said the HO.

'Only when she has to,' said Goldblatt.

They went around the patients briskly. Most of them were the usual Fuertler's bunch. They spent some time with one of Dr Morris's patients, a young man admitted two days previously with haemorrhagic lesions in his lungs and renal failure. They were waiting on a test result to confirm their diagnosis. The young man was scared and confused, as anyone would be. Goldblatt sat down with him and explained what the treatment would be if the result came back as they expected.

And then they were finished. The rest of the Fuertler's patients took about two minutes each. They had seen everyone.

They went back to the office. The HO pushed the trolley into place beside one of the desks. She sat down.

'What do I write for Sandra Hill's death certificate?' she asked.

'Number one, immediate cause of death, toxic megacolon,' said Goldblatt. 'One A, pulmonary fibrosis. One B, Fuertler's Syndrome.'

The HO wrote it down on a piece of paper.

'Happy with that?' asked Goldblatt.

'Yes,' said the HO.

'Understand?'

'Yes,' said the HO.

'All right,' said Goldblatt. 'Have you got much else to do?'

The HO took one of her innumerable pieces of paper out of her pocket. 'A few things.'

'There's no one booked to come in.'

'What about Sandra Hill's bed?'

'We'd borrowed that ourselves. Go home after you've finished what you have to do. Ludo will cover you, won't you Ludo?'

'I was hoping to get away early,' said Ludo.

'Ludo will cover you,' said Goldblatt. 'Won't you, Ludo?'

'All right,' said Ludo grudgingly.

The HO stood up. 'Well. Thanks, Malcolm.'

'For?'

'I don't know. Everything.'

'Did I ever tell you nothing gets in the way of lunch except a cardiac arrest?'

'Yes,' said the HO.

'Remember that. It'll be a lot more useful to you than anything else I ever said.'

The HO shrugged.

'And don't do Accident and Emergency. I forbid it.'

'All right,' said the HO.

'Really?' said Goldblatt.

'Maybe,' said the HO. She pushed her glasses back up her nose.

Goldblatt watched her. The HO would be all right, he thought. As all right as anyone ever was. He smiled. Good luck, HO. Do what you have to do to survive. But don't change too much. Don't lose the anger. Not all of it. May the smoke still come out of your nostrils once in a while.

'Anyway...' said the HO.

'You've got stuff to do. Go on. Go.'

The HO nodded. She glanced at Ludo for a moment. Then she looked back at him. 'See you around, Malcolm.'

'See you around,' said Goldblatt.

The HO left, closing the door behind her.

Ludo was still there.

'Don't you have a Dermatology clinic on Thursday afternoons?' he asked.

'Sometimes,' said Ludo.

Goldblatt leaned back in his chair. Ludo. In a purple woollen skirt and white coat, sitting in the doctors' office, just as he had found her on that first morning so many weeks ago.

'So how was the concert last night?' he asked.

'Malcolm, don't,' whined Ludo. 'She asked me. What was I supposed to say?'

Goldblatt didn't know. Suddenly he didn't care. He felt light. It was over. He just wanted to get out now. He just wanted to leave and go and find Lesley and throw her into bed. Laugh with her. Be with her. Recover the things in himself that had made her want to be with him all those years ago. Recover them for his own sake, as well. Tell her he loved her. Tell her that if he had to find the most difficult way, at least he had done it. He had found it, and there was no going back.

And tomorrow? What of the agony to come? He knew it must. What of the sense of loss? How long would it take to be dulled?

Who cared? Today there was no tomorrow.

He grabbed a results sheet, scrunched, swivelled, and threw. In!

'So the drink's off, I suppose?' asked Ludo, shaking out her long hair as if she didn't really care. She had been waiting all day, hoping that Goldblatt would ask the question for her. Now, at the last minute, she was forcing herself to be bold.

'I guess so.'

'Was there ever going to be another one?' asked Ludo quietly.

'I don't know.'

Ludo nodded, as if she knew what that really meant. But she was wrong. He had told her the truth. He didn't know. He really didn't. She didn't know how close he had come.

'Look, Ludo, all I would have done is...'

'What?'

Fucked you, he thought. And then got away from you as quickly as I could. And then come back for more.

Maybe she wouldn't have said no to that. Maybe that was all she'd ever had.

But that's what this world was. Or it was for him. Pleasure and pain, mostly self-inflicted. Passion and remorse. An endless cycle, one feeding on the other. Addictive. Destructive. He had to get out of it. If he didn't get out of it now, he never would.

He scrunched another results form and threw. The ball hit the rim of the rubbish bin and bounced out. Ludo picked it up ungraciously and tossed it back to him. He aimed and threw. In!

He wondered how much Ludo was in love with him. He hoped it wasn't much. Everything about her was so sad and slow. She didn't need something else dragging her down.

'Come on,' he said cheerfully, largely to stop himself heading down into the sink of all hopelessness where Ludo spent so much of her time. 'You'll be all right, Ludo.'

'I'll never pass the second part, Malcolm.'

Goldblatt laughed. She was probably right. 'Why do you want to?'

'It's easy for you to say! What else am I going to do?'

'I don't know.' His elation had returned. He was in danger of uttering platitudes. Trouble was, they seemed to be true. 'It's a big world, Ludo. That's all I know. It's a fucking big world! Go and explore it.'

Ludo grimaced. 'What about a coffee?'

Goldblatt shook his head.

'Come on, Malcolm,' she whined. 'Just one more. For old times' sake.'

'No, Ludo.'

Ludo lapsed into silence. 'Remember you asked me that question that time?' she said eventually.

'Which question?' There had been so many. 'The causes of polycystic kidneys?'

'No.'

'The causes of pneumothorax? The causes of hepatosplenomegaly? The causes of—'

'Malcolm! The one about the bat's CT scan.'

Goldblatt laughed. That question? Of all the ones for her to remember! 'Don't worry about it, Ludo. It's not worth it. It's a trick question.'

'What's the answer?'

'Do you want to know?'

Ludo nodded.

'If we were bats, what would our CT scans look like? Is that the one you mean?'

Ludo nodded.

Goldblatt shrugged. 'They wouldn't look like anything. They'd be noise, Ludo. Sounds. We wouldn't see the world. We'd hear it.'

'That's it? That's the answer?'

Goldblatt nodded. 'That's it.'

Ludo looked unimpressed.

Goldblatt stood up, unclipped his bleeper from his pocket, and laid it on the desk beside the phone. He took his jacket down from the hook where he had hung it at five o'clock that morning on the way in to see Sandra Hill.

'Good luck, Ludo,' he said, and opened the door.

Note on the Author

Michael Honig trained in medicine and worked at a number of London's teaching hospitals. He lives in London with his wife and son.